Stonedial

George Konrád

Stonedial

*Translated from the Hungarian
by Ivan Sanders*

A HELEN AND KURT WOLFF BOOK

HARCOURT, INC.

New York San Diego London

Requests for permission to make copies of any
part of the work should be mailed to the following address:
Permissions Department, Harcourt, Inc., 6277 Sea Harbor Drive,
Orlando, Florida 32887-6777.

This is a translation of *Kőóra*

Library of Congress Cataloging-in-Publication Data
Konrád, Gyorgy.
[Kőóra. English]
Stonedial / George Konrád; translated from the Hungarian by
Ivan Sanders.
p. cm.
ISBN 0-15-100619-9
I. Title. II. Sanders, Ivan.
PH3281.K7558 K6613 2000
894'.511334 21—dc21   99-045478

Designed by Lori McThomas Buley
Text set in Stempel Garamond
Printed in the United States of America
First U. S. edition
A C E G I K J H F D B

Stonedial

Passing Through

The hotel's hallways are long with plenty of brass and marble, and music seeping through the ceiling. I dozed off in the comfortable armchair and am awakened now by a strange black bird fluttering on the window ledge. It's still light outside, but no one can disturb me, I've locked the door. It's my special time, a blessed hour, I shall call no one. I've put out my things: a pair of glasses, a pipe, a fountain pen, a photograph. I like the neutral tidiness of a hotel room, it evokes no memories. Yesterday it was someone else's, now it's mine, in a day or two it will be somebody else's again. A bee is buzzing over the fruit bowl; I, too, circle my small living space, then stop in front of the mirror. This face I know. One day it's the face of a fugitive, the next day the face is everywhere. I've put my unopened mail on a shelf: they're all high-toned requests, terribly important, and therefore dispensable. The writing desk is in a corner, from there I can see the huge four-poster bed and an elaborately carved wardrobe with five doors, each concealing eight separate compartments. The two-tiered chandelier has eight candle-shaped bulbs in each row, spreading their light from under the high ceiling. From the advertising folder placed on the desk I learn that the wines and meats of Kandor please the most discriminating palate. The city boasts a cathedral, a medieval fort, and a lakeshore promenade that leads to an ornate, turn-of-the-century crematory. One of the paintings in the cathedral shows Death standing up in a cart, goading two oxen with a whip; stretched out around him are naked human bodies. *Ubi gloriosa victoria.*

I step out onto the roof terrace; straight ahead, I can see the lake, if I turn around I face Resurrection Square. The hotel's sandy beachfront, illuminated by floodlights at night, changes colors. In the noonday wind the waves surge, sprawl, and creep back again. A lone coast guard boat never leaves the horizon. The tide keeps smoothing out and breaking up the algae on the embankment stones. A fair-haired girl is stretched out on a board— low-cut bathing suit, bronze body, shaved pubic hair. The sound of rippling water is said to calm the nerves. A rush of air puffs out the curtain, and I step back from the guardrail. The trunks of birch trees around the swimming pool reflect the light, the children's swing creaks in the wind, white-breasted, dark birds flutter among the wicker chairs. A figure is swimming in the sky-blue pool, leaves fall in the water, an old man fishes them out with a long-handled rake. Solitary readers sit in the armchairs, the waxy green of a potted plant peers out from behind the column of the upper gallery, a waitress in white blouse and dark skirt stands ready, her tray pressed to her hip.

I am a guest here in Kandor, just passing through. I'll stay awhile and try not to get involved in local affairs. My present vantage point affords me the necessary distance. Facing me is the Gothic cathedral of questionable origin. The Romanesque crypt underneath it, not visible from outside, is authentic, as are the ruins of a Roman bath below, which can be admired by anyone with a healthy appreciation of the relative merits of the layers of time.

Kings were crowned on this square; rebels, plotters, and freethinkers were beheaded. There stands the courthouse and there the headquarters of the secret police. The place where I am staying welcomed travelers five hundred years ago. There was a hospice here, a night shelter for pilgrims arriving on foot or on horseback to visit the cathedral. In its tavern Franciscan friars, assisted by young novices, served wine. Students performed morality plays and grand seigneurs shared their cups of wine with women of easy virtue, bouncing them on their knees.

"Tell me, what kind of city is Kandor?" I asked an earnest-looking waiter the other day. "It's heaven on earth. I wouldn't want anything else. But not always. Today it was more like hell." He said this as if he were reciting verse. About a year ago, his wife died in bed beside him. She abandoned him while he slept.

He can't understand it, he still can't. Since then he's been raising their daughter alone.

The city has scaled the walls of the valley, and spilling over onto the other side of the mountain, it has continued to spread, encircling the slender volcanic peak, on top of which twelve giant rock formations mark both time and space. At the very center a thin strip of smoke rises from the depths. It's a barely visible message, some people can't see it. The Kandorans don't dare put a bench there. Stonedial, they call it. This arcane timepiece, this sluggish smoke signal, casts a spell on whoever approaches.

The ground plan of Resurrection Square resembles a rounded rectangle. The streets leading to the short sides of the rectangle are wide, those converging on the long sides are narrow. A few years ago the city's chief planner succeeded in detouring vehicular traffic and turned Liberation Square into a pedestrian mall. Before World War Two it was called Resurrection Square, now it has recovered its old name. The residents of nearby buildings looked puzzled when a reporter from a local newspaper wanted to know which they believed in more firmly, liberation or resurrection.

Extending over the eastern end of the square is the Crown Hotel with its four enclosed gardens. The rear wing of the building overlooks Old Market Square, where visitors may find several eateries. This is where flower vendors set up their stalls during the day, though nowadays the place is crowded with homeless people who huddle here amid their accumulated odds and ends. Prostitution, another old tradition in the square, hasn't disappeared.

THE ITINERANT PHILOSOPHER János Dragomán arrived in the city of Kandor, has seen his old friends—his onetime professor and his onetime lover—and learned that he had a daughter and a grandchild. The professor, about whom he possessed a secret, he will inadvertently murder and in the end pay dearly for this act. Otherwise Dragomán talked about how well he fared alone, how grateful he was for his advancing years, and how he planned to return to Kandor for good someday, if only to avoid the entanglements his frequent travels led him into. He said all this so emphatically that Kobra, his friend and former classmate, became suspicious. Dragomán didn't spend much time in Kandor, but he did manage to disturb the peace of mind of those close to him.

He arrived in town just as another former classmate of his, Antal Tombor, now mayor of Kandor, got a bit carried away with himself. As usual, Tombor didn't pay much attention to what was happening around him; what preoccupied him was how to make history, and how to put that history on film. "We'll just store all of this, these few years of our lives," he said. Kobra didn't understand what event Tombor was planning to cap with a grand finale on Resurrection Square. Did he really believe in a miraculous liberation, in a redemption that would prance around him like a happy mongrel? Tombor will stage a dazzling show in front of the newly restored City Hall, and naturally there will be trumpeters in red livery lining the steps, and performing monkeys and fire-eaters, and free lunches for the homeless.

A CRUMPLED HANDBILL lies on Dragomán's desk: "There's nothing finer than dinner at the diner." Dragomán remembers the diner in New York, near the piers. He sees giant trailer-trucks with silver pipes and fire-red cabs, and massive shoulders capable of lifting a grand piano. He also recalls a young floozy prancing past dark brick walls, piles, crates, and dimly lit bars. *"Ma morale est celle d'une papillon. Ce qui te convienne j'espère,"* she had said to him. Dragomán had a grand time in those waterfront dives, with their heavy and greasy food, and steaks as big as a truck-driver's hand.

HE HEARS A train whistle and is transported back to a railroad bridge. It's October, 1956, the wind is piercing cold. Below him are railroad tracks and a locomotive; in his belt, a submachine gun. Three men approach who also carry submachine guns. "Who are you?" "Who are *you*, fella?" "Come on, guys, are you friend or foe?" "Depends on who you are." "All I know is that we can pass each other in peace." "Right; but you cross over to the other side, and we'll stay here." "Any of you have a cigarette? And you won't shoot if I ask for a light, will you?" Dragomán trudges along on a bridge that won't end. The line of railroad cars passing underneath also seems endless. The deep breath he takes

4

goes on and on, too. He returns to his hotel room, the wind has sucked the curtain out of the window.

Boys love submachine guns. It's now or never, they say. Now's the time to hit that spire, or pump bullets into the old geezers who are so frightened they hide under their blankets. Yes, now's the time to set that hotel on fire, or bump off the reporter on the balcony. Not far away are irregulars, and sudden explosions, and children's beds in flames. Who can say which came first, the shots or the urge to shoot? Showing the flag or firing the gun? There always have been pursuers and deserters. Dragomán preferred the latter. Next door to his childhood home was a toy store. Before Christmas a castle would appear in the store window complete with bridges and ramparts and a bugler in the tower. It was all brilliantly illuminated, and the festivities inside went on day and night. Dragomán never wanted to be an armed sentry on the ramparts; he wanted to be the court jester who tumbled about in a garish clown suit.

A telephone call: Somebody who's supposed to see me tomorrow can't make it, unfortunately. Too bad, I'm sorry, too. I replace the receiver, relieved. Messages are slid under my door, requests, all of them. I've got lockjaw, my hand is numb, I cough, I shiver, I sweat. Let the activists act, I'll be a slacker, I'll be sick with a headcold. Being active means running yourself ragged, it means your engagement calendar is full. I try to steer clear of places where things happen. I flash a smile, I lecture, I dawdle, I do my thing. Arrivals, takeoffs, until one day there is no takeoff. I feel a tightness in my head, my brain must be wasting away. I've got several doctors' appointments, but I will not keep them—illness begins when the disease is named. Three times now I've received an envelope that contains another, smaller envelope, with an even smaller one inside, and in it a card with skull and crossbones drawn in gold ink.

Ladies and gentlemen, from the perspective of your comfortable anonymity, you are looking at a fallible human being who not only is content with his fallibility, he also raves about it. You see before you a typical professor, close to sixty, in a tweed jacket, cotton shirt, black shoes—his regular attire since high school. After his morning coffee he puts on his coat, saunters over to a building a few blocks from his house, walks up to his office, locks the door behind him, thumbs through a few books, swings in his chair, jots down words on a piece of paper, stuffs the paper in his pocket, takes out a bottle from the corner cabinet, pours himself a drink, gulps it down, and still can think of nothing to say, has no idea where to begin, all he remembers is the title of the lecture. But he's late, so he washes his hands and face, walks into the lecture hall, the students greet him, a glass of water has been placed near the lectern, he puts his hand on it for support, surveys the student body, then announces the subject of today's lecture, which somehow or other he'll have to elaborate, delineate, then wrap up. From time to time he looks out the window. Pigeons keep pecking at the red-brick walks of the campus, young mothers walk hand in hand with their children, swinging their arms back and forth.

Dragomán has spent the week in Kandor doing the very things he dislikes, exhausting himself at parties and receptions. Several times a day he finds himself in overheated rooms, where too many people stand around holding glasses, people who ordinarily would not seek out one another's company. The professor brightens up the scene; with a harried smile he asks questions and lets others shine. It's past midnight, the room is still full, there is general laughter. He takes up his position like a soldier, anyone can approach him and start a conversation—he must remain at his post. They take aim and fire away: each question makes him wince, but he answers with a smile. Now he walks anxiously through the lobby. Though thirsty, he won't go to the bar but will attempt to beat a fast retreat. Too late: a charming young lady turns up with a tape recorder and proceeds to ask questions. Doesn't he think it's wonderful that so many people showed up for the reception? Yes, amazing, Dragomán mumbles, and starts praising the very things that made him head for the door.

In the Crown Café, authors, editors, scholars, and activists sit in the same booth for hours on end. Coffee, wine, phone calls, handshakes, evasions, surrenders, promises, must-do tasks, tired fresh starts. Around noon he takes a few sedatives, then, in jacket and tie, stretches out on his bed. But before long the front desk calls: Somebody is waiting downstairs.

On the way to the café, in the winding hotel corridor, I see an open door; inside, a scantily dressed woman is applying lipstick.

An Oriental-looking man in a long cape and wide-rimmed felt hat is walking toward me: he bows politely and his four leashed Pekingese also drop to their knees. I return the greeting with a low bow. I have to wait a long time at the elevator because a woman in a wheelchair has sent one of her daughters back to the room for the third time for the right bottle of perfume, while her other daughter holds the elevator door. "You see, unpleasant odors must be neutralized by the right antidote," the woman in the wheelchair explains. "Without proper instruction, one wouldn't know that character flaws give off foul smells. We handicapped people are more perceptive; we can peer into people's souls." I adjust my tie in the elevator mirror on the way down. I see ice floes in the mirror, and a little boy on a narrow plank, getting into a frozen dinghy.

I've explored many a city around the globe, and wherever I stop for the night I reach the necessary state of drunkenness, so that even in crowds I feel protected by an invisible yet radiant wall. The desk clerk and the pianist in the hotel look familiar. Like foreign correspondents (which I am, too, between semesters), or like diplomats who delve into a strange land's strangeness, they have seen the world. I never tire of their company. Seasoned veterans, they've encountered a few heroes in their day, and even more killers.

I think of my Uncle Imre who had been a croupier at the Crown, and could also play the Gypsy bandleader's violin so expertly, the public couldn't tell the difference. The crazy Imre danced with a bottle of rum in his hands over the trenches on the Russian front. They shot the bottle right out of his hand, the cigarette from his mouth, but back then, in 1916, the Russians made sure he stayed alive. True, his folks had dispatched rum and sugar on dogsleds, so there'd be enough of both for Russian Christmas, but it was Uncle Imre who had given them the order. In 1944, however, he was shot summarily, even though for a time he had moved about freely on the arm of his young girlfriend, a little thin on top by then, but with a neat, fragrant mustache, a white armband, and all his World War One decorations—a privileged, exempted Jew. What enabled him to walk around so leisurely was that he no longer gave a damn. Instead, he kept watching the flames in the potbellied stove, annoyed that the split peas took so long to cook. His lady friend who sat with him for a while knew that he'd already settled his accounts. He hadn't had a drink in days, he felt like taking a walk, and she knew that what he wanted was some good schnapps—she even knew where to get it. They went to see a hauler who during the worst days of the war was able to smuggle smoked meat and homemade brandy into the besieged city. Uncle Imre bartered his fur hat for it, but he never got to drink his schnapps. The paper exempting him from the racial laws was torn up before his eyes, then he was shot in the head. The men who did it were first going to drag the woman to the "House of Retribution," probably to torture her, rape her, then throw her out, dead or alive. But she just knelt on the floor and kept looking at Uncle Imre, placing her hands on his shoulders. Finally they had enough. "That's it," they said to her. "Out!"

Only an Image

In the morning, at the cathedral, Dragomán read a Latin text in front of the altar screen. Next to him, swung over the transept, was a huge incense burner, held in place by twisted rope ten meters long, thick as a man's arm, and tugged rhythmically on a pulley by six hooded sextons, who could raise the contraption all the way to the frescoed ceiling. The bishop fed the glowing embers spoonfuls of incense, the silver and glass container exhaled clouds of smoke, the faithful were awed. A small, flat microphone was placed on a low table in front of Dragomán; he filled the church's lofty void with booming oratory. For a moment, he was lost, he panicked, but Alphonse, the loyal, cynical friend, quickly came to his aid. Everything was set out, he was told when to stand and sit, the bishop smiled at him bashfully, and proceeded to place wafers on the worshippers' tongues.

They came in droves, the international wizards and charmers, to perform feats never seen in these parts. Their arrival on an early-autumn weekend such as this is an event destined to fulfill all kinds of expectations. People are hard to please: if they can't get their fill of ordinary grape harvest revelers, they will be seized by an almost painful longing for more, for the unknown. On the first day the guests were welcomed at City Hall, whence they adjourned to the synagogue which now functions as a theater. At the many ancillary events the people of Kandor could enjoy spectacles befitting a circus or a fair, including unicycle-riding monkeys and doughnut-munching, jelly-mustachioed children. When the fair comes to town, and the magi parade, pickpockets come running, too. You may witness furious motorcycle chases, but

9

you may also get your head bashed in, and wind up floating in the lake.

Dragomán is one of those international shamans, and the handling of his day-to-day affairs falls to Alphonse, who gets along with millionaire socialites and well-mannered dictators as famously as he does with Lesbian tea-connoisseurs and parrot-training hermits. Alphonse knows every Venetian *principessa* and Bogotá druglord, or at least they are nodding acquaintances. Under his large nose, disdain turns into exaggerated humility. Deep-voiced, playful compliments, in his Russian-Jewish-French-accented English, are paid to an Oxford-educated baritone. Heis a born devotee of every outrageous avant-garde fad, but his breast pocket is never without a handkerchief, his lapel a carnation. Let his graying mane flow, his Mediterranean complexion and his clean-shaven chin glow. He would like Dragomán to stay, though they both know it's good-bye—they will miss each other sorely.

The delegates sat in conference for days. The tiny red light on Dragomán's microphone kept flashing, he didn't bother to turn it off. He was the moderator: he invited speakers to speak, and he spoke his own mind, cracking a joke now and then to relieve the solemnity. He also tried to keep track of who had his hand raised in the two-hundred-member audience, and what they were saying in their strange accents. He identified people according to the countries they represented, and made certain that genders, races, continents, and religions got equal time. He also knew whom he could count on to mediate between offended parties. He would have loved to dispose of the items on the agenda as quickly as possible, but there were motions to vote on, resolutions to pass, amendments to approve before they could move on. He criticized, firmly yet temperately, several heads of government, and didn't spare the leaders of liberation movements either, whether they were in power or still underground. There were fanatics, of course, who considered their cause important enough to kill for. He initialed the proceedings of the previous convocation, then pushed aside the pile of papers, which contained the international president's tony comments on all the wise and foolish things heard at that meeting, including his own. Somebody is asking a question, somebody else is inscribing a book, circulating a petition, yet another is most happy to have the opportunity to talk about his life's work.

Every other day a writer colleague is bumped off somewhere, because he poked his nose into something that was none of his reader's business. Or he may have shed light on curious alliances and conspiracies, on the deadly games played by hitmen and racketeers. Or perhaps he wasn't so eager to dine in a club frequented by ministers and generals, and didn't think more of a billionaire than of the man sleeping under a blanket of rags, a barefoot lounge chair seller who at the end of the day folds his display of untouched lounge chairs, piles them on a handcart, ties them down, and moves his business to the next location.

In the morning a TV crew arrives and sets up equipment in his study. As international president, he is worth the trouble, but what they really want to hear is how Kandor has enriched the world at large. The phone calls keep coming: like a frog shot through with electric current, he twitches into action and marches off to press conferences, receptions, luncheons, dinners. He grants interviews, gives lectures, and moves on to the next round. He is fully booked; between two engagements he might take a ten-minute nap, after which he jumps up, buttons his three-piece uniform, salutes, and is ready to perform again. Surrounded by dark suits and other understated evening wear, he switches from language to language, and defers to the hero of our time: the conference organizer, who has a genius for remembering all the names, and for cooing ingratiatingly into the telephone. Now he smiles into the lens of a camera amid a bevy of Far Eastern delegates; he bids them farewell ceremoniously, outbowing an exceedingly polite professor who has introduced himself several times during the day, and each time mentioning the name of the country he is from. One more coffee, one more cognac, Dragomán may still have time to deliver a short address. If only today's appearances were over. And tomorrow's, and the ones after that. He hopes the talking machine inside him will not fail him, that one word will bring on the next. A knock on the door, they've come for him, he's to be presented with a badge, on television. If your face appears on the screen, you've become an object on display, making statements about subjects you know nothing about. It's too much: the car rides, the appointments, the commitments, the frenzy of responsibility—being obliged to enjoy other people's company. He notices little besides the bustle, the race, the scrambling for position. All the high-minded rhetoric preys on his mind. He doesn't complete half of what he's promised, he simply forgets.

In recent years Dragomán has initiated a number of projects. He loves to conceive plans but is less keen on carrying them out. He gets upset if he has to appear anywhere on time. He's been to too many places where fault-finding and demand-making are the order of the day, where self-pity abounds. He has the plane ticket in his pocket, a hotel room awaits him in the next city. Keynote address the day after tomorrow, to be followed by a friendly panel discussion. He'll lecture in ceremonial halls, theaters, and classrooms. The red light will flash, he'll turn his head. The microphones in front of him will keep growing, and he'll get a nice round of applause each time. He'll speak between the main course and dessert, he'll speak in city centers in front of thousands. He'll chat with distinguished colleagues, opposition leaders, government officials. Views will be exchanged in fortresses and ancient monasteries. They will all want to give events a push, they'll meet to discuss which issues they should discuss at their next meeting. They will smooth out the wrinkles, cut away the edges, until what they say will not offend, will not *mean*—they will have interacted and separated. Afterward there will be long plane rides, distance, silence. Dragomán vows to change his life, and will do so again tomorrow. Yes, he'll cancel all his public appearances, he'll shut up for a change. But he must finish the game he has already started, he'll just go to a dozen more places—he promised.

Yes, he will resign, he will bow out. From now on, it will be his successor who will express his heartfelt gratitude to a cabinet minister; he'll tell the reporters tailing him to see the new man. He said it all in his last formal statement, everyone in the auditorium applauded his rhetorical flourishes. After his last appearance he can retire his public persona and reinstate his private self, the one that will not feel like giving solemn speeches in cathedrals and lecture halls, speeches enhanced by altarpieces, platforms, festive music.

Talking too much is as bad as overeating. God blessed humans with the gift of gab, but also cursed them with it. Some have grown so brazen, so vain, they refuse to hold their tongue and are comfortable only when they can gab away. He'll learn to stay away even from those who may seem quiet but are clearly itching to speak, whose organs of speech yearn for the old thrill. He'll be better off remaining silent for a while, for what can be more pathetic than an aging chatterbox.

When referring to the past, he finds he often repeats himself. Retrieved memories are frozen in time, no longer nourished by fresh currents. He experiences his stories in the form in which he has recounted them countless times. An old soldier keeps dropping his calcified treasures. The veterans of the 1848 Revolution were hailed as heroes, though not necessarily the most courageous among them, only those who lived the longest. At his age the face either shrivels or runs to fat; one's biography is inscribed in swells and hollows. As they pass outside his window, some of these faces, like a cracked sidewalk, blend into the scenery.

The stream flows through the hotel grounds right into the lake. Toward the end of the war a hole was drilled in the thick ice near here and the bodies of civilians—Jews, deserters, and other suspicious characters who'd been rounded up and shot—were dumped into the hole. Somebody complained that all those corpses might pollute the water, but the leader of the death squad assured him, and others voicing concern about water quality, that by spring the fish would have picked off all the flesh from the bodies.

Dragomán is not expecting anyone now, so he steps out on the terrace. He stands in perfect alignment with a cable car moving up the nearby mountain. Someone crouching in the car could easily target him with a gun, and vice versa. In the room the radio is playing Mozart's Requiem. *Dies irae, dies illa.* This day is the day of wrath. A researcher on death and dying has concluded that we depart in anger, not in serene acceptance.

A tabby cat hops about behind Dragomán, demanding attention, purring and clawing playfully. He had brought a sliced-up rabbit liver for the cat, which he immediately wolfed down, and then napped four hours on a camel hair blanket. On hearing Dragomán stir, he perked up, jumped in his lap, purred loudly, filled the room with life. Dragomán finally put him out on the terrace, but the cat eyed him from outside the glass door. "All right, come in," Dragomán said, and the tabby, with a victor's sneer, reclaimed his rightful place on the blanket.

In the afternoon he gave an interview to the editor of an anthroposophic journal, who submitted a list of questions highlighted in green. He presented Dragomán with an autographed copy of one of his own books, the back cover of which displayed the author's changing face. In each shot his dense facial hair was shaped differently. This man regularly changed domiciles, friends, identities. The earth has four billion inhabitants, he said, why should he lead the life of only one individual?

Whenever Dragomán wants something badly, or is afraid of something, he gets peevish. But then, some people sight UFO's, others are petrified of secret weapons or terrorists. Whoever wants to be afraid gets his chance. At the Crown café there is a lot of talk of people who are gone. Let's face it, bodies are unserviceable things, they break down and are disposed of.

The heavy mist hanging over the hotel's garden causes the green of the grass, the intense yellow of the hyacinths, to be imprinted on one's retina. On summer nights reconnaissance satellites streak across the starry skies. I wouldn't like to be up in that gadget, I have no desire to move from here. I've done many things in my life and lost many friends. I survived much happiness and much pain. I never thought about suicide for more than a few hours. Whatever happened to me is mine. My kingdom is right here, I do not live in exile.

Every night is a farewell party, I have my part in a shadow play. I try not to be judgmental, but like blood seeping through a bandage, personal taste shows through my attempted objectivity. I've been written up. I live my life the way I read a book. The only thing I don't know is where the book ends. Perhaps right here.

It makes no difference if life is eventful or humdrum; a peasant's redundant labors and a knight's fabulous journey are of equal value. I have within me the traveler and the staid bourgeois, the adventurer and the philistine, the navigator and the hermit, Don Juan and Oblomov. There are those who defy a thousand perils and set sail for distant shores, and those whose lives are fraught with danger here at home. And then there is the person who leans back in a café's velvet-upholstered banquette and imagines it all.

Some acquire wisdom even though they never leave their village. Some come by it only after circumnavigating the globe. But most people never gain wisdom, whether they stay in one place or are forever on the move.

Ten minutes from now I may tell myself to get away from this place. Maybe I'll cut short the cycle of repetition. Why haven't I gone everywhere I could have gone? Why didn't I become all that I imagined I could be? I love to explore little-known places, but because I am an outsider I cannot really get to know them. The locals can't because they live there. They are mainly interested in themselves. "What are we really like?" they ask the traveler, and by way of reply receive a few phony compliments.

Kandor is the kind of city to which the wandering dreamer returns when he gets homesick. A seasoned traveler, he knows a lot about the place and can infer even more from secret signs, as one does from a passing glance. I like to follow the path of a bird that just flew out of a window. I may be jostled in trains and buses, but I remain intact, body and soul, ensconced in my bubble of space. When I get back to my hotel room, a bed is there to receive me, a few familiar objects surround me. I carry my habits wherever I go.

What's good about the Crown is that it has everything I need: a restaurant, a café, a bar, a swimming pool, a nightclub, even a roof terrace, where from time to time I encounter curious characters. Right now I see the man in the wide-rimmed hat, whom I've seen before. He has a girlish face and crouches before his leashed dogs. Now he straightens up and asks me if I have a cigarette that might give him a high. We lean against the railing and inhale, looking skyward.

"Way below the things of this world and way above it," observes the stranger. "That's what's so nice about the tall building we blow the smoke on, don't you agree?" Seeing that I do, he tells me there is no need for formal introductions.

Transience, a night spent in a hotel room, could easily be the starting point of a more general survey. On my desk I find routine texts: schedules, agendas, reminders. My unknown future is the coauthor of these notes. What did I do? Nothing out of the ordinary. I got by. There are people who simply survive. I'd like to know, though, what actually took place in that jumble of happenstance.

I suppose sooner or later these notes, containing names, facts, moments of rapture, will be seen by others. For years I went to sleep knowing that they might come early in the morning and throw my notebooks into brown paper bags. I didn't want to write down names then, lest I get other people into trouble. Later, I decided to leave behind traces of my foolishness, for whatever is not written down doesn't exist.

The past, like a corpse on the pavement, is covered with a sheet. Between elusive happenings and the recorded words I insert only as much fiction as is dictated by an imperious mind and a capricious memory. It happens more and more that of all the characters in a story, I am the only one still alive. I have to answer all the questions. As more people I've known and loved pass on, I myself begin to embody history.

Where is yesterday? Stolen. I cannot tell the difference between the original happening and the image I created of it in my mind. There are no facts, only images. Can I order my imagination to enter with its flickering lantern the dim storehouse of an ancient evening? I've amassed a great many unretouched photographs, and they are all there in one large, unworked pile.

Reality is what was. As soon as it happens, it's transformed into an image, like the ship that's leaving the bay. Or the fat raindrop still adhering to the terrace railing but about to fall. Or the man with an umbrella making a turn at the far corner of the square. Their joint presence is real only for an instant, and it's real only for me. For them—for the ship, the raindrop, the man with the umbrella—it isn't. Has the moment I've already forgotten really happened? My consciousness captures an image, toys with it, lifts it into the realm of the unreal, thereby rendering it real. Memory is as remarkable as a match lighting up the night sky.

The Doorbell Rings

There's the bell, Melinda is here. She enters in a long black coat and tight-fitting black pants which, considering her slender figure and pretty ankles adorned with pointy black shoes, can be said to be flattering. No rings, no jewelry of any kind, only a black-and-white scarf slung over a white silk blouse. Add to this a pair of dark eyes that with the passing years have lost none of their sparkle, have been made no less bewitching by proliferating crow's-feet, and a well-cut, full mouth developing fine perpendicular lines, which some-day will pull her lips together like a purse string.

"My name is Melinda Kadron. I met this good-for-nothing in another novel foisted on you by the same author. But our story, mine and János Dragomán's, was never finished. You left me for the insane asylum, János dear, and from there abducted a girl with whom you roamed the world for three years. You barely thought of me all that time, wrote me only sporadically, the kind of evasive letters unfaithful husbands write. Now you are here in my city, in Kandor, which you'll surely regret. I am surprised you didn't bring that woman with you, for you did drag her to parties before, where she created scenes and made such a fool of herself that no self-respecting host wanted to see her again. Still, you insisted on showing up with her at dignified gatherings, where people are expected to behave. I believe you did it to annoy me. Old fool that you are, you tried to prove that you take pleasure in flouting the rules, while I scrupulously observe them. Yes, I serve the public, at my husband's side, doing everything expected of a mayor's wife. I go to receptions, I stand up straight, I smile

17

for the cameras. And I have no secret affairs. If you stick around, you can accompany me on my rounds, visit a child welfare agency, or come with me to the market. In between, we might drop in to the museum to see the latest exhibit. I can't afford to skip a single exhibit. I've been waiting for you, why so late? I kept calling the hotel; they must have thought me insane. You have no permanent address in Kandor, only this two-room suite, which could be yours, of course, if you'd be willing to embrace us. If you agreed to be a Kandoran even at border crossings. Whatever you are, a Buddhist, a Catholic, a Jew, past forty you must give some thought to what you want to do with your life, what you could do with it. There will always be people who are going to count on you."

Melinda Kadron is out shopping. Later in the day she'll fill out her husband's tax forms, answer his mail, visit the post office, the pharmacy, cook dinner, wash the dishes, speak to the children in their own secret language while feasting on macaroni and cheese with them. She'll also find time to pick up the spare tire and buy a wicker chair for the porch. For breakfast she usually has cocoa and buttered toast. She drinks very little coffee and almost no alcohol. She hates cigarette smoke but loves herbal teas, and is truly in her element at the flower show. Melinda clutches the shopping basket and says not a word. Dragomán is also silent. She sets the table for two and puts everything out: bread, goat cheese, peppers, homemade strawberry brandy, and the local, smoky table wine. Standing close to Dragomán, she pours the brandy, while he leans on the piano that was moved into his hotel room, courtesy of his friend Tombor. She lifts her glass, locks eyes with Dragomán, takes her closed fist out of her pocket and releases a parakeet. The bird immediately heads for the piano and screeches: "Whore! Whore!"

"My husband has an assistant, who is secretary, housekeeper, protocol chief, and chauffeur all in one. Sandra is her name and she also happens to be the wife of the man who is both rector of the university and vice-mayor of our fair city. She's very sweet to me, still I think she is after my queenly position. She wants too much, greed is in her blood. I am not saying she is crass or ugly or stupid, but there is something strange, almost extraterrestrial about her—for one thing, she is appallingly efficient. And she hooked Antal so fast, the poor man didn't know what hit him. She manages his busy schedule and has no qualms about cutting him off in the middle of a sentence, urging him to move on to the next topic, or telling him what to say at the next event. She jots down key words, discusses strategy with other advisors, reads and answers official mail, and in the office treats him with cool professionalism. Antal sleeps very little, his functions keep multiplying, his sense of duty has got the better of him, he squanders his strength, as if he knew it'll soon be over for him. If I were a worrier and not a fatalist, I'd be concerned about Antal. Not long ago he wrote out his will and gave me a copy. He made sure I'd have no reason to quarrel with my children. This whole mayor adventure is like a showy exit for him, he's atoning for his successes, for the fact that no one could ever hate him, at most they may have disliked him—in one way or another he had everybody eating out of his hand. Even today he gets what he wants, if not in the conference room then in the beer hall downstairs, where he makes deals with opposition leaders. They may not agree on everything, but they exchange absurd fishing stories, and the fellows enjoy his anecdotes. Lately Tombor has been regaling his table companions with rapid-fire one-liners, delivered with a straight face. He spends little time at home. Days go by without his seeing his children.

"Over the years I realized it wasn't me who helped you out of the loony bin with my cunning little ways, it was Nurse Brigitta. She took you to her room in the nurses' residence and caressed you in her bed until you cooed like a baby. I've taken account of your infidelities; but I also know that you're like a cat that wants to stay near the stove, close, and keep snoozing and stretching till all hours but does not disturb reading or writing. And I also know that your passion for telling tales, and for listening to them, ties you to me. Your friends are all here—I want you to be the mayor's alter ego. You also ought to finish my father's work; what he left behind are mere fragments. In short, you have obligations here. Ah, you used to snuggle up to me, put the moves on me, you rascal, but then, as if shot from a cannon, you would run, tearing your shirt off but keeping your hat on. Did anyone see my darling? Oh yes, they saw him take off in his ancient Jaguar and head straight for the border, and the insane asylum, only to get away from us. And you stayed there, literally dumb-struck, for six months. Don't leave me now, my dearest; if you are still up to it, if tobacco and alcohol haven't ruined you completely, start working on a new play. Come, I'll take you somewhere, I won't tell you where. My dream car, a real Russian Lada, is parked by the curb."

Dragomán asks lazily: "Are you comfortable?" It's a nice place I've got here, no need to move, we came here, so let's stay. It's not much of course, two rooms plus a small entranceway. And that big terrace in front of my window—part of the roof terrace, actually. Down below is Resurrection Square. Deluxe accommodations make for deluxe moments. I belong to no one, I owe nothing. When I've had enough I leave. Anyway, I came here only to give a lecture or two and to receive an honorary degree at the university. My next lecture is in N. I must be there Tuesday the latest, all the posters are up. We have a little time until then, this afternoon, at any rate, is ours. If you aren't too tired, you might want to take off your jacket: there would be one less barrier between us. Let me look at your hand.

My four-year absence is written all over it.

But let's not hear the abandoned woman's complaint. I left you among your loved ones, in the care of a friend who was named Man of the Year. When I close my eyes I still see you. To squeeze your hand is once again to walk into a trap. The last time I did, the Lord punished me, He took away my reason. I violated His command to go on. I must go on, even if it makes no sense. Everyone is charged by Him to do something. I was told to become an itinerant philosopher, a pilgrim-magus; I must push on to the places I haven't yet seen. Some get there by reclining in an easy chair. You are still a threat to me, you know. But I will enjoy accompanying you to the market Saturday morning. I'll get used to going places with you, and at a concert or the theater I'll doze off, knowing you are there to give me a gentle tug. When the moment is ripe I'll place my hand on your knee, I'll observe your face and wait for your inner smile to appear. I am curious about that, just as I am curious about how you cook, how you feel about my friends, how you feel about me. But I see trouble ahead if I let you be the arbiter of my affairs; if I let you take over my life. Because it would be perfectly all right then to keep my hands between your thighs at night until we both fall asleep and I turn onto my stomach—there is never enough room, you are the kind of person who takes up too much room. You would spread your long limbs and make those murmuring sounds that say I'm happy now, no one bother me. I will watch you wash and dry your hands and apply your creams and makeup and put on your stockings. With the passage of time you will look stunning, flawless, in a Melinda-ish sort of way, and everything on you will look more and more Melinda-like, your stockings, the point of your shoe, the edge of your sentences. I'll end up sitting in your hillside apartment on Leander Street, and everything outside will turn white…Help yourself from the fruit basket, and do look through the picture album, please don't let my chatter bother you.

A Village Room

In the middle of the nineteenth century this village room had been a tavern's taproom. The Jewish tavern-keeper who built the house used to rest his elbow on the countertop in the early-morning haze as expectantly as I do now. There were no customers at this hour, the light of the moon floated across the dewy grass. At such moments the tavern-keeper spoke to his God.

"You planted the desire for amusement in both young pups and grown men, O Lord. The villagers and travelers who come to my tavern hope that a few drinks will loosen their tongues, and that others will find their words amusing. They try to see who can shout the cleverest phrases across the tables. Whoever has the last word is king. When that man speaks, the others listen. One must be born a king, even in a tiny village. On ordinary nights we wait for that king."

A man in a smart overcoat with an upturned collar steps out of a rented car. His long hair does not tolerate a hat even in cold weather, his nose is tempest-tossed, there are bumps on his forehead. His right eye is stern, his left eye forgiving. The tavern-keeper and the guest look each other over, grin, then embrace, as if they both knew they'd been found out.

The guest takes a few deep breaths, the air on these autumn mornings is no less intoxicating than the plum brandy offered him by the tavern-keeper. Dragomán hears squealing: "Prepare your soul, Mr. Hog, they've come for your blood." He feels the light of the morning star between his eyes.

Dragomán's trademarks: slightly graying hair, a toothbrush mustache, and a silver-knobbed walking stick which, when twisted in the right direction, produces a thin-bladed knife. Another section of the stick houses a miniature brandy bottle.

He holds a small, oblong ebony elephant in his hand. When the object is pressed in the right place, a lid snaps open and Professor Dragomán, our onetime classmate and friend, puts a tiny ball of resin in his pipe and mixes it with green sinsemilla for better results. What he has is a cross between Afghan black and Lebanese red.

In the early-morning hours Dragomán begins to wilt, he's had his daily high, been turned on by the sense of his own importance, has generated scores of new ideas, laid the groundwork for one or two grandiose ventures and benevolent alliances. But then he cuts and runs, and everything goes back to where it was.

Another car stops near the tavern, but no one gets out. "You see?" Dragomán says with reproach in his voice. He can't help it, it's not his fault that a car stops and nobody gets out.

At most, he helps create situations; he highlights them. He can make sure that, if necessary, claws are bared and stubborn knees bent. Our world is full of splendid places, first-rate beds, and wonderful women; if only they wouldn't talk so much. Sharp, talkative women make Dragomán nervous, it's like not being able to shut off an alarm clock. He is no longer young, his one and only wife is dead, they never had children. He'd much rather forgo connubial coddling than the pleasures of a solitary life.

He sees Melinda sometimes, though they try to avoid each other. The childhood friend will not give the mayor's wife a bad name. Of course he does anyway, for while they haven't slept together, they take leisurely walks along the old castle wall, or sit on a cliff by the lake, and then visit a fisherman's inn or an out-of-the way tavern where they have mutton stew. They are seen holding hands, Dragomán gallantly helping Melinda across ditches and potholes. They ride their bicycles side by side. Or walk in opposite directions and act surprised when they run into each other. They also whistle short musical quotations at each other, an easy giveaway, for who else but Dragomán would whistle Bach's Toccata and Fugue in D Major so triumphantly; who else would resort to such an old-fashioned attention-getter.

Tomorrow morning he'll go with Melinda to the market and pick out fresh radishes, leeks, giant cauliflower heads, gobs of cottage cheese, and other snow-white wonders. He'll stand behind her, she knows exactly what to get. Dragomán's shopping tips are useless, he's better off carrying the black shoulder bag and minding his own business. Melinda will put a whole quince into her chicken soup and plenty of leeks, and blend in some sour cream at the end. While cooking, she may be distracted, or rather, pay attention to a hundred details and not even notice Dragomán. "What's that, dear, what did you say?"

Everything is wonderful, but Kobra knows it can't last. Right now the lake's surface is a mirror, but Dragomán has only to make a few moves, and he has unleashed a storm, churned up the placid water, produced mountainous waves. Mines explode around Dragomán, though he always manages to sidestep them. It's as if he were dancing the tango on a minefield. The mine analogy is appropriate, for he would hiss quietly and then blow up, without really knowing what is bothering him. He walks innocently from one tragic drama to another. Wherever he plays the inquisitive tourist, a revolution is sure to break out. There is an assassination in the hotel where he's staying? He immediately files an eyewitness report. The readers of his magazine are always eager to know what has happened to Dragomán.

Even if the report concerns an innocent boat excursion, they perk up, all agog, dying to know what happened. Something always does. For instance, a group of drunken rowdies harass a sailor, who smacks one of them across the face. The drunks then band together and throw the sailor in the water. More sailors appear and throw the whole bunch overboard, and then help them climb up the rope-ladder. The sailors as well as the drunks are overly polite to one another. But when everyone is on board, and they've even managed to push up the fattest attacker, a good rap on the chin sends the original victim over the rail and back into the water, and the whole thing starts again. And down below, the polite apologies begin again.

The reason Dragomán is constantly on the move is that he doesn't much care for sleep. One night he went on a local radio show to talk about how the greats of Kandor, unconventional geniuses all, had left home at a young age. He drank with them in the world's oddest bars; they'd reminisce about their salad days in Kandor. They are scattered all over the globe, and when they meet they first embrace, then push each other away, jealous of their new turf. The transient is always a welcome guest, the locals invite him and brag about the advantages of having stayed.

Dragomán has been in Kandor, staying at the Crown, for over a month now. His suite near the roof terrace is pleasant, his windows overlook Resurrection Square. By special arrangement with the hotel management he pays a monthly rate of $1,200, including all the amenities. They even fax his articles to his editor. He can work well on the terrace where tanned women in skimpy bathing suits loll in deck chairs.

During his sojourn in Kandor, Dragomán has visited Kobra several times, arriving at the oddest hour, confident that he can do no better than show up at his friend's house at eight o'clock in the morning, when that friend is about to sit down at his desk like a dutiful schoolboy to do his homework—or barge in after he's just completed his much-needed morning constitutional. Sometimes Kobra is all set to go jogging when the tall, sardonic figure of Dragomán knocks on his window, which Kobra keeps closed even in summer. None of Kobra's local friends would dream of doing this to him.

What's more, no one else has such an absurd face. Dragomán's nose is not exactly hooked, it curves gently at first, plunges downward, and his eyes, those huge blue eyes, peer upward, as though wanting heaven's blessing on his crazy ideas.

"It's a pleasure to see you among the regulars of my tavern, Professor Dragomán. A little borscht with a piece of smoked beef we can always rustle up for you. It will do you good, even this early in the morning, especially if you have a hangover. Or if you like, I will lock up and we can go for a walk in the fields, it's empty there now, we can take a long walk on the wet sand hills, treading on peat in our sturdy boots, happy that we've lived to see this day—it's Shabbat, after all."

"And you, Kobra, there is no escaping you, my friend." I turn on the radio and hear my old classmate yapping away. I switch on the TV, and there he is again, grinning and pontificating on how to keep a healthy balance between one's private and public life. The Olympian simpleton oozes common sense. I know, I know, you are a married man. That explains a lot.

"One thing is for sure: I couldn't do it. Balance, you say?

Where I live the soul has a way of dashing about in a room. I don't earn my keep if I don't send material to my paper. It so happens that whatever it is I'm supposed to pay attention to, I am not truly interested in. Maybe it's because of Melinda, though it's possible that the momentous changes in this place are not so momentous. There is a new vocabulary, a new set of tricks, new people concealing old greed with new slogans. A change in philosophy, a renaming of things, underlings learning to kowtow in a different direction—an underdeveloped country switching illusions in an attempt to catch up with the leaders of the pack. It can't be done. What they've got in the bargain are cheap imports, breathless overeagerness, and a mortal fear of being left behind. They changed trains not that long ago; they must change again. There's nothing here but provincial yammering and grandstanding. In these political times, my only interest is in Melinda. But if I get too close to her, I become weak in the head. I shed the tears of a cast-off lover on my hotel pillow.

But dear God, how nice it is to stretch out on that wide hotel bed, or jump on a bicycle in a pair of comfortable pants and ride along the open highway or down a country lane, then push and coast until I'm flat on my back in the grass, panting happily.

Like a proper gentleman he pays his respects to Regina. Among friends Dragomán usually takes the wife's side. If there is a woman in the house, she should rule. The running of a household, like that of a state, is a job for a chief executive. Kobra is better off abiding by Regina's decisions. No use trying to find out why she does what she does. He might as well tell himself: She's doing a great job. As soon as there is a child, the man owes the woman. In any case, a married man is not an adult but his wife's son; in return for a little warmth he's opted for dependence.

Dragomán never discusses with anyone where he is going or what time he will be back. He might, at most, inform the clerk at the desk. He can afford to pack up and leave. All his belongings fit into two shoulder bags. When he buys a new pair of pants, he throws out the old pair. He wears shirts that never need ironing; he washes them in the bathroom sink and in the morning they are dry. He can ring for room service whenever he feels like it. When he buys a book he reads it and gives it away. He finds that ever since he has given away his library, he's been reading more attentively. He learned in prison to appreciate books that came his way, by chance or on a warden's whim.

If I were a true cosmopolite, said Dragomán, I'd be happy everywhere. But the truth is I am unhappy wherever I am. When a person is nasty, a house ugly, a book boring, I say so—unlike my friend Kobra, who comes up with impossible, transcendental, and all-forgiving explanations for everything. He clings tooth and nail to the elemental, what's already come to pass, and will even abandon the present for fear of being swept away by future promise—which has to be false, since it can be broken—or taken in by a reckless vilification of the now. He rejects the contradictory contortions of two similarly mindless ways of thinking. Utopia, afterlife there, and a vale of tears and daily outrage here. How dull. That scoundrel Kobra knows well that this is all there is: house, wife, child, work, neighbors, early bedtime, starry skies, sunrise, thick walls, cool rooms easily heated in winter—he knows, in short, that man will always find a place to imprison himself.

This is what I kept mulling over on the boat which I boarded, though I had no desire to be on it. I got a choice cabin, yet I couldn't understand why I had to lie in my stateroom and listen to the drone of the ship's engines. Of course I could move to the deck, but there I would be expected to participate in the general conversation and entertain audacious illusions, which I had no stomach for. It always surprises me how passionately and vociferously refined spirits respond to dissenting opinions, even when they are voiced quietly and reasonably. At this point I would gladly have changed places with Kobra, that placid camel... Camel, buffalo, bear—in school he was all of these things, albeit of a slimmer variety. I would much rather have sat on his garden bench, or lain in his conjugal bed, with the captivating Regina's permission, naturally.

In the evening, however, I wandered amid strange houses, on an island's steep, winding streets, I moved from tavern to tavern, and then sat in a square, where in the moonlight I could look at the sea from three different sides. No ships were to be seen; on a wall behind me something unfavorable about Jews was scrawled. Under the palm trees, among glimmering cats' eyes I reached for my walking stick, unscrewed the top, and from a flat silver flask

27

took a sip of Jamaica rum. First glee, then pity made me laugh, and then cry. Rogues and idiots must bear the cross of their idiocy and roguery—they must live with themselves all their lives.

I ran down to the seashore and followed the receding waves on the sandy beach; I observed the dimmed blue headlight of a police launch. On the pier I struck up a conversation with a nice-looking fellow and played a game of checkers with a one-legged man. Standing on a terrace overlooking the pier, I rested my foot on the guardrail and scanned the bay, and across it the wooded hillside dotted with houses. All this belonged to me, I thought. I tried to become a character in other people's dreams, and then I no longer wanted to trade places with Kobra, though I was glad I had good reason to envy that grinning clod.

My friend's most irritable quality is his gentleness; it disarms dogs, cats, neighbors, crowds, though I do believe it is really a way of keeping his distance. His gentleness is psychic economy, sly indifference—it puts you at ease, wanting neither to antagonize nor to embrace. A clever way of staying alone. When I want solitude I run away. Kobra retreats into the glass cage of his gentleness.

You can see him sitting at a table or slinging a shopping bag over his shoulder—he'll bring you whatever you need. People come to see him, he tells them what they want to hear, after which he withdraws into his cave to juggle his shadows. Kobra is the kind of person everybody wants for president, while they see me as an outrageous entertainer. I can provoke, he can placate. You'll always find Kobra puttering about. Me you'll probably miss; I will have skipped town.

Kobra never learned to drive a car; I got my license at eighteen. For a time after my first exile I earned my daily caviar by driving aging, wealthy women to their summer homes. When I tired of them, which happened fairly quickly, I began a career in journalism.

I favored places where bullets cleaved the air, where avoiding police patrols was a daily pastime, and where the number of weapons seen on the street was always impressive. I was curious about the madness which matched up young men to machine guns, usually in the name of some lame ideal.

Dragomán can share a laugh with sleazy characters, it's not easy to shock him. He has a few friends wherever he goes and has a personal opinion of every country in the world. This is an insincere father-seeking country; here you either become a revered father figure, and therefore a charlatan, or a hopeless neurotic from too much dissembling. In any case, your existence tends toward excess. You too could become a first-rate father figure, my dear David Kobra. I appreciate your alliance with populist-statist factions—Heidigger himself supported these forces back when. The local variety is already in place, you made it up yourself.

At the Crown

Through the Crown's plate-glass window one can follow what goes on inside the café, as well as the activities on the square outside. I invite the reader to take a seat, preferably by himself, at a table for two, and observe those present. He may use a collapsible minimike or a camera concealed in a signet ring, if he has them handy. But I don't advise him to join me at my corner table, it might create difficulties. In any case, he will find Kandor only on special maps, and the odd thing about these maps is that they are available only in Kandor.

The Crown's heavy velvet curtains hang on polished brass rods. Seated at the table next to me, an angular man and a curvaceous woman laugh. On seeing me, Arthur, the old cabalist, stands up. He looked calmly at his wife, just as she shook off a moment of intense sadness with a smile. He smoothed a lock of hair away from her forehead, touching it with two fingers. "Yes, Arthur, we are still here." A big smile, then a gentle embrace. "A somnambulist demon," that was how Arthur had once described me. I may look dreamy, yes, but I arrive everywhere on time. Of course the right time is when I get there. And I usually find the people I am looking for. "What are you up to these days?" Arthur asks. "Still alive," I answer. "I am almost dead," he says. "Don't say that," I say. His wife finds my inane response amusing and invites me to dinner. "How does boiled fish with potatoes and vegetables sound? Call us, all right?" The other day I had an excellent meal at a waterfront bistro: homemade pâté, beef cordon bleu, a robust red wine. The long-haired, sad-eyed waitress told me that they buy their wine from a gruff vintner who was a complete mystery. He wouldn't give you the time of day and did you a favor by letting you have a bottle or two. There were strange-looking piles and even stranger contraptions in his yard, the door handle was so high you could hardly reach it, the gate always locked. But he made the best wine in the region.

I invite you, my friend, to Resurrection Square, to the Crown Hotel. Come to the café's pink marble-top table, sit on the brown velvet banquette behind the large plate-glass window. A home away from home for you, a spicier version of the real one. In 1918 to 1919 this hotel offered its rooms and services, not entirely by choice, to the general staff of two successive revolutions. After the war, when counterrevolutionists came to power, it became known as the House of Retribution. In the final days of the Second World War, the diehards of the Hungarian National Socialist movement turned its rooms into torture chambers. Arnold Kobra, at that time a host and merrymaker of the first order, watched the falling incendiary bombs from the hotel's roof terrace. Ostensibly under the protection of the Swiss embassy, he remarked that if the hotel hadn't been filled with prisoners, he would have loved to see a bomb tear into it. But it wasn't the hotel but Arnold that was hit, in the temple.

The hotel remained the site of physical suffering even after the postwar political changes; its updated facilities were now used by the newly installed security organs of the communist regime. Finally, in the more tranquil 1960s, when all the revolutionaries were released from jail, the building again assumed its original function and became one of the city's more venerable, if not excessively expensive, hostelries, its spacious halls the scene of important cultural events.

The manager, who likes to play philosopher, alludes to the crafty ways of the unflappable local population. "We never say no and we never say yes." I tell him I don't approve of this kind of relativism; it smacks of chicanery. But then why is it that I am always a little bored when exposed to the honesty of an either/or attitude? When a fellow denizen of Kandor joins me at my table, I always sense a snag between the speaker and his words, as if he were not telling me the whole truth, yet he leans too close to me as he speaks.

PETRA CALLS ME to the telephone. The voice on the other end says: "Before the week is out you are a dead man." Let's raise our glasses and drink to our health while the going is good; when the host is in a disagreeable mood it's not polite to invite guests. I've invited many, not knowing if all are still alive. I wish the dead happy birthday and offer condolences to the wives of the living.

May you be inscribed in the book of life. The year 5777 is not going to be any worse than 1993. What is recorded on paper is discarded like a heavy overcoat. Yes, madam, if you wish I'll check all my previous addresses. If I no longer live there, they don't belong to me.

What's the hurry, where are you off to at this dark and dismal hour? I am not going anywhere, let duty wait, I owe you nothing, and don't really care what you think of me. Sit at my table, if you like, eat and drink to your heart's content, ask me whatever is on your mind; but I tell you straight out: wild horses couldn't drag me from here.

Back then I sat in this very spot, surrounded by informers. As early as six o'clock in the morning I would settle into this corner seat, take out a pen, a bottle of ink, and my large notebook from my briefcase, and write furiously in my big hand, trying to find answers to the unanswerable. Two young women greeted me when I came in, Petra and Deborah, one of them small, the other large, one nimble, the other clumsy. When not busy they jabber endlessly. Back then there had also been two, a tiny one and a large one, and they wore high lace-up shoes with the toe-cap cut off. Then, too, the management was not responsible for articles left on the coat tree. Deborah used to be a discus thrower; then she made a fairly good living as a masseuse but grew tired of all the bodies. She wears shiny black blouses which, when she moves, balloon out. She mediates, soothes, encourages, and gets a nice tip for divulging confidential information.

A woman in a fur coat comes through the revolving door. The perfume she exudes is the kind that makes a woman all-knowing and fresh. She approaches with the loud clatter of spike heels. Her makeup is fresh, shades of pink flash across her face. What further defines her are quick drags on her cigarette, a nervous shudder, a heaving bosom, large earrings, and restless fingers playing with a shiny belt buckle. She sits at my table and asserts that Kandorans are awkward, dubious, not quite civilized, alternately insecure and overconfident.

Next, a long-haired, bearded man stops by. "You know," he says, "in my house I always have the last word. I open the door, say hello, and nobody answers. You still have somebody to come home to, don't you?" The slightly tipsy, hirsute guest lost his wife last year: she suffered a heart attack while brushing her teeth. He went into the bathroom to do the same and found his wife under the sink, still holding a glass and toothbrush, her eyes fixed in a stare. Ever since, this man has been feeling cold. One can always have breakfast alone, but for thirty-eight years he shared his morning coffee with his wife. He used to be a metal-pourer but then quit his job; two of his friends died of silicosis—they simply dried up. If there were proper ventilation at the plant, they would still be here.

An old girlfriend sits down at my table for a minute; I look at her tired face and listen to her smug, mirthless snicker—she strains to put the best face on her life. I hear a voice I often heard before.

A young boy, his head lolling sideways, is attempting to wriggle out of his wheelchair, his hands shaking. A tall, slender woman in riding pants bends over him. The boy tries to clutch at her neck but can't do it for long.

At the next table two lovers feed each other pieces of cake, and with their free hands grope each other's body. They can't get their fill of each other, or of the Crown's homemade pastry. They communicate without a common tongue; both speak their own but seem to understand each other well. The girl has a map spread in front of her and tries to explain to him how to drive out of the city. But they can't bring themselves to part.

Kuno Aba, my onetime history professor, joins me at my table. Now he is the rector of the university and vice-mayor of the city. He happened to notice me sitting here and dropped in to say hello—curious that I hadn't spotted him from inside. He asks me to go sailing with him, he is a water enthusiast. "It's too rough out there," I say. "Come on," he persists, "let's take on the elements and not each other." "You mean whoever survives wins?" Kuno has taken to speaking in riddles since his appointment as rector, and his vocabulary has become more sanctimonious. They say he is at the cathedral every Sunday, in the front pew. "Let's talk then," I say. "Now? Here?" he asks. "I find it uncomfortable to sit in a place like this with another man."

A cat moves across my field of vision wearing gold-rimmed eyeglasses, followed by the city's perennial avant-garde painter sporting a pointy, spectacularly colorful Egyptian beard. I watch the roller-skating narcissists on the square. The vociferous doomsday prophet is also in his regular spot, attracting, as always, a few attentive listeners. Several others examine the strips of rabbit skin interlaced in his beard. Wearing yellow boots and pulling her stockings up, good old Miss Imola is leaning against a lamppost. Now she bends over, shakes her behind, hits the legs of her boots with a switch and wags her stuck-out tongue. A man in a garish clown suit is conversing with a halberdier in steel-blue armor. The portrait painters and silhouette makers are out in full force, as are the show monkeys and the Peruvian and West Indian bands. In front of the café a skinny girl practices her cello; the coins collect in her open cello case. Two young boys amble along the sidewalk, arms around each other's shoulders. They are munching on apples, spitting out the seeds, convinced that they are the greatest. A third boy whizzes by on a bicycle, he too thinks he is the greatest. If no passerby obstructs my view, I can see the fruit vendor's stand and the bees buzzing over his crates of grapes; I can see him close his eyes. He also sells newspapers and porno magazines featuring huge melon breasts. A woman hisses: "Sex? Sex?" A young man counters, "Smoke? Smoke?" An old woman with pillar-like legs walks past the café window. She stares ahead into the air as though she has just recognized someone; she looks happy.

A thinnish older woman in a smart outfit lifts the veil attached to her hat and without asking for permission sits down at my table. "You knew I was coming, didn't you?" she says. "You knew all about me. I am into all kinds of mediations and exchanges; I relay messages from here and there, including the beyond. I also buy and sell china and jewelry. I can look into your soul, my son, I will bring you the perfect woman, your one and only bride. Naturally, you pay in advance. Show me your palm. Oh my God. I cannot tell you more. Only to be careful."

On the square an equestrian statue rears its legs. A saxophone blares from the jukebox, grappling with the high notes. One way or another, something has to give. Say a streetcar severs my legs. Or I open my mouth to yawn, a wasp flies in and stings me. My throat swells up and that's it. Another scenario: I sit in the grass and a tick crawls onto my testicles. I come down with meningitis, go soft in the head, chew on a piece of leather all day long, waiting for someone to visit me. It's no mean feat to get up every morning, year after year, put on a clean shirt and start the day.

There is no hour of the day like this. Rarely do the Crown's guests get to see sunlight this strong. The dipping sun aims a shaft, from the hip as it were, right in our faces. While a draft sways the cafe curtains, a stray beam goes haywire on the yellow parquet floor. My neck is protected by a scarf, I fidget with my cup and pen. There are always people who have time to sit around. In the fantastic light the gold mosaic muses would love to descend from the wall. Yet for me, the place itself—wherever it may be—is of little significance. This one may seem like *the* place, but then a train or a car can stop and whisk me away. Of all the earplugs I know, an American-made pellet is the best. Whoever doesn't hear the other is truly in charge. Nonbeing is the only secure state. I don't even have to move, I've already received my summons. I'll be fine in this hotel on what may turn out to be my last day.

My indolence keeps me from disturbing this temporary state with intemperate action. The matters I have to deal with daily are inessential, contrived, irksome. A concerned friend stops and says: "A jab here, a punch there. Relief at first, then the threats resume. Everything's become muddled; old friends call one another informers and spies, a foul smell rises from the ground and spreads like a disease. We're all grizzled old men spitting into each other's beards. How can you be so calm? Ah, they haven't done away with you yet. You're not safe anywhere. Even if you would like to settle down for good, they'll come and turn you out of your house."

These days his own body is sending him signals: beads of sweat appear regularly on his forehead. Although he keeps hearing kind words, Dragomán withdraws into his room. Yesterday afternoon, during an official send-off, he had to toast a friend with a glass of red wine, but after a few words he felt faint. He sneaked away, sat at his desk, felt uneasy still, lay down on his oversized bed, where he could hear the rain pelting his window.

Aggressive engine noises intrude, and the usual bustle, some of it purposeful, most of it senseless. A mad rush to produce things that have to be sold whether they are needed or not. People scurrying from one destination to another; pigeons, too, from rooftop to rooftop. Berries turn red on the vine, arms lift sheets from clothesline, clerks type messages at computer terminals to keep others busy.

At best, three-quarters of my life is behind me; if I am not so lucky, four-fifths is gone. And the remainder is getting shorter and shorter, even though the fun has just begun. I am not sixty but six, a first-grader starting the school year, peeping behind a dark curtain. I need a cellar, a tower, the cover of night. As a child I always searched for a good hiding place, in a thicket, behind a woodpile, under the piano, where no hand could reach in and pull me out, as if I were a cat or a rabbit. Accessibility may be a virtue, but it's one I don't care to practice. I have a thousand tasks to accomplish, I can't possibly do justice to them all; there is no telling which one will confound me completely. There's someone at the door with yet another request. Words are to push things away with, deeds are to draw them closer.

Yesterday he met a priest on the street who asked him who he was writing for. Dragomán said he wrote for God. When the clergyman asked if he believed God actually read what Professor Dragomán wrote, his reply was a shy smile. He hoped he did. He was aware of course of the endless number of words printed each day; and when he also took into account that the good Lord kept track of every fly, and could ponder the infinitely intricate inner life of each one, he realized there was nothing enviable about His divine occupation. This very second an infinite number of events are unfolding. God must keep an eye on each and every one, and must do it again the next second, without a break, which must test even His powers. Yet Dragomán continues writing to this overburdened God, informing and amusing Him, and instigating, too, urging Him not to suffer fools lightly, who are long-winded to boot. Why couldn't He doze off while they droned on or bickered? "Should I let them kill each other?" asks the Lord. "Ever since Cain it has happened many times, my Father. The story should be familiar to You. Since I began talking to myself, I've been addressing my words to You. It's possible to make searching observations even while pitching pennies or playing cards." At age eleven Dragomán sent God detailed reports from the Jewish ghetto. But then the pace of events quickened and he had to adopt a telegraphic style: "He's holding a gun to my head, he's waiting. He has lowered it now, he has stepped outside..."

Tombor

Antal Tombor was born to be mayor; he says little, hates to shoot off his mouth needlessly, yet the sound of appreciative laughter is often heard around him. The chin under his funny-looking hat is so prominent, no one wants to be on his bad side. He moves among his staff with a broad smile, exchanging pleasantries, while making sure his workers work. He can say the kindest things to the clumsiest clapper who forever gets his fingers caught in the clapboard, or to the silliest makeup girl who smears rouge on a hysterical actress's nose. Cameramen, soundmen, assistant directors all want to work with him—why shouldn't Tombor make an excellent mayor as well?

He carried off his latest stunt, a pseudorevolutionary campaign, with great aplomb, and as a result was chosen First Citizen of his city. One may well ask why the mayor, of all people, was picked for this honor, but that's another matter. Antal Tombor knows that you cannot direct a film democratically. If a crew member challenges him, he'll be fired even if he is the first cameraman. The director issues orders; people have to carry them out to the best of their abilities. He'll listen to everybody when he's ready, but when he is preoccupied he doesn't want anyone blathering next to him. An election campaign? Nothing to it, a show, a farce, he can do it. It's all in the presentation.

In the race for mayor, Tombor's chances were good: the timbre of his voice was pleasing, he wasn't yet gray, his teeth were fine, he still looked presentable. Women can always tell if a man is desirable to other women. Leaving his mistress's apartment, he'd notice their half-inviting glances. A room is permanently reserved for him at the Crown. When he arrives with a new companion, the doorman never lets on with a wink or a smirk. Tombor was elected mayor because he wasn't all that anxious to be one; because the sudden idea seemed perfectly reasonable; because everyone laughed when they first heard about it, and the comic surprise turned into concerted action. He was an independent, enjoying the support of all the liberal parties. None of the opposition candidates could smile so benignly.

Communism didn't get much out of Tombor. He saw the system collapse in 1956; it was a safe bet that he would see it happen again—it wasn't what you'd call a solid investment. He knew enough to avoid using their vocabulary; he devised his own language of evasion and subterfuge, full of verbal quirks and gags, adding to the mix a pinch of the Bible diction, a dash of Gypsy lingo. With party hacks he spoke about irrelevancies—astronomy, horses, haute cuisine—he made their heads spin with esoterica. They might have suspected that he was pulling their legs, yet they weren't offended; they could tell he didn't really hate them. He'd put his arm around their shoulders, he knew a bit about car repair and football and the construction trade—the apparatchiks embraced him. He looked in on the bigwigs now and then, he patronized them, and therefore was safe from bans and proscriptions. In the West, film directors have to break in the producers, here they had to take the party bosses in hand. "They thought I was cast in their play, but I knew they were playing a part in mine." He got away with much more than others, he was showered with prizes from East and West, journalists covering the award ceremonies were attracted by his laconic responses in French, and didn't mind that he answered questions about content with aperçus about form.

Tombor's guest list encompasses the entire political and cultural spectrum—avant-garde artists and academicians, rightists and leftists, conservatives and liberals in equal number, a representative sample of every circle and faction, featuring the showiest specimens. They can be shaggy, paunchy, or deformed, as long as they are impressive, memorable, and add color to his weekend gatherings. Tombor knows he's laying himself open to digs and thrusts, he'll be targeted by his rivals, but, as they say, if you don't want to lose, don't go to the races. And he does like to

39

go where things are happening. The office of mayor is more interesting now, it's possible to showcase urban democracy as though it were a play. Tombor will surely get it from the City Council after it finds that the sanitation people cleaned up the downtown area only after receiving a hefty bribe from the restaurant owners. And the city's leading citizens will most certainly have second thoughts about the police once they realize that rowdies and hooligans were allowed to go home, while harmless mental patients were back in the loony bin. What next, one wonders. What triple-edged knife will the rising star of the young liberals use to stab him in the back?

Actually, more and more people have been trying to discredit Tombor of late. They used to admire him, now they gloat over his indiscretions and are outraged that he won 18,000 German marks playing roulette in a casino. Everyone thinks it was a fix, though all that happened was that he had bet on black thirteen times in a row. Whereupon he grabbed his hat and coat, adjourned to one of the new brothels in a hillside suburb, and spent 2,000 marks on two charming girls, a thousand on each. The rest he gave to the city's welfare department, earmarking it for school lunches for needy children. It should also be noted that not long ago, after a city councilman had made an inflammatory statement at a meeting, His Honor jumped up and banged furiously on the table: "You little shit, care to step outside?" he shouted. The city father didn't feel like stepping outside, which Mayor Tombor didn't mind all that much. And before that there was a big-time real estate speculator who had the nerve to leave his wallet bulging with large bills on his desk. He collared the man in the anteroom, dragged him through several offices, and in front of the shocked secretaries grabbed his feet and dangled him out the window. Passersby looking up nodded in agreement. "Oh, it's just our mayor dangling somebody out the window. He does have a temper."

His constituents never get too angry with him; he does show up where he is needed. After a gas tank explodes or a roof collapses, he appears on the scene almost immediately. And he is also quick to visit the victims in the hospital. He hasn't taxed the city's merchants too severely, city services function tolerably well, and

Kandor has even begun to attract foreign capital—His Honor has established unexpected contacts with Swedish and Pakistani bankers. He can be so ingratiating when greeting foreign dignitaries that they have to reciprocate. And when he visits night shelters he makes sure he brings entertainers with him, and home-cooked meals for everyone.

Tombor is not really susceptible to vanity; being mayor is another production, another movie. He is basically a hardworking man, and now mayoralty is his project. If he decides he's had enough, he'll go into another line of work. Or do nothing. His children are grown, he could live on his pension and fish in the lake—the pike and sturgeon will bite for sure. At this point Tombor considers almost everything a game; he can afford to be mayor, but he can also afford to fail. He'll do nothing that goes against the grain, but if something makes his nostrils quiver he will have it as part of his prized collection. Tombor makes a note of every bright spot in the city, every new storefront and illuminated sign that enlivens the general dullness, although he also likes things to look gray, ash-gray, cement-gray—the shades he uses generously in his films.

Tombor has rented a lakefront hotel. It's the end of the season, which means attractive prices and an unrushed, courteous staff. The hotel is filled with Tombor's guests, who know one another and wander from room to room, socializing. Bella, the new owner of the place, has given every room its own distinct character. She sat in them, surveyed them, communed with each one. The building was old, the rooms needed antique or restored furniture, nothing must be uniform. "Every room's been reinvented," she said to Tombor with pride. The police chief of Balatonújfalu maintains order from a distance; he too will get his payoff for the weekend, plus a part in the movie.

Word got around that he was having big weekend bashes, like the one twenty years ago, in the village's Hubertus chapel, which Tombor had been clever enough to buy for a song from a hunters' club. The surrounding rocky peaks were too steep for the overweight hunters to climb, and the club thought it inappropriate to have a lift built for them at public expense. Besides, suspicious crashing and jangling noises were often heard from the chapel and no one could figure out the cause. It was Tombor, of course, rattling chains and ringing cowbells to scare off the hunters.

The host wanted his guests to introduce themselves formally in front of cameras and microphones suspended from tree branches. He procured the necessary funds for this expensive gathering from government sources and private foundations. Selecting with wit and daring, he invited a whole slew of friends and acquaintances, among them envious schemers and ill-wishers—a hotel full of dangerous characters. Many outsiders and hangers-on got wind of the event and now they prowled about the place like hungry wolves. Timed to coincide with the fall harvest, Tombor's September spectaculars have become all the rage. Water temperature is 20 degrees centigrade, the anglers have no reason to complain. Unfortunately, the merry-go-round has been taken down and the circus posters promising three-foot midgets are long out of date.

The invited guests know that tonight the eye of the camera, as well as those of all the others, will be on them. The invitation notes that all who enter will be spied on, eavesdropped on. Microphones gleam enticingly on tree trunks; push a button and start talking. This is the night of reckonings and revelations. A drunken guest hugs a tree and yells the truth at the full moon. The possibilities inherent in the material are endless. The profusion of random scenes may yield some remarkable footage. Let's praise aleatoric composition, for it exploits randomness. If the improvised scenes are riveting enough and the tension around the set electric, then the drama itself becomes rich and dense, though the director may still be in control. It's a collective production; whoever participates creates his own film...But that is how we were at the beginning of the nineties—artists turning irritable by the end of the summer; intellectuals getting themselves mixed up in politics. While grasping at the future, we let the present run through our fingers.

For Tombor concentrated time is more valuable than time drawn out. Around him people behave as if they have parts in his film, even those who don't. Yet Tombor always hints that this is all playacting, good clean fun—the show's on even as we speak. "Our director may need to decide whether he wants to be mayor of this town or its master of ceremonies," wrote a sharp-tongued columnist in the local paper.

It's a celebration, a time for ingathering and sacred ritual. The drums are beating, the sacrificial animal shudders with fright. What else could Tombor be than a secular grandmaster discussing politics with priests? Go ahead, sacrifice yourself, climb on the altar; you too could become a sacrificial bull, your head may be split open by an ax. "Hey, aren't you carrying this a bit far?" Dragomán asks. There is something grim about Tombor's resolve. Even a giant oak can be struck by lightning. A lumbering bear can be stabbed in the side by a bayonet.

Dragomán and Tombor are relaxing in an orchard. "You're the chief now, king of the jungle. Next to you I am a paper dragon. If you say it's a sunny day, everyone nods, filled with the heartwarming certainty that it is indeed a sunny day. It's a special gift, one has to be born with it. Your six-foot-four-inch frame radiates benevolence; people lose their mettle around you, and start spinning like so many minor planets.

"You are Kandor's First Citizen. The bourgeois has triumphed, private property is his obsession, he craves five-star goods and services. Discriminating consumers form their exclusive associations. And now you want to use your position as mayor to create outdoor urban theater.

"You may neutralize the young, low-brow radicals, but not for long. I watch them: their single-minded, unrelenting ideological hatred can target anyone: blueblood, prole, Jew, peasant, anyone who is easy to hate. The race is on to see who can produce the loudest bang. The puffs of emotional exhaust attract an audience, at least until the audience gets tired of the noisemakers who will eventually quiet down.

"Some of these leading gentlemen said good-bye to forty years, undeniably the longest continuous period of their lives. Did they simply throw them away? Were those forty years nothing but a mistake, a detour, a waste? Didn't they read or write anything worthwhile in those forty years? Didn't they ever find their sweethearts' gestures endearing? Or have a decent cut of meat, drink tolerably good wines? Didn't they ever take their children skating or to a ballet class? Or gaze at the stars, or at bundled-up infants?"

43

Every September a fair is held in the village, a strangely two-faced affair. In the valley, groups of elderly women pass one another; they arrived in chartered buses and now, led by their parish priest and holding their church banners aloft, they march in neat rows toward the village chapel. They will form long lines in front of four portable confessionals set up next to the church. They'll listen all night long to priests whose voices will resound in an amphitheater carved into the Valley of Mercy, in the hollow of a stone quarry, which therefore has singularly fine acoustics. The priests will take turns, every half hour another will preach, their faces illumined by spotlights. Farther back, lying on scattered straw with only the roof of an open shed to protect them, are the reluctant slumberers. It's a special honor to stay up all night and hear men of the cloth intone Christ's words. Some of the elderly women bite their own fingers so as not to be overtaken by sleep. On the hilltop, amid vendors' tents and gaudy sideshows, the Gypsy fair is under way. Here you can buy a car, a horse, a woman, and get married, too, for the night.

Tombor is gearing up for a major event. But then he has always been given to excess. More than likely the invited guests will not sleep much tonight, even though the hotel beds are quite comfortable. Right now, in one of the smaller pavilions, he is working on a special lighting effect. Different colors will blend, white sheets will luminesce in a sea of blue. The commotion will last only through the weekend, after which the village will return to its quiet self. The listening devices will be taken down from the trees, time will once again pass unmarked and unmissed. But this September he has carved a weekend out of oblivion.

Tug-of-War

The pull of gravity is far greater than Melinda's protests or her occasional declarations of independence. Early Saturday morning Antal slides out of Melinda's bed and crosses the garden to his workshop. After puttering about for a couple of hours, he can say he's accomplished something and deserves to get on his bicycle with his canvas shopping bag and ride out for milk and fresh rolls. On the way he'll probably meet Kobra and they'll talk—Saturday mornings wouldn't be the same without these chats. While filling their baskets, they'll outdo each other in flirting with the shopgirl and will also pick up the morning papers.

Antal puts the sheaf of newsprint in front of Melinda, who is the designated first reader. Friends of theirs have given interviews, their extended Kandoran family have become players in current events. Melinda is rooting for the right side, of course, and is a little sad that the majority do not share her enthusiasm. She is happy that the once shunned and ostracized are now stars, though she does regret that they've turned serious, considering exalted posts that a few years ago would have made them wince. Even their bearing has changed, they seem more masculine—more impersonal, too. They still want you to know that they count you among their friends, but you feel the strain; they seem ill at ease, duty calls, a mere apolitical chat may strike them as frivolous. A round or rectangle-shaped table awaits them in a council chamber, a conference hall, a press room. Because they have no time for anything else, Melinda perceives in their eyes a guilty conscience, a cooling heart.

When Antal enters the room, Melinda obligingly points to an

45

armchair across from hers. She can always interrupt the translation she is working on. Every Wednesday her friends come over and they chatter away in the living room or on the terrace. Antal, her husband, either joins them or he doesn't; he might even leave, though he'd rather stay. Actually, he prefers to sit quietly in a corner.

The mayor offered to marry his wife again, even though they were never officially divorced. He thought a lot about what happened between them, and admitted that he had acted churlishly; he was forever sidetracked, pulled this way and that; he knows now that curiosity is nothing more than divided attention.

A moment of truth is at hand. A showdown, and then order. We'll know once and for all who belongs to whom, and who is stronger. There's bound to be confusion when possession is not clarified. Victory as well as defeat must be clear-cut. Antal Tombor wants to possess both his wife and his city, and he won't tolerate any attempt to curtail his power. In his house everyone has a place, including Melinda.

In his lifetime he's reached out to many women, but with Melinda it's different. When he touches her, his fingers seem longer. When he takes her by the arm, he knows this is right. Otherwise he feels nervous, tired, old; he functions, but inefficiently. His sure touch is gone, he repeats himself, many trials may yield one good result, and even that is invariably her doing.

Antal loves to explore Melinda's private and public stratagems. He gave up long ago trying to comprehend his wife's fits of passion, her incomparable cerebration. Puzzles are not always for solving, though he has kept an eye on her relationships, while she thought to herself: Oh that simpleton; he thinks I'm so complicated. The truth is I am even simpler than he is. "Sometimes, not always"—their daughter Ninon has said—"Mama comes across as a genius, and then you seem like a big clod."

"EVEN WHEN WE quarrel I want you to sleep beside me; when you are abrupt and your offhand remarks sting, and you don't appreciate breakfast in bed, and awake muttering another woman's name—even then. For only people who fall asleep and wake up together belong to each other. I sneak out of the bedroom at six o'clock, but not before I look at your sleeping face.

When your father, Jeremiah, held Dragomán over our heads, I lowered my eyes in shame. He punished and tested us, and I never questioned his judgment. I can't even say that János was an interloper; I knew he was arranging Jeremiah's papers. It almost seemed as if the old man's spirit illuminated that upstairs room. János, the busy editor, never slept there. If he stayed late, he called a cab and went home. He knew enough to keep incompatible things separate, he had the sense of delicacy of the vanishing older generation. There really was nothing objectionable in the way János conducted himself."

One minute Tombor would like to sit with Dragomán in his workshop (for unlike Kobra, who is a dolt when it comes to moviemaking, Dragomán anticipates every one of Tombor's ideas), and the next he'd like to yank his old friend out of his chair and toss him into a corner like a pesky cat. Antal realizes that he is not complete without his wife. He wishes with all his heart that Melinda would always be there to torment him with her quick, sardonic wit.

Antal lays siege to his wife, he builds her into his life. What if I had no one, he muses, if all that surrounded me was cold dust. Others cry when they are alone. Melinda knows that there is enough of her husband to go around, and her own share of this old fool is quite enough, thank you. Ordinarily, she passes over his indiscretions, but sometimes she erupts. Tombor relishes these scenes; he wants all hell to break loose. Let the witch rant and rave. Or be like an iceberg. Or come at him with the kitchen knife. She does everything so magnificently. Trembling with curiosity, he waits to see how the scene will play itself out. Melinda's entry in her diary: "After I'd savaged and stomped on him, he was spent—and happy, like someone after a healthy bloodletting."

Melinda can be a little inattentive, she can look past Tombor; he, on the other hand, watches her constantly. When Melinda closes her eyes, she sees Dragomán approaching. Did her husband invite him here so he could blow his brains out? Or does he want to co-direct a film with him? Make him his right-hand man, his advisor, his spokesman, his representative? Does he want to appease him? Make himself suffer? Share the wealth? What?

On the streets of Kandor everyone eyes Dragomán as if he

were a flashy foreign car. God protect you, dear János; maybe tonight is the night when that oversized trickster will pounce. Or will it be tomorrow? Or never? Don't you sense danger? Do you want him to pounce? So you can strike back and knock him down? Your own blows are something to behold. Do you really want to see my husband stretched out on the floor? His eyes go dark? But perhaps it will all be quite friendly. We'll sit in the park near the lake and watch the ducks, or look across the water to the other side. Or ride our bikes to Tobacco Hill and walk up to the cemetery, and later, as the rocks give out the heat they've absorbed during the day, visit one of the cozy wine cellars. Under the strong moonlight we'll walk to the edge of the wharf, to be closer to the elements. No need to say anything about the pleasures of good eating. I will only mention the fried *fogas,* with its curled-up tail…You always thought, didn't you, that I was nothing but a cheap showgirl, a cut-rate enchantress.

The Fabric

As Dragomán alighted from the hotel elevator, he was greeted with a round of applause. Mayor Tombor took his arm, and the vice-mayor, Kuno Aba, his onetime political indoctrinator, now the city's leading light, rector, moral pillar and permanent fixture, went up to kiss him, or more precisely, to rub his beard against Dragomán's face. They crossed the square, their path cordoned off by police lines, with people on both sides leaning over the ropes, stretching out their hands, their faces aglow. Dragomán tried shyly to acknowledge the ovation. A flourish of trumpets from the galleries, and the man honored for rather sketchy achievements entered the university's ceremonial hall.

Not far from the hall was the bulletin board on which forty-odd years ago he had been exposed, disgraced as a "class enemy." He had darted up the stairs then, and at first could see only his high school graduation picture that looked like a mug shot. Next to the mug shot, the verdict: Expelled from the university on account of dubious family background, incorrect political views, dangerous comportment. Dragomán was declared history's refuse, out of place in a citadel of learning. He hadn't believed the judgment then; he didn't believe the tributes paid to him now.

These people wanted something from him. Kuno Aba read the laudation, Dragomán nodded off for a minute, but he did catch a subtle dig or two embedded in the homage. It was probably Tombor who had asked Kuno Aba to deliver the praises, and he obliged. Aba was ready to make the necessary gestures, ready to appreciate Dragomán's finer qualities. Forty years ago, even thirty years ago, the two had been leaders of a discussion group

49

that had met regularly at the Crown, and since then they had observed an unspoken rule: no public criticism of each other. Now they indicated with tiny smiles that they were not on the same team.

As for what happened there, in the Valley of Mercy, Dragomán had never told anyone about it. He'd never actually promised Kuno that he wouldn't, but Kuno knew that his friend would remain silent. The members of the special force were also not eager to talk. And the dead were in no position to say anything. Dragomán was the only witness who had no interest in keeping it a secret; it was his sense of decency that kept him from talking. He did it out of consideration for Kuno, of course, and for the regime which since has fallen. He had thought Kuno's situation tragic: good intentions, naïveté, complicity. Kuno hadn't yet begun to throw his weight around or start to rewrite history. He, too, kept quiet.

Another flourish of trumpets in the hall. Banners covered the walls—the city's flag adorned with antlers and the national colors with the prewar crown emblem. There was the inevitable schoolgirl presenting a bouquet of flowers. Dragomán didn't kiss her, a handshake sufficed. On the dais a parade of academic robes, and an honor guard that had to be the most resplendent on the continent. Tombor had staged a regular costume party, placing some of his uniformed boys in the gallery and turning them into trumpeters. What he loved most in his elaborate productions were these triumphal entrances. Dragomán noticed in Antal a strong desire to make a fashion statement even in politics. "Citizens, be dazzled" seemed to be his motto. The ceremonial cap was comically askew on Dragomán's head as he reached for the scroll and the fancy box. The largest size headgear seemed too small for his head.

He took a peek into one of the lecture rooms: the desks where he'd once read, ate, slept, or had fun with hand or leg, were still there. It had always been fascinating to watch a female classmate's expression change, the annoyed smile, when he reached under her skirt and stroked her leg—while behind the lectern the bellowing liars went on bellowing and lying, the subtle insinuators went on insinuating, and those who wanted to evade watchful eyes managed to get lost in minutiae.

Now both the university and City Hall embraced him, professors and students read his works. When they chided him Dragomán fell asleep. Kuno said it was all right to like Dragomán, but he was not the mainstream. He was not: God forbid he should ever be caught in the mainstream. Kuno, on the other hand, had it in him to be in the middle—so much the worse for him. Dragomán was still trying to keep his ceremonial cap from falling off, and was fingering his just-bestowed decorations. At twenty he had been branded a decadent bourgeois and expelled from the university. But what was he now? In the ceremonial hall, it was Tombor, his former classmate and intellectual interlocutor who introduced him as Doctor Kandoris and wished him to be *conditor urbis.* Yes, the honors were done by the great filmmaker, who, as mayor, is directing a film with endless scenes. He is also the husband of the woman Dragomán both fears and is attracted to—the woman he keeps running away from, because he thinks commitment is servitude.

What is going on? Would Tombor like him to get back together with Melinda? He encourages Dragomán to consider himself Kandor's writer in residence, its *Stadtschreiber*, and he would also like it if Dragomán could create interest in Kandor among his New York friends, bankers, in particular. Venture capital may follow venturesome curiosity—first a trickle, then a flood.

When he was last here, four years ago, he fell in love with Mrs. Tombor, née Melinda Kadron. The mayor's wife is forty-three now, her hair is still black, with only a few strands of gray. She continues to work as a school counselor and in her spare time translates foreign novels. The political changes of recent years have affected only her husband.

But then, with a suddenness that even he found puzzling, Dragomán left town. And he hasn't been back until now. He prefers not to talk about his misgivings. Kuno Aba has suggested that he help out the Circle of Memory, a group dedicated to historical preservation, though it's understood of course that each age rearranges its historical memory according to its own taste.

Dragomán was afraid to come back, he didn't want to live in the same city as Melinda. Only in motion can he be himself, and only mishaps can detain him or tie him down.

Tombor needs Kuno to be the leading spirit of his paternalistic setup, his little Kandoran monarchy. Without a clear-cut pecking order, citizens become confused. They must learn to respect their mayor in all his guises. Tombor needs to surround himself with academic types whose every third sentence is a piece of clever impertinence. He needs technocrats, too, who can translate their colleagues' lofty speeches into dollars and cents, and the saving thereof, and who can augment this gift with a modicum of modesty. They must make sure, moreover, that he doesn't die of boredom when being led on a tour of city projects.

Tombor has to pay regular visits to the labor exchange and attend every game of the city's soccer league. And he has to be on hand at every opening night and every concert given by the Kandor Philharmonic. At business luncheons and receptions he must use his charm and his powers of persuasion to solicit funds for endowments and charitable organizations, and he expects Kuno Aba to do his part in these endeavors. However, he also needs that defiant, naysaying spirit, the periodic appearance at City Hall of that counter-guru with sardonic, cosmopolitan airs. Let the bureaucrats and civil servants be caught between these two extremes. He needs Dragomán, in short, as a provocateur and seducer, to shake up the town's conservatism and complacency, tamper with entrenched political traditions, and jeer at the chorus of self-praise. It'll suffice for him to drop in once in a while—no need to unsettle officials excessively.

Professional ambition, integrity, dedication: Tombor demands these qualities from his subordinates, just as his predecessors did: men whose portraits hang in the corridors of City Hall. They are still all there regardless of their political conduct. For the most part they were intelligent men, moderately or extremely so, which also means that they were fools. For the sake of this or that political fad they deviated from ethical principles cherished by their family and friends. Yet they all possessed a fair amount of common sense, and an exquisite loyalty to their city; none of them intended to do it any harm, though they invariably did.

Tombor would like Dragomán to be his roving ambassador. He can't stand ceremonial functions, he only likes to direct films. In Cannes what interests him are the private screenings; he hates commotion and ostentation. Whenever he finishes a picture and the attendant hullabaloo has subsided, he loves to take solitary walks in the open country. Using his feet relaxes him; not having to think makes him happy. Tombor hates to extemporize and run the risk of stumbling over his words; he wants his friend to represent him, to regale his listeners with droll anecdotes. And if he, Tombor, must go too, he'll take Dragomán along, to keep talking when Tombor is too lazy. At official dinners he'll be glad to pass the ball to another member of his team, but it has to be a competent player. Dragomán can shine with his quotations and allusions, and step in for his mayor so brilliantly, he is bound to score. If Kuno Aba became Tombor's conservative right-hand man, then Dragomán could be his anarcho-liberal left hand. The mayor takes from both what he can use.

Antal, who likes to think he is of noble lineage, does pick and choose like a sovereign. By balancing between extremes, he believes he's grasped the essential, becoming himself the tongue of the scale. When he was asked the standard question: What book would he take with him to a desert island, he first gave the proper answer—the Bible, because it had everything—and then named János Dragomán. He needed the give and take, he said. As captain of the soccer team (for he had been that, too, naturally), Tombor had picked Dragomán first to be on his team. Tombor was a great center and chose Dragomán to cover the outside left. But Tombor also needs Kuno, to mouth solemn clichés, weighty phrases placing Tombor and his friends in a noble civic tradition. Words to take the sting out of the charge that the city for Tombor is one giant movie set. Actually, he loves sitting in his raised chair at City Council sessions. He invites earnest debate, delves into each item on the agenda, and calls the opposition's attention to weak points in his proposal. Let the woodpeckers tap away before it's too late, he says, and then proposes that they sleep on it. Good night all, let our dreams be our guide.

Kuno Aba's young wife, Sandra, is now the mayor's secretary, and it's rumored that before long all power will be in her hands. She made him get rid of his chief of staff and has assumed the roles of his English- and French-speaking foreign affairs advisor, chief spokesperson, and liaison with the law enforcement agencies. She schedules his appointments, writes his speeches, briefs him, preps him, and does it all with remarkable ease. She is far brighter than the other staff members and never takes offense when Tombor, with erratic stubbornness, crosses out phrases from prepared speeches, saying that's not his style. She simply rewrites them until Tombor says—That's me.

When still in high school, Sandra had a part in one of Tombor's films and at one point studied directing under him. But to please her father, and to be on the safe side, she also earned a law degree. She chose Tombor as her mentor, becoming one of his script-writers. According to Tombor, Sandra is good at sizing up situations, she knows how to be quiet and speak only when she has something worthwhile to say. She single-handedly ran Tombor's election campaign and even now accompanies him everywhere. All telephone calls to his His Honor are screened by her.

Tombor often spends the night in his office. He starts early in the morning, and if at eight p.m. he buzzes a subordinate, he is amazed that no one responds, the rest of the building is dark and deserted. Anywhere something occurs, Tombor is there, with Sandra in tow taking copious notes. Tombor makes the decisions, but it is Sandra who makes sense out of them; sees the wisdom in them.

The city is used to Tombor's long walks during working hours. He strolls through the market, stops at elementary schools, watches a rehearsal at the theater—he inaugurates, celebrates, ushers in, ushers out. He can improvise monologues on any subject, though he does forget sometimes where he is or why he is there. In crowded rooms where only one person speaks at a time, the mayor's eyes get droopy. But let it be said in his defense that he sometimes falls asleep in the mayor's chair, too, while one of his supporters is extolling the virtues of a mayoral proposal. The opposition's rhetoric puts him to sleep, too—though as soon as things become interesting, his eyes pop open, and he perks up. At least when I am walking I don't sleep, Tombor would say apologetically. If he didn't walk around so much, he would know far less about the city. Of course he has to stop now and then for a sip or a bite, which has led certain outsiders to conclude that he is pub-crawling with a pretty young girl during working hours.

If he has to, Dragomán musters all his academic and social skills and addresses conferences in Kraków and Prague and Budapest, sensing all the while the demise of the concept of Central Europe. They all wriggled out of the empire together, but the new leaders scoff at the idea of solidarity and turn up their noses at each other. They are in a race to see who can adapt to the West quicker, they strut their stuff, but there are no takers.

Dragomán brightens the arena with his harried smile; he poses questions, mediates, recognizes new voices. It's past midnight and the room is still full of people. All the new sages and big shots are here; eventually, they'll work things out with the older generation, everyone can say what they will, none of it is that dangerous. Underlings can easily trade bosses because they always know what lies behind the bosses' words. Styles come and go, but the underlings' versatile, adaptable face is here to stay.

Isn't this what you wanted, this slipping and sliding, which the human material is so good at? The aesthetic view of man does not relish an amorphous jelly-like state? Crystals are no doubt more pleasing, but they are also more brittle and fragile—while jelly can assume any shape. Anyone with that consistency is usually proud of his former stiff-necked self.

The obdurate and the willful should be banned; we don't want anything untoward to happen. Caves shouldn't crumble, walls shouldn't crack, no one should tear open your door, or strike you with a hatchet or stab you with a needle while pinning down your head and pulling back your hair. No one should kick you in the face when you're already down. There are people who can't take physical abuse in any form, they'd rather die. They get bullied, they despair, and jump out the window. Dragomán was beaten quite a few times in his life, his head was bashed in more than once, but he survived.

A student sits at Dragomán's table, badgering him with questions while pushing the red button of a tape recorder.

Why do you think that things are important only if people talk about them? Try to escape the jumble of words, the insidious tussle of idioms. At universities everyone invents a new terminology, which then grows with its author, and expires when he does. But if our favorite disciple, a parrot of our self-invented terminology, keeps on circulating these coinages, our immortality is assured. As for me, when I hear my parrot speak, I look for the exit sign.

I had a hard time in school; the first few days all I did was cry and fight with the other children. It bothered me no end that I had to stay in a room and couldn't leave. To this day I have the urge to quit places where I am expected to stay put. In such situations I just want out, the square is fine, there I calm down. Important people cross Resurrection Square with firm strides, whereas the nobodies, the good-for-nothings, wander about aimlessly. They shake their heads, they talk to themselves, or play chess on a bench, stretch their legs, strum a guitar, lie on a Ping-Pong table and cover their faces with their cap.

Do you want to be successful at all cost, ladies and gentlemen? I ask my students. Fight with all your might to keep up appearances? Past a certain age you are naturally considerate, yet don't much care what impression you make on others.

Please remember: our essential characteristic is ignorance, a progressively painful form of ignorance. What we may believe to be our common legacy of wisdom turns, in time, into vapidity. You must know that the idiocies of a given time and place will invariably assault your brain. But even at the zero point of your ignorance, keep thinking and disregard authority. For the most important questions put to us, there are no answers. It's enough to surmise that we are tiny and share our fate with others equally tiny. We are indebted to our forebears and to our offspring, if we have been blessed with any.

The thing itself becomes its own reward, ladies and gentlemen, not future prospects but the starting point, the place where you happen to be. You have been dealt a good or bad hand now, here, this is where the action is. Everything means something and you are always on view.

If you ask me, my friend, I would recommend remaining still. Greater self-control, a sober serenity. I am grateful that I am still alive and can still draw breath. Hats off to mellow perseverance.

What do I admire most? Zest, youth, the exertion of strength. I like the guy who breaks out of prison or absconds from his regiment; the one who wades through marshes and balances on a plank over a precipice, and uses a rope ladder to land on a secure branch only to light a peace pipe there, which will make everything moving up and down freeze for one timeless moment.

Good Feelings

In the fall of 1947, on the first day of school, all of us freshmen were lined up on the schoolyard's pavement to hear a cautious yet solemn welcoming address given by a skinny Latin teacher, our new principal. It was a cream puff of a speech, filled with air. He bored me, though not as much as he would bore me later. Everybody else, though, seemed interesting. No one was a total stranger, they were all vaguely familiar. I picked out several groups of faces in my new class, in a few days these groups would be individuals. I noticed that those sitting around me were not happy to be there either. I wasn't afraid that I might be called on to recite the lesson, but what did frighten me was the possibility of being exposed, that it would finally come out that I thought of school as a well-maintained detention center. For half the day the student is a prisoner: he can neither go where he would like nor stay at his desk to rummage around or scribble to his heart's content. Though otherwise receptive, I didn't like being around so many people so early in the morning, and was in no mood to listen to loud, eccentric schoolmasters. I could think of better ways to spend my time.

I was making plans with my desk mate to go to the cabaret that night, when the teacher pounced. He'd been waiting, eager to catch me red-handed, to prove once and for all that I was unprepared. When I produced the correct answer, he stopped me, suspicious that I was merely improvising. That answer was the only thing I knew. I was the kind of student who spiked his laziness with cunning. He's got brains, the scoundrel, the teacher would say, but he daydreams in class, or reads. Yes, the ruffian definitely has what it takes, but school is not what he has on his mind. Then one day the chemistry professor stopped at my desk. Seeing that I was reading again, he let out a roar. Was that why he was being paid? So that while he was sweating blood teaching us, I should keep my head buried in a book?

I would have loved to be a private student, a stevedore, a truck driver, a lonely pensioner on a long walk—anything but to have to sit in that classroom. I assumed school was a prison for the teachers, too; they had to come in every day and face a bunch of disagreeable, insolent adolescents. The chemistry teacher held up his frayed cuffs: "See that? I have no money to buy a new shirt. I have three children. Feeding them is a job in itself. They never get to eat ham or fancy sardines, like some of you young gentlemen. Why do you come to school, anyway? To humiliate your teacher? I fought in the war, I was in prison camp, do you think it's fun standing here lecturing you?"

No, we didn't think so. Life could not have been much fun for him. Waking up every morning inside that body would be discouraging enough. Or the thought that his red, bulbous nose would be his forever. And the same potbelly every morning, the same loose buttons on his jacket, the same darned socks. His love for his subject could not have been so great that he should want to share it with the enemy—young people whose eyes told him they were listening to him under duress. One of them was producing a series of obscene drawings, another was carving lines into his desk while gazing out the window, a third was conducting an imaginary orchestra, a fourth was squeezing tennis balls to make his hands stronger. Poetic glances are cast at the gray wall of the building across the street, but when the teacher called on someone, there was a defiant glint in the student's eye, as if he'd been violated. "Can you tell me what I just said? Summarize today's lesson, why don't you? You weren't here at all, were you? Has your spirit vanished like a fart in the evening air? Leaving only the cadaver sprawled out at your desk."

When the noon bell rang, we headed raucously for the door, despite admonitions to stay in line, let the others pass, have some respect, at least while we were still inside the building. Once past the swinging doors, or better still a few blocks away, we could finally let out the beast in us. I for one never slid down the marble-topped banister, which at one time had a ribbed surface and which had been worn mirror-smooth by numerous student bottoms, but once I reached the ground floor and pushed through the door, I too let out a sigh of relief. Free at last! Everything out here was great: the pigeons picking at horse droppings around the seltzer man's cart, or the Tango Café, where I sat with a sophisticated classmate, listening to him talk about women and jazz and the atom bomb.

It was a delight to look into the Babel Revue and Cabaret, at pictures of Lizaveta, the featured *artiste,* whose thighs were uncovered and whose backside was almost bare. And her orange sequin costume, and Joshua Strongman's saxophone rising out of the orchestra pit and bending toward those thighs, and the whole tinsel atmosphere, the exaggerated gestures and movements—all that was magnificent indeed. But how different these same people seemed when coming through the stage door. I tried to match the photographs with the ridiculous galoshes and snowboots, the skewed turbans, the worn-out features. Their faces did not elicit disappointment so much as compassionate admiration. How did they overcome their frailties on stage, we wondered. A large man in a fur hat led his trained bear down the street as though it were a dog, a Newfoundlander, say. The bear shuffled along, its nails knocking against the pavement. And how about that lanky redhead, Babette? One night she stepped out of a huge Buick and coolly let a tall man in a black coat walk her to her door and bid her good night with a kiss on her hand. The next day she arrived sitting on the "death seat" of a motorbike, behind her pimp who wore a checked cap and a leather jacket. He put his feet down and remained straddled on the bike as Babette, the elegant *artiste,* got off and planted a hot kiss on his neck.

I was becoming cynical and subversive, deriving inner satisfaction from attitudes which under the circumstances were an antidote to the compulsory optimism around me. I was filling up with a desire to snigger, to jeer, to bray. We drew a coffin on the blackboard and put our headmaster in it, and even attached a candle to the coffin. His was the next class, the sixth period of the day, and he was late—perhaps he'd already left, to be where we all wanted to go.

We rushed through the tall doors, onto the sidewalk, on a lark followed a kid and knocked the school bag out of his hand. In class, we kept laughing at a boy in the first row. We had rubbed garlic on his coat because we knew he had a date after school—let him stink to high heaven. When we saw his girlfriend outside, we said hello and headed for Brothel Row, where the ladies sat on long benches on the street. Some were waiting for us in the doorways. This seemed natural then, like buying bread or meat.

In their little cubicles the washstands were fitted with white bowls, into which they poured water from a pitcher, and then, from a bottle, added purple-red permanganate. We first had to take out our organ, which they washed as they would a sock, with natural, motherly solicitude, wrapping it in their thick fingers, wiping it clean, carefully examining it for signs of disease. Jars of quince preserve stood in a row on top of the cupboard. Then they lowered their ample bodies onto the bed and spread their legs so we could study what was between them. They did this quite leisurely, moaning in a deep but friendly voice. Afterward, they let us doze off in their arms, and even covered us with a blanket. Only later did they mention that they should get a little more for the extra service. Which was only fair. We climbed out of their beds and stepped onto a faded rug, and there was the washbowl again, and the uneven cobblestones outside, and new women in the doorways, clucking their tongues, pursing their lips, beckoning to new customers with their fingers.

In the afternoon you could ride a streetcar on an unfamiliar line to an unfamiliar neighborhood, where you could inspect every house—each had a unique personality, like our teachers and classmates, or like the passengers in the streetcar. If you looked more closely, the passengers seemed strange indeed. We were overjoyed when a horrid-looking person got on; a goiter, an unsightly bunion or boil was greeted with great excitement. I was also elated when I saw a man in the streetcar whose wrist was handcuffed to that of a policeman sitting next to him. The street is always more interesting than a movie screen. A film director guides our attention aggressively, on the street I am the filmmaker—just as in the library I choose the books from the shelf, or decide which girl to follow on the avenue. I go after her but am afraid to approach her; I wait for an encouraging sign. I look at the back of her head, her legs, the way she moves, I see her go into a building, I stop, and stare up, at bosomy stone muses, cary-atids, horn-blowing angels, and rooftop sirens and lightning rods.

I peek into courtyards and see tiny garden plots, carpet beaters, broken tricycles, longjohns swinging on a clothesline, huge jars filled with pickles, a dented rubber ball, a garden chair without a backrest. Decline and disuse have a certain sweetness, as do objects dying a slow death. But why should anything remain perfect?

To embark on an expedition into my youth, I would have to look up a few old addresses in the cramped urban space which had been my stomping ground. I must lead the reader down narrow streets which I walked daily on my way to school and, later, to university. With only a few breaks in between, I spent a quarter of a century in the same house in the middle of the city.

From our apartment I could see City Hall, a sooty-yellow, early-nineteenth-century neoclassical building, with a roof covered in ancient brown tiles. Since we lived on the fifth floor, what I actually saw on either side was a vast expanse of tiles, which time had marked with a profusion of discolored spots as visually intriguing as a network of cracks on an old wall.

But beyond City Hall I could see other rooftops and towers. Stepping up to the window, my visitors would invariably come up with the same cliché: "How Parisian!"—even those who'd seen Paris only in the movies. Above the maze of chimneys and roofs only the wings of birds and TV antennas slashed into the blue sky.

There were about thirty apartments in the building, most of them three-room flats. A post-eclectic, pre-modern façade, architectonic restraint, balconies that seemed to blend in with the wall face. The storefronts on the ground floor were rented to a greengrocer, a tailor, and a watchmaker. After socialism had won the day, the grocery store closed down—even though the owner, Mr. Daróczy, had pulled his handcart to the central market at four o'clock every morning to buy the best produce, and was so happy to inform the tenants that he had fresh goat cheese and strawberries, they felt like partaking of his joy.

The watchmaker's shop went out of business after its owner, a bald-headed, mysterious man, died. While still alive, he would roar with laughter whenever one of the tenants, a tall actress with

61

dyed hair, talked to her parakeet. One day this parakeet flew out the open window, descended the cavern of the narrow city street, settled on the sidewalk in front of the watchmaker's huge black tomcat, and, having no previous experience with that species, waited and waited, until the watchmaker cupped it in his hand.

The apartment above us was inhabited by a violin repairer, whose wife, a maturely attractive and desirable woman, walked down the stairs with an air of fragrant elegance. However, as our toilet and their kitchen window gave onto the same narrow air shaft, I often became the reluctant witness of the couple's routine dinner conversation. "Again you took the bigger piece," hissed the husband. "*Alter Scheissfresser*, you're jealous of the food in my mouth," came the reply in a hostile, icy alto.

It seems they couldn't manage to cut the meat into two equal slices, one of them always got the bigger half, and the other resented it bitterly. "All right, have it, it's yours, how disgustingly selfish can you be," said the woman with contempt. This cozy scene was reenacted daily, until one day the violin repairer—he had a magnificent head of snow-white hair and maintained the string instruments of the city's symphony orchestra—surprised everyone by dropping dead. From that day on, his wife, though still fragrant, glided down the stairs in black, and often quoted her dear departed, for he had something clever to say about everything, and was in general a loving, generous man.

The red-haired actress was younger and prettier than the widow; she descended the stairs in smartly tailored suits and trailed a cloud of unexotic, one might say workaday, perfume. "She's an actress," said a tenant in the elevator. "Yeah, a telephone actress," said another. Now and then a big, chauffeur-driven Hudson came for her, and once a car with diplomatic license plates delivered thirty-five red roses. She was quite tall, so when she said hello, she inevitably looked down on you.

In the summer of 1951, the same day she was deported from the capital, two other tenants were also kicked out of their flats: a Czech-German baron and a Jewish baroness. We, too, waited for the eviction notice, as one would for news about an epidemic raging in the neighborhood. The signed and stamped paper was usually delivered by the police in the early-morning hours, ordering the addressees to have their essential belongings packed by the following evening, specifying strict limits, and in any case no more than a few suitcases containing personal effects only. They'll come for us for sure, we thought, and transport us to our designated residence in some godforsaken village, which we won't be permitted to leave without the consent of the local authorities.

Some of the deportees we knew ended up in farmhouse kitchens with dirt floors. Their own apartments were occupied in short order by faithful party members, functionaries, security officers—people newly appointed to prominent positions, whose former domiciles, cold-water flats, in many cases, were no longer appropriate to their elevated status. Residences were found for them in the fashionable suburbs or in the city center, in the former homes of "class aliens" and "class enemies." Everything had to be left behind for the new occupants. Whoever now slept in their beds could also wear—if the size was right—the former owners' shirts and skirts. Worthless family mementos were usually discarded.

The building next door was, until 1949, a brothel. In the 1820s, ladies of pleasure decked out with flowers walked this very street, past the incorruptible gaze of Romantic poets. On this corner was the eatery where during the days of the 1848 Revolution poets consumed sweet rolls rather than crackling and beer, which later led to a court case. Guided by the assumption that after nibbling on sweets, one didn't feel like drinking beer, the brewer who rented out the premises forbade the cook to serve tarts and pies and such, thus infringing on the restaurateur's as well as his guests' natural rights. It fell to a young barrister, who was also an aspiring writer, to defend the sweet-toothed literati against the greedy brewery owner.

Our black-smocked watchmaker stood tall over customers who activated a bell, and his cat, when they opened the door. His living quarters, made up of a bed and a sink, were in the rear of his cramped shop. The dark walls were covered with an assortment of clocks, each with a different, lovely chime. He was the peculiar-looking man, with the monocle-like magnifying lens and the tiny tweezers between his fingers, who died shortly after the communist takeover. An olive-green curtain was hung inside his shop-window after his death.

Later on, I saw coarse-featured men slip into the store. It was rumored that it became a place where security agents met local informers. Once when walking by, I had the feeling somebody in there was watching me. I shot a glance in that direction and was convinced that an eye was peering through a gap in the painted-over plate glass, staring intently, without blinking, as if glued to the spot. Years later another man huddled inside the store, behind the white-painted plate glass. This man, it seems, had nothing better to do than to keep an eye on me and my visitors. The secret information that there was always a spy in there was blurted out by the caretaker. I found out that in the building opposite mine the security police maintained an entire apartment for the sole purpose of keeping me under surveillance.

If their aim was to intimidate me with their never-ending snooping and eavesdropping, they succeeded—up to a point. Though the lack of complete success wasn't due to my strong character but to the fact that I tended to get lost in my thoughts. I didn't even notice the black car with the tall antenna parked in front of my building, or a bit farther down, at the corner, where one of my neighbors, a famous tennis champion, liked to park his. He was furious that the security people took his favorite spot. There were always two plainclothesmen sitting in that big black car, one short and fat, the other tall and skinny, or one glum and the other cheerful, a tough guy and a softy—in short, always an ideal couple. Mostly they were bored; they smoked cigarettes, ate their snack, then their lunch, tracking me with their cameras and their bugging devices.

At times I actually thought that what they were doing was useful; after all, they collected information about me and my friends that future chroniclers would never be able to retrieve, simply because the participants' finite memories could not possibly retain it all. Let the sleuths be as diligent as possible, then, and note the name of every woman I had ever dated, and every wisecrack I had ever made at the dinner table. Let them serve the great manipulator, the secret archivist, who maintained this spy network as an adjunct of historical research. For scholars and graduate students examining this period, the Interior Ministry archives would be a gold mine. It didn't become that, though. After the latest historical turnabout, the professional snoops, in their first panic, burnt much of the gold mine. While the system was in place, no one could imagine their being afraid of anything.

In 1956 I passed all my exams, and after some practice teaching received my certificate. The army wanted no part of me, after I was branded an enemy of the state. A captain of the People's Army, at an indoctrination session, had tried to define enemy as he would a pair of trousers (which in army lingo was "an article of clothing ending in two tubular appendages"), but had got mixed up, whereupon I broke into a grin. That's all he needed. He switched from definition to illustrative example: "Stand up. Yes, you, over there! You see, men? This is the enemy. Cynically he laughs in your face." He sent me out of the room and told me that I needn't bother to attend future sessions. He was my guardian angel, this captain; I was through with the army for good—declared an incorrigible civilian. The rest of the men, those who had kept a straight face, went ahead with their abbreviated officer training in a nearby barracks during the summer of 1956. When the Revolution broke out in the fall, the local militia was disarmed, along with its brand-new officers. They returned to the city in army trucks and promptly joined the rebellion.

I got a teaching position in an outlying elementary school. I didn't mind being with the children; I could tell them stories. But one day a tiny bald man with a piping voice came up to me and told me to hurry up and hand in my lesson plans. "Who is the little fellow?" I asked my colleagues. "The principal," they said. "And what's a lesson plan?" I learned that it was an elaborate description that might take a whole afternoon to prepare. I rode home from the dusty, outlying neighborhood on the commuter train and then changed to a tram which took me past the university library. After a brief inner struggle—should I write up those blasted lesson plans or read the books I had borrowed the previous day?—I took my regular seat in the library's reading room, by a window overlooking the lake. On the wine-colored felt-top table I could even use my typewriter.

I must have been busy with my journal then. I would read the last ten pages and add two new ones. It was a mixed bag, this journal, consisting of quotations, thumbnail sketches, commentaries, reflections. The word count grew, the folder kept getting thicker, even though the typed pages were single-spaced. After a time, I was unable to keep track of the rambling fragments, each day I struck out in a new direction. Surveying the universe from the vantage point of my supreme ignorance, I perceived assimilable knowledge in every corner. In my more desperate moments, I found the infinite amount of knowable mysteries oppressive; either I would collapse under their weight or would have to clamber out from under the crushing piles. I didn't feel at all like scribbling lesson plans, sketching out each lesson ahead of time, and indicating the educational objective of each. I felt that such useless drudgery would do my semi-alert though still capable brain serious harm. I was always careful—out of pride, out of self-defense—not to fill my head with sawdust, or subject it to "sensible" tasks. While in high school, I resided in thick novels; in the early afternoon, after I got home from school, I would take long naps and wake up at ten o'clock. I really thought schoolwork corrupted, exhausted, and dulled the mind. Afterward I wouldn't have enough energy left to do real work. Students usually underline key passages in a college text, passages in which the author sums up, aphoristically almost, his main thesis, or at the very least says something worth remembering. That's how I tried to "read" the lectures I attended, but there was nothing to underline, the spoken text rolled by, the authoritative voice droned on, and my brain's editing function shut down; there was nothing to save and store, it was time to move on, to get the hell out of there—the classroom had become a mine shaft of boredom.

One can numb one's mind in so many ways, a student ought to be on guard. No delusions. He must know that all those deformed grownups are out to *re*form them in their own image. The idiots of this world want to turn out other idiots; they spread their high-sounding malarkey with the greatest of zeal. The bulk of what gets into print is rubbish. I was amused by all this, or upset, though mostly I was afraid that no matter how alert I might be, the buzzwords of the age would do me in.

But while making those rambling journal entries, my brain, this cumbersome machine, was at its frantic best, even my arms, my shoulders were in a state of excitement. This creative state—typing away furiously with two fingers, or simply jotting down key words—was more pleasurable than mere conversation. If others are present, they can interrupt and divert the flow of ideas.

But a polite man is considerate of others, he obligingly enters his interlocutor's world and soon feels ill at ease, lost, though he's been to quite a few of these cramped, murky places. Depraved mental fornicator that he is, he can't wait to get out of those dark hellholes. Let the paper airplane be buffeted by the wind. Let the drunken boat plow through the heaving waves.

Mental fornicator? In an espresso bar, divided into intimate little compartments but in keeping with the spirit of the times still called "Forward," the young Dragomán was groping the ample thighs of an opera singer. The singer was talented but no great beauty. Walking beside him, she trilled and warbled, and in bed she rumbled like a volcano. At half past eight in the morning he sneaked up to the fourth floor of a large apartment house, where she had a small flat overlooking the courtyard. There were sofas, plush ottomans, heavy brocades everywhere. You could do somersaults on the downy cushions and pillows. Quivering but firm flesh, a big nose, thick lips and thick vulva, but surprisingly fine, blonde pubic hair. Every new body is a surprise. In his youth, Dragomán thought he should conduct a comparative study of female anatomies. His experience was meager, his interest wideranging. He had to help Anna, the heavenly alto, squeeze into her corset. Afterward, he skipped down the stairs, taking two at a time. Dragomán felt pleasantly tired, something was already behind him, and the whole day still lay ahead.

Once afternoon in September of 1956—he had just got back from the dusty suburb where he taught school—he decided on the steps of the library to quit his job. He'd been imprisoned behind school walls long enough; should he now become a warden? He'd much rather meditate this afternoon on history and the intelligentsia, an excellent subject for a brand-new graduate in liberal arts.

He could earn money in some other way. For example, he might sell his future cadaver to the Institute of Anatomy; he and his family could live on the proceeds for two carefree weeks. Kobra had even more encouraging news. The city crematorium paid five times the minimum wage to volunteer cremators. It was a morbid gig, to be sure; they could see why it would be difficult to recruit people for the job, but Kobra and Dragomán quickly overcame their revulsion. Morally, there was nothing objectionable about it. They burned bodies only twice a week, the other days could still be devoted to their studies. They wrote a lofty-sounding letter, in which they expressed genuine interest in the profession, adding that they'd heard the pay was high. Since they considered themselves serious applicants, could they be further apprised of working conditions? The crematorium's reply was equally eloquent. The information the applicants possessed was correct in almost every respect: they were indeed looking for cremators, and were happy to learn that two such obviously mature and high-minded young men were interested in the position. Only the pay was lower than they had thought, about the same as that of a factory hand. There wasn't much interest in Dragomán's corpse, either. "You are much too cynical, young man," said a professor of anatomy who happened to pick up the phone when Dragomán made his inquiry. "Start taking life a little more seriously, and try earning your living by the sweat of your brow." After spending a night unloading freight cars, Dragomán could hardly keep his eyes open in the library. He did some translating and book reviewing, he tutored dim-witted youngsters, while Laura taught school. He also received a modest stipend from the Writers Union. If they had enough money for bread, milk, and a few apples, they were happy.

He sat in the library writing and reading, going without food or drink till nine in the evening. If he got thirsty, there was a water fountain in the washroom. But he was busy tracking down truths that apparently were still hidden from him. Every day he walked down the hill and into the library. Through the window Kobra saw him cross the bridge, his loose black raincoat flapping in the wind. There he was, all sparkle and glow, gesticulating and chuckling as he pranced along. At this time Dragomán was a superb self-entertainer, a one-man show.

They went to a milk bar where the breadgirl was captivated by their political and philosophical discussions. Dragomán asked her for extra sugar to sprinkle on his rice pudding. He burned up carbohydrates fast, he explained; that's just how his system worked. He looked skinny not because he didn't eat but because he had a super-quick metabolism. He could dry wet towels simply by wrapping them around his chest. He went on bragging this way to the breadgirl, who shook her head skeptically. "Wait till I wrap you in those wet towels," she said audaciously, while customers waiting to be served at the other table kept tapping their glasses with their knives.

From the milk bar they went over to the Club Café, where Tombor sat in a corner in the gallery brooding over his next film project. The semidarkness did wonders for his imagination. In his notebook there were only sketches and fragments—tiny letters, squiggles, and lots of blank spaces in between. Antal pointed to a table: "Sit down, I am not finished thinking." He thought for another half hour, without once moving his body. Then he jotted down two or three words in his notebook, and only then did he turn to his friends, relieved, as if he'd just put in a hard day at the office.

They went for a walk, but first stopped at a nearby butcher shop with gleaming yellow wall tiles. Here Antal reached into the fishtank every day, pulled out a wriggling carp, carried it down to the wharf and threw it back in the lake. "One day you'll get caught." "Never," Antal said. To make amends for the theft in the butcher shop, Antal would buy a jar of Hungarian-style tripe, the cheapest selection. But he was too embarrassed to admit that he and his girlfriend, Nora, ate this stuff, so he'd say it was for their dog. His winter coat, which used to belong to his father, looked good enough to pass. The butcher had a dog, too, and wanted to hear all about his. So Antal would regale the astonished butcher with incredible lies: his dog felled wild boars, his favorite delicacy was wild strawberries, he climbed up trees for quails' eggs, got along famously with squirrels, and could tell which mushroom was poisonous and which wasn't. One day the carp he stole leaped out from under his coat. The butcher saw it and seemed to understand all. "Here's some paper to wrap it in." "Thanks, chief," Tombor said with imperturbable good cheer.

While sipping Laura's tea, we talked about how the intelligentsia had first played the Bolshevist, then the anti-Bolshevist, how it re-embraced Bolshevism, only to become anti-Bolshevist again. We saw great thinkers turning every which way with the ever-changing true faith—weathercocks crowing salvation at all hours. We concluded that nothing was more alien to us than to pity those who had once believed and then became disenchanted. Whoever could be duped was a fool. The disillusioned

69

communists remained communists because communism itself was the object of their exertions, that's what they kept rationalizing and reviling; either way, they are still enthralled by it. They can't let go, and couldn't when they tied themselves to the undercarriage of trains, or when, after trudging through snowfields amid hissing bullets, they arrived in the West. And from then on and forever more, they go on exposing this one thing, this one play, in which they themselves were the actors, fighting for the cause as heroes or against it as villains. In this play the humorist is strung up, or he himself may become the hangman. Aesthetically, such people are the noblest former loyalists, we knew quite a few of them at the time, yet even they remained captives of communism.

Sitting with a bottle of wretched table wine and munching on bread smeared with lard and sprinkled with paprika (and taking note of Laura's dozing off by lowering our voices), we agreed that the liveliest adventure for intellectuals in the twentieth century has been the radically nationalist brand of state socialism, the type of society in which you can easily end up dead; yet we also concurred that there was no power like state power. Whoever does not wish to strive for power becomes a formalist, banishing all ethical and political biases from his mind. When that happens, there is only phenomenology, methodology, and professionalism, only Flaubert, Mallarmé, and Cézanne; then Sartre and Lukács do not exist. In which case you walk around the city like an old maid who in her dotage has only one thing left: her unscathed hymen. "Anyone able to preserve his impartiality, his ethical neutrality in the last twenty years must be a shithead," one of us said. After the rightist adventure, the leftist experiment came to an end, too; what remained was the library. The feats of hubris have been discredited, so let's study eternal things—our city, for example.

They frequented cafés galore: there was plenty of coffee and rum, and stories about a dreary reality that went beyond their clever banter. They all intended to take an in-depth look at Kandor, to dig up the facts, to engage in research, visit families— they believed that the history of one apartment never makes the next one redundant. Dragomán translated endless novels that barely made the grade. "They won't keep me out of hock," he grumbled, but paid for another round of drinks just the same. The only way to write about terror is the way Kafka did, they said, and the air in the espresso bar turned electric with true-confession stories about wartime resistance, underground derring-do, torture by secret police. They shivered with excitement when learning of unique interrogation methods; they mused on prison mythology.

"We should pay attention to our bowel movements even more carefully than to our brain functions," Kobra said. "You never had scarlet fever, you say? You may still get it." Reams of paper, voluminous notes, not enough finished, revised copy. What we wrote yesterday may seem worthless today.

Oh, but what a piece of work Kandor was: every day a new topic, each new idea quashed by the one before, we were one with the city. It felt good to take it all in on a crisp clear day from the chapel on Old Hill. Laura wore a soft, electric-blue winter coat. While walking along the lake, she swung her head a little, tilting it to the right, toward the lake. From this oblique angle, the city was even more breathtaking, its bridges like prancing horses.

We reached our conclusion: it's all in the draw, either they catch you or they don't. Here destiny steps up to you and tells you to get into the car. They'll try to grab you, that much is clear. So be suspicious, but also enjoy yourself while you are still free; tomorrow you may not be.

Who hangs out where? Whose favorite watering hole can you name? Who are the people you can count on? Suppose you were accepted into the young Hungarian intellectual crowd, which back in 1956 still looked up to their elders with reverence. It was like being a high school freshman. Respect was still alive for leaders and seers, for august biographies and long reading lists. It was an event just to come face-to-face with the bearer of a big name.

In the spring of 1956 the most incandescent name was Imre Nagy's. When this elderly gentleman went out for a walk, he could count on being noticed. What usually followed was a quick stare, recognition, and a dilemma: What now? Dragomán respectfully greeted Imre Nagy, who lifted his hat, and under his mustache there lurked if not a smile, then a polite readiness to listen. There was even the possibility of a brief exchange. But Dragomán didn't dare do more than offer greetings.

He was not one to be overly familiar with people; he didn't go up to his professors after class for a private chat, a chance to ask informal questions and show off his intelligence. Who was he, after all, to address the sixty-year-old Imre Nagy, yesterday's—and tomorrow's—prime minister?

Dragomán greatly admired Zoltán Kobra, David's older brother, who while sitting with his friends at the Crown told them casually that he'd gone up to see the "Old Man" and given him a letter from his boss, Attila Szigethy, in which Szigethy, a Trans-Danubian peasant leader, state-farm director, and MP, offered to deliver, in Parliament, a ringing indictment of Mátyás Rákosi's disastrous economic policies, which might just bring about the tyrant's fall. No one up to that point had dared to raise his voice against Rákosi in Parliament. Zoltán had sat for a while on the terrace of Imre Nagy's house on Orsó Street. At first Nagy was somewhat cool and cautious; he may have taken this young man for an *agent provocateur*. He withdrew into the apartment to place a telephone call. Fifteen minutes later the phone rang, he left again, and when he returned he smiled affably. The professor in him won out: a pensive old man proceeded to explain to his young visitor the benefits of a wait-and-see strategy.

"Does this mean that you agree with the strategy of General Kutuzov of *War and Peace* fame? Retreat, retreat, and when the enemy is exhausted by victories, attack?" "Yes," Imre Nagy said after a moment's reflection. Using Zoltán Kobra as his sounding board, Nagy tried to talk Attila Szigethy out of attempting some sort of coup. "You wait and see: the Politburo will come to me and place the party leadership in my lap."

Zoltán was interested in weightier matters than was Dragomán; everything he did had a symbolic air. Dragomán was content to walk the same streets that Imre Nagy did every afternoon. Years later he discovered that he stuck to the same itinerary and wouldn't think of altering it. Dragomán walked the way his father did, hands clasped behind his back, deep in thought. Unchanging routes, he realized, were a sign of old age, a pathetic self-defense. This path we know, we say. If we stray we might fall. We must tread carefully, we're frail. When we rise or sit, we need help.

The old man, already "The Old Man" even then, had been the same age as Dragomán now, perhaps younger—a round-faced, courteous, dignified gentleman. You could see in his eyes that he'd found his role, or rather, was still learning it, but it was his. He insisted on it, on being himself, which wasn't what we were accustomed to then. Being out of favor for holding firmly to principles was something entirely new and startling. He walked the streets of his city like an exiled, just king, an outsider who one day would surely return.

His ascent to power three years earlier had made it possible for Dragomán to return to the university. Imre Nagy had been responsible for the thaw. He allowed most of the regime's captives—political prisoners, internal exiles, deportees—to go free. Moscow, in one of its saner moments, had picked this man to rule over us. The fact that he chose loyalty to his people over loyalty to the empire, and stuck to his guns, though he knew he might be hanged for his stubbornness—this had to do with some inner force of character.

At the time, in the spring of '56, Dragomán had no inkling of the possible outcome, he considered himself an outsider, too, he'd been expelled for the third time from the university, although this time he did not consider the expulsion logical or inevitable, as he had before. "We are not in the same league, but we can live together. If Imre Nagy could do it…" Two years later Nagy did do it—without surrendering his dignity, he stood up straight under the gallows.

With a wide net he scoops up the past from the lake bottom: facts and events get tangled as they rise to the surface. The years run together and Dragomán doesn't feel like sorting them out. He liked to hurry down the stairs of his apartment, leave behind the yellow-tiled stairwell, and be off. He might choose Margaret Island as his first destination; he could go for a swim in the large public pool, where at six-thirty there were very few swimmers. After resting on the sundeck—at eight-thirty on a summer morning it could be quite hot—he might retreat to one of the island's shady coves, near the ruins of a medieval monastery, where there were benches along the waist-high wall remains and stone tables, placed there by the parks department. He could sit there for a while. Then, if he had money, he might have an espresso in a sidewalk café. He would unpack his briefcase and put everything on the white-painted cast-iron table: paper, pens, a folder, and a French novel he had to read and review for some extra cash. After a time he'd quit the café and there would be a random move from park bench to park bench. A good day had to work this way: finish the self-imposed tasks before noon, then there would still be time for some aimless loafing. He could go to the library, or visit a friend; he had until five, when he had to pick up the baby from the nursery. Laura had her last class from five to six. She already had a job; he was still a student. Or maybe he felt like getting on a bus and riding up to the Buda hills, and then chugging along on the narrow-gauge railway to a little open-air restaurant in the woods, where he would again take out his writing implements from his black briefcase and watch the leaves rustle in the wind, and the wasps and butterflies flutter under the tall pine trees. He looked for cozy hiding places, whence he would make his city more livable. In any event, he felt the city belonged to him—his daily wanderings entitled him to it. Every place he ever visited, remembered, or imagined became his; the whole city turned into his living room. He didn't consider a playground bench less grand than a study with padded doors. On a playground nobody lectured or sermonized; if someone started to, he got up and left. He was making preparations for a magnum opus, of which very little save some stray fragments survived.

Dragomán would write on the green metal tables of a hillside restaurant, under a huge chestnut tree, only a few tables away from a group of noisy beer drinkers, then slip the result, several pages of rough, verbose text, into his lockable folder. Sometimes he wrote on the stone tables of Margaret Island, or on the worm-eaten elbow rest of an old church. He particularly liked to ensconce himself in seedy cafés filled with seedy and somnambulant regulars, usually old men who argued over such questions as who was the deputy mayor when omnibuses disappeared from the city, or in which prewar year women's skirts began to inch upward. And while leggy waitresses sashayed between the tables with trays laden with coffee, cognac, and soda water, he dreamed about unwritten novels. What preoccupied him most, though, was the difference between maintaining one's integrity and keeping one's distance. "Don't give an inch," Dragomán said and hit the table with his long fingers. "Don't compromise, don't try to smuggle in the goods. They find out everything sooner or later." He continued writing relentlessly, so only freakish bad luck could hold him back. Writing made him feel good, he cooled off, as though he'd been making love; he returned home meek and mild. It took so little to make him happy, after all. Even the balcony could provide him with an idyllic moment. Laura was in bed reading, so he would disappear behind the folding partition and go on scribbling his—mostly unpublishable—sentences.

From his peregrinations he would always return to the Tango, to the company of royalists, social democrats, and other political has-beens, and ubiquitous informers fuming against the socialist order. From under the royalists' table you could hear clicking sounds from time to time. These distinguished gentlemen discreetly clicked the heels of their thick-soled, hand-sewn shoes whenever they uttered His Majesty Otto Hapsburg's name, which was quite often.

In the booth opposite Dragomán a well-dressed gentleman met a fine-looking lady every morning. The lady, arriving late, was always flustered, one might even say harried, if the word didn't have a slightly indecorous connotation, and there really was nothing indecorous about her state of agitation. After many years of marriage and a similarly long liaison, her husband was beginning to have suspicions. He had told her the other day: "I know, my dear, that you'd rather if I didn't walk you to the café." How very crude of him. Some people don't know their limits.

The door opened and in rolled a stump of a man. He pushed himself forward with his hands; and with his muscular arms he managed to raise his torso onto a chair and lean his body on the table. Before long he picked up the thread of the conversation and ran with it like a football player, scoring one goal after another, beating everyone to the punch line, and causing gales of laughter after each one. The student listened attentively, armed with pen and paper, convinced that the Tango espresso bar was still the best place to be.

There was another morning regular at the Tango, an art

historian, architect, painter, film director, avant-garde poet, mystic, prophet all rolled into one, a complex personality, in other words, and a rather corpulent, bald man besides, who liked to scrutinize the espresso bar's guests, usually with his left eye, raising his eyebrows a little—women too, especially if they were in the company of tall, robust-looking men. At first the offended gentleman would only stare back indignantly, his face turning red, but soon he would have to say something to the fat little clown, whose fingers, thick at the base, were long and slender around the nails: "You are bothering us. Be so good as to turn away, or stare at the ceiling, if you must stare. Or count the fringes on the tablecloth. But do stop sizing us up, sir, or I will belt you so hard you'll go right through that plate glass."

Just when it looked as if something like that might happen, another fixture, our perennial Baby, minced forward, making goo-goo eyes. "Why don't you ask me, sir?" she inquired. "I wouldn't mind…What I do mind is when a distinguished artist like yourself keeps eyeing people who are not even habitués of this establishment." The architect-prophet was the barely tolerated resident genius of the city planning commission, though most of his colleagues were rather fond of him. Later, when he and Dragomán became friends, the architect, who was given to despair but also to naïve amazement, asked him who his favorite character was in the Bible. Dragomán answered: Solomon—because he is said to be responsible for both the Song of Songs and the Ecclesiastes. Solomon had everything and nothing, but he did have the devastating knowledge that only a ruler possesses. This strange prophet decided that he had to protect his wife from Dragomán's advances; even in public he felt tears coming on whenever he thought that his wife might walk out on him, though he had far less reason to suspect her of infidelity than she had of him. "You cheat on her and then accuse her of cheating. You invite me to your house when your wife is at home alone, then make her tell you what we talked about. And then you suffer, because the two us got on well. Is this normal? Are you normal?" "No, I am not," the architect quickly replied. "But you are. And you, my friend, must learn to distinguish between that which is complex and that which is merely illogical."

One day it wasn't a satchel filled with books and notes that

Dragomán slung over his shoulder, but a Soviet-made submachine gun, a seventy-five shooter with cartridge clips and a perforated barrel. He had convinced himself that if rebels were handing out guns, he should take one home without hesitation. To counter the abuse of power, either public or private, it was best to grab a gun, though not necessarily with the intent of using it.

Deterrence, negotiating from a position of strength—these were concepts he picked up at that time. If he placed the gun between his legs with the barrel pointing up, or if he put it down next to him, within easy reach, people were more likely to listen, and there could be a peaceful and reasonable exchange of views. And if you keep a gun at home, in the linen closet so the child can't get his hand on it, you react differently to the sound of the doorbell at night. Dragomán joined the newly founded National Guard; along with many of his fellow students he moved about freely, with no commanding officer standing over them. Even if an argument broke out, no authority figure came to stop it. In the corridors of the university, in the lecture rooms, the library, the dean's office, gun-toting students wandered casually about. When the people are armed, there is no dictatorship. He accepted the proposition that you can't have a revolution without guns. You must take them from factories and armories, police stations and army barracks. On November 4, he realized that these guns had to be used; he had to join the fighters on the street. Laura tried to stop him, but he had to go, so he did. He never discussed the reasons, either with her or with himself. The neighbors, seeing the gun on the shoulder of his winter coat, hissed at him from doorways: "Are you crazy?" Bodies lay in the street covered with brown wrapping paper, people ran for cover from one building entrance to another, while a convoy of armored cars rumbled down the Grand Boulevard. From the tank turrets eyes darted from side to side, trying to locate the window from which an unseen hand might hurl a gasoline-filled bottle. With a terrible grating noise a frantic soldier turned the turret and began shelling a window: he thought he saw something move, or was it only his imagination? In any case, he managed to demolish a bedroom.

There are magical days; October 23 was one of them. In the 1960s, by early October controlled hysteria reigned in offices across the country. After working hours every typewriter had to be shut into cabinets, and before people left for the day these cabinets had to be locked. Counterrevolutionaries, whose devil's fangs showed through their hypocritical smiles, might sneak back at night, or, feigning overeagerness, stay after hours, and when vigilance slackened, type their subversive leaflets on the socialist state's antiquated Remingtons. There was no overtime, no one could stay late, in October of every year extra precautions were taken, the city swarmed with uniformed and plainclothes policemen.

Several years later, again on October 23—and it was no mere coincidence, surely—Dragomán was arrested in Laura's apartment. He thought he had successfully evaded his pursuers, and that they were no longer after him; time, he believed, was on his side. But one leaden autumn morning, as he sank comfortably into a velvet-upholstered armchair, and into Count Custine's book about imperial Russia, he noticed he was being watched by roofers working across the street, who were, naturally, state security people in disguise.

At first Dragomán laughed them off, believing he had outsmarted them, since he'd moved out of his place and thanks to Laura's generosity was living incognito in her apartment. But it was he who was outsmarted; he couldn't give them the slip—he might have shaken off a few, but there were many more than he had believed.

They went to the high school where Laura was a language teacher. Following proper legal procedure, they wouldn't enter her apartment in her absence, so they put her in their car and on the way home badgered her: Was Dragomán dangerous? Did he possess a weapon?

The burly colonel entered the apartment and when he saw Dragomán, he sank his right hand in his pocket and told him not to do anything foolish. Dragomán didn't know what he meant. Was he telling him not to take out his gun? They must have decided that if he was on the run, he was also capable of shooting. But there was no gun, not in his pocket and not on the table. There was only the travel journal he was reading, a reflection on the relationship between largeness of size and degree of obtuseness.

Custine's question—Why do big states want to become even bigger?—intrigued him. Small states are usually more refined and civilized. Since they are obliged to learn the rule that brain counts far more than brawn, they develop greater subtlety. The small ones fraternize among themselves, and have a good laugh in a corner when the big ones do something patently foolish. It's better to stick to human dimensions. Let the Russians be as big as only Russians can; let's not believe that our value can be expressed in square miles. Why don't they look to Siberia, which is theirs—what do they want from us? They get into all kinds of trouble by keeping their soldiers on our soil. What a shame that they've put themselves in this ridiculous position. If their fields are vast, they must think, so are their souls. But soul and space don't go together, not if fields under arms remain fallow.

Many years later, in 1986, I was explaining this to an Arab merchant in East Jerusalem, on the Via Dolorosa. Then I listened attentively to what my new friend, Amin, had to say. He flung out his arm in his tiny shop: "This is my palace, sir, so relax. No need to rush, drink your tea, it has mint leaves in it, it's good for you. We can also smoke our hubble-bubbles." He meant the waterpipe one can puff on for a whole hour.

"I will tell you my philosophy. Treat people gently, don't rush them, but make them feel that you can see through them. For example, I can see through you now. You *will* buy this pipe. I sell it to others for ten, but for you it will be twelve, because I can tell that you like it, and a man will always pay more for something he likes.

"I am building a youth hostel. It's slow going, my workers would rather smoke hashish than work, but I still pay their wages. If they don't work one day, they'll make it up the next. When they see I am not mean to them, they will not be mean to me. Because friendship is the most important thing in the world, more precious than anything else.

"It's the same with women. I welcome beautiful ladies in my palace: Scandinavians, Germans, blondes. It's a gift from Allah when I can touch the fine down on their long legs, tanned now by the sun. First they sit next to me, I thread pearls for them, offer tea, and explain that having a good feeling is everything. And it is.

"A man should be slow and tactful when relaxing and loosening up a woman, for when she first sits down she is all tight and wound up. What's most important for these lovely women is that they should feel safe next to you; they should want to put their head on your shoulder, and when you decide to touch them, you should feel slow stirrings—ripples in a calm sea—on their neck, their legs.

"Yes, go slowly; wait for the light, the inviting and promising light in their eyes, which encourages an honorable man to make his next move. And what those eyes say is this: 'It's fine with me, I may as well stay here with you, even though I have a date with a nice man who's waiting for me at my hotel. I don't know why I'm sitting here with you, you gap-toothed, gray-bearded, big-eyed Arab scoundrel...You're probably clairvoyant, too, because you knew from one look which bracelet and jewelry box I'd like for myself.'"

Amin smiles his way into her lap. Blond men are not very passionate, blonde girls will say, so they come here to the Old City, where for thousands of years blood has been thicker and passions run higher, in both Arab merchants and black-jacketed Yeshiva students. These blonde beauties need to feel guilty now and then. It may occur to them that they are not even alive. "And then our touch convinces them that they are, they are. Before we say our good-byes, I lead her up the winding staircase to the roof of my house. Let her behold the late-afternoon brilliance of towers, terraces, domes, and palm trees. One day, even if not tomorrow, she will come back and buy an expensive item in my palace. Look, my friend, how very big the space is between the sun and me, between Allah and me. You understand this because you are a little crazy; I can see it in your eyes. I am a little crazy, too. But remember: all that matters is feeling good."

Sandra

Sandra spells trouble, Dragomán thinks with a shudder. She is a collector, consumed by a cold fever, hell-bent like a shot arrow. This woman will cut my head off with a buzz saw, she'll castrate me in my sleep with a kitchen knife, pierce the chambers of my heart with a dagger, let air bubbles into my arteries, pour colorless antifreeze in my glass, and while I descend from Falcon Peak into the Valley of Mercy in a glider, aim a slingshot at my belly.

When Sandra swims in Kandor Bay, a whole school of piranhas gather and devour Dragomán who's swimming behind her. And when the unfortunate man emerges safely from these harrowing situations and returns to his hotel, to doze in an armchair over a decent book, Sandra sneaks up from behind and strangles him with a silk cord. She is about to slip a notebook that's lying on the table into her bag, when a hand grabs her wrist—it's Dragomán.

Sandra sits on the verandah, the wind ruffles her white blouse, while she pesters Dragomán to accept the post of writer in residence. As such he could spread Kandor's fame, or revile the city, if that's more to his liking. He might publicize the fact that the good mayor's bloodthirsty chief of staff bit him on the neck. Sandra will not let go of Tombor, though she remains the faithful wife of Rector Kuno Aba. She is with the mayor every minute of the day, and yet she finds time to write his speeches.

The mayor's chauffeur has come to pick her up and take her to the Thirsty Hunter Inn, a lakefront establishment on the other side of the mountain. The big black car hugs the center of the divided roadway, and without budging from there careens along at 120 miles an hour. Sandra enjoys the race, she is on her way to Antal. The time will come, she muses, when he will come to me. He'll get into the habit of sitting and waiting on the verandah. Let Regina and Melinda shine a while longer, pretty soon she'll be the toast of the party. She thrusts out her shoulders and stretches her legs. She has a knack for improvisation; people will want to know what she has up her sleeve. Her fingers and toes are all well formed, her nails have a sculptured look. It may be hot, but she doesn't perspire. She neither drinks nor smokes. As always, she thinks it's a perfect time for precise, purposeful work. Nothing is free, every word, every motion has its place in the play she is composing. Sandra readily grants that the mayor's presence projects calm, but she is interested in creating excitement.

The rector arrives. Kuno Aba is a square-jawed, angular man, stately and polite, who now celebrates this city of murdered princes and princesses, dedicating it, like a coronation robe, to the Queen of Heaven. Living with her but never touching her, he drove his wife, Ágnes, to suicide. Sandra was only five years old when in a playground Kuno Aba picked her out—first the child, then Ágnes, her mother. It was Sandra's feet in dainty white patent-leather shoes that he noticed, and after that he couldn't take his eyes off her. The little girl, sitting on the swing, sensed that she was being watched. When Kuno Aba figured out which of the women there was the mother of this adorable child, he sat down next to her and they began to talk. That same year he successfully separated her from her husband and married her.

On one occasion Ágnes asked her husband for permission to travel to Budapest for a weekend to visit her girlfriend. Kuno Aba did not give her permission to go. Come Friday Ágnes informed her husband in a short letter that she did not accept his prohibition, and gave her friend's telephone number. He should not call in the evening because they would probably go to the theater or to a concert; after midnight, though, she'd be in. A reasonable and chivalrous husband might be expected to take back his rude prohibition and tell his wife to have a good time.

Kuno Aba did not call. She didn't telephone him either, but extended her stay in Budapest by a day. One of Kuno Aba's colleagues mentioned that he had seen Kuno's wife at the Maxim

Bar. Kuno didn't inquire further. At the dinner table he told Sandra that Mummy had fun last night at the Maxim Bar. Kuno Aba was happy to confide in his adopted daughter. He sat on her bed and they held hands. Kuno Aba realized that it would have been an overreaction to tell Ágnes that she'd be condemning him to a life of solitude if she defied his prohibition. So when she came home, he was polite, but in the evening he carried his bedding to his study, and from then on he slept there.

At first, he would wake with a start several times a night, but he resisted going back to his wife. Their garden was surrounded by a high stone wall. It was easy to leave this house but much more difficult to come back. Ágnes felt faint at times, she reacted to changes in the weather, to a full moon; premenstrual tension also drained her. Kuno Aba responded coolly to plaintive or quarrelsome tones and seemed unapproachable; at night he locked his door. He began having nightmares; he groaned, cried out, and these sounds could be heard in his wife's room. At breakfast she would remark that he must have had a fitful night's sleep.

EVER SINCE AN insidious flu epidemic swept through Kandor, everyone seems more fatigued and run-down, even the mayor and his wife, but deputy-mayor and university rector Kuno Aba is definitely not tired, if only because he's banished from his vocabulary every word that connotes weakness. A vegetarian diet, weight lifting, yoga, daily laps in the pool, horseback riding in summer, skiing in winter—all these are part of the rector's regimen. He plans to live to a hundred and intends to do his most important work between ninety and a hundred. He has trouble with a slipped disk, occasionally his knee hurts, but he ignores it; at most he winces now and then.

The sage of Kandor must make the grade as a hunter, too; he must be able to shoot straight, bad leg and all. A pheasant, hit by his pellet, tries to get away, but after a few steps falls over. Kuno Aba's upper lip curls a little. He knew he'd bag it, it couldn't happen any other way. He apologizes for his cockiness; being a good shot requires, among other things, practice, and he has it: sessions at the rifle range were also part of his routine. Afterward he might draft a new law, taking into account every one of Kandor's interests. The historian and jurist lobes of his brain invite the constitutional law expert in him, and it holds the stage until the evening program gets under way at the municipal concert hall, where during intermission he has to evaluate the performance, in light of the difficulty of the pieces heard and other artists' performances of the same program. Even if he stays out late, he'll be in the swimming pool at six-thirty sharp the next morning. His driver picks him up and they are off. The driver appeared when Aba was only department chairman—as an academician he was entitled to a chauffeur-driven car. He took his driver wherever he went, he took good care of the man. Hot or cold weather has no effect on Kuno Aba; he has utter self-control, his muscles, too, are under his command, even though due to an injury that dates back to the street battles of the '56 uprising, he cannot move his right leg without a twinge of pain. Affability is not his strong suit, though, his naturally cool temperament notwithstanding, he can be charming with intellectual rivals, is capable of praising Dragomán, for instance, even though their value preferences, as he likes to put it, are very different. But remaining relevant is a top priority for him.

His universalist attitude does not preclude comments such as: "A gentleman doesn't do that." Or: "Where we come from it isn't done." When he says this, Kuno Aba looks as if he were smiling, though all he does is curl his upper lip. When it comes to exposing foibles, Kuno Aba is never at a loss. He savors other people's mistakes, dwells on them in detail, reiterates them with gusto. To which one is supposed to respond with a smile. At length, though, when the target of his gibes has finally had it and is ready to punch him in the face, he goes on to a new subject, and on that one, too, he is dazzling.

"As a teacher I am never lenient," he likes to say. He will not put up with young people's shenanigans. Truth does not tolerate scatterbrained sloppiness. What students need is a solid base, a clear sense of direction and focus. Doubt is the privilege of ripe old age. A student must realize that exceptional people find their essence in service that transcends their individual needs. All our energies must be concentrated on our goals, ladies and gentlemen. You must stay the course, finish the race, sweat it out, run out of breath, and if in the process you sprain your ankle, moan if you must, but do it quietly. You must learn to live with pain and suffering. When you are older, you will look back on your trials with gratitude.

The survival of a city, a nation, depends on the cooperation of its notables. The individual's job is to get by. The task before a city or a country that has existed for a thousand years is to make sure that it will be around for another thousand. The farther back its collective memory reaches, the more easily it will find the strength to renew itself. Make it a crime, ladies and gentlemen, to be irreverent, or worse still, indifferent, toward tradition.

Kuno Aba agreed to serve as vice-mayor and assumed both ideological and administrative responsibilities. He permits no disarray of any kind; he detests crude improvisation, frivolous informality. Young people should live for their country, learn to obey, so they may eventually rule. A junior officer should smile for the umpteenth time at a general's joke. He need not roll on the floor. And a young man should help a lady on with her coat, feminist notions notwithstanding. Current fashion must never be allowed to undermine the ideals of chivalry. Sometimes a nation can afford to trifle with its core values; it can afford to show off its international mutants, which is what Professor Dragomán is. It's wonderful to have such people in our midst, but Heaven forbid that our vagabond honorary doctor should have too many followers. Professor Dragomán spices up our lives, but more than a pinch of this spice is too much.

Kuno Aba explains to Kobra how to graft the branch of a pear tree to an apple tree so that apples will grow on top and pears on the bottom. He recommended to Kobra that he use a scythe instead of an electric mower to cut the lawn. Or better still, he should get two lambs. They will run to the garden gate as soon as he opens it and follow him inside. Lambs are much smarter than most people think, and are also easier to train than human beings. For us teachers the very thought that everybody can be molded is an incredible temptation.

Kuno Aba is in favor of re-spiritualizing the world. Let the church again have temporal power. Runaway secularization and independence have led to political irrationalism, new pagan cults, and the extremes of communism and nationalism. Aba is organizing a gathering of neoconservative pundits in Kandor. Let solid, fundamental values prevail once more. Europe should reclaim its leadership role; we need a hierarchical order. America, ever more a crazy quilt, is fast sinking into third-world chaos. Russia has nothing new to offer the world. Japan is unoriginal, the Germans have grown intellectually timid, the French have become nostalgic archivists. The new Europe should beware. Kuno is a man of continuity, order, and conservation. He feels that the true Hungarian virtue, the best Hungarian strategy, has always been endurance and survival—triumph through submission. The rector is not in favor of the pedantic separation of talking heads and swinging fists. Universalist creeds are only for the brilliant few. Ethnic consciousness is desirable, but so is mutual respect among ethnic groups, a sense of ethical community. The ethical motive, in Kuno Aba's eyes, is *ab ovo* transcendental.

With his own sturdy hands and using rough-hewn stones, Kuno Aba enlarged his father's house, whose porthole-like windows had always fueled vivid fantasies in him. Kuno Aba was careful to keep these fantasies alive—people still think of him as a kind of seer. It's said he can read people's minds. This is the house where he kept his wife Ágnes and his adopted daughter Sandra. In Sandra's mind there is a Kuno file, though her brain can retrieve other files as well: a counter-Kuno file, for instance. Sandra has more than one self, and her different files cancel each other out.

KUNO ABA IS a monarchist. It makes no difference to him who the king is, though he must be a man of breeding. A king personifies the unity of a multinational political entity. What he has in mind is a Hapsburg king, if only because there is a long tradition behind him. Those who wish can rally once more around Vienna or, better still, Budapest. The king should reside in Buda Castle. Offer potential member states a customs union; undo the treaties of Versailles and Trianon by rebuilding a Central European empire. There was always a need for a buffer between Germany and Russia, and the Monarchy is just that. The reigning Hapsburg king would divide his time between Prague, Bratislava, Vienna, and Buda, and would be surrounded by a corps of multiethnic advisors. We badly need a Middle European union, a confederation, a commonwealth. The days of the nation-states are over, they only led to disputes and wars, so good riddance. We are not West Europeans; regional differences to us mean something more, something else. Regimes should reflect local conditions—they should resemble us. Let's be done once and for all with fascist and communist experiments. For Kuno Aba, a Central European dynasty can much more easily symbolize unity than can the national representatives of a republican government. But Kuno Aba is thinking not merely of an aggregate of nation-states but of a more inclusive homeland, one that would offer a radical solution to the minority problem. Everyone would become a citizen of this commonwealth. Local self-government would be the starting point, the basis of it all; state and federal structures would be superimposed on it. Multilingual education would be mandatory, and an international language might be agreed upon—why not English? There would be a common currency, of course, and free customs zones. Take down the economic barriers and there is immediately less pushing and shoving. Kuno Aba makes no secret of the fact that within this Central European union the Hungarians' position would not be half bad. Students might be exchanged; they could tour the federation, study in different places, and get a sense of the largeness of their interdependent homeland. Restore the upper houses, the institutions based on birth and rank. Respect for tradition implies the rehabilitation of the values of the historical aristocracy. It's in the interest of every nation to ensure its own historical continuity. A great deal can be learned about this from the Jewish experience.

KUNO ABA STOOD in Melinda's living room and stretched out his arms in the direction of the verandah door: "Whoever wants to join this Central European union can do so, and those who don't want to jump on this bandwagon will perhaps hop on the next one. The great multinational companies are also behind it; we have plenty to discuss with them, above all, a state organized along territorial rather than national lines and held together by a supranational aristocracy: the hereditary kind as well as a financial aristocracy. This Central European union would be based on the inescapable realization that we are Eurasians. The eastern regions of this entity would be obliged to look more openly toward Asia. It's impossible not to, when you're close to the Black Sea,

Russia, the Balkans, and Asia Minor. I've discussed this with my Turkologist friends; in academic-literary circles we are actively pushing the Turkish connection. The outlines of a Central European and Middle Eastern alliance are beginning to appear on the screen of our own imagination; it will be the creation of the marginal ones, the eclectics, the second tier. I can attest to the idea's positive reception by many Lebanese, Palestinians, and Israelis, as well as Greek and Turkish Cypriots. We are in the same boat in many ways; the solidarity of the poor is an attractive ideal. It's entirely possible that before true European union may be realized, one of its main pillars, a Central European nation, may be born. Germans and Russians cannot be members, but this patchwork empire would be on good terms with them. Our Central European union will be proud of its multifaceted, multicultural character, of an individualism that hasn't quite jelled, of individuals and communities that still go their own way. Thus, even people used to smallness could have the satisfying feeling of belonging to a great country. Just as Americans have been granted the privilege of feeling big and powerful, and even people who have been oppressed elsewhere can achieve dignity through U.S. citizenship, the Central European union could make an Albanian or a Serbian feel that he is part of something big. Kandor should be the center of this empire, just as Bonn is the capital of Germany. At the university of our city, in the cellar of its cathedral, in the museum, we find traces of successive cultures. Here in Kandor, newspapers in Serbo-Croatian and Romanian were once published. Kandor would not be the capital of a nation-state, as Budapest is of Hungary. The Ottoman Turks were here, too, and left behind their minarets and mosques. At one time, French, Armenian, Serbian, German, Slovak, and Polish settlers made up the bulk of Kandor's population, and in the last century its middle class was increasingly Jewish. The remaining Jews, descendants and survivors, would like to feel at home in Kandor. And the reason they would is perhaps that this Central European union is not merely a plan for an empire; it's a strategy for survival, and it was the city of Kandor that nurtured this plan. Devotion is needed to make it a reality. You can't be a good Kandoran if you are not seduced by the idea of this union. At the cathedral a cleric friend speaks about finding our true calling, becoming reconciled with our neighbors, learning to rely on ourselves and not wait for handouts—reintroducing transcendence into our earthly life. A new religion may emerge from a Central European union. Children at graduation ceremonies will vow to promote friendship among the many peoples of the empire, these multilingual united states, where the most profitable occupation will be that of interpreter and translator, for proficiency in more than one language is merely a technical problem. The giving hand is the union's most potent symbol. In this connection theological discussions are conducted about the sharing of bread. Giving is a key concept in the metaphysics of *Dasein.* To embrace is also to give. The concept, which unites Christians, Jews, and Muslims in one monotheistic, pluralistic ecumenical whole, says that you, too, can be messiahs and anointed saviors, you who give of yourselves to a few or a few million people. This idea embraces and honors all the peoples of the region, as well as their unique traditions. The linkup might begin with an association of mayors, a worldwide network with members from the four corners of the globe, a globe that can then be seen as a luminous whole. The earth is a divine exception, since we know nothing about life beyond it. The religions of the world need not be fused but simply made more aware of earthly life, so that each faith can learn to respect the other. We do indeed need a new regional universality that will snatch back folklore from the clutches of nationalism. The challenge of the millennium is to achieve a kind of global spiritual consensus. That is why there is a large Buddhist temple here in Kandor, why Jews have their yeshiva established, and why mullahs, with the generous support of local government, are founding an Islamic research and education center: they all sense something of the interactive spirit of the place. A major flaw of West European thinking is its inability to place itself in a Eurasian context. Western man's limitation is that he cannot understand immobility. The West created a culture of self-indulgence; the process of re-spiritualization must manifest itself in service to others, to the world, to Earth itself. Superimposed on a network of autonomous local governments is a universal alliance of citizens forming intertwining communities, all of us with equal rights.

"We are also citizens of a unique, Central European political nation. Far-flung civilizations embedded in a landscape, variegated networks of substructures—these make up the earth's living core. States can be established only when these vast networks are already in place. But the culture of endless growth, of acquisition and accumulation, cannot be maintained. It's a dead end, a crime against the universality of our planet. The question is: In which corner of the earth will the truth spring up? A great ecumenical pilgrimage is in the making, everyone will come here next year—Kandor will be Europe's cultural capital for a month. The mayor of Kandor will proclaim, in French, the creed of the new century, the needs of planet Earth, the tenets of the Central European union, the equality of regions, the interconnectedness of cities and provinces. Yet, since all that we believe in is a surmise, a flickering image, why not attempt to present a visual illustration of Kandorism? This living picture is Kandor itself, as it is. Our hoped-for union considers age-old conflicts obsolete, a misunderstanding. Our mutual interdependence is so obvious, it makes us laugh. We grow into each other; conversion means nothing more than understanding. If the earth is to survive its mistakes, we must all become saints. There are saints and there are criminals; but a criminal may believe that he is a saint. Nobody can be sure who is or is not a saint. Earth is God's favorite, and on this earth Kandor is a most precious spot"—Kuno Aba can attest to that.

A Cave on the Roof

Dragomán shuts himself in his hotel room. He enjoys his cave, he swings in his swivel chair, walks around barefoot, rests his elbows on the large brown desk, and gives a start when the maid knocks on the door to ask if she can clean up and check the minibar. The walls are soundproof, the floor covered wall to wall with chocolate-milk-colored carpeting, which got Dragomán into the habit of kicking off his shoes and walking around all day in a pair of baggy pants and a flannel shirt.

He writes the way he walks, letting his material meander at will—he'll find out sooner or later where it's heading. He carries his manuscript wherever he goes; he's written near the lake, in the woods, on top of skyscrapers. He's also used to a teeming Kandor, the busyness of Resurrection Square. The people of Kandor, a curious and gossipy lot, like to be near the action. In the cafés the atmosphere is always intense, there is tension both inside and outside, the two are in balance. But that is where Dragomán finds his daily enchantments. He likes the city's mayor, but he can also understand the groups of squatters all over town, though for the skinheads who are likely to bash his face in he has less sympathy.

He can imagine a map of the city on which certain places fade or darken according to the frequency of his visits there. The most memorable events of his past conjure a particular section of the city, a room, a flat. He walks along, he notices a house, he remembers something. If he were prevented from walking this way, he would develop amnesia. Every walk is casual, capricious, and, in its own way, perfect.

Dragomán is a latter-day celebrity; he scrutinizes the monsters, sniffs out dictators, to get a better idea of how base base is. He was always there where people flew at each other, dying to know what monumental absurdities felt like. People say curious things about him; they try to figure out whether he is a scoundrel. Young essayists the world over consider him a demonic guru. When he is around, the existence of secret networks strikes one as both humorous and terrifying.

The year 2000 calls for a new mythology. People like to be near Dragomán, they stay close, becoming his escorts, his groupies. They watch this adventurer as he keeps reinventing himself. The firm of Darnok can use an older cult figure, not a product of the youth culture but someone whose manners go over well in the media and who is also dapper enough to be appealing to the fashion industry. Darnok is an international organization; to them Dragomán makes good business sense. There are people who would gladly buy the same kind of hat or nickel-plated water bottle he owns. Svetozar takes note of everything and submits his reports. All the people at Darnok want is for Dragomán to follow his star. They suspect that before long he will turn up in places they could never dream of, and then that will be the place to be at. That's why the man with the scarred lips is always on his trail: to help him out of jams, to make sure he continues to pursue his dangerous diversions.

IT'S HARD FOR Dragomán to get things done. And harder still when he has to appear on time. He is lazy and likes those evenings best when nobody calls him from the hotel lobby, nobody pierces his protective shell, when he doesn't sense self-conscious nervousness all around, when nobody wants anything other than what they already have.

People look for him here at the hotel; they sink into the lobby's soft armchairs. After they've waited an hour or two, the desk clerk may suggest that they come back later. They go outside and wait for him to emerge from the revolving door. They all want something from him, of course; crafty beggars, madcap inventors, crooked entrepreneurs try to interest him in their solid-sounding schemes.

There is a Venetian princess staying at the hotel who intends to set up a foundation, and would like him to turn her palazzo into a retreat for world-class intellectuals. She is willing to assume the cost of running it. The *principessa* has buried four husbands; now she is interested in Dragomán.

After the noonday peal of bells in the cathedral clock tower, he takes his shoulder bag, which contains everything he needs, and goes down to the reception desk to collect his messages and drop off his mail. "I am a responsive person, unlike Your Laziness," he likes to tell his friend Kobra.

He returns late in the evening, his rounds completed; with each round he feels he's reached the end of the road. The traveler never thinks he's found the true path. It's all random tramping through sidestreets. The observer mustn't cause a scandal. Unobtrusiveness is key. Let the busybodies go their way; it's not for him to get involved in other people's affairs, to say what should be done. Fretting, fussing, fighting—there are plenty of other people to do that. Action takes away from one's concentration. Real work requires lowered eyes, unbroken calm.

If he were to get up from this chair, this table, with which he forms a triangle, leave his cave, he would first step out onto the terrace. He could sit in a deck chair from which only treetops are visible: aspen and birch, pine and ash all around. If he craned his neck, he could see gardens encircled by rows of raked leaves: the baroque horticultural fantasies of an old woman, and the more disciplined, classical rectangular flower beds of an old man. The old fusspot, the woman would always say about her neighbor.

One can also focus on stone nymphs, miniature pools, moss-covered columns, things just a little overdone—triple gateway arches and turrets. Let's have something more here, an extra dash of ornamentation there; whatever struck the builder's fancy was carried out, on the cheap. Still, every house has character: lions and angels on each façade, the exuberance of the late nineteenth century in the thick walls. The lawns are not annoyingly perfect, but their unkemptness is also kept in check. Here everyone is tidy or untidy in his or her own way.

Now the eye glances over a tennis court, where every afternoon children troop in, warm up, serve, and nimbly return the ball. Mothers sit in parked cars and read, or chat on street corners. A familiar-looking old gentleman appears with his cane; he is ninety years old, and his strolls, which must last an hour and half, trace an ever-shrinking circuit. Cherries and strawberries, mushrooms and flowers are on display at the greengrocer's. The only way to walk is without intending to accomplish anything. Four large, white-bellied pigeons keep fluttering in varying formations in front of the old man.

In a stone-faced, Bauhaus-style building exactly forty-five years ago, Dragomán came to a girl's birthday party carrying a bouquet of flowers. He'd been brought here by a classmate who told him with a wink not to be shy, to talk to the pretty birthday girl. Years later he rented an apartment in this building and used it for secret trysts. He could also work undisturbed in the tiny flat; he could hide his manuscript in the linen closet. He realized that his whole life had been haunted by a fruitless search for a truly safe hiding place.

Cyclamens, vermilion roses, lemon trees. An attractive, long-legged girl with a tennis racket leans on her bicycle. In a sidewalk restaurant the neighborhood driving instructor is eating lunch, a dog stretched out next to him. Middle-aged couples wipe their plates clean with bread and drink red wine. Nothing's the same, prices are going up—the fate of aging lovers. A church huddles up the street, threatened by change; it doesn't reach out or up, it just wants to stay put. Some of these stocky people never left the neighborhood either. Young girls in pretty blouses; pale pink and reddish brown flowers; an elderly lady in a white suit walking to the playground with two white borzois and two grandchildren carrying plastic pails and shovels.

He notices his former boss walking by with his dog. The man had no qualms about dismissing him at the request of the security police. Now all he can remember is what great friends they were.

DRAGOMÁN CARRIES AN old woman's shopping basket: soft gooseberries, young kohlrabi, celery stalks, mushrooms, garlic. She makes the sign of the cross when she sees the bloody jowl of a freshly killed pig hanging out of a truck window. A tall, thin young man in glasses wearing a hooded jacket throws two sides of pork onto his shoulder and with manly strides carries the carcass into the butcher shop.

The old scientist shuffles up and down his long balcony. Now and then he pauses to drink his tea, then gets up again, and with his rubber-tipped cane continues shuffling. At ninety, this is all the activity he can manage; he no longer wants to see strangers.

The hill's tranquillity, a motionless pine tree, a Labrador trying to squeeze its head between the fence posts, untrimmed, dense shrubs hanging out of gardens, reddening ivy, backyards kept up just enough so that their neglect won't show—all these are the precious ingredients of a historical moment.

Wind shakes the leaves of yellowing poplars, the creeping vine on the walls is fading, no one sits in the garden chairs now. A swing creaks between the cherry trees when the wind catches it, a pigeon coos as it moves along, crows have descended on the trees in the parade ground, bird feeders hide under ivy-clad façades. The smell of hot apple jam wafts from a balcony; under a window a piece of ornamental pottery catches the eye, though the wall behind it peels and molders.

HE OFTEN VISITS Kobra in his house on Old Hill. Their other classmates have scattered to the four winds, but Kobra stayed. Dragomán would love to understand Kobra's secret, the art of serene resignation, which enables him to feel good about having stayed.

The peripatetic professor visits Kobra and the two withdraw to a stone cottage open on two sides. Suddenly there are wineglasses and pipes on the table; restlessness has suddenly displaced restful calm. Kobra tries to persuade Dragomán to stay, he needs him, he says, though he is careful to feed him the sentimental line about home bittersweet home in small enough doses. Just the same, whenever he hears Dragomán's voice, he brightens up and laughs into the telephone. "What are you two cooing about?" Regina would ask. When Dragomán visits, Regina knows he hasn't eaten yet. With him it's either feast or famine, now it's the latter; he'll only have tea and buttered toast.

He left Kandor in '67; it had become much too boring. The boredom suited Kobra; for Dragomán it was unbearable. He wanted to have fun and test his capacities. He was past asking what was allowed and what was not. Whatever he read or heard or said seemed like a cautious tautology. He wanted to study saints and monsters, was eager to meet sages, size them up, and watch them reveal the depth of their wisdom. He could respect the professional in a pickpocket, even if it was his own wallet the fellow was after. Let Kobra continue to write long novels; he, Dragomán, preferred sudden insights. He didn't sit at his desk too long—he'd rather use his feet than his behind. Things had to be grasped rather than described. He tried to experience everyone's truths, even if they were mutually impenetrable. His body was his own, and the Earth. Not everyone can be a vagabond, but anyone with an inclination should become one.

He and Kobra trek over to the other side of the mountain for some wine at a friend's wine cellar. Back in the stone cottage they analyze it until the wee hours of the morning. The next day Dragomán doesn't even want to think about getting up, he closes the window and pulls down the shades in his room, which looks over the garden. When Regina calls him for breakfast, he mumbles something about Interpol, that it must be behind the campaign being waged against him. He is in fact a longtime supporter of International Pacifists, a secret organization that promotes the cause of peace by periodically assassinating a warlike world leader in the hope that this will have a moderating effect on his successor. It's better to do away with a single despot, so the argument goes, than allow him to cause the death of thousands. Dragomán's reasoning may be compelling, but he can't get the police to agree. Heads of state, even if they hate one another, don't appreciate headhunters of this type.

Dragomán arouses all kinds of suspicion. One of his lovers was implicated in a conspiracy against a Latin American dictator. He is friendly with anarchist civil rights activists and is the founder of a magazine called *International Dada.* He is the conduit for the secret society of metropolitan magi. Interpol does keep an eye on Dragomán; he is in touch with too many shady operations. Intelligence gatherers, when they realize how far afield the good professor tends to wander, make sure shadows have him covered at all times. Interpol is also aware that under the heading of media study, the firm of Darnok does the same.

"I'm being written up," complains Dragomán. "Watched from a nerve center. They tell me to just do my thing, but I keep thinking that I am being followed, programmed, controlled. You told me some odd things, too." He grabs Kobra's hand. "Are you also writing reports?"

Kobra smiles. In Dragomán's eyes is the sobering light of a sudden realization.

"You yourself are Darnok. You are the great spider, I only seem like one. You weave your web from here, and keep making me over, deciding my ultimate fate. Please don't tell me what to do. I know what role you have in mind for me. I should be the absurd romantic dreamer, while you calmly sit on your behind. I should be the tempter, the instigator, the mysterious vagabond—everything that you are too lazy and cowardly to be."

Even while talking, Dragomán keeps jumping up. Then he goes to the gristmill and borrows a horse. The young mare is overexcited, Dragomán wears her out and returns in the evening, disheveled and wound up, in time to play with the children and chat with Kobra's mother.

Roaming

School desks. From them he looked out at a world of wonders, a yellow wall on which a sign in raised letters said: BAKERY. He couldn't have been more than eight; he hated school even then. Much later, in his third year of high school, he sat at a desk from which he could see a young woman in a window across the way, wearing a black slip and black stockings. Sometimes she'd only have on her bra and girdle, and then slip into a flowing dressing gown. Ass, tits, fresh rolls, round loaves—adolescents are always hungry.

The cardsharps of the class offered good money for Dragomán's seat; they returned books they had won from him, and were willing to finance an expedition to the local bordello, but he couldn't be dragged away—even during class his eyes were glued to the window across the street. "She must smell great, probably of musk or myrrh," he opined. He'd only read about these fragrances, but he loved to make his friends look stupid.

Theirs had to be the dullest geography teacher ever. Following the latest directive, he discussed in excruciating detail the coal, oil, and steel production of each of the Soviet Union's member republics. The growth rate, one had to admit, was phenomenal.

The woman leaned out of the window, looked down at the sidewalk—was she waiting for someone?—while her breasts almost spilled out of the low-cut brassiere. Dragomán had nothing against Mr. Tóth, the geography teacher, who twirled his pointy mustache with noble resignation. Whether he conducted a lesson in geography or in drawing, his performance, though adequate, was pathetic. Mr. Tóth's uncharismatic ways were beyond remedy.

"May I open the window, sir?" Dragomán asked. "I have a headache." The good-natured teacher, with an underdog's compassion, was genuinely concerned about his boys' health. So the suffering student took the opportunity to shield his mouth with both hands, pucker his lips for a kiss, and dispatch it through the open window.

Until now he hadn't seen that this woman had the wide and massive legs of a drill sergeant—a herd of wild boars could run through them. And her forehead was narrow, suggesting modest brainpower. But even when he realized all this, he conceded that her bosom, though perhaps too ample, was nevertheless shapely. The migraine-afflicted young Dragomán blew a few more kisses her way.

The kind of women he could only dream about at seventeen he could easily have at twenty-three, in 1956, in the spring of that year, to be more precise, on an uncertain, overcast day. He was walking with Mari and her dog. Mari was a sharp-witted, worldly-wise girl who liked to sit in her stepfather's lap when she was little and was even more eager to do so when she got older. She liked having a secret understanding with this man, and liked, too, that he summoned her as soon as her mother walked out.

She had her own room, and for privacy she hung mattresses on the door leading to her parents' room, so hers was accessible only through the bathroom. She walked around her large, unmade bed in a long T-shirt and short pants, and when Dragomán sat down, her long legs swayed at eye level in front of him.

Dragomán never liked to make dates with her in advance, he noted with satisfaction that any time was a good time, that he'd always be welcome. As soon as he walked into Mari's room, she would lock the door. The windows were closed, the red linen shades pulled down. In the strong spring light that filtered in, their burning cigarettes turned green.

Mari's stepfather would knock on the door with any excuse he could think of, and Dragomán was also unnerved by Mari's five-year-old stepbrother who ran around with a pocketknife. "If you come at me with that knife one more time, I'll smack your bottom," he said. Naturally, the parents were offended.

He frequently sat with Mari at the Tango. The couple opposite them, always the same couple, glanced approvingly at Dragomán's choice. Mari, who was somewhat clumsy and easily distracted, always flicking the ash into her saucer rather then the ashtray, was about to give a large sum of money to some con artist who desperately needed to see his children in the country. She had to be talked out of this folly, and it was an old waitress named Baby who did most of the talking, basically because she, along with the other waitresses, liked Mari. Even the populous Gypsy family that sometimes showed up at the bar sought her out; they could tell she empathized with their problems. Once the Gypsies were discussing, with the other customers' active participation, why the young Gypsy husband couldn't perform so his wife might enjoy it also. Liba, who for years was the number one whore at the Tango, was present when the young wife told her husband: "Go to Liba, she'll teach you." "I can teach him," Mari offered generously, motivated no doubt by pure altruism. "Let Liba teach him," Dragomán suggested. "All right," Mari said.

AT THIS TIME Dragomán was spending a lot of time in and around his old high school, since Lona was a teacher there. From the editorial office where he dropped off his occasional book reviews, and the press cafeteria where he could talk to anyone worth talking to over a cup of coffee and a brioche, he went straight to the school. Lona invited Dragomán for her final student-teaching session. Dragomán sat in his old classroom, at his old desk, watching Lona teach her class. Across the street the seductress of old appeared in the window, still wearing a black bra and black panties, looking flustered on noticing Dragomán, who again pursed his lips, which in turn made Lona lose her concentration. After the class she lashed out at her incorrigible friend.

"Look at me," Lona said, and Dragomán knew he was going to be slapped in the face, and knew, too, that he was going to take it, and would not even think of striking back; it was best to get it over with.

In the ensuing showdown the window business came up, of course, the appearance six years later of the same woman at the same window, the possibility that she had freckled breasts, his infantile fantasies, and the slap just received, with which she was trying to keep Dragomán within the broadly defined limits of adult behavior. "You are what's known as a hebephrenic, my sweet. The symptoms are clear: an uncritical nature, a complete inability to discriminate, to choose, a tendency to grab at everything with childish greed."

Mari's beagle was sniffing at a scraggly acacia tree, and then he peed on it. The tree was in front of the house opposite the high school, its bare branches reaching all the way up to the third floor. Dragomán tossed his head back in surprise. "That's where the mysterious Kunigunda lives!"—for that's what he called her.

"Let me see," Mari said. "Is that her window? The third on the right? I know her. We trade sweaters sometimes." They walked up the stairs and found her at home. There were lots of German books on her shelves, which did little to lessen the pervasive cat smell in the flat.

"My cat is not nice," the mystery woman began. "She is jealous. My little niece was here the other day. I played with her, kissed her on the cheek, whereupon this wretch disappeared for two weeks. Abandoned me just like that. We met on the roof; she hissed and tried to claw at me. Then she came back, depositing a dead pigeon with its throat cut open at my feet. My Nelly has her moments of generosity, but don't think she ever lets me pet her. She doesn't know what it means to purr. When I come near, she scratches. She detests me, I think. It happens. I often ask myself: Why live with an animal that detests me? She's not as mean to other people, mind you. I bet if she came in now, she'd be nice to you.

"Of course I recognize you. Schoolboys love to look at me; and I let them. But my boyfriends were always such huge, hairy beasts, the little schoolboys didn't dare come up and ring my bell. You were scared too, though from your school desk you played the big shot. You even threw me kisses.

Mari went into the other room and sat down at the piano. The mysterious Kunigunda had an amazingly versatile bed equipped with drawers and secret compartments. If she needed a pair of tweezers or a paper clip while lying in bed, to say nothing of delicious edibles—sticky raspberry-flavored candy was an especially handy treat—or old picture postcards from Venice or

Biarritz, all you had to do was pull out the appropriate drawer. There were also numerous bottles and vials that could be sniffed with pleasure.

"My only loyalty is to a cat that hates me. I take care of her, I'm good to her, but she sees through me. I won't let her in now because she might jump at you. If I lock her in the closet, she starts tearing up my clothes. If I put her in the bathroom and you felt like taking a shower, she might lunge at you. She pops into my bed at the worst possible moments, spoiling all my fun. It's really nice of you to spend time with me like this. But how come it doesn't bother you that Mari is here, too, playing, if I hear her correctly, Rachmaninoff. I'll call her back, shall I?

"There you are, Mari, dear. Open the drawer with the brass knob; that's where I keep my jade collection. And in the larger one next to it, you can find pictures of my boyfriends. On the back of each one I wrote their address and phone number. Take your pick, dear, as many as you like, in exchange for this timid admirer. Open that little cabinet, no, you don't even have to get up, you can take out the bottle of rum and glasses. This bed is like Noah's ark; it helps me get through hard times."

DRAGOMÁN LOVED COLLECTING the fees for his freelance jobs, first at the radio station, then at the newspaper. In between, he met people, bought a bottle of champagne, or in a fit of eccentric enthusiasm, a pet hamster, which he presented to Mari, who wasn't sure she liked it. Then they went to see Kunigunda, who was in the middle of brushing her hair. The wire hairbrush threw off sparks, the curve of her neck was especially tempting. Dragomán made as if to bite it, Kunigunda screamed, while Mari grew less and less happy with her hamster. Almost desperate, on the verge of tears, she began to stare at her own hands, as if noticing how lovely they were, until this moved her to tears.

Dragomán wandered from city to city, country to country, woman to woman. He always found rationalization for his sojourns, but he knew well that he was after women. Yet they always controlled the relationship. He left to chance who should call or visit or insist on meeting—if they were more determined, they deserved him. He had no regrets about any of his love affairs; the art of living in the moment he learned from women.

Most of his lovers wanted Dragomán all for themselves. He was given to pangs of guilt and exaggerated politeness, so he met them even when he had no desire to do so, and often attached moral significance to things that had little or none. Considering every phone call an obligation, and every evasion a serious omission, he still found his sense of duty and priority to be changeable.

More than once he had settled down next to a body: her curves, her touch, the timbre of her voice, her smell were more appealing than anything he'd ever experienced, and he didn't feel like moving on. Only you? Only me? At a certain age impassioned obtuseness is highly prized. In a marriage the best thing is a beautiful church wedding. If there's no mystical bond, he'll forgo the civil ceremony.

"My accomplice, though never my ally," Melinda said of him. The only time Dragomán felt like studying a menu, tearing to pieces a mediocre book, thinking up an apocalypse or a redemption, or simply turning into a curious little side street to try a new café, was when she was with him. Then he felt she could give each moment its due. If he said something intelligent, Melinda would be sure to appreciate it; if what he said was ordinary, she'd be the first to exhale disapproval. When she smiles, because for once he has bought the right flowers, he is happy. When Melinda speaks, Dragomán hears every word; with others he absorbs far less. When Melinda speaks, there is no enlightened self-interest, no careful deliberation: then, Dragomán jumps up and runs through flaming hoops.

Enter Olga

Cool, rainy weather. The wind blows in leaves through an open window. A call from the reception desk: A young lady is here. Her name is Olga Dragomán.

"Send her up."

A knock on the door. A slim, pregnant woman stands in the doorway. Big black eyes, a searching, suspicious look.

"Mr. Dragomán?" He nods. "Do you think it is possible that I am your daughter? My name is Olga Dragomán. As you can see, I am expecting. If your answer is yes, you'll have a grandchild, too, not just a daughter."

"Let me have a closer look, then. It is possible. Please come in."

"My mother's name is Bella Olajos. Remember her? She is a midwife in Kandor. You met her at the lake. She wore her thick auburn hair in a bun then. You had just left the Academy building and accosted her. 'I am a stranger in town,' you said, 'and I am looking for a place to eat. Won't you join me?' Mother was tired and hungry; she'd cleaned off a dozen newborns that day. You ate at the Fishnet, then went for a walk. You also dropped in at the Tango bar, where you discovered that my mother had several friends who didn't like you. After you left they followed you and let you have it, sustaining minor injuries themselves. Mother dragged you from the scene and took you home. And that's when I was conceived."

"An unfortunate incident with a happy outcome. How *is* your mother?"

"Would you like to see her?"

"I wasn't planning to."

"I don't remember what you were saying, but there you were on TV. One of the regulars at the Mousetrap smirked. I happened to look at Mother: her face hardened and turned red. 'Olga, that's your father,' she said. From the time you left Kandor, Professor Dragomán, and then the country, my mother stopped looking for you. A friend told me you were in town. I didn't want to call you; I wanted you to see me in person."

Olga stood, seized Dragomán's hand and pulled him to the mirror.

"Do you still have doubts?" He didn't. His daughter made herself comfortable, clasping her hands over her belly. "I wouldn't mind having a cup of tea, I may have caught a chill."

Dragomán called room service, and while on the phone, with his back to her, he kept glancing at her in the mirror. It's unmistakable, he thought. The shape of the nose, the cut of her eyes, the lips. Could he put his hand over the baby, his grandchild, he asked. The waiter wheeled in the tea cart. Leisurely, Olga ate a few biscuits, sipped her tea, and took a good look at his personal items in the room. It was still raining outside. Dragomán poured a little rum in her tea; his hand trembled.

Later, Olga reached deep into her handbag and took out a slightly creased photograph. "And this is Habakuk Dragomán, bearing the name of my elusive father. The children's court went along with it. Mother wanted it this way. It's a stupid name, she said, but she insisted on it just the same. And when Bella has her heart set on something, there is no arguing with her. A nice-looking boy, no?"

"Yes, yes," a stunned Dragomán said.

Olga quickly took back the picture and sank it into her bag, a fine black leather bag fading into reddish brown with wear. Inside, bunched-up tissues concealed the general chaos.

"Habakuk Dragomán is only three years old, but he is a regular little prophet, with a highly developed sense of justice and an uncanny knowledge of his true worth. He'll say to me: 'Mommy, a beautiful child shouldn't be spanked; it would make him very sad.' I cannot stand to see him sad, so we hit the hand—mine— that would dare to hurt him. Listen, Professor, for your grandson it's nothing to assume the spirit of forest animals, or any other creatures, for that matter. He climbs high and jumps down; he knows no fear, or pain. When he sings or paints or dances, he does it with his whole little being. You may want to stay here, with us, your daughter and grandson; you could be the hermit of Old Hill. Of course, you could lecture in one of Kandor's great halls, too. You could also plant seed onions, train the vines over Habakuk's sandbox, watch the wild vine creep over a trestle put together from logs sturdy enough to support the child's swing, because he has to start in the pit and swing to the sky. We have a child, your grandson, and this child is king. I am pregnant again by the same man, a trumpet player in a jazz band, who rarely comes home. I saw a documentary once, which showed that during an abortion the fetus tries to escape, it defends itself from destruction. I decided then that if I ever got pregnant again, I'd keep the baby. As far as the trumpet player is concerned, neither Mother nor I care much for temporary solutions. 'Don't think you're getting a real father,' Mother told me. 'First he'll settle in, make himself at home, then one day he'll take off.' He does come back, my trumpet player, making both of us very happy. But on the third day Habakuk usually pulls me aside; 'Do you think he'll still be here tomorrow?' When my man asks if there is somebody else, my answer is a simple no. Habakuk misses his father, and he'd love to have a grandfather."

Dragomán muses. The young woman's offer interests him: fatherhood, grandfatherhood—a clear-cut business, with no amorous entanglements. He's finished teaching a semester; he is free again. Olga continues her enticing speech:

"You'll soon meet Habakuk and see how solid the child is, and how slippery in his wisdom. He's a philosopher, I tell you. His feet are miraculous, his smile a triumphant challenge..." There is a notebook on the table. Olga casually picks it up and starts reading from it: "Your egomania will be your undoing. No searching observations, only me, me, me. And afterward, penitential self-effacement.

"Are you berating yourself, by any chance? If you need a whip, I can be of help. I am sure I am every bit as sharp-tongued as you. I have taste; I can tell when something is beautiful. I am not rich, but I do like the finer things in life. I cannot abide repulsive odors, for instance. Apples on the radiator are fine, but you might want to air your slippers. You don't happen to have any hazelnuts, do you? Or a tangerine? By the way, I wouldn't like you to ask me what I do for a living. The skills I have, nobody is interested in. I am also pretty expensive. With my child and my bulging belly, I need someone to support me. This sometimes causes friction between me and Mother. She's a little thickskulled when it comes to understanding that it's her job to support us, my children and me, until the day she dies. It's fairly clear, wouldn't you say? Mother is not poor. She owns one of the best taverns in town. Ever hear of the Mousetrap? She is about to make an offer on the Crown Hotel. She had a studio set up for me, that's where I do my sketching, although I haven't sold any of my drawings."

"I wouldn't want to become too involved in your intimate affairs," Dragomán said, and moving to the farthest corner of the room, settled himself in a rocking chair. "Tell me, my dear, were you also sent here?"

"Yes, I was. But who else?"

"That bald man with the cane chairs and the bird cage. He follows me everywhere, grinning and waving from a distance. He wears Tyrolean pants, and when he gets near me, he offers his services in a low whisper. There is also the woman who walks around with a rat on her shoulder, sucking pensively on the rat's long, pink tail. Neither of these characters ever let me out of their sight."

"Everyone is followed," Olga remarks. "When I was a child, a man followed me to school every morning, whispering obscenities in my ear. He was careful to do it when no one else was around. I guess that's how he amused himself on his way to work. One day I told my mother about it. She had a truck driver deliver a bucket of pig shit, and without saying a word splash it in the whispering pursuer's face. My mother doesn't take her complaints to the authorities. She is an amazingly strong woman, a lioness, and she wants me to be one, too. Come around and see for yourself. Mother prefers young men. She can afford to go out with twenty-year-olds. If you come over to the Mousetrap, you can see Habakuk and have the meal of your life. No one—and I mean no one—can cook like Mother. Mother also rents out rooms, you could move into one of them. It'll cost you less than the Crown, and will include three meals a day. You'd get the best room in the house. A magnificent silver spruce stands under the window."

"That's how it is when you have people snooping after you," Dragomán said pensively. "There's a voice hovering in the air, the voice of a tagtail, a tempter. He could be your agent, your impresario, your manager, she might be a waitress in the espresso bar who will say, in a declarative rather than interrogative voice, 'A little more rum.' If I turn on the flickering idiot box, all I see is someone trying to fob off something on me: Buy it, eat it. But even that is nothing compared to some of my visitors. A little lady walks in who is capable of turning my life upside down. She knocks on my door and within minutes I've acquired a whole new family."

Olga rests her tea cup on her belly.

"The ultrasound says it's going to be a boy. I can hardly imagine another boy as brilliant as Habakuk. Do you know what I'd like my big boy to become? The founder of a religion. I'll be his spokesperson. With a job like that I can't very well waitress more than four hours a day at the tavern. I'll need time for my spiritual duties. Those drunken fishermen are not exactly rude, but they can't keep their eyes off my lower body. Between you and me, my relationship with that part of my body is rather cool. I sense quite a distance between myself and everything else."

"The fact of the matter is, Olga, that the similarities between us are striking. It's nice to think that on a night like this, when darkness descends on the Northern Hemisphere, an old rake like me is suddenly blessed with a daughter and grandchildren, although my own contribution to your being was but a single night's pleasure. From now on, the old codger will dine on carp and stuffed cabbage in a family circle. He'll praise the holiday nut roll prepared by his queen for a night, and disparage similar endeavors by other, lesser bakers. And all this without having to tie the knot. Would you show me that photograph again?"

"I understand people generally get to feel this way about Habakuk. It's easy to be captivated by him. He gives assignments to everyone. I never saw anyone so sure of himself. Last week he was sick, he looked drawn, he wanted to be held. But even then, of the two of us he was the stronger. When I feel a pain in my chest, I hug him and feel better."

"I would need that, too. You know, Olga, inside me there's a madman who keeps knocking down walls with an ax, all the while roaring with laughter. He doesn't know yet that it will take just one bad move for the house to come crashing down on him. But in the end life is fair; first you take, then you pay. Inasmuch as I give credence to your dubious proofs, you have indeed acquired a Papa, in the foolish hope that Papa will always pay. Don't forget that you, too, may have to pay for your foolish curiosity. You'll end up high and dry with, well, nothing. I for one am getting used to this nothing, and have my own spiritual exercises to perform. But now, on a dark day like this, when my hands and feet throb with pain, I find myself in the middle of a touching Christmas story. To be honest, I have grown a little weak, I need someone to lean on. Of course I don't know if there isn't a ruse behind this visitation. Perhaps all I see before me is an apparition. After all, no one has ever showed up at my door claiming to be my daughter until now. I've lived with the knowledge that once I am gone I'll leave no one behind, not even a household pet."

But what if the enchantment is real? What if Dragomán really is a grandfather? Nonsense. If my grandmother had four wheels, I'd be calling her a car. For the most part, Dragomán hates that wet blanket called common sense, though he does listen to it—that's why he is still alive. Let's just see what happens as Dragomán goes over to that undeniably warm and friendly place called the Mousetrap.

The Mousetrap

Dragomán became a grandfather, and a father, too, of course; all at once he was given something—exactly what, he didn't yet know. A young woman appeared in his hotel room, an expectant mother, who showed him a picture of a little boy and told him the boy was his grandson. The woman's name should have been Olga Olajos, after her mother, but the court permitted the use of the putative father.

That's how craftily Bella Olajos, the dark-lipped midwife, bound her child to her elusive lover, and twenty-four years later, in the fall of 1992, this erstwhile love child is frightened—of what, she herself doesn't know. She has premonitions, she says, and apologizes for them. She is still young, she points out, she wasn't alive when gun battles on city streets were common—the sound of a firecracker is enough to scare her out of her wits. At such moments a girl needs a father to say something lighthearted and clever to her, and assure her that everything will be all right.

That's why she came to Dragomán; she saw him on TV. With those eyes, he had to be a relative, she decided. His narrow face was all too familiar, and that gaze, too, boring into people, peering upward, checking if he was being understood—she would recognize that look anywhere.

Kobra is also encouraging Dragomán to move into Bella's house in Balatonújfalu. He might want to settle down in his old age, his daughter and grandson are there, soon there'll be another, these are certainties—not the vague longings of the heart, but the undying assertion of blood ties. From the village he could commute to Kandor, and if he felt like it, he could teach a class at the university—that would be enough to satisfy his professorial needs. He makes enough money to live comfortably, even if he were to give himself over periodically to sheer idleness. He might get tired of Kandor quickly, in which case, with Regina's permission, he could take their two boys over to see Habakuk.

He loves to wade through wet grass in his heavy boots. But what if Kobra and Regina don't let him take their boys on an excursion with Habakuk? Why then he can go on a bike ride with Habakuk alone. He'd install a child seat, on the crossbar, not in the back, so Habakuk can be in front, between his two arms; and while pedaling through corn and alfalfa fields he can smell the boy's head.

Riding with a beautiful three-year-old is a continuous triumph—smiles at the boy, smiles at Grandpa. They understand each other perfectly. At any given moment Dragomán has to guess who he is, for the child undergoes one metamorphosis after another. Now he is a thrush singing on a treetop, now a worm in the bird's beak. But he might also transform himself into a weed that his grandmother leaves growing in front of her lakefront establishment.

Dragomán sees himself commuting between two places; he cannot give up Resurrection Square. *Enfin, je suis citadin.* You know what you are? A spoiled, aging roué. Yes, but he still insists on his freedom. When he is here, he longs to be back in his hotel room, though he's already inaugurated the table in the garden, under the walnut tree; many a sentence that received final approval was born there.

Around noontime he wheels his bicycle out of the garage and rides over to Balatonújfalu, where Bella owns a house with rooms to let, and a tavern with a large and lively clientele. The house is located on the corner of Owls Nest and Hempseed Streets. Green metal tables with oilcloth covers are set out in front, under the chestnut trees, while the backyard is more private, with Habakuk's swing set and sandbox, and lounge chairs placed under a walnut tree and a lilac bush. There is a ramshackle structure with missing roof tiles and three walls that Olga has come to call the bus stop. "If you placed the trestle and a chair near that quaint ruin, you'd be sure to come up with a few good ideas." There is a small apartment on the first floor of the main house—

they'd love to have him there, all three of them. With his two shoulder bags he could move in and make it livable in no time.

Bella Olajos is still good-looking. Here is a sixty-year-old man face-to-face with a forty-seven-year-old woman, and next to them their pregnant daughter and grandson. He's decided to rent the entire floor from Bella for the season. "It'll cost you three thousand marks, darling. One day your grandson will put that money to good use." Dragomán eats Bella's cooking; no shared bed, only shared suppers.

Bella is the owner of the Mousetrap. One of her lovers had run off with her money, and she herself had run afoul of the law and ended up in jail. But as far as she was concerned, it was not an issue. She grew tired of women whining about their sad lot, so she struck out on her own. She started small, ran a bar at the edge of town in rented space. It took years before she was able to open a nice lakefront tavern.

"You're going to have to leave if you get yourself mixed up in politics," she had told her daughter. Before the big political changes Olga had typed forbidden manuscripts for her friends. And when Olga asked about her father, Bella would only say, "A transient."

Bella also bought a disco with striptease and other erotic attractions. There is no money in the till, being in business is one long struggle, sometimes she has to hire hoodlums to beat up her creditors. She also dabbles in real estate, both as agent and as contractor. She has gone bankrupt a few times, but something could always be salvaged, and the Mousetrap brought in some money. However, what is Bella's is not automatically Olga's. If her daughter wants a cut of the profits, she'll have to work for it. From Bella's vineyard one can see all the way to the lake. Silver Shell is the name of the valley, and next to it, where the woods start, is the Valley of Mercy.

By Heaven's grace Dragomán now has a daughter and a grandson; he needs a retreat on this mountain near Stonedial, too, where he could sit and watch the smoke rising. It gives him a warm feeling that there is a Buddhist temple nearby, its location having been chosen after careful calculations by Tibetan monks far, far away. The spirit mushroom of serenity sprang up in this distant landscape.

The hillocks rising out of the green plain know they are touched by grace, and this quiet knowledge, and his friends' secret enchantment with this spot, have permeated Dragomán's consciousness. His ego needs the particular: this tree and that row of vines, a sheaf of straw, a lonely poplar, the outlines of the pointy mountaintop, the many caps and aprons. He needs a house where he is left alone, where he can live on very little, where death is paid as little notice as an old household animal.

Sitting comfortably in an armchair, Olga lets out a sigh. Her smile is so sweet and open, Dragomán is embarrassed and looks away. She had finished reading a book, taken Habakuk out for a walk, and is getting ready now to cook supper—she has invited guests for the evening. On the table are copies of *Die Zeit*, *Les Débats*, *The New York Review of Books*. Olga has to be well-informed, up-to-date on important issues and intellectual trends.

Habakuk's saxophone-playing father leads a vagabond's life. He sends them money, turns up now and then, hits the road again. Olga and Habakuk speak of him with stars in their eyes. He telephones when he is on his way; when he does finally show up with a suitcaseful of toys, Habakuk has eyes only for him. He is supposed to come again, this very month, but they cannot be sure.

Olga lives with her son at her mother's place at the Mousetrap Inn and waits for this man. She has a computer, so in the morning she types sloppy manuscripts; somebody usually dictates the material to her. Several of her friends bare their souls to her, and she discreetly corrects their spelling and grammatical errors, and prunes back their more offensive adjectives.

Days go by; it's been raining. Dragomán is in no hurry to go anywhere, he prefers to linger on the verandah—today it's the center of the universe for him. In the evening he is at the Mousetrap. When he first passed through the blazing torches of its entryway and walked into the bar, Bella smiled: they recognized each other but refrained from recalling the past; they remained on formal terms. Every tavern Bella has ever owned was called Mousetrap. She moves around the country, followed by her mice. Bella lives her life, preferring truck drivers for companions, yawning after each encounter, and never neglecting her day-to-day affairs. She is busy with the tavern, the house, and the children, who run back and forth between the garden and the tiny landing stage on the lake.

Bella mentions one of her competitors, a certain Georgette, whose inn is glitzier, and far more expensive, than it was only a few years ago. No more small talk around the bar; grim, hulking waiters inform you coldly that your order will be brought to your table. These waiters even know some German. Georgette doesn't understand what old Bella knows instinctively: that a good customer likes simplicity. She prefers her little Mousetrap, a cozy and unpretentious place in the country, where the customer doesn't mind if the owner's child is always underfoot. The customer doesn't want trained gorillas for waiters, he wants to see a sweet-looking barmaid.

Everything loses its magic, says Bella, once it becomes too successful. Let things remain a little flimsy, unfinished. Whatever's too good, or worked out in detail, isn't that interesting. Then it's no longer you inventing yourself, but others making you over. It's much better to plod along, barely making it—you still get sympathy that way. Bella put out a few small signs, you have to look to notice them. "You are what you are, but only so long as you are not it completely—so long as you are still trying to be it."

Sit quietly in the garden and wait for them to come. Perhaps they'll never come, or they may show up tomorrow morning. It's the bench that counts, not that they might appear, after all. Pitch-black rain may fall from the sky. Dragomán tells himself to be as inconspicuous as possible: in his noiseless sneakers and thick woolen socks he can be all but unnoticeable, tactfully invisible. It's unlikely that anybody would push him off that bench.

With age he is beginning to have a better grasp of what it means to be alive, what it takes to breathe. The wind whistles louder between the branches, but now only the sound of birds and dogs, the drone of a distant car engine can reach him. The swallows must be close by, their chatter, too, grows louder, the roosters crow late into the morning, even the ducklings have something to say. Freshly washed lace curtains flutter on a clothesline.

To a man lying in a meadow, the sky is a giant beaker. If he stands and turns around, he dominates the landscape. You can walk on rain-softened ground or on freshly mowed hay, but the springiness of a beaten trail feels better under your feet—that thin strip which others have pounded until it became nice and solid.

Walking is its own reward, it serves no other purpose; it is simple progression in space—leaving home to go somewhere and then coming back. There are still large meadows out there where he won't run into anyone, and silent trees and curious flocks of crows—places where he can spit at will. The row of poplars rustles evenly. But now there is also an even hum in his ear, it's been there ever since he noticed that his hearing was going. A man follows him everywhere with a cane chair and a traveling bag, which appears to be light on some days and heavy on others. A young woman has appeared on the horizon, carrying a pet rat on her shoulder.

Dragomán's pursuers usually enter through the front door, while he sneaks out through the garden, hides among the man-sized cornstalks, then cuts through the neighbors' backyards. He's always loved to turn off main roads, pull away, clear out, or play possum. The cornstalks, like heads of bushy hair, sway in the wind, then stand straight up.

He steals back into the garden under lowering skies. Now he rests his elbows on the stone wall and contemplates the tumble-down shed in the neighbor's garden, a stone structure surrounded by a sea of nettles and a few apple trees. He scrutinizes the collapsed door frame, the crumbling plaster between the jagged stones.

His thoughts have grown heavy, but now they rise and begin to circle over the village, the lake, the city. He sits on the garden bench, a Bible lies on the long worktable, and on top of it, a bread knife. The stone wall gleams in front of him, the wind moves the pine branches, he turns on the portable radio, the news is on, good news, bad news blend together and fade away, garbled, until there is no news at all.

There is unperturbable cheer in Dragomán's face; he is a child of luck—sixty years old and he's still around. He is grateful to fate for granting him a daughter and a grandchild, and soon another. He growls playfully at his daughter's belly. Olga is convinced that her soon-to-be born baby needs such grandfatherly growling.

Olga spends hours in her room with her books and notes and diaries, her silk handkerchiefs, her herbal teas, her reveries. Dragomán is getting used to Olga's quirks, they are becoming familiar to him, so if she should suddenly stop worrying about having eaten something unhealthy or being cold, or about cigarette smoke irritating her throat (which she wraps in silk scarves to ward off a sudden chill), then Dragomán would probably think something was amiss. These days Olga's goodwill knows no bounds: she cleans the house from top to bottom, rearranges the furniture, prepares Chinese lemon chicken with specially marinated, sun-dried peppers. The Riesling she serves with it isn't bad either.

Guests gather on the verandah, Dragomán is the host; he is either excessively cordial to them or totally oblivious. Bella and Olga look in on the party from time to time. Those who sit on the verandah rest their eyes on a range of colors, from pale yellow through varieties of green to bluish red.

There is nothing wrong with the place, everything works like a charm. He sees himself running between stalls in a marketplace, clutching a submachine gun. He lowers himself on a rope from the fourth floor of a building onto the tar-covered roof of a garage. From there he slides down the drainpipe and hits the street. No one sees him escape.

He swims on his back in the Sea of Galillee. The pebbles on the lake's bottom reflect the sunlight conveyed by the waves. Pursuing a camel, he descends on a rosemary bush to the pit of Gehenna.

Now he is in a blue-and-pink setting at an American airport. The coffee is watery, the cake much too rich. In this country he could roam at will for thousands of miles in any direction and still remain connected. As for the human element, he may as well be traveling between two identical points, he finds the same things everywhere. Yet their abundance holds him in thrall.

In his student days his favorite fantasy was crouching in an industrial cable car that ran across the Hungarian-Austrian border, near the Brennberg mines. Even as guards were busy shooting at escapees on the ground, one could roll across the border in one of those cars. In more recent years there were those famous East German balloonists, and people who dug tunnels under East

Berlin, and swimmers in diving suits who were often caught. Wherever he is, Dragomán checks out the back door.

He takes his grandson Habakuk to see his playmates, Kobra's two sons, Zsiga and Döme Kobra. Zsiga likes to mimic and mock Döme, yet at times he explains things to him with an older brother's patient kindness. "You know, Döme, and you too, Habakuk, you are silly little babies still, but one day you'll learn." Little Döme's speech is quite refined: "Would-you-please-thank-you, Zsiga." They hold hands on the way to the sandbox, but once there they start pummeling each other. They have their routine. Döme screams, Zsiga stops his mouth, Döme quiets down, Zsiga removes his hand, Döme starts screaming again, and so it goes.

Habakuk runs up a hill. He is a bird, a droning airplane. He drops on the ground and tells his grandfather who comes running, that he's heard an explosion; he hates sudden, sharp noises. Using horse chestnuts as ingredients, the boys cook and bake, and after much sweat and toil present the elaborate meal, potatoes, meats, pancakes, to Regina. Now they're busy taking things apart, and then with much drilling and hammering reassemble them. While they are at it, they repair Grandpa János, too. In a flash they turn themselves into tigers or trains, or they may give chase to the ducks and turkeys, pet the kitten, and climb over the garden rocks.

The sunset sky is purple, lights go on at the station platform, poplars loom beyond the railroad tracks, there is a light drizzle, you can smell the wet leaves. On his way home, Dragomán waits for his daughter and the child. A train arrives every fifteen minutes: students, workers, vacationers come and go, all connected now to the larger world. They can leave anytime for Kandor, Budapest, or for that matter, Rome.

They celebrate Habakuk's third birthday. Dragomán opens the door and finds the child sitting alone in his mother's armchair; Olga is still in the bathroom. Interrupting his thumb-sucking, Habakuk lets out a plaintive wail, but once he sees his grandfather he is more or less content.

Olga appears in a red silk dress, and the three of them wait for the guests to arrive. Three candles are placed on the birthday cake, but not the trick kind that go out when you blow them, only to start flickering again a moment later. Children's eyes stare at the tiny flames; it's no good dragging out the solemnity. A smile shouldn't last too long, birthday goodies are better if they are not too sweet. With one puff Habakuk blows away the magic.

The cake is excellent, the drinks too, though things do get out of hand after a while. Mimi bites Rozika, though she meant to bite Habakuk; all the same, Rozika's mother is upset. Motherhood is servitude, but it does make you more aware, it toughens your spirit. Olga just stands there in her beautiful silk dress, and the look of pity and compassion will not go away. Father kisses his daughter's hand, with the three-year-old birthday boy standing next to him. He is a homegrown, carefully nurtured specimen—kudos to his maker.

Yesterday Habakuk walked up to his grandpa: "You are very old, aren't you?" "Yes." "Then you will die soon. I know, that's what happens to old people: they die." Having said that, he left Dragomán and ran up to the attic. Habakuk's hair is blond, his skin is tawny, his eyes are burning coals. All in all, an intrepid soul, at one with himself.

Dragomán shuffles down the stairs and out into the garden. After taking a drop of the yellowish brandy, he trudges over to Bella for a cup of coffee. "Bella, *bella mia*," he croons. The manager likes to serve her customers in her bathing suit. Last night she saw Dragomán on television. "Grandpa János, I had no idea you were a celebrity, why didn't you tell me? I know, I know: great men are always modest, only fools show off. But tell me, darling, what do you think of all the changes taking place in this part of the world? Oh, but how silly of me. You're on vacation, why should you discuss politics?"

Dragomán rolls up his pants, adjusts the handlebar of his bicycle, and goes for a leisurely ride. The furniture in his room is whitewashed pine; he has everything he needs. A telegram is forwarded to him, inviting him to give prestigious lectures for impressive fees. He throws it among the letters that require immediate attention and that he'll never look at again. When they are no longer timely, he'll throw them out.

There are gardens that seem so large and deep, its trees fade into the darkness. The only room in the house where the light is still on is the professor's. But he is in the garden. Between him and the house are those hard-to-avoid tree trunks. He is drunk and the rest of the household is away. Whatever doesn't interest him he promptly forgets. He is almost happy here, though his instincts warn him of impending danger.

He set up camp in this verdant lakeside garden with surprising ease. The rich vegetation disregards the infrequent horticultural interventions. Even the shutters and the carved balcony railing are green. The trestle table and the bench he managed to make his own the very first evening he was here. Now, pressing his back against the wall, he feasts his eyes on giant plane trees. A lantern, a typewriter, a notebook, a pipe, a glass, outline the small space between his eyes and the table, a space he can measure out wherever he unpacks his traveling bag.

Can this minimal space be one's real, portable homeland? He can no longer count the number of times he has moved. The teacher in him does not want him to get used to abundance in any form. When he leaves, he carries with him not only his meager worldly possessions but his daily rituals and routines. In hotel after hotel he spreads out his belongings and then packs them up again. One day he'll unpack and there'll be no follow-up. A snail must leave behind his quick-to-dry trail with a certain sardonic pleasure.

Let's wade into the storm, let's ride the waves. Not slip into bed but into a watery grave, and be spotted by a helicopter after our bloated body has risen to the surface. On second thought, let's give liquid diet and yoga a try. What's best at such times is a hot bath. I'm barely alive, he mutters in the bathtub. He arrived in the village with a bad cold, then rode his bicycle, walked down to the landing stage, sat in the sun, all of which made him even sicker. But then he pulled himself together, and now his complexion is no longer pasty, he is beginning to be himself again.

Habakuk steps out onto the verandah. He can be happy and unhappy with total abandon. He has olive skin and blond hair, his eyes are smoldering black, his look is forever restless, daring to take anything on. Now he rides a giant Siberian husky.

Dragomán goes into a store and before he can say what he wants, the shopgirl screams: "Help, a holdup man!" He visits a charming little church up the hill; he hears groans from under the stone floor—human refuse they are, from a halfway house, in one horrible pile.

In a deserted side street Dragomán has the feeling somebody wants to run him over. But he knows: Life is good even if it's bad, for what's bad can also be good. And the good is better still. But this fleeting nothing? This hardly anything? This false start? Could this have been his life?

Where Were You?

"Where were you on October 23, 1956, and what did you do on November 4, 1956?" The question was put to Dragomán by a young reporter, a new university graduate, whose poems, reports, editorials, and society columns fill the pages of a brand-new local newspaper. On October 23 he didn't take up arms but on November 4 he did. Why it happened that way he couldn't really say. He remembers a bright, beautiful morning. The 23rd was the day the first issue of *Experiment*, a new literary and political monthly, was to come out. Dragomán was the journal's newly appointed assistant editor. He sat in his corner room that day alone; the rest of the staff had gone to a meeting. It must have been around ten o'clock when he decided to stop working on the slush pile. His drawer was filled with poems by portly accountants and hard-luck sagas penned by mustachioed veterinarians. At the time everyone was expected to have had a difficult childhood. An attractive biography had to begin this way: "There were ten children in my family and we often went hungry."

Every job and college application, every official request and appeal had to contain a curriculum vitae with a precise description of one's parents' social origin. Dragomán usually began his with "I come from a middle-class background." That was why on every list an X was placed next to his name. This meant he was a "class alien," unreliable, barely tolerated, and easily removed if the authorities so desired. Next to other names there were more attractive, regular letters: W for worker, the best possible classification, P for peasant, which was also good though not as good as W, C for civil servant, which was neither good nor bad, and P for professional—that needed further looking into. But that X! The letter itself was strange, suspicious. A good Hungarian name did not begin with X, it had to be a cosmopolitan name. He was branded with an X, therefore he was dangerous. It wasn't the first time this happened to Dragomán. They had placed letters next to his name before, either J or Isr., depending on whether the explicit "Jew" or the more euphemistic "Israelite" was deemed the more appropriate classification by compliant compilers—people who no doubt belonged to the decent and reliable majority, and may have even enjoyed drawing up lists of undesirables.

Later, yet another designation was put next to his name. In the 1960s discrimination based on class origin was abolished, and the official classifiers switched to the criterion of loyalty. Whoever was not against us, said János Kádár, must surely be with us. Such people needed no special letters in front of their names. And the country's ruler for thirty-three years, its local overlord, its iron-fisted dictator turned paternalistic leader, truly believed this. The new openness, the notion that those who are not hostile to the regime will be treated kindly, had a profound effect on people. At last they could now be part of the undiscriminated-against majority. Why be in the same league with those who were unreliable of their own volition, who were enemies of the state not on account of their birth but out of free choice? These disagreeable individuals did indeed foul their own nest. This was the time when being a dissident meant you were restless, quarrelsome, crazy.

Suddenly he was part of a procession. He stepped off the curb and found himself among like-minded young men and women whose faces seemed prematurely long. Some walked arm in arm, waiting at each corner for state security men to appear and break up the marching columns. People leaned out of windows with curious, terrified, encouraging faces. The news vendors stepped out of their kiosks—the real news was there on the pavement. All the cafés were open.

He joined the crowd with slight misgivings. Though he felt justified in being there, he knew he had marched like this before, on May Day, with thousands of others. There were organizers among the demonstrators whom he remembered from the old days. They were out again in full force, directing the crowd from cars, acting as if they knew exactly what to do. But there were new leaders too, who came up with new slogans. Whoever devised a clever jingle or even a silly-sounding rhyme was applauded by an appreciative audience; the new expression rippling through the crowd.

They knew they had to act: at least knock over something and burn it. It was rumored that in Poznan fires were set by the demonstrators. And why not? Can one imagine an honest-to-goodness peasant rebellion without people setting the manor house on fire? Cutting or burning the communist emblem of wheat sheaf, hammer, and five-pointed star from the middle of the red, white, and green Hungarian flag seemed like a harmless enough alternative. It took some skill, however, to remove the hated emblem without damaging the rest of the banner.

Dragomán wasn't comfortable witnessing the more vehement scenes, just as he hadn't much cared for the rhythmic marches of old, the unruly, malodorous physical closeness of high school assemblies. He had an aversion to the cult of the collective, and disdained everyone engrossed in communal activity. He felt his native skepticism threatened by the revolutionary fervor of those healthy plebeian forces.

They were all here on the street, the brightest and the best, including those who in the past had been able to break into song at a moment's notice, or form a circle and dance as soon as the procession came to a halt. Now they marched quietly: no song, no dance. Dragomán had skipped most of the earlier marches; this one he didn't.

There were people, of course, who marched for a while and then quit the demonstration. Streetcars stopped, old ladies waved from the sidewalk, tots in strollers waved flags.

There were so many marchers, marching against the very ones who in earlier years had stood over them and watched as they filed past. University students came in droves, the same students who pored over the history of the Communist (Bolshevik) Party of the Soviet Union, the book supposedly written by Stalin himself, which discussed not only the intricacies of ideological deviations but also his prescription for resistance and revolution.

Party members marched alongside the politically uncommitted; but the loudest and liveliest were those who had also been loud and lively back in '49. A famous poet in the crowd signaled broadly with his hand and cried out in his pleasantly deep voice: "People, here comes the revolution." But he'd said the same thing before, and what had come was rule by a revolutionary elite, and along with it his own glory days. Now he, like others on the street, was disgruntled, embittered, clinging nevertheless to his former idealism. But they all had to do that: their vocabulary was as modest as their wardrobe; they'd never been abroad, they were stuck in the old phraseology. They could only play with the one deck they carried with them.

Dragomán was tolerant rather than aggressive, though his mild manner often combined with tenacity. He carried a submachine gun but like a civilian, as though it were an umbrella—it was good to have it handy, he might need it. He was no revolutionary; in fact he thought the movers and shakers were dilettantes at heart, but during this season of breathtaking exposés he was also of the opinion that they couldn't possibly do a worse job than the present rulers.

He recalled the political pilgrimages and processions of past years, at which he had to show his face now and then, and repeat the slogans, if not at the top of his voice, then at least in polite agreement. Those marching around him had done the same, with more self-assurance perhaps. After a time Dragomán had absented himself from the ritualistic demonstrations, just as years later he would sneak away from solemn conferences. He had felt ill at ease at those giant rallies and found something slightly ludicrous about every subsequent demonstration that signaled a historic turning point.

At such events many people do get swept away by the emotions of the moment; there is always someone who feels compelled to step into the line of fire, open his shirt, and shout: "Here I am, you curs, shoot if you dare." Such a dramatic stand usually causes the guns to be lowered, but who is to say that there isn't a gloved hand holding a revolver ready to shoot into that gallantly bared chest? It may also happen that the murderous officer will become a general someday, and the victim who survived the revolver shot will get so despondent over the injustice of it that he takes his own life. There are times when emotions surge, vital instincts do not function, and in an ecstasy of self-abnegation people leap into the abyss. Mothers with infants in their arms carry a flag through a hail of bullets.

A man about to be executed adheres to a secret script. He walks under the gallows or into the gas chamber, he stands before the firing squad, he takes off his clothes at the edge of a mass grave, and he does it with lame and petrified submissiveness perhaps, but still at the required speed. The victim at this point is no longer passive. He enacts his own death, rising above his murderers, already a free man. He will do this much for them, he will stand there, why shouldn't he? In a moment he'll disappear into the void, whereas they remain to live with this act. As the executioner packs up his tools, he must know that the condemned man is the hero of the day.

For it is he, the victim, who is the one serious and solemn participant in the ritual of death. He does not make light of it, his self-respect demands that he have a high regard for the ceremony. Why should stepping on a stool be considered different from other routine motions, like jumping up, standing at attention, clasping one's hands behind one's back? If one gets accustomed to prison formalities, the ceremonies of captivity; if one obeys meaningless commands and naturally submits to the guards' will; if he speaks only when spoken to and remains silent when no question is put to him; if only what his prison guard expects and approves is to be considered true and real and worthy of note; if for the sake of his hoped-for survival he adheres to every single prison regulation, from when he can smoke to when he can relieve his bladder, then his participation in his own execution is nothing more than an extension of the almost automatic prison routine that has kept him alive until now. If he hadn't rebelled before, he certainly will not rebel before the firing squad. If that's what they want from him, his life, he will hand it over. If this is the last act of the prison drama, then he will stay in character to the very end.

Staying in character, Dragomán realized, is the essence of all oppressive systems, and this role-playing must have a profound effect on human relations in such systems. Whoever is below obeys and works, and receives special favors in return for his obedience. He wants to be liked, of course, he is a loyal and enthusiastic subject, and will remain so as long as the propaganda machinery of the state remains unmovable, as long as the controlled media roundly condemns everything that deviates from the prescribed norms.

But if the voice of authority falters; if the citizen is compelled to think for himself; if those at the top haven't played their parts well or done a good job of thinking for the people; if the underlings don't receive clear-cut orders—then there is confusion, dissolution, and revolution cannot be far away. At such times the citizen is tempted to do some serious thinking. He begins to lose respect for the ceremonies of self-renunciation, he joins his fellow citizens in a march on the main square, and switches his allegiance to another set of leaders.

Revolutions are festivals of self-sacrifice, hence they are hardly normal phenomena. Many people gather in a square, even though they know they may be shot at, and may even be targeted for massive retaliation by armed forces. And then begins a tug-of-war to see who is more determined, whose moral stand is more forceful. At one end there are more and more people, at the other fewer and fewer; the balance is upset.

An opposition that had been minuscule, almost nonexistent, has swelled into a huge and formidable force. No organization is needed, people flock to the square of their own accord, their heart summons them. Sensible family men and women arrive, people who ordinarily avoid conflict and confrontation. Now they plant themselves before the barrels of guns. Otherwise cautious individuals display death-defying courage. Those who used to keep their eyes lowered now stare down the armed soldiers. At such moments these timid rather than daring citizens do partake of the sanctity of a collective experience. Having overcome their fears, they radiate a celebratory spirit.

At such revolutionary turning points, it's not enough to stand and wait in the square, one must move, from one historical symbol to another, and knock down statues, open prisons, occupy communications centers, take over printing presses, radio and television stations. People wave flags from the balconies of public buildings, and then push forward a famous but timorous humanist intellectual, who upon seeing the enthusiastic crowd utters lofty and moving sentences of a kind that seldom leave his lips.

Like a conductor, he directs the mood of the throng; sensing their vibrations, he unconsciously adjusts his rhetoric, and if sensitive enough, takes full advantage of people's innermost desires. If the orator is unable to do this he'll soon be hooted down. Prophets and showmen win the day. Whoever has not experienced a crowd in raptures keeps yearning for it.

Order of the Day

After the '56 uprising was put down and the city filled with Soviet tanks, many of Dragomán's friends set out, along with thousands of other men and women. But even as this wave of humanity lurched toward the border, choosing this more sensible alternative, he did not consider moving to a more tranquil spot. Beyond rational explanations and sheer inertia, he simply stayed. He waited for the arresting officer, the retaliation, and then the relief; he waited for new women, for loneliness.

He became a stroller without destination, finding something appealing in every neighborhood even if what made it special was its unique ugliness. Every memorable event is spatial, everything happens somewhere, every incident is connected to a place—the way a snail is attached to its house, an oyster to its shell, a cat to its favorite corner by the stove. There are things Dragomán recalls only in this or that place; they emerge from the depths. A memory may be inscribed on a bare wall. If he hadn't found himself on a street corner, if he didn't pass by a doorway, the story they evoked would vanish.

Ever since he was a child he has dreamed about wide-open spaces without people. He liked to brood undisturbed, like a hen, and he didn't let circumstances overwhelm him. He would wait and see where a stream carved a bed for itself. Matter has a way of letting us know what it wants to turn into. Only afterward, and only for an instant, do we discover its true design. These flashes reward us, until we stumble, inevitably, into a pit.

Dragomán sits in his room, somebody taps on the window, it's almost dark, the street lamps flicker. It's her: Laura. She walks softly, Dragomán lets her in. She says she came to visit, but will soon have to leave. She'll come again if all goes well now. No, she can't stay more than a half hour. Considering she's been dead for seventeen years, a half hour is a maddeningly long time. All her letters are locked in a drawer, Dragomán takes them with him wherever he goes, but never touches them. Laura left, Dragomán stayed, and he would like to stay awhile longer.

Good times, bad times, what does it matter? The future holds neither reward nor punishment. Those who want to talk to him can find him. Dragomán will spread out the carpet of curiosity, but there are things he doesn't wish to share with anyone. The older he gets, the less patience he has for weepiness, gooeyness, touch-me-not squeamishness. Till four in the afternoon he is a misanthrope, he cannot take the smell of humans.

When he sees someone lose his temper, Dragomán wonders: What did this guy have to drink? What's eating him anyway? Folly is impressed with its own foolery, it loves to show off, bluffing is its strongest suit. As they get older, even sensible people love to hear their own voice, and go on and on—it's a confirmation that they are still here. Dragomán's guest talks, therefore he exists. What did he do for a living? He talked all his life, he gushed, he oozed.

Dragomán himself harbors no resentment against anyone, accuses no one, makes no demands, does not feel he gave or received too little, is bored by self-pity, and wants no part of infantile, self-revelatory togetherness. He reassures everyone that they owe him nothing, and if they are thankful or apologetic, he tells them there is no need.

In any case, whatever happened, happened. Every occurrence is stuck in universal time, it cannot be dislodged. Neither forgiveness nor forgetfulness can undo what was done. If Dragomán committed misdeeds, his punishment is that he committed them. He lives with his sins; they stand around him like bodyguards, like jailers.

Dragomán loves to hem and haw; when it's his turn to speak he'd much rather tell a funny story than make a significant statement, which irritates serious thinkers no end. But then, there is no pleasing everyone.

His mind reels in a pitching boat; he is asked to come down for a photo session. Embarrassed, he smiles as he descends the narrow staircase; reporters with microphones crowd around him. He manages to say something, not quite what they wanted to hear, for he is evasive, as usual, but he is with the president, and the photographers run after them, and on their knees, on tiptoes, they record the handshake. Dragomán smiles again, the president, too, tries to pry loose his thin lips, there is champagne but no champagne glasses—security men run to fetch them.

Summer returns, the air is motionless. For days the leaves on the willow tree barely stir. Dragomán presses his back against the stone wall, his head and back seek out the stone's pleasant dents and protrusions, and he sways back and forth with his eyes closed. Now and then he sips from his drink, he straightens out, and when he is sufficiently high, he reaches for his pen.

An airplane also appears to gear itself up before take-off. A weight lifter, too, performs odd little rituals before his enemy, the dumbbells: he walks around them, closes his eyes, shakes himself before lifting. The sun hides behind dense clouds, a summer storm tears through the garden, and afterward a rainbow connects the miller's house to the retired eye-doctor's cottage. Dragomán walks into his room: through the window he can see his grandson rollicking in the rain with his playmates. The rain stops, and a few old women come out to admire the rainbow. They are joined by a tractor driver, a landscaper, a cowherd, as well as the village winegrower, locksmith, and stud farm owner.

Dragomán's living quarters are conveniently remote from the bedrooms and the stables. Dinner preparations are under way. Dragomán plays a game of catch with Habakuk, after which they pick cauliflowers, onions, and string beans for dinner. Then Habakuk settles into a green wicker chair under the parakeet cage, listening to Olga's bedtime story. Each evening she embroiders on the same tale, adding exciting new twists, though the hero of the story remains Habakuk.

A stream runs under the old wooden bridge, the apple and plum trees are bursting with fruit, a hen went berserk in the neighbor's backyard. It's been raining a lot, after a long dry spell, the grapes began to shrivel on the vine, the plant sucked back the moisture from the almost ripe fruit. Now the earth drinks in the water greedily.

The professor leans on the fence and looks out at the cornfield, a duck quacks behind him, the clouds belly out in the sky, a light breeze rustles the corn blades.

Now Dragomán leans against the stone wall. He drank too much last night, so he feels distant and dull, and is merely polite, even with Habakuk. He sits in the gazebo, or in a hut at the edge of the garden used to dry corn husks; it's drizzling again, the clouds weep, the air fills with mist, birds chirp lazily, the elderberries are almost black.

After he spends a few days in a neighboring country, the old people in the village invariably ask: "You've come back from strange lands, have you? And what did you see?" He saw ramshackle houses, fruit trees, cats, ditches, bicycles, an old man nodding in a tavern, a cheerful barmaid. He walked through an unlit village, across a wooden bridge, toward yet another tavern by a river.

Back home, he drank brandy with a young man who was happy enough with a cup of coffee. His job was to drive the professor home, so he listened respectfully to the old man's stories, and then told him with some embarrassment that he'd heard Dragomán had once had an affair with his mother. That's right! She was that lovely young thing with the coffee-colored skin from the rare books shop. She would laugh until tears ran down her face and nestle up to Dragomán like a child. Once she told him she was pregnant, but she'd already done something about it; she didn't want to upset him with the news.

He returned home with this young man, who drove carefully and stopped now and then to rest. In a nearby village an elderly woman offered Dragomán cherry brandy, a piece of freshly baked cake, and the story of her grandmother, who had emigrated to America, became rich there, came back and bought half the village. But she lost her fortune to a crooked lover. The woman also complained that she didn't see her grandson often enough, a good, kind boy, though a rascal, too. She told Dragomán she was dirt poor, but she didn't expect much from life, so all in all she was content.

The young man pointed out that if they were going to stop in every village to drink brandy and listen to stories, they'd never get home. Dragomán found this voice, this gentle persistence, familiar, though it did not at all remind him of the girl with the coffee-colored skin. He slept the rest of the way, or at least closed his eyes.

"What an impossible character," Bella says, reflecting on what had become, twenty-five years later, of the excitable, fiery young professor she had once known. "Melancholy overtakes him, he turns lifeless, locks himself in his room and pushes everyone away—except the little boy. He disparages, he sneers, his own being fills him with gloom. 'Where would you like to go?' I say to him, 'what do you feel like doing? I'll take you anywhere,' but he doesn't answer. When somebody comes to see him, he'll reluctantly play the professor for a while, then throw off the part like an old house coat. When I open the door, all I see is a tired, stiffly smiling mask. There are newspapers all over the verandah, he glances at them and throws them down. When I look at him, he turns to the wall. He won't tell me what's troubling him—what we don't talk about doesn't exist."

DRAGOMÁN SAYS HELLO to everyone in the village, talks to people on the street, about the weather, if nothing else. Then he goes shopping, pays bills, trudges up and down the hill, helps carry bags, peeks inside women's unbuttoned summer dresses, repots the oleander plants into large tubs, or just stands in the lush garden.

He's come to admire the green carved wood railing of the upstairs balcony, he domesticated the trestle table and bench his first night here, and has learned to contemplate the plane tree while leaning against the stone wall. This is what he wants: to be always outside and watch the hill from the garden bench—to experience it in the sighing wind as though it were a birth, a beginning; to whistle in the arbor, free of the chronicler's responsibility, to mark arrivals, to tolerate the strong sun, to feel the ground under his feet...

Dragomán visits friends nearby, he explores the countryside, walks up to the Stonedial daily to look at three bays, listens to the rushing streams, the rivulets racing down Old Hill—he has no desire to be anywhere else.

His is a bare-bones lifestyle. From the university library he can borrow any book he likes. He grabs his rucksack, hops on his bicycle, and rides into the city. Or he wanders off to the other side of Old Hill, into the stone quarry, which years ago was a labor camp. He had to coil electric wires in a cold workshop from morning to night—he was serving time in 1957 for God knows what misdeed. His most serious crime—shooting a Soviet commandant—the authorities didn't know about.

From here he looks down on a large plateau, which is at the foot of a rock formation and the looming Stonedial. There, in the Valley of Mercy, young boys were killed during the war. When Dragomán goes on these excursions, he takes a pair of field glasses with him, sketches the terrain from different angles, and snaps pictures. In the abandoned stone quarry, in that great stone basin, he settles onto an old wooden bench. The trail winding up the mountain is lined with currant and blueberry bushes. In a clearing Dragomán even finds a four-leafed clover.

This region was a place of rest for aging veterans two thousand years ago; retired legionaries tended their vineyards here. The different races that settled in these parts were not violent; they coexisted, mingled, and had no desire to kill one another off. The landscape taught them moderation. They doctor the wine, it's true, the water is a little hard, a strong wind blows from narrow-mouthed caves. Old men with rucksacks trek down to the general store every third day, otherwise they don't move much. Between watching the flight of an eagle and a roving deer, they have their eyes fixed on time, or what's left of it.

A man will go far if he allows his feet to guide him. He treads on wet green footpaths, and on the banks of a stream the rustle of poplar trees accompanies him. Herds of cows approach as he lies down against a haystack and disperse when he stirs. While still on his back, he watches crows' etchings on a white sky.

In the distance, near the abandoned ruins, a black dot gradually turns into a glider. A helmeted pilot in goggles aims his gun at Dragomán, and then shoots a rabbit that springs out of the bushes. On the television news this morning he saw the burnt face of a colleague, an eminent philosopher. While he was opening his mail at the breakfast table, a letter bomb had exploded in his hand. Dragomán must travel to several cities and raise his voice in behalf of several noble causes, which is why he is sitting here on the garden bench. Reunions take place with growing frequency. Former classmates gather, veterans of '56 and '68, unfashionable old dissidents and insufferable, revenge-seeking newcomers, old-style self-promoters and up-to-date trendsetters—they all put on their name tags and deliberate on other people's suffering, demanding armed interventions in places where body bags contain other people's bodies. With a few strategic faxes he is able to rescue a few colleagues stranded in a besieged city, and several more from prison. He does manage to settle a couple of ugly disputes, work out a few compromises.

A uniformed driver picks him up and drives him to a distant town where they first stop in a pub for brandy and coffee. Then polite moderators in several different lecture halls wait their turn to conduct informal interviews with him that last over an hour. There is applause before and after the cozy chats, which continue through dinner, with more talk between the main course and dessert. They drive home late at night. He is tense and nervous before every appearance—in N., a town of ten thousand, as much as in New York. No part of him desires these performances, these well-rehearsed apologias. At the end of each he is presented with a vase and told that they have seen a true European among the white natives. He wishes he didn't hear this line anymore. Whoever is lionized will sooner or later be brought down. First the buildup, then the comedown. They invite him, insist that he come, then demand to know why he came. Out of vanity, no doubt. In truth, he likes dividing walls; there is no need to appear in person when he can appear in print. He is not much interested in what others say about him; no one's judgment carries that much weight. He'd love to pull back, retreat, but in the meantime the car is racing at ninety miles an hour, in N. the audience is waiting, the hall is almost full, and he promised he would be there.

AFTER SUPPER HE hears a story about a funeral. In the 1960s it was rumored that the county's leading politician had shot himself during a hunt and died. The casket was closed, not even the family was permitted to view the body. The man's daughter jumped up, tore open the coffin and saw that it was empty. But she was quickly pulled away and sedated. The empty coffin was buried with due pomp, in accordance with official funeral regulations.

The next local party boss was an avid hunter; he and only he had the run of the woods around top-secret Soviet rocket silos. Because the area was off limits to everyone, the game quickly multiplied. When he felt sluggish, he did his shooting from a car. At other times he took aim from a helicopter: the floodlights startled the animals and he gunned them down from the air. A herd of boars came to drink from a pond every afternoon at five; he shot every last sow and piglet.

He was a tall, strong, wicked man who liked to humiliate people; they all feared his wrath. "I'm coming over to blow your brains out," he would say to show his displeasure. His way of dismissing a subordinate was to tell him simply: "Beat it!" He practically demolished the old town center and had a huge party headquarters erected in its place, and a few high-rises with apartments for his apparatchiks. He handpicked his attractive young communist female associates, and presented them with a cottage and a kid. He was in the theater every opening night, sitting in the center box. During intermission toadies surrounded him, waiting for the ultimate critic to deliver himself of an opinion. After the performance he adjourned with his entourage to the actors' club for a drink.

Four aging, pudgy men can talk about nothing but this man, his shadow lurks in their memories. He was responsible for all their failures, the cause of all their missed opportunities. They feared him all their lives, and wanted desperately to figure him out; they grew old trying. One of them, a schoolmaster, had been followed years ago for weeks on end: "I was emasculated. I've lived in fear ever since. I had it in me to succeed, but used my energy instead to stay out of his way. I kept to my garden. Now he is finished, and so am I."

A picture postcard shows a clenched fist about to deliver a blow; on the reverse side it says: *Memento mori.* A letter begins: "Watch out, you scum." At a meeting a new party boss calls Dragomán a traitor to his country. In the grocery store a strange woman tells Dragomán that she likes him very much and hopes he'll have the strength to fight his battles. She calls expressing a few thoughts about battle. A male voice asks on the telephone: "Is this Professor Dragomán?" After hearing him say yes, the stranger intones: "You are a dead man."

Dragomán buys a new pair of pants and takes them to an old Jewish seamstress to be altered. The woman hugs him and with tears in her eyes tells him that she is frightened. One of her neighbors, a gendarme officer before the war, has never stepped into the elevator with her. But just yesterday he did, and with no witnesses present, of course, he asked: "What's your view, madam, on emigration? Don't you think it would be wise for you to do what the Russian Jews have done?" Her grandson asked his teacher in school: "Why are there so many swastikas in your grade book? Who is it meant for?" "You," she said. "Your kind."

The Jew-baiter is always indignant. How can anyone say that he is an anti-Semite? He does maintain, of course, that the source of the country's troubles is a furtive, wicked minority. Faced with them, the well-meaning majority flails helplessly, as one does in a bad dream. "Do you consider yourself an assimilated Jew?" a fellow professor asked Dragomán. He said no. "A dissimilated one, then?" He wasn't that, either. "But how is that possible?" Why can't the Jews ever become part of the society in which they live?" Dragomán says that he personally feels no compelling reason to blend in.

What Has the
Orange Branch Done Wrong?

Tomorrow, or the day after, we will visit Kandor's cemetery, where our relatives lie buried. I will stand in the rank, knee-high grass, amid sunken graves, touch the tall black granite tombstones, and read off the names of family members killed in the camps. Uncles and aunts had lined up dutifully, with their coats over their arms, following orders issued by local gendarmes. The train pulled in, they got into the cattle car assigned to them and were taken away.

Some came back, not many, and most of those left again, in 1948. One day, after dark, they clambered onto trucks, voluntarily and in secret, and rather adventurously crossed several borders, settling in the end in Israel, in a seaside town which nowadays is hit occasionally by rockets fired from southern Lebanon. There, too, they saw one another daily. A cobbler took his three-legged chair with him, sat on it while working, and told the same jokes he did back home.

I stood behind the cobbler's grandson in a video arcade. The boy gripped the joystick, near crashes came hard and fast, but he avoided the danger with amazing agility. The console lit up and buzzed, he won extra points, and a chip for another game. He put away the chip, and having had his fill, like a tired victor he skipped down the concrete stairs onto the sandy beach.

When I managed to get away and roam the world, slightly drunk and alone, and get on and off trains and buses at will; when I thought it was restlessness that had seized me, I was obeying a command. The object was always the same: to move, to exercise my feet. A pedestrian may be knocked down or shot at, but as long as he is alive he is up, and flies even when he walks. He is not moving his feet, his feet carry him. He trudges along Kandor's mazelike alleyways, not knowing if at the next corner he'll be turning right or left. People materialize at his side, then disappear, but he doesn't mind being left alone. Desire, dread, hope, ambition—he'll have none of it; he wants only the tranquillity of a sun-drenched square.

Dragomán felt nothing resembling mortal fear when his airplane was buffeted by turbulent winds over Kandor's airport. Trapped in the valley, dangling above the lake and the city, the wide-bodied plane flapped and fluttered in the raging storm, like a torn-off piece of newspaper. It would have been fair to say then: This is it. But once he'd convinced himself that the end was near, that there would be no reprieve, he felt nothing but simple curiosity. He would have had to clear out soon anyway. He's begun to mistake the merest trifles for meaningful signs.

He is happy, of course, that he can still be here, that he can grip the armrest of a chair. After all, for a writer, even uncomfortable situations are comfortable. For him, cold is not cold, hot is not hot, he never wants more than what he has. He writes about the things he sees. A correspondent is not motivated by self-interest, he is neither vain nor selfish, he doesn't hate anyone, he doesn't whine. If he were blind and mute and lame, he'd find amusement in his own breathing. He doesn't impose on anyone, he is polite at all times, like a Chinese diplomat.

I am your faithful servant, Father, just one of the multitudes, who is thankful for this warm drink, for being able to follow the downward glide of raindrops on that window pane. Sitting at my regular table, I order coffee, brandy and mineral water, as I did forty years ago. While waiting for my order, I close my eyes and soak up Kandor's familial air, the bubbling laughter. This amorous old couple, or one just like it, was here forty years ago. I look at them and they turn away. The man gently takes the woman's hand in his.

They were partial to gold-leafing when they built the Crown. They also favored walnut and cherry wood, and insisted on covering the floor in marble and upholstering the chairs in leather. Mere accidents saved this turn-of-the century splendor from subsequent uglifying changes. The heavy chandeliers cast a soft glow

on the wall hanging, on which a bare-breasted black woman offers a dainty cup to a blue prince.

Petra the waitress is small rather than large. She is neither
skinny nor chunky, and has shapely, mobile features. Her nails
are painted red, her earrings and necklace are gold, and she never
runs out of questions. Springing to the sound of music, she is easily amused and amazed by anything funny or odd. She wiggles in
front of my table, her fine little hand always in her hair—I like to
look at her stretching lazily.

Petra is afraid of armed bandits, crazies with lead pipes. Her
sister had something terrible happen to her. She was getting out
of her car when two husky young men grabbed her, took her car
key and waved good-bye: "So long, darling. Don't make any
noise or you'll be sorry." To make their threat more convincing,
one of the guys showed her a curved dagger. Her brother-in-law
happened to spot the car on the Boulevard; by then a thin little
man was sitting in it. Her brother-in-law is a weightlifter, he
made the little man get out and called the police. The officer said:
"Let's just call it a traffic violation. Look, mister, you have children, and so do I. So many people have accidents nowadays."
Petra's brother-in-law makes good money; he is a locksmith
and installs protective bars on windows—business is booming.

Am I interested in a gun with a silencer? An old lady across the
street is selling them. Do I know that Kandor's whores are famous throughout the region? A lady friend of hers was deserted
by her husband, so she hired a Ukrainian hit man, a hero of
Kabul, and for five hundred dollars he bumped off the unfaithful
husband. Now she is sorry, but only because she found out that
she had paid too much—she could've had it done for three hundred. The landing dock next to the police chief's private pier
belongs to a well-known gangster. While fishing together, they
communicate in fractured phrases and get along well. Here at the
Crown, the suite next to mine is occupied by four Middle Eastern
men who are in the habit of whipping out wads of hundred-
dollar bills. They got into a brawl over a blonde whore and
pulled out their guns. Two of them were killed, the other two got
away without a scratch, swearing vengeance. Now they criss-
cross the globe in hot pursuit of each other. "Don't think, my
dear professor, that strangers can't get into your room if they

want to; anyone can get his hand on a magnetic card with the right code." The man with scarred lips and the bird cage passes the café and looks inside.

I ask for a glass of white wine. At the next table a group of female teachers are huddling, trying to decide what to order. A young one sweeps back her long hair, looks at me and hums: "I'm going to bite out your eyes, my darling."

"Look at that strapping young man in the doorway," Petra whispers. "He is hulking but polite, his language skills are impressive. The hotel manager has him on loan from the local mafia. If he were to dismiss him, there'd be a fire here tomorrow, though first, as a warning, a canister of tear gas would land on the floor."

Drawing aside a velvet curtain, the manager emerges from the dark, mingles with the guests, inquires if they are satisfied with the service, offers suggestions for the evening meal, then steps into the elevator and rides to the rooftop bar.

Loose-limbed youths in fashionably shabby clothes sit at a table: glasses clink, strange music assails Dragomán's ear. An older boy instructs a younger one: "Before they can get you, you ram one of them with your head and break the guy's nose. If it's done right, you might also have given him a slight concussion. Walk up to him and whisper between your teeth: 'I'm going to slice your head off.' " Nobody can be sure that his head won't in fact be sliced off.

An old woman steps up to Dragomán's table, her bleached blonde hair piled high like a wig. She is wearing a lot of makeup and blood-red lipstick. "Did you bring it?" "What?" "So you didn't bring it. You're a champ, Doctor Kandoris. It's too late to get out of this thing, darling. You could pretend that you are an internationally known scholar, but it's your ass that's on the line. We're in this together, you and me, you can't just forget about us. But if it's a bodyguard you want, I can get you someone good, a retired bouncer."

The scar-lipped, straw-hatted Svetozar is always about with his inevitable bird cage. My random walks are witnessed by eavesdroppers and snoopers. Svetozar sidles up to me: "At your service, master." He opens his jacket and passes his hand over a miniature Tommy gun. A drunk, an otherwise jovial livestock dealer, tried to pick a fight with me. Svetozar hit him on the head with a rag ball that had a steel pellet in the middle. His aim was flawless, the man lay stretched out on the floor—the shock brought a smile to his face. I ask him to sit down; I know he likes beer. And Svetozar, for perhaps the first time in his life, ventures a criticism, saying that in the evening I might also consider drinking beer instead of wine. Too much stimulation before going to sleep may be harmful, and beer puts you in a more acquiescent mood. You accept the unalterable fact that night is near. He again offers to spirit me across any border if I feel too confined here. Then, Svetozar, a representative of the Darnok Corporation, disappears just as suddenly as he had appeared.

Darnok is an international outfit with interests in everything from sensitive military hardware to show business, from genetic engineering to hotel management. Svetozar claims it's worth it to them to have an agent equipped with a video camera, a folding chair and a bird cage trailing me. Naturally he must spy on me relentlessly and submit detailed reports, though his job is also to ensure my safety. It's enough for him if we exchange glances in the hotel breakfast room; he plies his trade with the utmost discretion.

"I shadow you, that's certain. In fact, if the need arose, I'd be ready to provide additional services. But now and then I disappear, and reap the benefits of your groundwork. I look up the important personages you have been in touch with, and using you as a reference, invite them to make a selection from our firm's wide-ranging goods and services. We sell everything, you know, from sewing needles to pre-packaged, cable-ready religious programs and the latest high-tech weapons. On request, we can spray laughing gas or angel dust on an entire province. Not long ago the International Anarcho-Pacifists ordered a large shipment of both. And oddly enough, the little lady who placed the order was seen in your company. She hardly reached up to your bow tie, if I remember correctly, but standing on tiptoe she did pat your cheek, and then moving through the tables, poured salt into the coffee of a gentleman who was eagerly explaining something to his neighbor.

"Thanks to you, I get a share of the profits, and also benefit from the goodwill you leave behind. Sometimes the ladies you leave behind are also mine, ladies who are interested in every-thing I have to say about you. I don't want to exaggerate, but I have plenty to tell them." Svetozar assures me that he will keep on following me. He doesn't believe I can ever free myself from the swirl of controversy that erupts in the wake of an interna-tional wizard such as myself.

"I am afraid, sir, that you will become embroiled in something that may be of interest to our company's strategists." If I do get myself in a scrape, I should let him know, call this number here, and he'll come running from the bottom of the lake or from in-side the Stonedial, if need be. In any case, if he may be permitted to offer a suggestion, I should be a little more wary of people, a little more cautious. And quit Kandor as soon as possible, for I could only end up a loser here.

As Darnok is a huge, multinational concern, Dragomán and Svetozar's travel expenses are an infinitesimal item in the com-pany's budget. Whoever produces recorded images of the world, in a way owns the world. The resourceful Svetozar sells the pro-fessor's pearls of wisdom to newspapers. When the good doctor warms to his subject, he doesn't much care if the camera's red eye is on or off. Svetozar pleads with him not to discard anything of his, but Dragomán cannot be relied on to save every scrap of paper. On the other hand, chambermaids everywhere are more amenable, so when Dragomán is out, Svetozar rummages through his wastepaper basket, scooping up anything that looks to be of interest.

He will not be shaken off. If Svetozar stays close to the master, something remarkable is bound to happen. "I see that you need me," he will say. And the professor is crazy enough to need Svetozar's help. When traveling from one city to another, they are never in the same compartment but always on the same train. Dragomán doesn't even have to reach for his suitcase or put on his coat—Svetozar knows enough to bump into him in the break-fast room and ask while they spoon their fruit salad: "Where to this time?" "Kandor, Hotel Crown," a resigned Dragomán an-swers. The rest is up to Svetozar.

The master sits in the Crown's outdoor café with his eyes closed, his face turned to the sun. "Svetozar, when I give you the nod, we can go. Whatever happened here in the past couple of years was cooked up here. It's all homemade, you can tell. If the perpetrators look like a bunch of bunglers, they must be. Why was I in such a hurry to come home?" Dragomán must be drunk, otherwise he wouldn't deign to talk to Svetozar. He leans his head against the back of his chair and closes his eyes again. Svetozar comes up close and snaps a picture of his face. "Or have you come to hate me, to Svetozar, old friend, that you are ready to take advantage of my weakened state?" Svetozar's eyes fill with tears; the professor must have misread his intentions.

At any given moment, Dragomán believes, his life may end. In one step, from the table to the bookshelf, it can happen: a slip, a fall, and that's it. But by what right does he wish to remain alive? The chambermaid keeps his room clean. He gets up at six o'clock and has breakfast at seven. He doesn't get sick, because he gets up early. But what is this stick in his hand disguised as an umbrella? What is the pressure he feels under his left shoulder? What about those symptoms of disequilibrium? Every day we bury someone we know; a familiar face vanishes, replaced by several unfamiliar ones. We are all contemporaries, waiting for our turn to disappear in the wings. We buried an old idol whose books we had kept under our desks as students, and read on streetcars and in bed before school. While sitting in a café he turned his head, looked out the window, into the distance, and finally hit upon the answer. Fine hairlike strands floated, gossamer-like, before his eyes, he complained about it, was afraid he was going blind. Now he lies in a box, the show is on, sobs, black veils, the *circumdederunt, yisgadal veyiskadash,* our beloved brother in Christ, our beloved Jewish brother, so much has happened to you, which, in reality, comes to nothing. Friends of the deceased don't dare greet one another, look down, and clasp their hands over their stomachs. And then the bereaved show up at the dear departed's flat, rummage through the closets, pile papers and photographs into crates to be stored in basements and attics. The silver candelabras they will put out, the witty sayings they will recycle. Our friend's face is sketched out by the words chosen to describe him. What he did and when: a series of decisions can make up a character. He came full circle, they thought, when he gave himself over to the Lord of Time. But what happened was that in front of a bakery, on the sidewalk, he let out a cry, fell back, and his heart cracked.

Dragomán takes the elevator from the roof terrace down to the garden. He is preoccupied, as though looking for someone. Guests stroll among the plane trees, blue spruces and magnolias, the gravel crunches under their feet. He then steps into a theatrically illuminated open space where figures emerge from the shadows, perform for the crowd, playing themselves, and you don't know who will step out of the darkness next. Someone whispers that two inmates, newly released from an asylum, have strayed into the garden. Silent waiters move about with their trays, members of the audience sip exotic drinks. On the other side of the old hotel gleams the swimming pool, the white-skinned birches reflect the light, a swing creaks in the wind.

Why does a stranger in a rowboat aim a gun with a silencer at Dragomán? He hits the branch of a potted orange tree, three centimeters from Dragomán's neck. It's late September, time to put on a jacket. Dragomán stands on the terrace. There is a knock on the door, Dragomán opens it. It's Svetozar, the agent of Darnok. His lips are still scarred, but his bird cage is not with him. "Nothing serious, I hope," says Svetozar. "Somebody had it in for that orange tree," Dragomán says and points to the mangled branch. He walks up closer. "This is where I was standing," he says and turns his head. With his right hand the Darnok agent pushes Dragomán to the floor. The rowboat is still there in the water, and the orange tree has lost another branch. "Target practice," Svetozar concludes, and with a spyglass tries to get a better look at the boatman. It's the bearded lady, no?" Dragomán asks sardonically. "A professional, in other words." The agent nods. "The bearded lady must cost the company an awful lot of money, which proves that I am worth it." From the recesses of his jacket Svetozar pulls out a small gun with a telescopic sight. "In self-defense we are permitted to destroy an enemy," he says. "It's enough to blow a hole in her rubber boat, my friend," Dragomán counters. "If the bearded lady can't swim, so much the worse for her. Who told her to shoot? She could grab the oar. Let her swim to safety. Afterward you could ask if she'd be interested in playing a part in a tableau vivant I plan to stage on Resurrection Square. Provided she is not an idiot and her beard is real. Tell her I'm inviting her to tea at the Crown."

A chauffeur comes for me, the car speeds down a highway

lined with plane trees. We stop in front of an old mansion. As soon as I enter I am taken to the bathroom. A cold jet of water, a slippery tile floor, I stumble and hurt myself. Men in canvas aprons put me in a bed with netting around it. My hands are tied behind me, I lie naked on my stomach, and with my mouth pick up kernels of salted popcorn thrown on the floor. I am left alone with no water to relieve my thirst. Then the sun beats down, as I sit with my eyes closed in the doorway, on a warm step. I pick my nose and mumble quietly to myself.

No News

On Old Hill Dragomán brightens up; here it feels more natural to him to be lowered into the ground. To lie in a cemetery, on this hill, might even be enjoyable. In the morning he gambols in the garden and splashes himself with cold water while breathing rhythmically. In late September the air grows cooler, the nighttime dew clings to the grass, and the sun casts stealthy rays on the stone wall.

Some inner force thrusts him out of bed each morning; he'd rather be without than within, he no longer knows why. Living in the same house with his daughter and grandson sometimes seems like touching the spikes of horse chestnuts—he can feel the protrusions. He builds until the day he dies, though the plans change every minute. He himself is the building, and there's the constant threat of a crash, a cave-in, a breakdown. Whatever happened to him is his, he survived mortal danger and minor inconvenience, worked at odd jobs, lost people, but he still considers himself fit to live. The only thing that surprises him is that it was all so brief.

He put up with his vexing country, then kept tearing himself away from it, belittled it, argued back, made excuses for it, boasted about it. He almost sees Kandorans now as members of his chosen family, and in a fit of goodwill accepts all his forebears, embracing them in his heart, praying for this insufferable lot. He's dashed out of the house in anger, roamed the world, returned, stopped at the door, and got exasperated all over again. He did leave this place once the great danger had passed, and the idea of capitalism was reintroduced piecemeal. But he decided to study the real thing. He had to straighten his spine and stretch his body; he needed Western curiosity to counter Eastern sluggishness.

It is commendable that Melinda doesn't chain him here, it's better to avoid her house on Leander Street. He'd rather visit Kobra on Old Hill, even if it means that Melinda might drop in, with Tombor at her side. They might sit around the huge trestle table and drink the local smoky Riesling, though some may prefer stronger stuff. There'd be fresh farmer cheese and tomatoes and peppers on the table, Regina would bring out her home-made cookies, Kobra would fill the glasses, Dragomán would take a peek in the fridge.

Zsiga, Döme and Habakuk would play in the sandbox, go on the swings, then climb the stone wall. They might also sneak out the back door to look at the horses, or run down to the stream to do a little fishing. Or they might frolic in the meadow, in the alfalfa field, in the tall grass strewn with red poppies, and then watch the ducks from the lake shore, or catch tiny fish for bait with a dipping net—tonight they will want to go out on a boat with the real anglers.

The grownups might disperse in the garden—the pear trees are irresistible; and there is the open cellar, you can just walk down and with a siphon sample the secrets of the different barrels. They could also visit the neighbors' friendly gardens, and walk through the sedge, along narrow planks, down to the flat-bottom boats and row out on the lake. Or they might just lean against the stone wall, settle into lounge chairs and let their eyes rest on the fiery-gold roof of the neighbor's house.

Just now he dozed off on the bench and dreamed of Lona. She rang him up: her voice was warm and clear, it took Dragomán a while to realize it was she. When he did, he responded with a laugh. For years, when they were separated by several borders, he kept her photograph on his desk. During his vagabond years, whenever he felt low, he thought how nice it would have been to stay with her. He kept rereading Lona's letters, scrutinizing her bold, shapely characters.

He could conjure the well-cut nose, the pale brown skin that kept its hue even in winter. Lona had an air of independence about her that was remarkable; she stood apart not only from her husband and Dragomán but from men in general. She always found her way out of tight spots and could easily forget lovers when her curiosity led her elsewhere. I'll call you, she would say, sounding like a no-nonsense boss. She'd let us know. And we could only hope that she would, that the sun would shine on us once again. She indulged her fancies, received complete strangers with gracious curiosity, criminals and madmen included, and was unfazed even when these characters threatened to kill themselves.

He sauntered down to the Gypsy tavern for a glass of apricot brandy. It used to be a German tavern, but now the lower end of the village is heavily Gypsy. He greeted people amiably, shook hands with the thickset tavern keeper, who was also the coach of the village soccer team and the most respected man among the Gypsies, the chief, one might say. If someone got drunk, he wouldn't give him another drink but would send him home to sleep it off.

Standing by the entrance is Gabi, a sixty-year-old pensioner, a bachelor who attends every funeral in the village, and helps dig the graves. After a tragic period in his life, he decided not to marry. He pulls out a plastic case containing a stack of photographs—the first is of an attractive young woman with fleshy cheeks and a warm smile. "She had a good heart," Gabi says. He thinks a lot about her and takes out her picture often; she's no longer alive. The last time he visited her, in St. John's Hospital, in the mental ward, she said to him: "Take me away, I'll marry you." She was a bad alcoholic by then. Once he ran into her in a snack bar; she'd bought a plate of vegetables and was carrying it to one of the metal tables. She was drunk then too. "Gabi, don't you recognize me?" He turned away. That photograph was taken in 1953. They didn't get married because of the age difference: eighteen years. "If you were only five years younger, I'd marry you," she said. When she was still healthy, she'd often come for a week's visit; they would commute to work together. Gabi bought lots of meat and did all the cooking—he'd been a cook in the army. "A Jewish boy—the company clerk—told me to ask for kitchen duty. I said to him I was no cook, and couldn't bake, either. But the clerk encouraged me: 'That's all right, you'll learn.'" There he is in that picture, in the top row, looking well-fed and stocky in his uniform. "I was like a bull then." After he was discharged from the army, he got a job in a textile plant, and the woman visited him often. They lived well, picking fruit off the tree and drinking good wine. She was divorced and had an apartment in the city. She didn't want to move out here for good. And Gabi didn't want to live in the city; his father and grandfather before him had lived here and were buried here. "There is nothing nicer than this village. That's why I stayed alone, I just couldn't see myself leaving. Even though this woman was prettier than all the others I'd known." The last time he went out with a woman was fifteen years ago, but that ended, too. His parents died, and so did his sister, his older and younger brothers, too; he has no one. He doesn't work anymore, he lives on his pension. He worked for thirty years at the textile factory, it took him forty-five minutes to get there by bus. Now he never leaves Old Hill. "A bit of Switzerland, that's what the newspaper says about us. Look at the mountains, and those outcroppings in the valley; it's as if a beautiful woman were lying here—look, that's what it says in the newspaper." In earlier times farmers with thirty acres to their name tended vineyards, smoked their pipes, drank home-grown wine, ate home-cured ham, distilled their own brandy. And though they drank at home mostly, seven tavern keepers made a decent living. At carnival time, there were five dances to choose from on a Saturday night—the lads and the girls had their dance, and the married couples and the old-timers had theirs. "I didn't want to have to go down to the market from a third-floor apartment. I grow fruits and vegetables for free here in the garden. Need tomatoes? Apricots? All you got to do is go out and pick them."

City women create their own space in the country: they exchange rare plants, have new windows cut into their peasant houses, build fences, set up the heavy garden furniture, watch falling stars at night, and even find time to write or translate three-four pages a day. They make plans for the weekend, draw up blueprints for a new house, design a gazebo, make the old mill habitable, and work on refilling the dried-up stream. They explore the countryside on horseback, ask the shepherds not to scorch the meadow, cut the grass along the drainage ditch, bicycle to the dairy farm for milk, pick peaches and peppers in the garden, collect the eggs laid by the hens, ride downstream, in a canoe, all the way to the lake. Or they stay behind to rake the soil, dry the hemp, barbecue meat, sip wine, or get acquainted with a new neighbor. Leaning back, they may simply gaze at the stars while dreaming up a plan for a new bathroom or a new winery: crushed stone here, a cluster of hollyhock there—a new folklore is being born in this old spot.

In the still sunny garden he hears the popping of flare guns: a storm is approaching. His eyes stray to his daughter's window; maybe he should break the silence, and not smile when she makes one of her impassioned speeches. She's wonderful when she gets angry, and unbeatable when it comes to high-minded inanities. A peck on her head is enough to make her break into tears.

He feeds crumbs to a swan couple when they emerge from the tall reeds with their three young. The parents are snow white, the cygnets are covered with gray fuzz. He laughs at a rooster as it settles comfortably on a mound over the wine cellar. Before crowing in earnest, he summons the hens to a meeting, making a big to-do. The hens are unimpressed, they go on pecking: they heard, they heard, and they couldn't care less.

For some time now Dragomán has noticed that even a little is too much. Freshly washed white shirts on a clothesline flutter in the wind. He is almost happy here, though his senses smell danger. He's walking the banks of a stream, now and then he hears cawing, grayish clouds move across the sky. Every day, for several hours, he strides along, drawing strength from the earth. He sees no one in the large meadow, the cows lie down peacefully, the tedious hang glider circles overhead. In the thicket a butterfly hovers between giant petals, birches sway evenly in the wind. Dragomán doesn't think all this coming and going is a mere accident—the early-morning bicycle rides, for instance, across the field and over the tiny bridge spanning the stream, past the lookout point and the crucifix that's overgrown with wild hemp. Every spot is sacred when you suddenly rediscover it.

From a cellar in Old Hill, where he tasted more varieties of wine than could be soberly appreciated, he comes down the hill ever so lightly; his two feet under him seem to fly, the air's thermal action moving him up the inclines and down the descents. And then, surprise: he finds himself in front of the ivy-clad Mousetrap Inn.

The inn's patio looks out on the hillside and the lake; an old armchair on the terrace promises rest to a weary body. Suddenly, car doors slam, guests alight, high-spirited company streams through the garden door—these people have been here before. They settle themselves in the pretty arbor behind the house. Dragomán has certain conditioned reflexes: he offers wine to the guests, sees to it that everyone has a glass, that their jaws keep moving, that they are seated comfortably and their conversation is sufficiently lively...

The guests have left. Whatever he commits to paper about them afterward, he leaves behind like an old coat. The one constant is the bed on which he reclines. Early in the morning he goes for a swim in the lake, then sits back at the table—a listlessly stretching graphomaniac. He hears shouts through the window. He is neither good nor dutiful; he does not succor victims, whose numbers in any case are myriad. Let those who do not consider themselves victims stand there, and those who do line up here. As expected, there are only a few here and a whole crowd over there. And you, professor, aren't you a victim? No, I am not. In the morning he never says much, and retreats whenever possible. It's raining again: tiny puddles collect in the hollows of flagstones, the oleanders rejoice, the roof tiles glisten. He offers wine to the intelligent questioner and answers his questions in detail.

He has no authority, no one's beneath him, he can't even give orders to his grandson, he waits things out in silence—whatever he has, he already had yesterday. It feels good to walk in the thick grass of the Old Hill garden in his black sneakers and his pullover with a leather patch on the sleeves. He contemplates with approval the stonecrop on the gable roof. Even taking a breath can turn into a rare pleasure. It rained a lot overnight, a strong northern wind blows, swaying the fir trees' crown. The wind knocked over the flowerpots on the terrace and keeps a yellow rubber ball rolling along the wall. It bends the willows and stirs the acacia branches. The slender trees enjoyed the rainy night, they filled up with moisture and suppleness. Beneath a rich dark sky, rich dark leaves.

Dragomán doesn't have to go anywhere, so he allows himself to let go; it doesn't bother him that nobody agrees with him. At least in the village no one feels like shooting anyone. A shopgirl says: "No news, thank God." A cuckoo and a kite circle overhead.

But at night, in a dream, they asked for his papers, he had to surrender his passport, on account of some old criminal charge, which he knew was without merit. He hung about alone, drank a lot, was overcome with fear, sat in his car and drove off. Near the border, he got out and wandered off in the direction of an endless wire fence with photoelectric sensors. The border patrol caught up with him, but at the interrogation he would not emit a sound. And for a year afterward he wore the striped pajamas of mental patients in silence. He turned into a narrow-faced, bristle-haired, wide-eyed inmate. He squatted for hours, mute, behind the imposing French doors of the mansion-turned-asylum. Now and then he rose, and stepping on the black tile squares, and only on the black ones, he pranced about with mincing airs, then squatted again and looked at the park wistfully. But he never walked through those imposing French doors.

In Laura's Company

1952. A long, narrow lecture hall, a class in history, body odor, the professor addresses us as "dear students," which is better than "dear comrades." As is my custom, I conceal myself in the last row and then, leaving my body behind, sail through the window. I surround myself with a few well-meaning people, the miner Cibulka and Kabarkó, a peasant. They were admitted to the university after a six-month crash course, which earned them a special high school diploma. They had been "singled out" and told to study, study, study, a great honor, they thought. If all goes well, they'll be teachers of Russian.

The two are clumsy, shy, and also somewhat foxy overage students. During the war both were POW's in Ukraine. They survived; they'll surely survive this learning experience. I lend them a hand, prompt them, while they regale me with stories and get into fights—their beds are next to each other in the dormitory. When Kabarkó receives a food package from his wife, he eats most if it himself; but when Cibulka gets something from his family, he, representing the working class and its vanguard, the miners, demonstrates a higher morality: even before opening the package, he lays it on the table and calls everyone over. He had been a foreman in the Donetz mines, and the Soviet comrades were well pleased with Tovarisch Cibulka—he showed the men of Donetz what a miner from Hungary was capable of. Before long, his name was on the honor roll. The professors at the university were less pleased; oral exams were not Cibulka's strong suit. Although he took copious notes in class, what came out was a bewildering agglomeration of words. Kabarkó was sharper and liked to show off, especially if he could shine in front of Cibulka, who had no recourse but to expose Kabarkó's calculating selfishness with his tired barbs.

I never saw one without the other, the two were inseparable. But then they did part ways. The day the '56 Revolution broke out, Kabarkó was about to return to his village. When he passed a truck from which weapons were handed out, and saw how ineptly the young city slickers were wiping the rifle grease from the freshly uncrated machine guns, he couldn't let it go. As an ex-serviceman he became their instructor for the next hour. Afterward, he still wasn't satisfied with their handling of firearms, so he stayed with them and led them in battle, setting fire to three Russian tanks. When young Russian soldiers occupied an old, half-destroyed building, he and his men went from room to room with hand grenades and finished them off. What annoyed Kabarkó most was that his squadron, which included Gypsies, drank a whole keg of brandy. He ascribed it to Gypsy frivolity. Kabarkó continued to look after his men, and only after the revolt had been crushed did he return to his village and his wife. There he was picked up by Cibulka himself, who came for him in a big Pobeda car, for by then he was a newly appointed investigator working for State Security.

During the interrogation Cibulka called his friend by his last name, which was a great strain on him. The use of the typewriter also caused some head-scratching, but he had to prepare an official report. Kabarkó, with gloating politeness, pointed out Cibulka's spelling mistakes. To make matters worse, Kabarkó's peasant craftiness got the better of him and he denied everything. "Is there no decency left in you?" a shocked Cibulka demanded. "You would even deny that we were roommates?" "We were never roommates," Kabarkó insisted, whereupon Cibulka became so incensed, he punched Kabarkó in the mouth, and decided to let somebody else handle the case—this lying scoundrel made him lose his temper. He had to be a kulak son of a bitch, he fumed, even if his mother *was* a penniless servant girl. His superiors told Cibulka it was okay to be angry, and he changed his mind and remained in charge of the case. The next day he apologized to his friend for having been too free with his hand. In wrapping up the investigation he made sure his friend was spared the hangman's rope and got off with a three-year jail sentence.

Kabarkó served two of the three years, during which he made a valuable contribution to the prison economy, working in a vast cornfield as a gang leader. When Cilbulka visited him there, he was told that Kabarkó once again played the boss. They filled sacks with straw and carried them on their backs to the barracks, and of course it was Kabarkó who showed those nincompoops how to fill a sack evenly. The two sat opposite each other at a long pine table, not saying a word. Kabarkó's wife sat next to Cibulka. Like her, Cibulka brought sausages and black pudding from his village; by then he'd gone back to being a miner—his fellow inspectors had made fun of his clumsily worded reports.

After his release from prison, Kabarkó also turned his back on his college education. He was among the first in his village to grow tomatoes under hothouse conditions, covering the plants with plastic sheets. He rebuilt his house, but then his wife succumbed to cancer; and he, while walking home from the hospital one day, was felled by a heart attack. The veteran miner Cibulka, now gray and gaunt, trudged sadly behind the coffin at the head of the funeral procession. He had been left by a younger woman, and relieved of all his earthly possessions by her and her truck driver lover. They piled everything on his truck and drove off.

Early September, my second academic year; sunlight streams into the lecture hall. Why must I sit here? Why am I at the university, anyway? What an incredible waste of time. A shaft of light hits Laura's head, she sways an untamable shock of hair, making it flicker between bronze and rust. As I look at her—she sits up front, with the eager beavers—it seems to catch fire. I couldn't take my eyes off that head for long, I stole glances at it when she moved, which was often, because she loved to chatter and turn to one side or the other, flanked as she was by two refugees from distant countries. We had all kinds of revolutionaries—even Cypriots, Bosnians—among our classmates, and they were all busy courting Hungarian girls. They told her she was as beautiful as a fly, and couldn't understand why she was so taken aback by the compliment—they meant butterfly but mixed up the two Hungarian words.

A disciplined, serious face, a fantastic snub nose, a sardonic fold at the corner of her mouth, ivory whites around brown irises—I kept looking at her for days but did not dare talk to her. My intense scrutiny extended to the heels of her shoes. She could use a new pair, I decided, and her not having them was not a political statement—it simply meant that she had no money. From time to time I landed odd translating jobs. I'll get her an assignment, too, I thought; and if she can't do it, I'll finish the job myself. A working relationship would require that I talk to her once in a while.

"Listen, you want to make some money?" She did. The next day we met in a pastry shop and then visited a museum. In front of a van Eyck Laura quietly collapsed. Her eyes were closed. I knelt beside her and placed my hand under her head. Her long hair made her head feel soft. Before long, though, she opened her long-lashed eyes and smiled with bashful uncertainty. She didn't understand what had happened; neither did I.

The next day we went to the movies. Before embarking on a joint translating project, we would have to get better acquainted. Upon leaving the cinema—I was expounding on something—Laura again ended up horizontal. It was no tumble, but a gentle slide and collapse onto the pavement at the streetcar stop. I wasn't so conceited as to interpret the strange occurrence as an overwhelmed response to my words or to my person, and asked her apprehensively if she might be pregnant. Oh no, out of the question. True, she had got married last summer, but still, she couldn't possibly be pregnant.

The news of the recent nuptials did not make me happy. But where was the husband? In Leningrad. He was a third-year medical student, on scholarship. Young love, eternal troth, frequent exchange of letters, her in-laws were both workers–turned–factory managers who'd been party members from before the war. Lali, her husband, was a highly gifted man of solid character. They had been soulmates for six years, and since their summer nuptials—Laura was nineteen, Lali twenty-one—physically intimate as well. They both lost their virginity, with each other, after the wedding. "He told you he was a virgin? Hm." Both of them would have considered premarital sex immoral. The wedding took place in the summer; Lali knew exactly when it was safe to do it: in the middle of the lunar month. I nodded: Lali was a man of science, after all; he ought to know. Even his wedding he timed scientifically. He quickly makes her pregnant, I thought, then leaves, and urges her from afar to stay strong. Giving up his scholarship and attending medical school in Budapest would be an act of desertion—the party might even expel him for it. The son of two worker-managers and prominent party members couldn't be that irresponsible. The party sent him to Leningrad to study; to put his personal feelings before duty would be a sign of weakness—he could never forgive himself. Once he successfully passed his exams, in both academic and ideological subjects, then, fortified by superior knowledge, he would surely be offered an important position back home. To stay here now because of Laura? No, she would despise him if he did; he had to remain true to himself. He had the ambitions of the rising working class, with a mission to fulfill. He came from a humble background, before the war they had lived in a two-room flat—he *must* reach the top. Lali often said that one must demand a great deal of oneself; the steel of one's character is tempered by life's hardships.

In any event, Laura was surprised when I expressed a contrary medical opinion and encouraged her to see a gynecologist. The situation was potentially serious, since abortion at that time was a punishable offense; a doctor performing an illegal abortion could receive a five-year jail sentence. A retired gynecologist in their building, who was also active in the local party cell, and whose dachshund went out for a walk by itself, determined that Laura was indeed pregnant, and told her that under no circumstances would he perform the operation. Laura was nineteen and poor. Her father was dead, her mother had a modest pension. She and Laura gave English lessons, and they lived very modestly. But as we know, hardship steels the character. Soon, though, Laura made peace with her condition; besides, the fainting spells had passed.

I LIKED THE rhythm of my days: mornings at the university, then the library, and after five, when most husbands returned to their families, I, too, rang the bell in the yellow-tiled lobby of Laura's apartment building. Out came Mr. Rétházi, the slightly hunchbacked caretaker in his visored cap. He was a crabby old man with a stubbled chin and a long, red, always moist nose, and none too happy about having to take people up in the elevator. His grumpiness seemed to contain a special message for me: Go on, step into that cage, if you are shameless enough to show your face. We know all about your coming here. The husband's parents are bigwigs, but you must know that, too. They can break your neck, if you don't watch out. (In the fall of 1956 he may have seen me walk around with a submachine gun, but even then he wasn't likely to denounce me.) I got out on the sixth floor and turned right.

From inside I could hear those lovable, quickening footsteps, which, as the weeks went by, became heavier. The door opened with a decisive swing; through the pebbled glass the newly arrived guest's shadow could be recognized. To the usual foyer smell was added a very unpretentious perfume, and Laura's natural sweet smell, reminiscent of vanilla pudding. I somehow connected the pastry shop smell of pregnant women with the matchless smell of fresh-cut hay that hovers around babies' heads. Every house has its own smell. Laura's hit my nostrils as soon as I entered. In the foyer the emanations of old leather suitcases mingled with that of pigeons that nested outside their bathroom window. Laura greeted me in a loose-fitting red dress. We shook hands; after a few months there'd be a light peck on the cheek. And we'd race through an alcove into her room. Inside, I'd be relieved that no one had seen me and I didn't have to say hello. I wasn't exactly welcome here; felt more like an intruder. Laura would bustle about for a while, but soon she'd stand there with her coat on. Her belly was getting bigger, and the doctor had suggested that she take long walks.

Sometimes, on the street, we held hands. Or the wind would blow Laura's hair into my face. In the movies she might drop her head onto my shoulder. A fellow student like myself was permitted to touch her when helping her step over the low wall of a ruined monastery. We wandered through deserted loading docks near the waterfront; it was nice to stroll in the falling snow, a neat little snow cap would form on Laura's head. Now I could imagine her as a child fighting with boys older than she was. The story went that she would throw herself at men with such fury that when a lady from their building took a closer look at the grubby little terror, she cried out: "Oh my Lord, could this be Doctor Barta's little girl?"

We spent most of our time walking, good exercise for expectant mothers. It was winter, so we clambered up the wooded hillside in hiking boots, leaving circuitous traces in the snow. We'd be chilled to the bone, our faces were red; so after such excursions I'd be invited into Laura's deceased lawyer father's study, where important books bore penciled N.B. markings. Laura's deep voice, and her opinions, delivered laconically, with a wry face or a chuckle, lifted me into the rarefied circle of the initiated. When I was with Laura, I knew I was in a good place, sitting in the most comfortable armchair, holding in my hand the best available book.

This lakeshore was the center of my universe; it's where Laura and I would stroll on the gravel walks of the rose garden on cloudy rather than moonlit evenings. For the longest time I did not confess to Laura that I had feelings for her other than brotherly affection. I did not desire her with any great passion, but I did want to visit her every day. At six o'clock in the afternoon I wanted to sit in her room. Ensconced in one of the two armchairs that were turned toward each other at an angle, I simply wanted to chat, and thought it a feast when with tea, she offered me a piece of toast. We took our meals at the university cafeteria, so we were both on the lean side, and always a little hungry. But one wasn't supposed to pay attention to such things.

Laura's mother shuffled off every morning to the soup kitchen run by the Jewish Community, where for a reasonable sum food was ladled into the battered dishes she fished out of a canvas bag. The fare wasn't good but it was edible. One didn't comment; neither the soup kitchen nor the community itself, supported by American Jewish groups, was worthy of comment. Aunt Erzsi and I preferred to discuss literature; she loved to recite poems by Goethe and Schiller. She read mostly German books with Gothic print; in her literary salon of long ago, the poet Endre Ady was once a guest. She spoke with great admiration of her son-in-law; she could talk about medicine with him. Her own father was a doctor, too, and that's what she would have liked to become, if only because she was a hypochondriac. I couldn't expect Aunt Erzsi to regard me as highly as she did the lawful Lali. The frequency of my visits became suspicious, ominous. If Aunt Erzsi opened the door, I could tell from her slow approach that she was not thrilled to see me.

The lighting in Laura's room was pleasant, the flowers arranged attractively in a Chinese vase. From time to time I had enough money to buy a few stems for her myself. The furniture, its feel, its warm brown color, became cozily familiar. And when Laura was busy in the kitchen, I liked to sit at the glass-topped desk and jot down some high-minded foolishness, in keeping with the spirit of the times. I watched Laura's belly turn round under her red dress, and hoped she would have time to go to the movies with me and have supper afterward. I was planning to become a philosopher and novelist then, but at home I was translating Russian texts on chemical fertilizers and underground granaries. I always kept enough money in my pocket so I wouldn't be embarrassed when it was time to pick up the tab. And when I was broke, I sold a few of my books, or took clothes to the pawnshop—my summer suit in winter, my woolens in summer.

Then her time came and family power reasserted itself. Mothers, mothers-in-law, and Juliska the cleaning lady took over. The beautiful baby girl arrived on Laura's twentieth birthday. I wanted to visit Laura when the mothers weren't there. Borrowing a white robe from a doctor friend, I sneaked into the maternity ward to see the woman of my dreams. Her head lay somewhat languidly, tentatively, on the pillow, her skin was paler, her eyes brighter, more triumphant and more mature. I stood there, flowers in hand, savoring the pleasure of my illegal entry. I marveled at Laura's otherworldly radiance. The baby on the nurse's arm was like a message from the other side; she looked quite serious, nothing was inscribed yet on her skin, her palm a mere outline.

And then, at home, I held the baby, and burped her, too. The women were too bashful to have me witness Laura's struggles with that clumsy baby as she kept urging her to take the nipple, suck on it, act on what was supposedly instinct. Babies were s upposed to suckle and wheeze contentedly, and create a vacuum around the nipple with their toothless gums. I sat in a high-backed armchair in the foyer with my back to Laura's room, listening to the noises from inside. She nursed. Now for the weighing in. Good: the right amount had been consumed. Another round of joyous burping, brightness all around, and now I could rock the baby a little. "She looks good in your arms," Laura said, and I blushed, which I did easily. Summer vacation was approaching, the end of the school year, and Lali's homecoming. In the meantime, a slight bump in my road to success: I was expelled from the university.

The local party secretary was a man with a limp, and implacable when it came to unmasking enemies. He discovered that my grandfather had been a wine wholesaler; contrary to what I'd put down in my curriculum vitae, he had had as many as eight employees, not just two or three. I had also concealed the fact that I had a cousin living in America. True, she was there as the wife of a diplomat, but still, I had neglected to mention her in a questionnaire. They quoted my political views, and the disciplinary committee felt that I wasn't worthy of the people's university. Actually, these proceedings came at a good time—I was beginning to feel overconfident. I'd already led a history seminar, I even got paid for it; I thought I no longer had to make a secret of the fact that I had brains. Until then it seemed improper to demonstrate that I already knew much of what I was supposed to learn, for that might have been construed as an attempt to outshine students from working-class backgrounds.

The previous year, before I befriended Laura, Irene, my girlfriend of several months, had suggested that I spend more time in the communal study hall, attend national defense training sessions, including rifle practice, participate more often in popular circle dances, and read Stalin instead of Marx, so that the collective would consider me one of their own. It didn't help my image, cautioned Irene, that I was seen in espresso bars, that I wore a suit and tie sometimes, or greeted people a certain way and looked at women too openly. I could stand a little self-improvement, she said, and should start by casting off my bourgeois individualism, in particular my disgustingly possessive and contemptuous attitude toward women, which made me act more kindly to pretty girls than to ones not so pretty. Irene tried hard to convince me that good looks were inversely proportional to inner beauty.

My life was fairly limited; I visited the library regularly, roamed unfamiliar sections of the city, and to earn extra money translated something about Moscow's skyscrapers, or an account of a farm cooperative's evening entertainment. In the afternoons I dropped in at the university. Irene was still in study hall, and she agreed to join me in a dark corner for an intense kissing session.

Irene was a funny, nervy girl. She loved to tease: her tongue, her wit, her feet were all quick, and she laughed a lot. She also had a large nose and a unique smell; I couldn't decide whether it came from the detergent she used or from her body. I also wasn't sure I wanted to marry her. She kept returning to the subject of marriage while trying amiably to free me of my bourgeois prejudices.

I did what I could. I even stood guard in front of a gilded bust of Stalin. At my right was Irene—she'd been nice enough to think of me, I could thank her for this honor. The giant head was placed in a round-arched niche; we stood at attention for an hour at a time. I looked straight ahead, fully cognizant of the solemnity of the situation. This plaster copy made me feel closer to Him. Everything here happened at his behest. Upon hearing his name, audiences sprang to their feet and applauded, vigorously at first, then rhythmically and, in a sort of coda, even more clamorously. The shouts at rallies were combinations of various sacred words and names. Fear alone can't make us clap. The one we are cheering lives in us. I wasn't just a reluctant adorer, I couldn't help revering the scholar-leader. The master historian is by nature mysterious, taciturn. According to one of our instructors, who would soon be imprisoned, Stalin read two fat books every night. There was a window in the Kremlin, high above slumbering Moscow, that was always well lit—his window. While the people slept, their leader was awake, watching over their dreams. "Why, of course," said my instructor when I inquired if Stalin had mastered speed-reading techniques, for how else could he finish two long books in a single night. His "of course" wasn't entirely convincing. Then again, why shouldn't he be endowed with superhuman abilities? My instructor, incidentally, was also a Stalinist—a victim, that is, of a Stalinist show trial.

One day I accompanied Irene to a remote district of the city;

the trip lasted over an hour, we held hands in the streetcar. Our destination was the modest one-family cottage where she lived with her mother. Her father had died; she spoke very solemnly of him, he embodied the very best qualities of the working class, she said. Her mother was a refined little woman who worked in a textile factory and used the word "comrade" all too frequently when talking about her co-workers. She received numerous awards and scrolls, which were all framed and hung on the wall. Irene also won a junior cross-country race and a bronze medal in the "Ready to Work and Fight" movement; she excelled in marksmanship. Irene was a member of the party, of course, and at party meetings her eyes radiated a knowing seriousness; she belonged among the elect, the secret society of stalwarts and initiates.

The big moment—the consummation of our love—I kept putting off. Irene was still a virgin, and it fell to me to turn her into a woman. Though we often discussed where this would take place (neither her house nor mine was a suitable location), and she no longer held fast to her belief that we must be married first, I, in a sudden turnabout, began praising the biblical idea of marriage, and found all kinds of reasons why we shouldn't go just yet to the youth hostel where, as we had previously planned, in a room with a beautiful balcony we would become man and wife in body and soul. If her mother happened not to be at home, and we put away the pink doll and the lacy cushions from the living room couch so I could stretch out and she could snuggle up, my advances were rather perfunctory, and the slightest resistance on her part cooled my ardor and elicited expressions of remorse from me. I promised I would behave most honorably, and that I did.

When summer came I was drafted and ended up in boot camp far from the city. I quickly forgot Irene, who warned me before I left that what she, rather ambivalently, had denied me, she would now give to Andor Késmárki—all the more as she and Késmárki were ideologically much better suited, and there was nothing more important in a relationship than a shared worldview. That Andor Késmárki went to great lengths to acquire the right attitude could be discerned in his speech. Although the son of middle-class Budapest Jews, he began to speak in dialect, affecting the idiom of the region where the country's wise leader hailed from.

There was no safe hiding place for lovers in our apartment either; we were crowded enough, privacy was an unaffordable luxury. Oh, those old-fashioned Budapest apartments! How much sly maneuvering was needed to keep those three- or four-room apartments intact. How our parents worried that they would lose their apartment, that it would be assigned to someone else, that dividing walls would further diminish their meager living space, and they'd have to crowd their already much-reduced possessions. The grander apartments had long since been broken up. Strange little passageways came into being, and tiny rooms with tall ceilings. And also vipers' nests, venomous hatreds, for in these newly formed communal apartments, bathrooms and kitchens had to be shared. And if a hostile co-tenant happened to be sitting on the toilet when you had to go, you couldn't count on human decency and fellow feeling. They carved up anterooms and kitchens and everything else left over from the old days; and they let the newcomers on the other side of the wall know that they were there only because they had the right background, because they were the darlings of the new regime. The new tenants, on the other hand, felt that historical justice had placed them in these flats.

Part of our apartment was allocated to a young and very reliable bureaucrat and his working wife, who would greet my parents with a curt and cold good morning, and more often than not with just a nod. Of course they could hear what went on in our half of the apartment. The BBC world service, for instance, which my father listened to every morning at 6:45. Ta-ta-ta-taaaa. This is London. For my father the BBC was the only reliable source of information. Whatever Radio Budapest reported was naturally a pack of lies. Our new neighbors had every reason to hate us; they had to justify their intrusive presence. Besides, they found it intolerable that a larger part of the apartment was still inhabited by the original owners.

It was true that on our side we wallowed in bourgeois culture. On a sofa covered with a thick Oriental rug, I read Proust and Mann and Huxley. On their side, the young couple's bedtime activities became audible—a crescendo and diminuendo of gasps and groans. I tried to concentrate on my book, but a female voice, so very different from the one uttering a curt hello in the morning, made it impossible. The choked and shameless moaning and screaming our co-tenant produced every other night between nine-thirty and ten inevitably distracted me. I thought I should perhaps turn off the light to convince them they were alone, but I decided to leave it on, otherwise I might wake them when I turned it on again, for most nights I'd read till two in the morning. Here I was steeped in decadent idleness, engrossed in highbrow literature, while they went off to work in their government and party offices, and even in their free time had the common good in mind, working on increasing the population. In a sense, they were entitled to occupy the best room in our apartment and make love in our bed. I heard her voice through the glass door, it got me all excited, but I tried not to imagine exactly what our voluptuously vocalizing neighbor was doing with her husband.

This was a different kind of takeover from what we had during the war, when Hungarian army officers took over the same room, originally my father's study. On their way to their room, where we had set up the requisite number of beds for their use, they tiptoed through the living and dining rooms. These officers were convinced that, thanks to the superlative quality of German arms, they would win the war. This view was shared by gimlet-eyed state bureaucrats with toothbrush mustaches, who, being Hungarian fascists sympathetic to the Nazi cause, learned to hate my father and his entire family. Actually, the new tenants' resemblance to these officials was remarkable.

I set myself the task of trying to understand the other side—the position of the expropriators and nationalizers, those who placed me in the "X" category, declaring me a "class alien," a bourgeois enemy, who from a socialist point of view was eminently untrustworthy. Even as a child entering school, I began to realize that our well-to-do, middle-class lifestyle evoked hostility in most people, including poor Jews. We did not flaunt our wealth, though we did ride to the ice-skating rink in a fancy carriage, and took strolls on Main Street in our sailor suits and white gloves, with our nanny in tow. Why was I entitled to so much more than other people? Just because we had so much more?

There would come a time when we would have much less. The greater your fortune, the greater your responsibility, Father once said. The rich man is the one who has a little more of everything than his neighbor, even in a concentration camp. I admit it's high-handed, sneering generosity to say: Take it, it's yours, make the most of it, but I did borrow the socialists' argument for relieving the bourgeoisie of its property. I thought it was only fair that we now yielded our place to those who would say, like children: It's my turn now, you've had the bicycle long enough, and who were not really interested in knowing to whom the bicycle actually belonged.

In the morning I usually arrived late for my classes, which wasn't too smart because guards stood at the entrance and noted the names of latecomers. One morning, over the heads of the guards I noticed two display cases, one for "Heroes," the other for "Shirkers." One's name could get on the second list just for being late, if an overeager administrator so decided. One day I discovered my name and photograph among the shirkers. I didn't like myself in that photograph, it showed a dreamy, well-bred young man, and my first foolish impulse was to fume about how unflattering it was. Only slowly did it dawn on me that that was the point. I was being expelled as a class enemy. I was forbidden to set foot in the building.

Around Laura I felt protected somehow. Her mother was there, Aunt Erzsi, with her sure taste and refined manners, giving English and French lessons to youngsters. She shuffled past in her oddly lackadaisical yet carefully considered manner, the daughter of a well-to-do Jewish family from southern Hungary, with musical, literary, and even medical-scientific curiosities, proclivities, and prejudices. She had reason to be disenchanted with her life. Even as a young woman she walked slowly, with tiny steps, stopping and pausing along the way. Her husband always strode ahead, and the small distance that was always between them must have annoyed them both. In their fairly large though cluttered apartment there appeared, for the purpose of lending her moral support, a whole host of aunts: Aunt Manci, Aunt Magda, and so on. At first it wasn't easy to tell them apart, but once I overcame my shyness and sat down to chat with them, I could see their life experience, a warm, impish wisdom, inscribed on their wrinkled faces. They saw each other daily, yet they always had something to talk and reminisce about—husbands and other family members who died in ghettos and camps, turned into airy memory by poison gas and bullets, though in their dreams they were a substantial if mysterious presence.

The head of this assemblage of aunts was Uncle Vilmos, who before the war was the owner of a publishing house and printing plant, the friend of famous writers and something of a rhymester and merrymaker, a still-lean, white-haired, slightly stooped, eighty-year-old former urban sophisticate, and these days the retired employee of the Red Star printing plant, still consulted when problems arose in the trade. He visited his former wife, Aunt Ilus, twice a day. First in secret, at seven-thirty in the morning, huffing and puffing all the way up to her sixth-floor apartment. The real reason he didn't take the elevator was not to save the few pennies he'd have to give the caretaker, though even that made a difference—the real reason was that he didn't want to give away the secret of his illicit relationship with his former wife. The relationship consisted of a question and a paper bag. The question was "What's new?" The answer: "Nothing." And the response to that: "Thank God." It was worth climbing the stairs just for that, for the peace of mind. In the bag there might be a croissant, perhaps only a half, or just the tip, an apple, the end of a sausage, a piece of cheese, a few sugar cubes, a cookie or two, just a little *nosherei*. If you took the bag, you were not going to starve. He might bring her a book too, which he referred to the day before. Now he brought proof, pointing to a passage from Heine or Tocqueville. In the afternoon Uncle Vilmos came again with Aunt Magda, his second wife, taking the elevator this time and keeping silent about the morning visit.

In the late 1920s Aunt Erzsi left her well-established and well-to-do husband for Doctor Barta, a more romantic and imposing, dreamy-eyed lawyer. There was a divorce, a new marriage, and multiple moves, since Doctor Barta was constantly looking for new and better living quarters. He spent his mornings in the city, and whenever he saw ads for apartments to let, he went to look at them and then came home in triumph. Here's our new address, he would say and describe in great detail the advantages of the new place. But his wife, after going along with the first few moves, dug in her heels. No more moving, she declared. If Doctor Barta wanted to move, he could do it alone, without his wife and child. Thus, the cherry wood dining room set with the chinoiserie in the glass cabinet, the high-backed armchairs with the fluffy cushions, stayed permanently in the massive, arcaded apartment house owned by the Arkádia Insurance Company. During business hours he would wait in his new office, actually the rearranged anteroom—for clients, litigants with money to burn; but only rarely did such people seat themselves in one of the fancy, richly upholstered chairs.

Then Barta would get up from his huge, glass-topped desk, walk out onto the balcony, lean against the stone parapet, and look down. After resigning himself to another clientless day, he would take a book off the shelf. He liked to read the same ones over and over, and if he found a particularly memorable or noteworthy phrase, he drew a thin vertical line in the margin with a sharp pencil. I never knew this man, and wondered sometimes why he found this or that paragraph intriguing. At other times I nodded, Yes, that sentence *is* worth rereading.

Doctor Barta tired of legal matters, so even fewer clients sought him out. His income was less than sufficient. Luckily, his wife, after her first marriage was dissolved, and as part of her divorce settlement, kept all the valuable furniture. Doctor Barta's older brother contributed to the household expenses, as did Uncle Vilmos, though nobody was supposed to know about it. Nevertheless, Barta never forgave his brother for marrying a non-Jewish woman and becoming a Catholic convert himself. Though he rarely went to synagogue and didn't observe the religious laws, Dr. Barta considered his brother's act a betrayal, and on his deathbed extracted a promise from him that he would return to Judaism. In tears, the brother promised, though I don't know if he ever did. The truth is that Barta himself was not religious, and he didn't raise Laura to be religious; his education, too, was strictly secular, though his moral sense was strong: he didn't allow himself to be unfaithful to his wife. Their older daughter died at a young age, after that little Laura wrapped herself in silence and spent most of the day under the dining room table playing with her doll, not uttering a sound.

During the war Dr. Barta contracted tuberculosis in the basement of a large apartment building where he and his family hid, posing as refugees from Transylvania. They survived both the Hungarian Fascist takeover and the last bloody days of the war. Bombing raids were nothing compared to what the Arrow Cross thugs perpetrated. They took over one of the apartments in the building, where they tortured their victims and then hacked them to death. They fled the apartment a few days before the Russians entered, but left human limbs and skulls in the stove and numerous hundred-dollar bills among the pages of an encyclopedia. These bills were later picked up by an officer of the new police force, who went straight to the bookshelf and took down the *Lovas–Mons* volume of the Révai Encyclopedia.

After the war Dr. Barta's condition deteriorated and he stayed in various tuberculosis clinics and sanitariums. Perhaps he could have been saved, for about that time a new drug, streptomycin, appeared on the international pharmaceutical market and was said to be highly effective in the treatment of tuberculosis. But the drug was not yet manufactured in Hungary and had to be imported from Switzerland at an exorbitant price. The Bartas were about to sell their Persian carpets and porcelain figurines, but it occurred to them that the new drug might not be effective, after all, and in any case, Aunt Erzsi was not decisive enough but a rather wavering, brooding type—she simply couldn't decide to whom to sell the remnants of her dowry, and for how much.

The lawyer died before they had a chance to acquire the medicine. Laura never let her mother forget this and was pitiless about it. She remained a good daughter, she cared for her mother, but kept her distance. She had rendered judgment and there was no acquittal. Rest assured, she told me, that she would sell any damn carpet if *her* husband became ill.

LAURA. TENT-LIKE RED tresses, a smallish face, softly furrowed forehead, arching brows, inquisitorial deep brown eyes. She had a tall, slender girlish figure (first to tan, last to lose it), a supple walk, and springy arms. Our love grew less secretive, we now went everywhere together, and kept up appearances, but just barely. A year later, in '54, it seemed natural that we should get married. There was a photographer, a newly purchased white hat, which Laura liked enormously, I less so, but the bride was so enamored of it, she would say yes to her groom at City Hall only in that hat.

A somewhat older woman with thick legs, a broad-rimmed black hat, enveloped in a cloud of heavy perfume, was leading away a decrepit little old man from the sashed registrar's table. Not a good omen. When I went to pick up Laura's divorce papers, I ended up at the desk of the same smooth-skinned justice of the peace. The same black-hatted woman was again getting married, to another decrepit old man. Apparently, she had used up the first one, and turned specialist in legacy-collecting. Her ankles even thicker, her hips even broader, she was once again trailing a heavy cloud of sweet perfume, and her face, under layers of makeup, was an impenetrable mask.

Memory might be given to exaggerated boasts, but the truth is I became a man at the age of twenty when I and Laura (who was only three weeks my junior) went on a premature honeymoon in Balatonújfalu. I had called up to make a reservation at the Hotel Móló. It was late August, 1953. Stalin was dead, and after a conciliatory speech made by the new premier, Imre Nagy, I, an expelled, disgraced student, was hoping to be able to continue my studies. For if not, then in October I would have to begin my two-year stint in the military, most probably in a special unit for enemies of the state. Not an enticing possibility, though not a bad place really for serious thinking.

After leaving the station, the train ran into a dark tunnel. At the time lightbulbs were used sparingly on trains, it was quiet and dark in our compartment, a perfect opportunity for some real kissing. Delicate, fragrant lips, a still cautious, timid tongue, a hint of a fuzz on her upper lip. The tunnel was long. Before this there had been only one real kiss on the lakeshore, after a long, long walk; a single peck on the cheek upon meeting or, in a more daring mood, two pecks. Not like nowadays, when ladies offer their lips out of sheer kindness, which doesn't necessarily signal a readiness to offer more.

Lali, the husband, had returned to Leningrad, a medical student on special scholarship He would come back three years later, armed with a superior Soviet medical degree; in between he came home for summer visits. He was back for a month that summer, too, he liked the baby, but then one day Laura told him that she didn't want to live with him anymore. Five months earlier, on Laura's twentieth birthday, after the birth of his baby, I had rocked the week-old infant in the husband's absence. Now at the end of August, she was nice and big; already weaned, she was on formula, so she could be left with Auntie Erzsi for a few days.

The previous November Laura and I had confessed our love to each other. This train ride, in effect, was a breakout, an act of rebellion. Where could our love be consummated? The most obvious place would be in Laura's bed. But at Laura's Auntie Erzsi still ruled supreme. For me to spend the night there was out of the question. Why? Because such was the delicate balance of power between patience and recklessness. And we might have been embarrassed ourselves to let our parents in on our secret love life—I was also reluctant to bring her to my parents' place, where in the next room my father, a light sleeper who stayed up late into the night, was always "resting" rather than sleeping. We needed a room of our own, where we could lock the door.

The Grand Hotel at Balatonújfalu seemed a little too extravagant, so we settled for the more modest but still charming Hotel Móló, with its attractive terraces and windows looking out on the lake. It was breathtaking even to imagine the moment: With key in one hand and our light luggage in the other, I would enter the room and invite Laura in with a gallant gesture. In the lobby, after making it through the revolving door, the porter looked a little askance at me, but then handed her a key with a heavy copper weight, and along with it, for show, another, much smaller key that opened the cheapest room in the house. Not being married to each other—our identity papers made that plain—we were not permitted to sleep in the same room. But we could visit each other, there was free passage in the corridors. To impede that traffic, they would have had to place full-muscled lady monitors on every floor, à la Soviet Russia. But conditions in Hungary were more flexible. The bellhop showed us to our real room. Both of us expressed our delight a trifle more effusively than would a seasoned hotel guest, and the tip likewise was too eagerly offered, and excessive.

It was almost evening and still warm. We did it, we were over it. Until then I hadn't considered any lovemaking worthy of a wedding night. I worshipped Laura, saw her as a higher form of being, so the question for me boiled down to this: Dare one physically possess a higher being? The thorough inspection of a beautiful body, the overcoming of lingering resistance—all this took inspiration and yielded vast excitement. I thought I had to serve her above all, thus the series of assaults and retreats was a little too self-conscious; I was afraid to let go. After supper, it was back to the sheets, our creased and sweaty battleground. And then, sudden nighttime awakenings, followed by quick, clinging sleep, and then a new sneak-attack—nothing on that beautiful body should be left unexplored. Sighs, a barely audible singsong, two chests rising and falling. It was getting light outside, but we were still at it. Now was the time for her to confess that she'd always thought about me, always; and now was the time for me to make a vow: my life of dissipation is over. (As if there had been so much dissipation.) We exchanged marriage vows there and then, before God if there was one, and before each other if there wasn't. We gave our lives a proper form even as she was committing adultery and I was guilty of abduction. Solemn overstatements, all of them, but the vows, even if not forever, did last for seven years.

After the honeymoon, back to secrecy. One room and a single bed; we had to learn to lie straight, whether near the wall or on the other side. But even at night, after being startled out of sleep, it was permitted to make love. Sneaking out in the morning was a problem; I didn't want to run into Auntie Erzsi. It was best to disappear at five a.m., after the janitor unlocked the gate downstairs. But it was not advisable to go into the bathroom at that hour; the thing to do was to slip through the foyer and wash my face in the kitchen sink. The charade began the night before, at twelve-thirty: Laura would walk me to the front door, and after making all the appropriate noises, I'd bid them a loud good night and slam the door. And then I'd take off my shoes and tiptoe soundlessly back to her room—we'd even try to synchronize our steps. It wasn't a bad performance, but I could never be sure if we really managed to fool Auntie Erzsi.

The Voice of Kandor at Night

The Voice of Kandor at Night, a brazen voice in the studio of a pirate radio station. Imagine a tall, grinning male with a boxer's nose, and a black-haired, wide-eyed, twenty-year-old woman with an impudent look. Her name is Rebecca and she snaps and bounces as she turns from record to push-button to switch, as do her pointy breasts, which I watch through the glass partition of the control room, and which attract the attention of every dirty old man in the studio. I always have them sit with their back to Rebecca, so she bows at the well only to me, and gracefully pours water into my jug. She also puts disks on the turntable, and answers the telephone, screening the more obnoxious calls. She signals if the lines get jammed, and knows instinctively who has something interesting to say. Luckily nobody knows where the broadcast comes from, or else the crazies of the night, the stabbers and snipers, would invade. No one will ever find me here. I look out on the city, Kandor all around; we sit up here, just the two of us.

Rebecca, want a cup of coffee? Let's have some music! Put on that subtle saxophone. What's his name...Steve something. Sex isn't what's on my mind—let the girl run around in her spare time with whoever she likes, up here in the tower she is mine. I can tell what she's thinking from the record she puts on; sometimes she ends a conversation by turning on the music, as if on cue. This is highly irregular, but I put up with it. If I continue gabbing, she says, "You *are* a compulsive talker, aren't you?" That's exactly what I am, why else would I talk into the night. Mornings are even more dangerous, she goes one way, I go the other, she in her car, I in mine. If either car breaks down, the other offers a lift, but one is not supposed to accept it. What are taxis for?

We don't tell each other much about our backgrounds, only as much as I make up on the air. Sometimes we play it for laughs and carry on lengthy dialogues. She pretends that she is a caller and that she is pregnant. She's not sure who the father is, but she'll keep the baby and call it Edward. She knows for sure it's a boy? No she doesn't, but she'll call it Edward just the same. I see. She has no idea who the father is? It might make him happy, I hypothesize good-naturedly. Perhaps it's you, she answers demurely. But I never touched you, madam. You do keep looking at me, though. Through the glass she thumbs her nose at me, while I listen to new voices on the phone, and respond to sob stories that people unload only to a stranger in the night.

It's better to remain anonymous—the Voice of Kandor at Night. I don't want people looking for me at home; I use a different pseudonym every night, sometimes I give myself female names, my listeners are used to my shifting identity—one has to take precautions, if only because one can find just about anything in the outdoor markets, including guns and babies, in the color and quality of one's choice. Murder is not uncommon in Kandor, and contract killing is more affordable than ever. Yet life goes on: restaurants, taverns, shops, spas are full, and so are the people, of themselves, mostly, but they're also fed up with each other, with me. As long as no one's pointing a gun at me, I keep talking.

Dear listeners, you know who Kandor's troublemakers are, every child in Kandor can name them, the Bitchovs, the Pestniks, the Fagovskys, it's them we despise and vilify; there may, of course, be good Fagovskys, but the best Fagovsky is a dead Fagovsky. And that goes for the Bitchovs and the Pestniks, as well. I suppose I could apply for a gun license, but I won't. I can kick, I can run—I have long legs.

Every morning I run up to the Stonedial, and from there to the cave baths, where ancient Romans (or was it the Greeks? the Hittities? hey, Rebecca!) immersed themselves in water and steam amid huge, torch-lit columns, where every splash and flash of light held a mystery, and someone always went under in the otherwise transparent, mirror-smooth, red marble pool.

I'm forever on the run, I race through continents, and I kick, too, like, my horse Toy, who attacks everyone except his master. As for safety, the Lord protects me, as He does every simpleton. And if He is with me, who can be against me? Here we sit, then, on top of the world, I don't even know which floor, but way the hell up, surrounded by bullet-proof glass.

But excuse me, we're close to the hour; I look to my left and read the news and weather off a TV screen, as well as important local news. The latest car thefts, for instance. Or that the head of a mad fox has been found—whoever did the butchering should report to the health department for a rabies shot. I do the work of a drummer boy, a town crier. A show is canceled on account of the star's illness. I read the names of the deceased, the injured, the missing. I announce news of forthcoming balls, public meetings, processions. And, ladies and gentlemen, I will tell you who said what about his neighbor.

It's different, of course, when there is a break-in, when the security people ensconced behind the revolving door are not vigilant enough, and three hulking men push their way in, the beefiest of whom has fists as massive as paperweights. He also has numerous gold teeth, and several gold bracelets on his wrist. He used to be the driver of a famous crime boss, and ruled the road from an armor-plated limousine. When he switched on his high beams, those in front got out of his way fast, even seasoned truck drivers took fright as he scorched along the highway sitting perfectly straight at the wheel, his head grazing the car's ceiling. Most of the time he didn't utter a sound, but when he and his gun were called upon to perform, the job was done.

That car of his knew no obstacles; he'd look through the bullet-proof glass at the pitiful clunkers; he drove a custom-made job, a real beauty, manufactured especially for the previous boss. The present one simply inherited it, along with the château and the antique four-poster beds. If he is one of the burglars, arrived here after having finished off his current boss and several members of his inner circle (a destructive gang, they all deserve to be eliminated), then we're in for some unpleasantness.

If these three come up in the elevator, these three more or less veteran gangsters, then Rebecca will whip out two Uzis from her bag, I'll crouch behind an old safe and start firing. I'll be a regular Schwarzenegger, I'll vaporize the intruders, the reinforcement too, the whole swarming lot. And if they climb up on fire-ladders, we'll pour hot tar on them. If, however, they resort to stinkbombs made of, say, rotten shark meat, then I'll give up. There is a limit.

Nevertheless, ladies and gentlemen, we're prepared for every eventuality. We may even try to reason with them, they *are* human, after all. If they must knock somebody off, why us? Let it be someone we'd like to see dead anyway. People need us, and we can use the publicity. The old and new bullies agree on one thing: they both like to show off, flash their intellect. But they also want to pour out their heart on the airwaves, and be heard by those tuning in to Kandor at Night.

Yes, ladies and gentlemen, they want to be here with us, and we with you, our sleepless audience. Here the insomniacs communicate with one another. Or with those who wake up, leave the radio on, doze off, wake up again, give a listen. And we shoot the breeze with you, the callers, the public at large. Rebecca screens the calls, you can get through only via Rebecca, I'm very sorry, that's just the way it is. Rebecca decides, and she is always right, the technical end is her responsibility, I am merely the chatterbox who makes sure that as many of you as possible get on the air. Then it's Rebecca again, more music and commercials.

I ask you, ladies and gentlemen, to hold off putting the two suitcases in your car; don't flee yet, spend another night in your bed. Calm down, stop entertaining gloomy thoughts. Believe me, friends: this is not your final hour; not yet. Don't call our home-grown tedium an apocalypse.

If you ask me what's sweeping this land, I will tell you: your stupidity, that's what. A new kind of gooey logic, full of semantic atrocities. One caller promises to gouge out my eyes, just wait and see, they're watching me, there'll be little fuss, they'll blow me to bits. Or they will place some of that invisible, self-adhesive explosive under my car. I'll get in and good-bye Charlie.

Another says, Vanish if you know what's good for you. Kandorans, as everyone knows, can be divided into upright citizens and scumbags, and the division is so precise, you can never be sure which half you belong to. If you're a scumbag Kandoran, you clear out as you are, you can't take anything with you, not even books. That surprise you? You think we'll let you take community property, national treasures? The greatest danger is posed by cosmopolites, of course, those who have a life outside Kandor. We'll comb the city for such traitors. We respect minorities, but anyone with an ounce of self-respect is first and last a Kandoran. (In between he can be something else.)

What I read to you, ladies and gentlemen, are excerpts from the manifesto of upright Kandorans, who made it clear (by fax, actually) that their next target is your favorite nighttime talk show host. They have already bumped off two who preceded me. They work from a list and keep at it until the job is done.

I met a Kurd not long ago, who is in a similar situation. His friend was already sent packing, one more to go, then it's his turn to be deported, but he has cancer and might die in a hospital bed before they come for him. His wife is pregnant, so the timing is bad either way.

Almost daily I get calls that a time bomb has been placed right under my office. The bomb squad has to be called, the offices are evacuated, police dogs sniff every corner, but so far they have found nothing. We've stopped reporting the threats, because these fellows never follow through. One day they might, though, and then we'll all be blown up.

My job, dear insomniacs, is to keep talking to you. And don't be frightened, don't crawl under your bed to sniff out explosives. Relish the fact that we're still alive, that hope springs eternal. And though the inflation and mortality rates have jumped a few percentage points, the night is glorious. The sardonic visage of a full moon over Kandor illumines our madness.

Tattered clouds fill the ruddy sky, a nasty wind is blowing, but on the hotel lawn rich ladies in fur coats have gathered around the buffet table. They are here because everyone else is, because they cannot afford not to be. They've already shown off their jewelry, their physical imperfections were also on view, but what now? They want to be something, but they can't decide what.

Flabby bodies glisten in the sauna; under a sheet of bluish-yellow mist bald-headed old men daydream. Perhaps the wind will blow away the dust, and tomorrow will be a nice day. It's always tomorrow and the next day; your Doctor Pangloss is generous with his promises. Tomorrow you'll be happy that you are not blind, if you aren't already, and that you don't have aches and pains, if you don't already. And if you do, why then you'll hope for a little relief. If we know of no better place than our planet, then on the vast surface of this grain of sand called Earth why shouldn't we fix our eyes on Kandor, its promenade, where gents in apple-green topcoats peek under the parasols of ladies in pink? There used to be public hangings in this square, and when that stopped, gents in gray looked under sea-blue parasols. Times change, no one peeks anymore, people for the most part stare straight ahead.

The observer now notes pouts and pursed lips; mouths breaking into smiles, swelling in laughter, are less common. It's no longer customary to greet strangers on the street, though your Doctor Pangloss has contradicted himself again: today he engendered a few smiles as he walked from the tram stop to his hotel, carrying a bunch of snowdrops.

He brought it for—who else?—Rebecca. In her dreams Rebecca wandered off who knows where, her fine shoes barely touching the cobblestones, which brighten up under legs like these. Piano legs! I mean table legs. No, broomsticks. No, I take that back. Spindlelegs. Not that either—a wisp of opium smoke, red wine poured into a glass. An eight-thousand-year-old Hittite idol. That's no good, Rebecca knows they are fat, those fertility goddesses. And my witch of a colleague is more knowledgeable than temple hetaeras.

Why all those scarves around her neck? Why is smoking not allowed when she is in the studio? Why must she win every argument? Why does she have to approve every necktie I put on? Why does she see through people long before I do? Why a smile that penetrates the very core of your soul? Rebecca would never advise anyone to jump on Doctor Pangloss's bandwagon. She would maintain that nothing is more doubtful than universal goodwill and curiosity, with which your host now turns to you, ladies and gentlemen, and urges you to be patient—while he still has the floor. But here comes that played-out character, the international president of the metropolitan wizards, I have to let him go on, seniority, you understand, he just turned sixty.

Professor Dragomán is my guest tonight, I'll be spending the next couple of hours with him, but you may join in the conversation, ladies and gentlemen. We're sitting in this dimly lit studio, refreshments are served, everyone may smoke whatever they have on them, our callers can ramble into the night, and give freely of themselves.

Rebecca, don't grin at the president, don't be too sweet, he's spoiled rotten as it is, let's not permit him to take over; he came, he saw, he won, but now the city gates are wide open, on your way out do play your swansong, maestro. Show him your ass, Rebecca, not your face.

He lives right here, under the studio tower, and shows up sometimes on the roof terrace, green now with creeping ivy and potted palms. We invited his friend, too, the mayor of Kandor, whom everyone reviles and adores. They love to grope him even as they run him down. His Honor spends more money on public celebrations than on maintaining city streets. His fingers reach far, and in the most mysterious ways. The mayoralty has brought out qualities in him that even his friends have come to fear. He's demonstrated that he can be utterly ruthless; he knows how to let people go and how to exact revenge, all in good time, of course. He also showed that he can forgive but never forget.

Let's respect our veterans. Mr. Dragomán is the liveliest of them all, we were lucky to grab him for an interview, he is forever on the run, always in transit, tomorrow he may gone. We wouldn't be damaging his reputation if we revealed that people pay money for his counsel—many believe he is the brightest of the lot, yet he gets mixed up in scandals all the time. Last night, for instance, he hopped on a table in the Ecstasy bar with the manager and squirted seltzer on a couple for no good reason, they had done nothing to him. He doused them, then stepped outside with the gentleman. When he came back he straightened his jacket and told the lady to take care of her doused partner. With his ogling he managed to irritate just about everyone in the bar.

Mr. Dragomán can be seen on the roof terrace with his grandson, or in his favorite cane chair; he sits around in his black trousers and white shirt, with Habakuk on a stool next to him, the little boy of Dragomán's natural daughter, Olga.

The mother of said Olga is Bella Olajos, our noble-hearted landlady, the director of the Crown Hotel, majority shareholder and venture capitalist of our fair city, who began small, with the

Mousetrap, then took over the Tango, and now has claimed the Crown, too, as her prize—the steps to the top are steep indeed. Bella Olajos can now afford to host artist gatherings and charge her guests next to nothing for the privilege of attending.

Mr. Dragomán spent a lot of time at the Crown in his youth, mainly in the bar, cozying up to Baroness Rosamunde, the barmaid. The baroness was widely known for her unsurpassed cappuccinos as well as her extraordinary breast size—many of Kandor's culture heroes luxuriated between those formidable mounds, people after whom streets were named later. Baroness Rosamunde sometimes dreamt that entire streets ran through her, bridges, hills, ships floated on a river that flowed across her belly. It's understandable that Dragomán would be interested in topographical descriptions where ribs are avenues, and from the pelvic bone one can look down on an ocean. Seagulls circle over the white railing, oh, I hear music, let's hop over the navel and get close to the columned pavilion where the band is playing.

There's Dragomán again, leaning on his elbow and watching his daughter, a young lady whose conspicuous slenderness and pregnancy are not, strange to say, at odds with each other. For her the Baroness Rosamunde is like a St. Bernard. Olga Dragomán is in need of protection because her husband, Berci, is away, playing the trumpet in the four corners of the world, though not that often in Kandor. But when he comes, he caps his brief sojourn by making Olga pregnant. He also brings presents, a whole carful, for Habakuk, who is terribly spoiled, with an ego as big as the Crown Hotel.

Habakuk is either the great leader or a quietly brooding melancholic sitting on a stool next to his grandpa. Do you know this one, he asks: "I go home, and just for fun, chase my folks with a machine gun." No, Dragomán hasn't heard this one. He tells his grandson about the ventriloquist who can make people say all sorts of crazy things; when he's around, people simply talk differently. Habakuk listens intently, then asks: Would you like people to be stranger than they are? I think they are strange enough already.

They leave the hotel, hand in hand, and we see them on the square, in front of a bell-ringing ice-cream cart. Dragomán inspects bottles in a liquor store; Habakuk stops in front of a jeweler's store and a fur salon. Both of them pause in front of a gun-and-dagger emporium, then disappear behind the door of a beer hall, we can still see them inside: Habakuk gets a piece of cake and a sip of Grandpa's beer.

In the pub Dragomán starts up with two regulars famous for their Jew-baiting. He sat with them both in jail in 1958. He quizzes them as to whether they can still fit into their pants, and whether they can bend down and reach over their belly to tie their shoelaces. Don't they get dizzy when they straighten up afterward? He tries to explain to them they are actually Jews (which in the case of one of them is half true, at least in Nurembergese), and what's more unpleasant, the accident occurred on his mother's side. His member, however, is untouched, the foreskin had not been surrendered, in lieu of his heart, as an offering, to the Hebrew God, so he is free to argue that the Jews have not fit into Hungarian society the way the Slovaks, the Romanians, or the Serbs have; they've kept their separateness, will never be Magyars, for in their pride they reject the very essence of European civilization—Christianity.

Dragomán hears him out, then says simply: The Bible is mine, I'll take it with me—it's Jewish literature. The rest is yours. The holy pictures of that Jewish woman with her son are mine, too. I'll take them to Israel, where you want to send all the Jews. And I'll take you there too, friend, I'll take everyone who's hung up on this Jewish thing. And I may even have a few kind words for your mother. The peddler Jew will carry you on his shoulder. We'll stop at the eastern end of the Mount of Olives, where the garden entrance is blocked by a cemetery, to prevent the Messiah from going in. He's a Cohanite, you see, and a Cohanite cannot enter the cemetery. Don't you understand? Everyone's a Jew: Christians as well as Muslims. In their heart of hearts none of them believes in this business of Ascension and Second Coming. They scoff at the idea of a blood tie between God and man.

The most improbable of Jews—the prophets—were in reality writers who stood in the marketplace and spread the Word to those who cared to listen. One elbow leaning on a long trestle table, they pushed back their hat, grabbed their beard, turned and twisted it, trying to squeeze out the right answer. They thrust their head forward, closed their eyes, made all sorts of temporizing noises, and then put into words their version of the Law. People put questions to them and they answered—sheer mumbo-jumbo sometimes.

Secluded, in agony, silent for days, they were seared by the truth, which each time began with them anew. They knew something about what connects God to man. They did not stand on ceremony, they turned to Him—no intermediaries for them—they were blinded by the light in His eyes. They bowed, their bodies shook, but they remained standing, never knelt, didn't touch the ground with their head, never turned away from the Lord, always carried on a dialogue with Him. Whatever they did, they asked for a blessing, they couldn't even urinate without Him, they dragged Him into everything.

You are right, my dear Kálmán; Jews *are* terrible creatures, responsible for this strange intimacy. They began this trend, these shady dealings with God; you might say they invented conscience, this disagreeable figment, this bloodsucking phantom, this feeling that one owes something to someone and can never settle the debt. They deserve to be hated, I can well understand you. Only thing is you, too, are one of them. So there's nothing left to do but lament the Jewification of this great country of ours. But rest assured, friend: in time, you'll be Yiddified, too. At the end of your life you'll understand it better, now you're still in a fog. It's true that Jewishness is also just so much malarkey, like everything else we talk about or believe in, especially if we foolishly take them to heart—still, the wise Jews are among those few who suspect that groups differ from each other only in the way cows in the same herd or horses in a stud farm do. But now, Kálmán, old man, you must excuse me; Habakuk the prophet, who's sitting right here, has to make kaka. Maybe he doesn't have to, he's just tired of listening to my speeches. Habakuk's frequent question to me: "Papa Jani, why do you talk so much?" is completely justified. My reply to him is usually: "Because my head spouts like a fountain." "Bend down, then," Habakuk would say and twist his grandpa's ear: "Okay, I turned on the tap."

The Voice of Kandor at Night has a direct line to Habakuk. We'll ask him whose voice he wants to hear. Mommy's, of course, always Mommy's because nobody is more beautiful. Girls are stupid and smelly, and they're touchy and whiny too, he'll never ever fall in love. What's this business about kissing on the lips? Licking each other's tongue? Yuck! Habakuk would actually wipe his tongue with his hand. He'd never do anything so yucky, the only wife he'll have is Mommy, who is pretty and always smells nice. She does have a few white hairs, but that's pretty too, and her face is as smooth as if she were still in nursery school. She has the reddest shoes, the longest legs, and she is the fastest swimmer around. Nobody can make chocolate cake or macaroni and cheese the way she can. Just because she always loses at Memory doesn't make her dumb, and being bad at foosball doesn't make her a klutz. She looks good even when she's mad. Habakuk comforts her and tells her she'll get better. Lately, when they play Memory, Dragomán has joined them, and of course he ends up last.

Lona

On October 23, 1956, early in the afternoon, Dragomán met Lona on a street corner. A dilemma: Should he leave the demonstrators, or should Lona join the march? The question was decided in the spirit of the moment. Though she should have gone home to her husband, she stayed; and Dragomán, though he didn't know where Laura was, assumed that she, too, had been sucked in by the marching throngs.

They kept marching; Dragomán's hand held another hand; Lona looked unusually pretty, her eyes ablaze with double excitement. She was exhilarated by the march and enjoying the hand that moved up and down her back. She had got married and told Dragomán about it only afterward. But they overcame this technicality in no time, and made up for the oversight, first in a boathouse, then in a country inn, and a third time at home, in Lona's little alcove. They proved that what's meant to last will indeed.

Lona hated the voice of the overage classmate marching next to them, who during the compulsory military training sessions at the university goose-stepped ecstatically, and though in the last stages of pregnancy, swung with her big belly left and right like a soldier, and saluted solemnly as she rattled off the expected idiocies. Now she was marching next to them, shouting different slogans.

Lona was highly sensitive to smells, and could describe in minute detail the odors emanating from her fellow students. Her bathroom shelf was filled with an array of toiletries, so it was dangerous for a married man to sleep with her in the afternoon;

The scents would not rub off, even after showering and scrubbing.

Their long-lasting friendship, divided into discrete chapters by periods of estrangement, was regularly rekindled by Lona's intriguingly compact features and her throaty whine. Her essential self was a pool of honesty deep inside a gorge of jeering laughter. You ran there for relief, and hovered over it like a coot. Or dipped into that pool while in bed or in the Tango Café, where they could rarely avoid grim-faced policemen checking identity papers.

"You play me like a piano," Lona said in 1956. A Kantian history major then, she knew everything about the Hungarian Age of Reform, and spoke about the indiscretions of romantic and early populist literary figures, or about Count Széchenyi's *samizdat* activities in a Viennese insane asylum—about a very different world—as though talking about her own family. She loved to see through their deceptions and pretend to be interested only in that period. Considering how much she knew, she didn't wear thick glasses, and her frequent excursions in French and Russian Romanticism notwithstanding, her behind did not become less shapely.

The authorities invited her father to emigrate. He had been a highly respected figure in the banking world; his expertise, he was told, would be valued anywhere. But he was reluctant to leave behind his enormous, three-meter by three-meter bed, which he used as a couch for reading during the day. His forced resignation as the head of the country's largest bank enabled him to devote himself entirely to his outside interests. He translated music-related literature, everything from composers' memoirs to musicians' biographies, and while working he listened to the appropriate music. Every day he revised five pages of text. Most of the time, though, he just relaxed on his huge bed.

In order to keep his distance from the newly installed co-tenant, he had his apartment partitioned. Walls were raised in the remaining section of the flat, too, so that he and his daughter would not be in each other's way. He'd call her on a specially hooked-up telephone before coming to visit, and see for himself that in contrast to his own habit of lolling about all day, she stood at the top of a movable ladder in front of the highest shelf of a room-size library. Lona inherited some real estate, which she traded, in exchange for rare books, to private libraries and antiquarian book dealers. And as she also came into possession of her grandparents' library, she had to decide what to choose from up there. She didn't want to think about Dragomán. The stepladder was rigged up with wheels and a bicycle chain, so she could glide like a wading bird, from one tall bookcase to the next. Sometimes she took a bottle of rum up with her, and when she descended from her lofty perch, she placed two candles on her desk, which would neutralize the cigarette smoke while she studied. She smoked the cheapest brand, it could be smelled on her breath when we kissed.

When it snowed Dragomán would go down to the Danube to play his harmonica. Lona would look out of the window, and if her husband wasn't home, she would tell Dragomán to come up. The husband was a quiet architect, who one day, when Lona was feeling particularly lonely, had moved into her flat with a suitcase. Actually, he fell asleep on the couch, and stayed. Lona didn't have the heart to throw him out; he kept the house in order, went shopping, cleaned, cooked, relieving Lona of all these mundane tasks. She could go out and take pictures of courtyards, old apartment buildings—photography was her other passion, and her architect gladly developed her photos.

You cheat on me; I cannot count on you. Why must you wait for me on a park bench, in the snow? My husband is right here in bed with me, we went to sleep late; and you sit under my window, torturing me with your presence. Sleep with me, then; I want to wake up next to you. But no: you're a married man, you've got to keep up appearances. You're a lying bastard, you deceive me and you have deceived Laura, and you force me to hate and pity my best friend.

I will not see you again, Dragomán said, pacing frantically. He's had it with women.

Laura gave him his walking papers, too. His infidelities came to light: a note from him fell into her hands—Dragomán had a date with Lona, who never waited more than twenty minutes. "Take your belongings and get out," Laura said in a choked voice. "I never want to see you again." It was a good thing he lived at Laura's, this way he could be kicked out, and after begging for forgiveness and working his way back into her bed—the departure and arrival platform of his wanderings—a semblance of order could be restored.

It should be pointed out that Lona's thighs were heavier, more muscular than Laura's, or those of the other women in Dragomán's life. On the beach in the summer she wore only bikini bottoms, so the large pink areolae of her nipples could be properly admired. Her full upper lip quivered expressively when exchanging a wise smile with Dragomán. Large eyes, mouth, and nose, brown shoulders, trembling lips—she could be satire one minute and elegy the next. Dragomán could not easily forget her hoarse groans, or that unusual smell, a mixture of body odor and her favorite perfume, the name of which he could never remember. One of her specialties was the conspiratorial chuckle; she had a cabaret singer's high-handed, sophisticated humor—in a college student it was captivating. Lona learned everything that could be learned; and if she wanted, she could get him to see her anytime, that very day, even if all Dragomán wanted to do was tell her that it was over, that they were through, that he'd already put her out of his mind.

Lona made Dragomán promise that for the next two nights he would not make love to Laura, and to make sure, she smeared lipstick on the tip of his penis. If that red spot was not there tomorrow, she warned, she'd throw him out on his ear. I can't even take a shower? Dragomán asked. You'll take one here, Lona said peremptorily.

Incredible. Yet her possessiveness did not cloud her judgment. Then again, she had had designs on Laura's man from the very beginning. In fact, she wanted everything of Laura's, and had even in grade school—her pen case, her hair ribbons, her slender build, for as a child Lona was quite a bit heavier than Laura. And she coveted Laura's sharp intelligence, her quick way with words.

Laura kept those around her in a state of tension; she possessed a formidable verbal memory, she knew every cliché in the book, and therefore could not help spotting tiresome repetitions. The contemptuous put-downs, the furious insistence on originality, the flashes of light that filled her walnut-brown eyes when someone said something clever, and her tuning out when she felt the conversation had lost its intellectual sparkle—all this drove Dragomán to ecstasy and despair several times a night.

She would say to him: "János dear, can't you be an acrobat tonight, or a seer? What *can* you do if you can't even hold your own in an argument? Kobra, that dullard, trounced you. Oh, you returned some of his serves, but—surprise, surprise—he lobbed the ball back every time, ironically almost, or should I say sardonically?"

While Laura said these things to Dragomán, Lona remained quiet, looked around, shook her imaginary feathers, and at the right moment wiggled her hips. Lona was more kindly disposed toward humanity, she could have been a nurse, a midwife, a medicine woman, a fortune-teller, a ringmaster's wife, but instead she was a college student majoring in French and Hungarian literature, a budding scholar with positivist tendencies and an affinity for literary biographies.

Dragomán and Lona were taking a walk along the lakeshore. For no apparent reason, they started talking about why the Jews undressed so obediently before being shot into mass graves. Why did those in the second row, seeing how people in the first got mowed down after they'd stepped out of their clothes, still go ahead and take off theirs? Why did they feel it was their duty to make their executioners' job easier? Why didn't they jump on the guards? They could have disarmed them, there were more of them, some could have escaped, surely. It wasn't even certain that the first to resist would have been killed. Why this paralysis, this resignation? If they want us to die, they seemed to be saying, so be it, let us die. Whoever was chosen to be a victim played the role dutifully.

SOMETIMES THEY STOOD at the metal counter of a greasy "people's diner" eating bean soup, a filling gruel with lots of beans floating on top. If they were lucky they were able to finish it, but more often than not, one of the awful regulars of the place appeared before them and began moving his toothless gums along with theirs, grinning provocatively and baring his lone tooth. "I am helping myself to your leftovers, in the name of proletarian internationalism," he announced when two-thirds of the meal was gone, insisting on the remaining third. Dragomán gave in first; he put down his spoon and surrendered his soup along with a piece of bread. The champion of proletarian internationalism was not loath to eating somebody else's leavings, and he didn't look undernourished either.

The day after the revolt broke out, Dragomán sat at home listening to the conflicting news reports on the radio, trying to make sense out of the previous day's events. Then he went out, bought a loaf of bread, and even managed to find some meat and powdered milk for the boy. He also stopped at the Writers Union where, by virtue of a few published reviews, he was a stipend-receiving member and where right now canned goods were being handed out. In one of the editorial offices four men held on to the corners of a table. They had once sat here, but were dismissed for political reasons. Now all four laid claim to the desk.

In the following days he visited City Hall and saw his boss in the chief executive's office, occupying the tall leather chair behind the presidential desk. A friend of his, duly solemn-faced, was ushering in the new petitioners. The editor-in-chief thus replaced the mayor, and the former chief, a party stalwart, stayed at home. The editor-in-chief rang him and told him that under the circumstances it would be better if he didn't come in; that way no harm could come to him. An armed guard would be dispatched for his protection, just in case.

His friend, a gifted young ethnographer, let people in to see the chief editor according to a system that was as inscrutable as it was impressive, while the new boss ordered the secretaries around and took possession of the official seal. People accepted the new state of affairs and crowded into his anteroom, waiting in line for a stamped and sealed permit to requisition cars, occupy houses and offices. They all sought funds for pet projects. Dragomán was genuinely surprised to see so many people vying for a piece of paper.

But then, he, too, showed up in that executive suite. He wanted to take over the journal from his former boss, the chief editor. You go ahead and assume the mayor's duties, he said, and let us younger people run the journal. We no longer need mentors to look over our shoulders. As a self-appointed correspondent representing his avant-garde journal, he interviewed the leaders of brand-new political parties; there were former army officers and bishops among the founders.

He saw the fast-talkers, the wheeler-dealers, the wily sentimentalists, the lovable old and the brand-new SOB's—all jockeying for position. He walked through the square just as bullets began to fly; scores of people were injured. When the ambulances arrived, he, too, grabbed a stretcher and ran to help. He was given a journalist's pass, though he never had to use it; with his Leica and his red scarf he looked the part.

He pretended to be a war correspondent, and asked permission to ride with important delegations. Every morning he joined the revolution as if he were going off to work. He saw a man being hanged from a tree by a belt twisted around his ankles. The men, and the women helping them, did their job quickly and efficiently. A finicky little man spat on the corpse: "Phew! You, too, were thick with the Russians." A broad-faced boy in knee breeches ambled over to the corpse and with a pocketknife etched a five-pointed star on its back. There were people who simply stood and watched. An old woman finally said: "Even that wretch had a mother." "Then let her cry over him," said a man with a nondescript face, and kicked the dangling corpse. A Swedish correspondent appeared with his escort. "*Vous savez, les passions révolutionnaires sont démesurés,*" the escort said and quickly pulled him away, but the Swede took another peek. "It's time to calm down; party headquarters has been occupied," a man with a toolbox said, a plumber probably. A shaky-voiced fellow stuttered: "At least another hundred should be strung up next to this one. Then we'll finally have peace in this city."

DURING THE DAYS of the revolution Lona had time on her hands and joined Dragomán on his forays. She knew that he would always take her where the action was, but she also agreed with him that whatever she did, whether staring out the window or pounding away on the piano, it was a way of reflecting on the events. They sat in the Tango bar, waiting for Kobra. Late as usual, he appeared with a submachine gun slung over his shoulder and a patriotic armband. He was in a hurry. Rosamunde brought them coffee and reminded him sharply: "Umbrellas, canes, machine guns have to be checked. Old lady Gizi will watch it for you. Why do you have to carry this thing around anyway? You won't use it." "It can't hurt to have it handy," Kobra said and left.

After days of street fighting, a scream rang in Dragomán's ear: "Jewish assassins!" He went home, stood next to Laura on the balcony and listened to distant gunfire, which died down, then started up again. A flare streaked across the sky. This was not his war, Dragomán decided.

When a man was hanged on a lamppost in front of the Tango, Dragomán remained silent and continued to play the piano. "I was afraid to do anything," he later said to Lona. "The hanged man was a member of the secret police. But why should a man be hanged for being a policeman?" He posed the question in English, and paraphrased something from Sterne's *Sentimental Journey*. A young man with a tommy gun asked: "And who are you?" Dragomán raised his finger: "Don't shoot the piano player."

The regulars had already gathered at the bar: a rich American farmer in a garish parka, who by midnight took up the entire dance floor (perhaps he stayed in Kandor only to dance the night away), and the son of the Finnish ambassador, who got drunk and kept dropping his wineglass. The call girls, as usual, sat at the bar.

Our hero's father, Döme Dragomán, who used to play the piano in cafés and bars, had told him about the time he was a slave laborer in a stone quarry, where Jews had to play Sisyphus: roll heavy boulders from morning to night in icy weather. Now the boulders were not for a pianist's hands, so he had no choice but to escape, which was as unlikely a thing for a piano player to do as rolling stones up a hill. But that's history for you: nothing is what it's supposed to be. A pesky nutcase comes along and says that from now on everything will be different, and Döme Dragomán no longer belongs in the Tango but at some stone quarry in the Balkans. What was he doing in the Balkans? A few days were enough for him to note the sound pattern of rolling stones, the rest was a waste of time.

The popular sportscaster also hung out at the Tango, as well as a Brazilian military attaché with his platinum-blonde girlfriend; the deputy head of counterintelligence; an Olympic boxing champion; an obscure veterinarian from the country; and behind the bar, the inevitable Baroness Rosamunde. Reigning over the motley crew, however, was Camilla, the hotel manager's wife. The manager, a famous fencer, had been put in charge of both the Crown Hotel and the Tango bar in recognition of patriotic merits, but in the fall of 1956 he was coaching a fencing team abroad, and left the running of the two establishments to his wife, whose business savvy was beyond dispute.

Camilla walked in like an empress, and looked regal even when nonchalantly patting her stomach under her blouse. She preferred sundecks that allowed nude sunbathing; she was tanned in April, revealing a trim body to her Maker. The price of such fitness: daily gymnastics, massage, hot and cold showers, and a hundred laps every morning.

Camilla was as comfortable preparing filet mignon or a hazelnut torte as she was standing in the spotlight in a glittering evening dress, microphone in hand, announcing the next attraction. If she had to, she could also belt out a popular ballad to a misty-eyed audience. Everything about her was both captivating and practical, and the same could be said about her sexual habits. Extraordinarily inventive in voice and gesture, she was equally original in her choice of rings for her ears and fingers. As for her backside, it was an ass to reckon with.

At eleven o'clock every morning Camilla sat on a bench at the public swimming pool, applying suntan lotion to her brown legs. Around her would gather a philosopher, a divorce lawyer, a jockey, watching her smear cream on her skin, and listening to her gossip and boisterous effusions—the effects of fast-acting stimulants. *Mes pauvres sottises,* she would say. There was also a journalist in her circle, a man more likely to write confidential reports for the secret police than newspaper articles, if only because in the former he was not constrained by censorship considerations: he could crack jokes, call a spade a spade—his superiors demanded clarity and candor. These members of Camilla's court were in a position to report on the intimate connections between the manager's wife and a group of anarchist students; but they didn't badger her as long as they could hang around the hotel where Camilla reigned. Though not over everyone. Over her daughter, for example, she didn't. Dragomán, it so happened, had the opportunity to get intimately acquainted not only with the elder Camilla, but with the younger one as well. Even back then there were lounge chairs on the roof terrace and the hotel guests, after taking a dip in the pool, could come up and get a splendid view of Liberation Square. Dragomán, if he was chasing after one of the help, could hide in one of the attic rooms. In fact it was in one such room that in the summer of 1956 the younger Camilla's legs, those memorably slender, shapely legs, sailed through the window, followed by the rest of her, bereft of clothing.

It was the summer of Dragomán's moral decline. Anything goes, he declared, no more taboos. The past was rubbish. Fascism was rubbish, and so was communism. We could dispense with everything that seemed morally weighty then.

You may put your hand on the woman next to you. Desire what she desires. Buzz in her ear, enjoy her smell, and believe that she's the first woman in your life. Lie to yourself and to her. Let her feel that this afternoon, because she sneaked into your room, stepped right through your window, is the high point of your life.

The roller coaster of earthly delights was going at full swing: up and down, in and out, people shrieked, they felt their hearts in their throats, felt light as air, they wanted more and more and still more. Why was this afternoon so different from all other afternoons? Why was even the streetcar ride home special, the return trip to loved ones to whom you didn't breathe a word about the afternoon orgies. You experienced moments of liberation, illumination, you felt you could do anything to anybody.

Dragomán sat at the Tango's piano; franks and beans were served at the next table, to a man with a large forehead who periodically banged the table with his fist: "No more international morality. What we'll have here now is Hungarian morality."

Outside the café window armed civilians paced back and forth; a Gypsy boy, wearing a blanket for a coat, dragged a machine gun behind him; now and then he stopped and fired a round in the air. Dragomán and Laura were walking home, with the child sitting on his shoulder. It was drizzling; the shooting had stopped, the streets were deserted. A car headed toward them, screeched to a halt, turned around and took off again. Swarms of crows descended on the park; fog settled on temporary burial mounds, Soviet soldiers slept under a circus tent.

The streetcars, except for certain lines, were running. The power stations, the gas- and waterworks, the telephone company continued to provide service. Doctor Bíró from next door set out for the hospital, dashing from doorway to doorway in his white coat, waving his doctor's bag like a flag. It wasn't clear who was shooting at whom, but it was clear that people were being shot and needed a doctor.

Children didn't go to school, women stayed home, too, and men went off to work to plan strategy. It was true that plants had to be maintained, but there was also a general strike; the frightened looked for help to the bold and bright, who seemed just as helpless. The heroes were the ambulance drivers and the bakers, and the women from the village cooperatives who sent truckloads of fried geese to the hungry city.

In the open corridors of apartment buildings the exchange of news and information never stopped. The chairman of all the revolutionary committees, a rugged-looking man in a leather jacket, rode around in a jeep and issued orders with scientific precision. The city lives, he said, so keep forming your committees and associations.

The elder Dragomán continued to play songs without words on the piano. Members of a tourist club organized fall excursions in the trouble-free woods. A businessman bought and resold, sight unseen, a shipment of Argentine canned beef. Children collected cartridge shells and marched around in helmets. A van delivered coffins. Do-it-yourselfers continued plastering walls and tiling roofs of their cottages. At dining room tables children played dominoes and checkers. Well-known actors were heard on the radio; humorists told the Russian troops in no uncertain terms to go home. Neighbors felt free to ring each other's doorbells, and were glad they could talk more candidly now. Children stayed close to their mothers and they all looked marvelous together—four-five women and a dozen kids. Flyers appeared in store windows and on advertising columns. A boy smeared flour paste on a wall and put up a sign: "We demands longer recesses and hot chocolate for everyone."

Dragomán decided to read Tolstoy to prevent himself from being prejudiced against the Russians. He and a friend held impromptu debates about constitutional reforms—how to combine revolutionary action with representative democracy—in the university lobby, a gathering place for budding philosophers and Sinologists. They peered into the locked bookcases, searching for the latest acquisitions. On benches and in the corridors they found newspapers, broadsides, announcements.

Not long before, on one of the lobby's massive columns his name had appeared on a list of disgraced students, together with that stupid graduation picture, which showed him with his hair slicked back and wearing an idiotic expression. Yet it was the most "stable" time of his life: he had graduated with honors, even in math. He was ready to take on the world—in that clear-sighted period, how could he look so inane?

One of the guards said his aunt had told him that there were prison camps all over the Soviet Union. His aunt had been in such a camp, but was let out because her sister went to bed with an NKVD colonel. These camps were everywhere in Russia, she said, they stretched endlessly. Why not build a barbed-wire fence around the whole city, Dragomán said, and declare it a camp. Kandor *is* surrounded, a fat, always well-informed journalist said.

The head of the revolutionary executive council got hold of a gunboat that could be used as an escape vessel. The cave experts were on the alert, ready to spirit away the revolutionary leadership through subterranean passageways. An actress looked up Tatyana's letter to Onegin; a nice reading would please everyone now. The Russians would see it as a fine gesture, properly dignified, and her own compatriots would not think she was sucking up to the captors—after all, *Eugene Onegin* was a classic, from the last century.

I TRY TO revive shrouded memories, I remove the dustcover. An excavation in my head: image leads to image. What happened after the Revolution, during the so-called Years of Reprisals? Public discourse succumbed to brute force. In such times one reads long books, and is given to elegiac discourse with friends, in the gentle glow of a lamp. The ordinary citizen turns his back on politics; there is so much to decry and jeer at, he'd much rather exchange information with trusted friends. He feels guilty when thinking about those languishing in jail. Why they and not me? But then he takes a walk along the Danube embankment, sits on the bottom step, and realizes that he doesn't long for the naked lightbulb, the brown brick wall of a prison; he has an aversion to institutional order, to communal life in any form. He releases his guilt—a paper boat—into the river. He is inclined to believe now that it was the hyperactive types who worked their way into prisons or into emigration. He is ashamed of himself for harboring such thoughts, but he doesn't try to stop them. The slow ones who cannot stand long meetings, the undisciplined dreamers, the idle loafers, the quiet brooders never bring on themselves the full ire of the authorities, at most they irritate the police. They will always be watched, and the watchdogs will always wonder whether or not to recruit them, but the odds are they will never be thrown in jail.

Accident

Y ou have to take this on now," his friends told him in the early months of 1990. He must act as moderator in debates between intelligent people on interesting subjects. His colleagues' engagement calendars are full, they devise duties for themselves and for one another, develop useful initiatives, take stands on important issues, or elaborately justify why they won't commit themselves. They take it to heart that their institute, their firm, their university, is in a sorry state. Tossing in bed at night, they rack their brains: What could they do to make them flourish again?

He answers listeners' questions in a newly opened literary café. He does the same in a youth center, in a newly formed club of independent intellectuals, in a municipal library, at City Hall, in a tea room, in an art gallery, in the castle courtyard, on the main square. At times he declines invitations on grounds of illness, or comes up with some other excuse—he prefers not to leave his daughter and grandson; the bicycle ride to the pier or a walk up the hill is enough exercise for him.

But isn't it true that once you get involved, you must keep it up? If you stood up for A, you must do the same for B. If the academy honored you, you owe something to the academy—or your church, your bank, if you happen to be a priest or a banker. Without personal involvement, one may think the thing itself does not exist.

The audience's confusion is deceptive, they are all searching for magic answers, abandoning one religion and quickly adopting another—they are greedy and fickle, in quest of a master, whom they find and then try to forget. In time disciple and master both become passé, until someone rediscovers them. And then it's time again for questioning?

He tries to scurry past colleagues in lobbies. While roaming the fields he tries to figure out why he ever agreed to sit in an auditorium or a lecture hall and preside over the proceedings, or submit to photographers' cameras, their flashing inhibiting the flow of his own thoughts.

In Balatonújfalu and Old Hill no one can afford to be idle; the women are anxious about the grape harvest, they'll spend days bending over the vines, especially the old stalks—trellis vines require less effort. Everything that grows has to be put by in bottles and cans. There are cucumbers and peppers to be sliced, squash to shred for animal feed, and plums to cook for *lekvár*. The pears are waiting to be preserved, too, the grapes are ready to be picked; when you touch them your hands get sticky; wasps hover over the clusters.

Last week Olga stood in the city park in the rain, under a black umbrella, along with two thousand others. From the lit-up stage all those attentive faces under colorful umbrellas looked appealing. For four hours they listened to poems, songs, and speeches. Dragomán had respect for an audience that ignored the rain.

Habakuk was first in his kindergarten class in running and swimming, and he insisted on seeing those gaping, ferocious dinosaurs in the movies, though when one of the computer-generated synthetic monsters spat up something vile, he said, Let's go. He trembled and whimpered and decided he didn't like horror movies; it would have been better to stay home and help Mommy bake cookies.

A friend just back from Serbia said that old people there had simply given up. They stopped joining early-morning bread lines. So they don't eat, they quietly waste away, what's the big deal? The seven o'clock news shows the maimed corpse of a child. The mutilators, the burners of live flesh, the rapists, the snipers, all claim to be doing it in defense of their country.

But here in the village all is peaceful. Across the river the wild boars are getting restless, and hunters keep a sharp eye out. The wind has dispersed the clouds, a bit of sunshine hovers on the wet rooftops. It usually rains at night, but by morning it clears; wet days are approaching, it will drizzle continuously and pour from time to time. During dry spells Dragomán walks in the fields; the sheep huddle together, the goats butt each other—filthy animals, a shepherd says and shakes his head.

He doesn't feel like taxing his brain, he lets the wetness trickle down his back in tiny rivulets. Let the dye run in the folds of his clothes, let the blood stream down, let it all happen. Time stands still, only he runs round and round—midday and midnight are whenever he comes to rest.

Accompanied by Olga, he goes to see a neighbor, the mother of two sons and a daughter, to wish her a happy birthday. The two sons are married, as is the daughter. They all live in Kandor, they all have children, on holidays and family occasions the family gathers in Grandma's house; fourteen people crowd into her small cottage. She prepares beef stew and veal cutlets and nut and jelly rolls, the women make themselves useful, the men watch television and drink to each other's health—Dragomán sips home brew, Olga drinks a little wine, which makes her exceptionally friendly. Before the young leave in the afternoon, they will stop by at the church.

Their other neighbor, a young man, wouldn't dream of living in any other part of the country, there's so much work here. In the morning he has to decide whether to go to the vineyard, hoe the potato field, or fix a broken faucet. He's happy to know there is oil under the lake, but doesn't think much of the marine biologist who approved the introduction of new breeds of fish, for they gnaw on the fresh shoots in the reed bank, and the lake gets choked with mud. On the other hand, he would like the town to put in floodlights at the soccer field, so they could have night games.

Habakuk wants to go to church, too, he thinks a lot about God these days. Olga allows herself a little sarcasm here. But Habakuk, whose notion of good and evil is like that of the patriarchs, says gravely: "Mommy, you can't say these things, because God knows perfectly well what you are thinking, but you can't know what *He* is thinking."

Olga stays on the verandah reading when Habakuk goes to

mass with the neighbor's children. At lunch he will nod knowl-edgeably: "Yes, Jesus was God's only son, and he was killed. But what did God do, what kind of sin did He commit to make them kill His own Son? Olga says, it's only a story. Each religion is a different story.

Then Yom Kippur was mentioned, Habakuk brought it up: "You know, the thing you were talking about in the car, that we have to do a lot of thinking about the dead, about sin." Yes, he was right for bringing up the subject, but Grandfather didn't feel like talking just now about the dead or about sin, he'd rather dis-cuss family get-togethers. He praised the neighbors for having these nice gatherings from all over the region. His own family is scattered all over the globe, but mostly in a continent called the Beyond.

He sees the treetops under a thin blade of a moon, and around them the northern stars. In the morning Habakuk is taken to kindergarten, and on the way he studies finches and hamsters, and says hello to lots of mommies. His family is full of tough, uncompromising characters. On Yom Kippur eve, he will go to temple to atone for the errors of his ways, which he can expect to repeat in the new year.

Olga went to Budapest for two days, Bella is away, too, Dragomán is alone with Habakuk. Everything is more casual now, though the most important chores are fixed in the boy's mind: the rituals of bathing, drinking, tooth-brushing, peeing. Habakuk climbs walls and trees, races down the road on his bike, leaving his grandfather in the dust. He can use a monkey wrench, has seen a pig being neutered, and wonders whether a pit dug in the sand and covered with branches is a real trap that can kill an animal or just break his leg.

Dragomán makes macaroni and cheese for Habakuk, he is rea-sonably good at dominoes, they go on long bicycle rides together, and have dinner in the garden. He gets better and better at grand-fatherhood. They receive guests on their own, and there's not a crumb on the kitchen table, plates, glasses, silverware are all in place, though they make silly faces throughout the meal, and get even more unruly afterward. Olga will be back tomorrow and will give them a piece of her mind, which will instantly deflate the two gentlemen's conceit. But until she arrives they're not the least bit afraid of Habakuk's mother. The dessert they gobble up first, and then tackle the main course.

What's a hero, Habakuk wants to know. Somebody like you. Why? He likes getting up better than going to sleep. You like heroes? When I lie in bed and he appears before me full of ideas, I say to myself: Save me from all heroes, O Lord. Should I go out then? No, I am not in bed now, stay, I want you to. Is Mommy a hero? Yes, she is, all the time. And what's a fallen hero? Habakuk asks. One who gets killed. Everyone who gets killed is a fallen hero? There are people who say that a fallen hero is someone who had killed. That's silly, Habakuk says. Then, after some head-scratching: You know, Papa Jani, only a person who lived can die, so let's say that everyone who's ever lived is a hero. And then I am a hero, too, because I get up every morning. Can a little boy be a hero? Yes, I think so. But a person doesn't have to be a hero, does he? Not if he can help it. But sometimes you can't avoid it. Then you have to be one. Unfortunately.

ON HIS WAY back to the city, Dragomán stands on an escalator and watches the faces of people passing by on the other side; they look back, the low-key glances barely registering. Who among them is worth talking to? Whose face reveals a beguiling inner smile? Who is a potential murderer, an informer? That man in a hat most probably would not turn Dragomán in, even if it was in his interest to do so. But that one with the briefcase over there probably would, and rob him and spit in his face for good measure. This one could keep a secret, that one is a blabbermouth. These seven youngsters are like barnyard animals; they wouldn't lift a finger if one of them were to be singled out, they wouldn't hide their friend or help him escape, they would hand him over. Rough-hewn faces, all—they'd never appear in a chocolate ad. During the afternoon rush, the people of Kandor are on display; they dress fairly well now, unobtrusively, they don't talk much, their smiles, too, are controlled, sparing. Discreetly, with re-strained eagerness, they look over the more unusual-looking pas-sengers and skip the duller ones, although a few discriminating youngsters give the old-timers a long, encouraging appraisal. Two girls standing next to Dragomán discuss the highlights of a vol-leyball game, their quivering leg muscles firmly supporting them.

Both of them know they'll have husbands, a home, children—nothing fazes them. On the train Dragomán sits down and closes his eyes—now he feels close to the people around him. He wouldn't mind if the roaring subway suddenly became one of those old-fashioned trains and cut through the suburbs above-ground. Before long there would be conversation: Where are you off to then? The subway pulls into a station, the doors fling open with a thud, Dragomán is jostled along by the crowd onto the escalator, where he now watches those descending on the other side. He looks back at the tunnel, the depths he emerged from. Moving up, he sees there's farther to go, the light is far away.

At the Tango a group called Skins sounds raw; over cappuccino Dragomán and his good-looking friend Marton conclude that the Lebanon red he got him was the best ever, it glistens for hours, it opens up new vistas. Sirens screech from the speakers, drums reverberate, followed by the rattle of machine guns. A blond boy, the back of his head shaved, slumps on a bar stool and dunks a croissant in his coffee. A saxophone wails, its ball is muffled, what comes out sounds like a goat's bleat. An older man's growl blends with the heavy-metal music, his gray mustache and skimpy ponytail sway to the beat. A woman in red pants, leather jacket, and cowboy boots is making entries in a notebook. A rat creeps on her shoulder; when she pauses in her writing she licks the rat's pink tail.

Dragomán returns to the Crown, the doorman greets him with a friendly hello, his mail has been placed in his room. From the roof terrace Resurrection Square and the hotel's garden look captivatingly beautiful, Dragomán thinks he's a fool not to be staying here permanently. A visitor rings the bell, a young man introduces himself. Dragomán doesn't catch his name, but the visitor proceeds to tell Dragomán that he's read his essay on the esthetics and erotics of fire. He wishes he himself had written this brilliant piece, it would have been even more convincing, one would have got a better sense of what fatal attraction to fire means—he could tell Dragomán was not a true fire worshipper. When he set fire to one of the Kandor's nightclubs with a can of kerosene, the joy he felt while fleeing the scene was ineffable. He doesn't have much time, he believes they're after him, he didn't try to cover his face when he came up. Time is of the essence, he decided—he must meet the author. How did he find out his room number? Let that remain a secret. But what he'd really like to ask is if he could still hope. The maestro should take a good look at him, front and back, he wants to be the maestro's lover, he'll cater to his every desire. You're too kind, but no thank you, Dragomán says. He offers his young visitor some tea. I like it with lots of sugar, the boy says. While Dragomán goes out to the tiny kitchen to get more sugar, his guest leaps over the terrace railing and falls six stories, landing on the side of the blue-tiled swimming pool. People rush over: He's dead. Dragomán sits down in the rocking chair. Come what may.

Fifteen minutes later the police are at the door. That boy may have been thrown from the window. So he was the one who set fire to the theater. But why did he come to you? Was he an old friend, a former student? You didn't know him, you say? Never met him before? He knew you but only by reputation? The erotics of fire, hm. Could there be some connection between your writing and the fire at the theater? To the young police officer, who was only doing his job, Dragomán seemed increasingly suspicious. He would let him go only if the mayor gave his word that his friend would not leave Kandor.

"You can't leave now," Tombor said to Dragomán as he got out of his car in front of the police station. He hurried up the stairs, took Dragomán by the arm, who turned on him: "I won't stay another minute in this crazy town. And your word of honor is your affair." Tombor bowed his head. "Just joking," Dragomán added, "I'll stay. It's easier to slip out of handcuffs than from your official word of honor. A madman barges into my room, jumps out of the window, an overzealous detective thinks I had something to do with arson at a music hall, as well as other acts of madness, all because of something I wrote. You really think a writer is responsible for his reader's obsessions? Some guy appears from nowhere and leaps out the window—it could happen to anyone."

The incident caused shock and revulsion among the hotel guests; they kept eyeing Dragomán, and seeing him in the elevator, demanded an explanation. "I have never defenestrated anyone," Dragomán replied. "Why would I throw a complete stranger out of my window?" A silver-haired lady looked rather mysteriously into the elevator mirror: "I assume you've heard of *actes gratuites*. One may get a sudden urge to throw somebody out of the window." "Has this ever happened to you, madam?" Dragomán inquired. "And to you?" asked the silver-haired lady.

A Would-Be Assassin
in a Long Coat

In the early-morning hours of November 4, 1956, when cannon fire woke up the city of Budapest, I lay next to Laura on a narrow daybed off the kitchen, in a small alcove that used to be the maid's room. Laura had left the bed we shared in her own, much larger room around three a.m.—she must have been cold and wondering why I wasn't beside her. Actually, I'd been up most of the night writing a paper in which I entertained a single question: Why is it that what seems so natural now—a parliamentary democracy—for years did not seem natural at all? Was it lack of imagination? The belief that only what's possible is natural? I'd kept myself awake with cup after cup of very strong tea, and now I was cold, too. Cuddling up to Laura I tried to fall asleep. The day before—November 3—I was awash with hope and confidence. We had become a neutral, multiparty democracy, it was our turn now to show what we had in us. My friends and I could finally launch our new periodical, *Experiment.* My gun on my shoulder, I had gone to see the director of the publishing company, and he had surprised me by acceding to every one of my requests. "It's agreed then: we'll publish your journal in sixty thousand copies." From now on, I decided, what you see is what you get. I won't need the gun that I kept in the linen closet, although it was reassuring to know I had it; I'd better not surrender it just yet. If armed men should come for me, if anyone should threaten to take me away, I would shoot…I kept musing in the dark, while pressing against Laura's behind. At twenty-three I was still close to the daydreams with which I amused myself at thirteen. There was a sag in the old daybed which brought us especially close.

The moment of awakening was the same for just about everyone. Women and men sat up in their beds in exactly the same way, the men pretending to be military experts—yes, that sounded like a T54 tank. Everyone turned on their radios to hear words that would be quoted decades later in every newspaper: "Soviet troops entered the territory of our country with the clear-cut purpose of overthrowing its legitimate government. Our men are fighting on." But if that's the case, we will, if not jump, at least stagger out of bed. I couldn't have known then that by the time I stepped out of the building, the legitimate Hungarian government would already have sought asylum at the Yugoslav embassy. It was dark in the maid's room where Laura and I were snuggling, but she already knew what was on my mind, even before I had actually thought it. She knew that I wouldn't stay put, I'd have to go, they were shooting outside, even if not in the immediate vicinity, my country needed me. I was summoned by a categorical imperative and the voice of the Lord, so it was all right to make love one more time, I had it coming to me. At times like this, reasonable people stay in bed.

The better class of people go off to battle in clean underwear, after their morning shower and breakfast of soft-boiled eggs and tea. I traipsed down the stairs with my machine gun slung over my shoulder; nobody stuck out their head as I passed their doors, though I did hear faint squeaks as they opened and closed the peephole cover. On the street, to my left, I saw a column of tanks rolling down the boulevard, an endless line moving from east to west. I concealed myself under the arcades of tall buildings, and inched closer to a main thoroughfare. A man called out from a doorway and pulled me in: "If they see that gun, they'll blow your brains out." Come to think of it, why was I carrying that weapon? There were crates full of guns at the university. I needed to get there, and not think about why. But then a quick decision: I ran home, put the gun back in the closet, drank another mug of hot tea, slipped a copy of Merleau-Ponty's *Les aventures de la dialectique* into my satchel, and set out again. On the boulevard, a space opened up between two columns of tanks, so a few pedestrians risked crossing. Soldiers on top of an armored car looked on impassively. Quick, into a sidestreet; someone might see me from a window or through a doorway. In an empty lot weapons were handed down from a truck. We heard news about successful rebel resistance.

I arrive, the guards recognize me, I go up to the dean's office where the revolutionary committee is supposed to be meeting. I see only a few people and then spot Lona wearing blue ski pants and a blue-and-yellow pullover. She holds out her hand with natural dignity. What's up, you want to know? We are just hanging around, printing leaflets, consulting, making phone calls, keeping the channels of communication open. Plenty of guns and canned ham to go around. The Russians haven't yet attacked the university building, and we haven't targeted them either. Most of the government buildings have been taken over, but the university is still ours. I call Laura to tell her I am all right, there is a lull in the fighting. Laura says she's making bean soup for lunch with the leftover smoked meat.

Wandering about, turning up everywhere, are the more eccentric and bumptious humanities students, who for various reasons are convinced that history cannot march on without them. Let's face it, I am one of them. My conceit knows no bounds. Several pairs of eyes are on me, I am not alone, what I decide to do has weight, moral significance.

Existentialism reached Hungary, or at least my intellectual horizon, in the mid-1950s, though it was a distillation of an earlier generation's war experience. In war, things happen without rhyme or reason; one does whatever one does to fill one's stomach, to survive, and one may make it even if it means losing a few friends or killing a few disagreeable individuals. This generation provided belated moral justification for the things that were behind them, things that had to be remembered, unpleasant as that may have been.

Lona held forth on Camus. I also read *The Stranger,* and believed that no other novel had opening lines quite as mercilessly perfect. Lona was more advanced: she also read *Les Noces,* and translated a chapter from *The Myth of Sisyphus.* She kept nodding: this was real literature, dark, sharp, an immediate classic. But any writer who pleased Lona was not good enough for me. The only way to guard against envy is to love, Goethe said that, and I was bent on heeding his advice—I tried not to hate Camus. I could have countered her praises by scoffing at the existentialists; and if I had said clever things about them, Lona would have anticipated the next disparagement with interest and a degree of uncertainty. But I tried not to express too many opinions. If something was new to me, I tried to see it on its own terms, even if it was not really to my liking. We talked about the Surrealists: poets, painters, a parade of names. Lona's diction was slow, precise, deliberate—nothing she did was ever hasty. I'd show her how a gun worked. She might be wearing Chanel Number Five and a silk scarf around her neck, but she watched intently. A painter's name was mentioned, a "real" one—before long the word "authentic" was used.

It was common knowledge that I was her number-one love, while her husband, Emil, a passive, pleasant enough man in duck trousers and a tweed jacket, merely escorted her everywhere. He listened to the conversation, but interesting words rarely left his lips. I knew him as an editor and could see the considerable slack he gave her; she could leave his side to join me for an intimate chat by the dark window. Keeping my eyes on the street below, I put my arms around her, my chin close to her ear. We heard a rumble, a tank made half-turn, its turret popping into our field of vision and aimed straight at our window. Leaning against the wide window frame, I tried to see what this tank was up to. Nothing much, I surmised, but the moment was extraordinary enough for me to want to breathe in again and again the fragrance of Lona's hair.

Guard duty over, the couples dispersed to study halls and classrooms, taking with them their folding mattresses and blankets. Lona returned to Emil, I didn't even look to see which way they went. I had things to do in the room where leaflets and flyers were being produced. This was the intellectual unit; what we had to do was to dissuade the occupying soldiers, in Russian, from committing shameful acts, and shock them into acknowledging the Marxist truth that no nation oppressing another nation can ever be free. In my version the Russian sentences turned out a little convoluted, the text read more like a term paper than a leaflet. It was voted unanimously to shorten and simplify it. I agreed to the cuts graciously, but I did not compose any more leaflets.

The night passed: distant screams and gasps. I don't remember where I slept, I may have found space on one of the gym mats, or in a room piled with uniforms and quilted jackets. The university came alive during those few days; trucks stood at the students' disposal in the courtyard, and on the upper floors were crates filled with guns still greasy in their wax-paper wraps. There were also piles of wood shavings needed to protect the more valuable goods, the shipments of cans of ham and peach preserves Otto Hapsburg had sent to the heroic Hungarian youth. I thought I was watching an endless movie: human apparitions, Russian soldiers or Hungarian students, faded in and out puffing and blowing, and I watched them so they would be seen, and instilled in the mind, since events gain meaning only after the fact. During the night someone discharged his gun accidentally while cleaning it, and though the room was full of people, no one was hurt.

I slept for a few hours, then lay awake asking myself, What am I doing here? Humanists with guns, one of my professors had remarked. There were no small-town boys among us, at most a few miners. There were, however, quite a few young instructors from blue-collar families who taught Marxism-Leninism. And of course Jewish boys—poets, critics, enthusiastic skeptics. The radical fringe, in short. Most of my classmates felt it was best not to get involved in these events, just as one didn't get mixed up in street brawls. But I did get involved. A large crowd watched a fight at University Place. Two men were beating a third; they knocked him down, he stood up, they knocked him down again, he rose again. I walked over; my friend Kobra followed reluctantly. Now we'll have to fight? Could be. We might have to, but should we? Why can't Dragomán keep still? Why must he be the one to set things right? There is no need to fight. Watch me. "Don't hurt that man. Aren't you ashamed of yourselves? Two against one?" The sort of things one says to children. And instead of letting me have it too, with a gesture that said: You know, he's right, they let the poor devil go, tucked in their shirts, smoothed their hair, and the people on University Place had to look elsewhere for excitement.

The students sat in a circle; some of us had already killed someone, most hadn't. By early morning the discussion still centered on the same issue. We students, who had come together from various schools and universities and were joined by girlfriends and boyfriends, had to decide who the enemy was, and what we were fighting for. Were we here to defend the university? Should we let the guns and mortars set up on top of Mount Gellért assault and destroy it? Or should we fight on to the last bullet, our last drop of blood, retreat from room to room, and perish in the rubble? Whether posterity declared us counter-revolutionaries or martyrs was their affair. A young man from a poor peasant family, his own face full of stubborn lumps and knots, felt we should hold out. Let's stay here and become an island of resistance, he said. With other such islands we can keep the fire of resistance burning until the world's indignation forces the Russians to negotiate, and eventually they will recognize the neutrality and sovereignty of Hungary.

We only had to define this "until." Until when, exactly, do we resist? The last bullet? The last drop of blood? The humanities students were of the opinion that ordinary Russian soldiers were not guilty. Over the past several days we had talked with them. I even ate with them in a makeshift mess, where, as members of the hastily formed National Guard, we laid our weapons on the floor. We ate and talked—the Russian boys said the same thing as the Hungarian policemen: they wanted to get this over with and go home to Mother or to their sweetheart. But they couldn't, of course. Orders are orders, brother; you break our hearts, but we still have to shell your apartment buildings. So we thanked them for their good borscht, picked up our weapons, and went on our way. And remained alone with our doubts in the early-morning fog.

Then suddenly the fog lifted, and sunlight illuminated the windows. I came forward with a suggestion. We couldn't hold out for more than a few days. There were pockets of resistance, but in a matter of days it would all be over. We must plan an underground network, I said; for the time being, our main task should be to prevent the establishment of a collaborationist government. We must get rid of the quislings moving between the Soviets and the civilian population. I got excited justifying my own strategic position. But we all felt the weight of our own decisions; there was no higher authority telling us what to do. Should the general strike continue? If so, for how long? Should we go on shooting from cellars or attics, like desperadoes, with blind determination? But shoot at whom? The Soviets? There were too many of them, and too few collaborators. The Soviet soldiers did what they had to, while the cooperating Hungarians, we felt, were traitors.

We must use terror against them, fire indiscriminately at militiamen, assassinate members of the traitorous Kádár regime, to frighten the waverers and discourage them from accepting the new state of affairs. The occupiers must be isolated, ringed with hostility, to make them realize that they were alone. And we should set up an underground government, a truly revolutionary polity, which the populace would embrace, and continue where we'd left off on November 3. What was needed, in short, was the creation of another, invisible, state. It was an attractively youthful idea, although how the spirit of an independent government could be reconciled with the use of terror wasn't clear. Some approved, the more mature among us shook their heads, and the oldest person there suggested that I take a gun, go out on the street, size up the situation, and if I found that I could actually shoot a collaborationist militiaman, do it. Then I should try to get back before dark and tell the others about my experiment.

"Be careful," a guard says as he lets me out on the street. "It's quiet now, go that way." So a man with long hair, wearing a cheap winter coat, leaves a university building to take a stroll. He feels his pockets: pistol, switchblade, apple, fountain pen, notebook. He's got what he needs. Stay close to the wall now, blend into the gray plaster wall of the Red Elephant Inn. This is the place where professors and students, after receiving their paychecks or stipends, would head, and feast on meats set out in large, sectioned serving dishes.

A burst of gunfire; somebody pulls me into the restaurant. "I see you have a pistol in your pocket," the waiter says. "You keep feeling it. Relax." The cook says, "I am Wilma. You recognize me, I hope." And she puts a nice piece of meat on a slice of bread. "What brings you here," asks Dezsö, the waiter. "I'm on my way home from the university, and I thought I'd take a look around." "You can stop shooting then, we're outnumbered," Dezsö says.

Wilma and Dezsö came in to keep an eye on things and thought they might as well have a little snack. "There's still plenty of us left," I say. "Don't start shooting from here," the waiter warns. "I have no intention of shooting." "You can't fool a mother, young man," Wilma says. "Here, take this piece of buttered bread. When you reach into your pocket, grab it instead." And they pushed me out the door as fast as they'd pulled me in.

People saunter between the tanks, the soldiers inside smoke. The large bakeries are operating at full capacity, in the local bake shop they say there'll soon be fresh bread. A long line of people wait outside. There is a sound of machine gun fire, and everyone presses against the wall. Fortunately it came from the next street over. A truck has arrived with fresh bread, the driver gets admiring glances from the crowd. Anyone taking home a whole loaf of still warm bread is buoyed by this quasi-military victory.

I meet my neighbor Diósi, who wears a bulging knapsack on his back. "Where have you been?" To the Baku nightclub, he tells me, where he filled his sack with bottles of good liquor. Looting is in full swing on Rákoczi Street. The Russians broke into a few shops, and the mob followed them inside. But in this revolution even the mob shows restraint, though Mr. Diósi, a respectable businessman, is not ashamed of having swiped a few bottles of brandy from the Baku bar, perhaps heeding a patriotic instinct—punishing the Soviet Union by degrading the capital of one of the member republics. Every sip of this brandy will be a little punishment. The image is familiar. In 1945, at the age of twelve, I saw Ukrainian soldiers breaking into perfumery shops and lifting industrial-size perfume bottles off the shelves—bottles from which the shopkeeper would measure out smaller amounts. They knew exactly what they wanted, Chat Noir, mostly, that was the best for drinking. Arms around each other's shoulders, they took big swigs, belching fragrantly. And the locals took what was left over.

On November 6, 1956, the city inside a ring of armored cars seemed to revive. The general strike was on, but children needed bread and milk. Everyone had the day off, everyone walked the streets. Militia members in their gray quilted jackets mingled with the crowd. The same street corners, the same faces, but they gave the tanks a wide berth now, didn't fraternize with the enemy, people no longer believed that the intruders could be persuaded to leave peacefully. They walked around the tanks as though around roadblocks.

Loden coats, windbreakers, and even some finer garments. I am wearing a long, scratchy, heavy rather than warm overcoat, with a deep inside pocket where I keep a pistol. With this pistol I must bump somebody off, though I still don't know who. If I manage to carry out my plan, I will have justified it. The deep pocket can also hold books and a notepad.

In the distance a man in a gray coat and gray hat walks, carrying a tattered flag. Someone fires at him but misses. Dust, rubbish, broken glass, severed wires, turned-over vehicles, breakdown and disorder everywhere. But then I step into a telephone booth; the phone works. I call Laura; she picks up. "I am on the street, I still have to do a few things, take a look around, I'll see you soon. No, I can't stay, I've got to come back." "Why?" Laura asks. "Who says you have to?" "See you," I say curtly and step out of the glass booth, on which a brand-new bullet hole with cracks radiating in all directions tells me it was time to end the conversation.

The question remains: Whom do I bump off? Can I sit in my easy chair reading books when justice demands an armed defense? I have a right to carry a gun, I am officially a revolutionary, a member of the National Guard, I even have a piece of paper to prove it. I do feel like carrying out my plan, and proving that I am not just playing with words but mean what I say. I will shoot someone with my Browning, which I found among a stack of handguns. I have a sentimental attachment to Brownings, my father kept one in the dressing table, above which, in a mirror held up by angels of a Baroque bedroom set, he could spot an intruder. A man protects his own. Should he hear a suspicious noise, he gets out of bed and with a flashlight in one hand and a pistol in the other, walks toward the source. Later, I couldn't stop laughing at stories of husbands who, bent on protecting their families, mistake their wives for burglars and shoot them by mistake, even though the poor woman was only coming back from the kitchen with a glass of water.

I'm all set to find my victim, bearing in mind that I may have to stab him with my pocketknife. There has to be someone, a henchman of the new rulers, a traitor who must be dealt with accordingly, a member of the new police force, or better yet, somebody really important. Yes, I will roam the streets; by tonight I have to become a murderer, if only to prove that this was not a farce. For if I don't find anyone to shoot, then my carrying this pistol and this knife is nothing, an adolescent prank. In these situations one must anticipate, which doesn't of course mean that I should bump off the first person I see who's gone over to the enemy, though he may deserve that. My would-be victim has to be someone who's using force to oppose the will of the majority. He started it, he's working with the foreign occupiers. He's taken up arms against us, and by God, he'll perish by force of arms.

Until now I had not joined the ranks of the rebels; it didn't suit my character. Fighting alongside self-styled guerrilla bands or paramilitary units, however colorful their garb, held no attraction for me. What suited me was to wander about in my long overcoat, wait for my victim, stalk him, confront him, and shoot him. But not immediately, not the minute I saw him, not on the basis of some identifying mark or insignia, like an armband. His death could not be impersonal, but should be tailor-made for him. The victim must deserve the death he dies; and for that I must first make his acquaintance.

Then again, I could go home and spend the day with Laura. We could get into profound conversations about these matters, which would probably end in a rebuke from her. I should sit down and quit being so impetuous and stupid, she'd say. Or, if I was so restless, I ought to take my knapsack and try to get some food, our supplies were running low. If I didn't feel like doing that, I could read something worthwhile, stretch out on the sofa and consider that while my body is frail, all those tanks on the street are not— they constitute reality, whereas I with my vest-pocket arsenal am a self-created illusion.

It is our duty to resist, another voice says, even if we know we can't win. The revolution succeeded in destroying the inner core of the old system; we have to compel the Russians to negotiate with us. An underground government must be formed which would be in a position to negotiate. There must also be a government in the West, a government in exile, that can represent the legitimate revolutionary Hungary before the United Nations. If the occupiers do not find collaborators, sooner or later they will be forced to compromise—if the Hungarian question can be kept alive till then. This is most important. The cause must not be allowed to fade away, the question mustn't be taken off the agenda. The existence of a guerrilla movement would prove that the country could not be pacified. If the world sees that Hungary remains defiant, then with UN mediation or intercession, a compromise could be worked out between an underground or émigré Hungarian government on the one hand and the Russians on the other. Even then we would only work on easing the pain of defeat, insisting, for instance, that no more people be imprisoned, and that political prisoners still held should be released. We could say we will experiment with some form of enlightened, self-reforming communism in return for a looser association with the Soviet bloc.

AMONG THE PEDESTRIANS I notice Andor Késmárki, my former classmate, the perennial crusader and purifier, who had a knack for creating theories out of his obsessions, and whose paranoia enabled him to discover actual conspiracies. Here was the always unexpected visitor of the past few years, who would appear suddenly to acquaint me with his latest readings and offer me a critique of new and dangerous philosophies, always keen to find out what I thought. Here he stood: tall, attractive, clean-shaven, like a movie actor fully clothed in Marxism-Leninism, over which he wore the quilted jacket of the new militia, and over his shoulder, a gun. Why did fate have to bring me this idiot? I should have it out with him, he deserved it, if only because he wanted me to marry Irene, whose single incontrovertible and invaluable virtue was an honest-to-goodness working-class background. Was he my man, then? Should I finish him off? I urged myself to watch my step, to find the right word, the right move. Should I call out his name and then shoot? His face would reveal a double surprise: recognizing a fellow student, then being shot by him in the stomach. And what would I do afterward? Run? Or stay and explain to other sterling patriots that the man was obviously a traitor, because he had joined the new militia? The majority would surely not approve of the man, but it was doubtful that the same majority would approve of the execution-style murder of a young man named Andor Késmárki.

I didn't have a chance to think it through, for at this point Késmárki greeted me. "How are you then? May I see your identity card?" There was sardonic curiosity in his eyes. A few days earlier he had appeared in front of the law school, where I was on guard duty, protecting with machine gun a meeting of the Young Intellectuals' Revolutionary Committee on the second floor. "Will you let me in?" Késmárki had asked. "Only if I have to," I said. "You are here spying, I take it." "That's right, I'll look around, listen, and maybe learn something." It was clear to me that Késmárki was a secret agent; his philosophy was a secret agent's philosophy. I reached into my pocket now, fumbled about for my ID card and pulled it out. I could see that the militiaman in him felt the fumbling took longer than necessary. He looked at the card, which had Laura's picture tucked into it—I'd slipped it in there so it wouldn't get creased.

"You are not permitted to place any other item inside your ID card. I hereby confiscate the photograph," he said. "At this point it may be premature to detain you. But may I remind you that I am authorized to conduct a body search. Go home to your wife, and don't let yourself be talked into anything. And don't worry: arresting officers usually come to the house, they don't catch you on the street." Késmárki saluted and turned around. Now I could easily shoot him in the back.

Laura has rearranged my room. From the depths of her closet she pulled out a tapestry and a bedspread. She also covered my table with green velvet and placed a Buddha-faced Chinese vase on it. She picks up my coat and is shocked at how heavy it is. She notices the revolver. "You carry this around? Why?" "Just in case." "In case what?" "You never know." I don't dare admit to her that I'm on a trial run, that I have to deliver a scalp by the end of the day. Instead of complying with Késmárki's directive and returning home to Laura, I should have gone after him and given him the works. We should emulate the resolve of assassins. Instead I compliment her on the soup she made and on her decorating skills. I put on my heavy coat. Laura doesn't move from her chair, and offers only her forehead for a peck. On the table I notice Merleau-Ponty's *Les aventures de la dialectique.* In the stairwell I hear the neighbor's dog yelp.

On the street corner, cautious footsteps and leaflets from the Soviet commandant: "Resistance will result in heavy reprisals." At the university the guards welcome me back. "What's going on?" "Utter confusion and helplessness," I tell them. I got nowhere with my plan and so the group morale is weakened. I return the gun to the head of the revolutionary committee. At the dean's office the majority is of the opinion that we cannot undermine all ties between the enemy and the collaborators; the instruments of power are in the occupied hands. What remains is continued harassment. In time, the majority will inevitably submit to the occupying army. If we continue the armed struggle, we become fanatics, assassins. But if we lay down our arms, we have laid down our arms. We settle for a modus vivendi, latency, we choose a cautious, long-range, historical strategy. I tell them about Késmárki. There is not much debate; if they attack, we defend ourselves. But there's been no attack. Then we receive news that several students at the school of art have been shot, and the authorities are combing through the nearby buildings. If more students are found, they'll be dragged to the courtyard and summarily executed.

One of our more mercurial classmates arrives and urges us to go to the barracks at the edge of the city. He's got hold of two trucks, we should hurry, that's the place to be now. But why should we go there, I ask. People are being mowed down. How? With mortar fire from a hilltop. But how can we fight back from the barracks with only machine guns? You're right, we can't. Then why go there? Don't you understand? We die together. I *don't* understand. Lona wants to go, I don't let her, I hold down her hand as she is about to clamber onto the truck.

A Soviet officer approaches with a white flag and hands us a note in Russian. If we don't vacate the university by the following morning, their tanks will demolish the building. If we want to save our school, we should go home. So we take our papers and one by one sneak out of the building, leaving behind a truck, a cache of weapons, and dozens of canned hams.

Several days later I stand guard at the entrance of our apartment house. Behind the closed gates of the building, the male tenants serve as sentries in two-man shifts. I didn't bring my gun; I left it in the linen closet. My partner is a famous concertmaster, a coolly polite, absentminded man blessed with a large mother-in-law and an equally large wife and children. Panting, roly-poly creatures with heads lolling sideways surround this still-angular man, who's done the best he could: he reduced his practice time, so the sound of his violin is heard less frequently. He's even begun to resemble his family. The concertmaster didn't expect history to produce a more reasonable turn of events. "Everybody abandons you eventually. And you don't believe it until it happens to you. We Hungarians have always paid a heavy price for our leaders' gullibility. We believed the Germans. Where did it get us? We believed the Russians, and look what that got us into. Now we believed that the Americans would help, that the Russians would relent and not dare do this to us, because of world public opinion."

I thought at the time that the world would overwhelm me with its richness. I'd surely have something to write about. It's all there before me: reprisal, resistance, concealment, a wide range of human responses. The heroes and scoundrels are out in full force. "We shall abandon ourselves, too, in the end," says the concertmaster. "If you hold out, you'll notice that your friends are still here but saying different things. Be skeptical, young man, especially when hope stirs. Hope drags you down into the pit. Which could mean a mass grave. I have my music, at least. I cling to my violin, I exist through it. I understand you chose the art of writing. Develop a secret code, that's my advice."

Before long the shops are open, there's finally something to eat. The Writers and Artists House distributes care packages to its members. As the assistant editor of a new literary magazine, I am entitled to a few packages myself. The old-timers hold meetings, but when bullets ring out in Könyv Street, one of them throws himself on the floor and curses himself, in French, for having come back from Paris. Stray bullets graze the walls of the building, but they are merely warning shots from a tank rolling down the street. We turn off the light and watch from behind the heavy curtains as two boys with machine guns race across the street and jump over a low garden gate. The door of the house is locked. They look around helplessly. There's nowhere to go, all the doors are shut tight. "We should let them in here." "Are you crazy? You want them to start shooting from here? And invite the tanks to converge and blow up the building?" So we don't let the boys in, and are relieved to see that they've turned the corner. On all the shelves, there are papers and official statements exuding dignity. People still come in now and then, a group arrives from the Russian headquarters: the country's leading intellectuals are invited for talks. To talk or resist, that's the question. The hotheads and the realists are locked in a debate, but the steam has gone out of it, it's all empty rhetoric and grandstanding. At this point, we still can't imagine that people like us will be kicked out of this building and from every university and editorial office. That the losers will disperse and won't feel like commiserating with one another.

The Incident

Word has it that Tombor has been preparing for this day in a big way; in the garden his assistants and his groupies are in a state of excitement. Now every encounter and conversation is fast becoming history. He wants to see an explosion of stars, is inviting his guests to step right up, participants as well as onlookers—he wants hundreds of hours of tape of this happening, this extravaganza.

It will take place down at the bay. Tombor reserved rooms in the city's better hotels, the police will patrol the roads leading to the festival, throngs of out-of-towners are expected, he had a large area by the lake roped off for parking. As you step out of your car, you get a whiff of oxen roasting on a spit, and before you start mingling, a chef in a tall hat offers you a piece of roast on a slice of bread and a glass of wine.

The stage manager of the affair keeps his distance from the spectacle. With whimsical randomness he's assembled a motley cast of characters. He oversees the preparations: the cameras and microphones fastened to the tree branches, the Chinese lanterns with their unusual glow, the floodlights placed on pedestals emitting colorful beams, and the huge barges moored in the lake and fitted out with dance floors. He walks into the control booth and trains a camera on his wife in the distance, scrutinizing her from various angles as she walks from her garden to the church ruins and back again. As mayor and filmmaker, Tombor could pick the perfect setting for the occasion: the hillside next to the church ruins and the sacred spring, right by the pilgrims' chapel where

Gypsies hold their annual fair. If unexpected things happen, so much the better.

He invited his former classmates and political associates, artist friends and drinking companions. Extremists of one kind or another, he felt, must be brought closer together; it's important to have them seen assembled. He also invited the new loudmouths; every new bounder is offered a seat—either he'll hold on to it, or he won't. Actually, it's not people who make up the show but a new set of rules, and Tombor understands the essence of the new style. He has an acute sense of what the world around him needs, and he is pleased to oblige. He is also capable of doing nothing. He jogs in the woods, the soles of his feet welcome the ground's springy softness. He rests on a tree stump, looks at the mossy bark, presses a pine cone, lets his eyes travel up all the way to the clouds, inspects the cracks in every rock, and keeps an eye on the pheasants strutting in the valley, along the bank of a stream.

At the mayor's side is Kuno Aba, the rector of the university and deputy mayor of the city. Aba was in third grade when Dragomán entered first, yet the impossible happened: the two became friends in the schoolyard. As time went on they raced their motorbikes, itching for a collision; they tried to beat each other at Indian wrestling, or to see who could eat more apricot dumplings in one sitting, or to memorize more Latin words in an hour. They competed at composing Dadaist sonnets while lying on the beach with their eyes closed. They took turns winning. Not even at school dances did one have a clear edge over the other.

Perhaps that was why they had divided the city between them, as well as every other area of mutual interest. The blond prince and the black prince agreed that Kuno was the classic Machiavellian, practical, while the cynical-romantic Dragomán could never be persuaded that some things *are* real, or at least correspond to what's real. He dared to put moral outrage above mere experience, believing that if one goes along with whatever happens, one's thinking becomes as flat as a toad run over by a truck.

In his last year at the university, Kuno Aba conducted a history seminar, and also served as guide to a group of cave explorers. Dragomán studied English, Kuno studied German. Dragomán learned English from his grandmother while walking her to the tennis court, whereas Aba learned German from his mother, whose father had been a law professor in Berlin. Kuno Aba was better at rhetoric, capable of bursting into oratory with an utterly straight face, and charming his interlocutor as he made a fool of him. Dragomán was low-key, exaggeratedly so, verging on self-mockery.

On November 10, 1956, the occupiers decided that rather than going after the rebels, it might be better to lure them out of their mountain hideout. A whole caravan made its way up the winding road. The commandant himself shouted into a bullhorn: "We win, you lose. We are many, you are few. Resistance is foolish. Come out and hand over your guns. And go to biblioteka to study. You must serve world peace and eternal Soviet-Hungarian friendship."

From the cave's mouth Dragomán took aim. He asked no questions, he didn't think, he fired and hit his target. As a child Dragomán was quite a marksman with an air gun. At fairs he'd win furry monkeys and kaleidoscopes. Since 1944 he's been of the opinion that if they hunt you down, you'd better know how to shoot back. A hunter would think twice before shooting a rabbit if he knew that the rabbit had a gun. That day in the woods Dragomán was particularly annoyed. He wanted to take pictures, and a sharpshooter shot his Leica right out of his hand without even grazing him. All the same, he now had a murder on his conscience. True, for someone like the commandant a chest wound was an occupational hazard. Still, a sniper has reason to be appalled at himself.

Thirty years had to pass before he would pick up a gun again and shoot. He went on a field trip in Israel, accompanying a fellow professor, and agreed to be an armed escort. It never occurred to him that he might have to use the heavy machine gun he lugged. But when fire opened nearby, he pulled the gun off his shoulder fast, and flat on his stomach, began firing back. For a long time nobody moved, he motioned the children to stay down and crawl back. His guess proved correct: another round crackled right next to him. Again Dragomán lost no time, but a man riding a tractor on a hilltop was faster: he noticed another Arab behind a pile of rocks, and was probably a better shot than Dragomán, who thus became a killer a second time.

Both times he had reason to fire his gun; the Soviet colonel in '56 and the guerrilla died holding their weapons. Both times it was an even match, his targets were prepared, trained to kill, waiting for the opportunity. All Dragomán could say was that he was quicker. Those two also had a chance to bring him down. But he bears the responsibility for getting into these skirmishes in the first place. If he hadn't shot the colonel, then perhaps the pro-Soviet authorities would not have dealt so mercilessly with the armed students emerging from the woods. And he did say yes to coming on the field trip as an armed escort.

Once, returning from Berlin, Dragomán told a young girl at the Kandor airport, a student from Scandinavia, that the taxis at the end of the line were cheaper, she should take one of those. The Mercedes cabs parked up front, their drivers, the "hyenas," charged twice or three times the regular fare. One such hyena got very angry, but Dragomán ignored him and kept walking toward the end of the line. "I'll bash your skull in, you bastard," the hyena said. "Scared to turn around, eh? I'll rip your guts out, I'll see you rot in the jewghetto." Suddenly, Dragomán turned around and swiftly kicked the man in the stomach. By now the other hyenas came over, but a taxi rolled by with a weight-lifter-looking driver at the wheel, whom the hyenas didn't want to cross. Dragomán got in; the driver said he was impressed with the youthful energy of that kick.

Inside the car Dragomán began to expound on his theory that what was feasible was never desirable, and what is desirable is not practical. There are no good nations. The generosity of the wealthy? All the beauty around here comes from arm dealer's profits. A civil society? The tyranny of conventions brooks no exceptions. The masses can be self-indulgent, grasping, stingy, and selfish. Or they can be community-minded and selfless. Better to be a philistine than a revolutionary. It's less disturbing to have them shopping at the mall than starting a new movement. The individualist may be too concerned with money, but the collectivist is a fanatic. Since man cannot be saved from death, it makes no sense to speak about utopias. "What do you think of all this, my friend?" "Every word is pure gold, chief," the cabby said enigmatically.

Kuno Aba owns a house by the lake, where he spends

weekends with his second wife, Sandra, his first wife having committed suicide. In the garden Aba is now relating a somewhat re-
touched story to his guests. Back in '56 he fought alongside the
students. Six of them died; he was injured and managed to limp
home. The burden of memory was harder on his first wife than
on him.

In an impromptu lecture series held in his house, Kuno Aba
made a return to an ancient and sacred golden age sound desirable indeed. But since the time for that much-longed-for return
has not yet arrived, and because in private Kuno Aba speaks with
contempt about the masses and democracy, about a decline that
has been going on for several thousand years, producing epochs
that are a far cry from the great age of demigods and heroes,
whose secrets only he can unlock—anyway, for all these reasons,
as a practical matter, our job is to wait and bear witness.

A teacher is always responsible for his student; no relationship
is more noble than that between master and disciple. Kuno Aba
recommends compromise and pretense. Recognizing the reality
of the existing balance of power, he feels it his duty, as part of his
rescue mission, to be a member of every elite that comes along.
Let's learn to navigate our flimsy boat in the swirling currents of
time, which never seem to favor us. In the interest of the institutions entrusted to our care, let's form a good working relationship with the powers that be. For the good of the city, we request
an audience, one that is morally justifiable, with whoever is in
power.

Requesting an audience is not tantamount to submission. Do
not sell yourself to the potentate of the hour. You are here and he
is there, sitting on the other side of the desk. You address him
from a realm of knowledge so abundant, you may as well appear
modest. Try to mollify the ruler, who is by nature vain and snob-
bish, and would therefore like to see the custodian of certain
knowledge on his side. But never turn into a courtier; be a styl-
ishly infrequent guest at court. Impress on the knights of the moment the need for continuity, so that they will have a sense of
tradition, and feel one with those who once lived here.

In 1990, a year of momentous changes, Kuno Aba became rector of the university, and at the same time deputy mayor in
charge of cultural affairs. In a teasing manner he relates to

Melinda, the mayor's wife, his differences with his childhood friend. "I got married around that time, and managed to keep my bride's identity from Professor Dragomán, for he might have stolen her from me, using his all-condoning private brand of mysticism to confuse not only himself but my poor bride as well. At that time, thanks to the appearance of two snow-white pigeons and the illumination that followed, I became a firm believer in the power of extrasensory knowledge."

Kuno Aba told Dragomán: "Your rather idiosyncratic notion of freedom, sir"—at times he was quite formal with his friend— "allows you to go to bed with a different woman every night." Dragomán nodded his head guiltily. "The wanderer sleeps in a different place every night. It's a cruel world, you can get killed easily. There are dangers lurking everywhere, so you either crawl into a nonexistent mouse hole, or celebrate your wedding night every night."

Dragomán has had his fill of writing, reading, traveling, and meeting people. After a time, roaming feels like running in place. He is through professing, he's seen so many versions of the same roguery, he knows that good will never supplant evil. It's all madness. One kind today, another kind tomorrow. Grin and bear it. Have a nice day.

As an urbanist he was pleased when Tombor invited him to be one of his advisors. But then he learned that his friend intended to make him a spokesman, a speechwriter, a roving ambassador. "Are you mad?" he told him. "If God needed a speechwriter I'd write one or two for Him, as I do for my illiterate neighbor in the village, as a favor, but that would be it. What you want to do is press me into service. But don't you see? I am not part of any *we*...Oh all right, let's see what I can do for Kandor. My grandson does live here, after all."

Nobody knew that it was Dragomán who had shot the Russian commandant in '56. For his activities on the university's revolutionary committee, he was sentenced to a year and a half in prison. He spent the time on a prison farm and was not released until the spring of '59. After the commandant was shot, the Soviets began shelling the forest hideout. They needed someone who enjoyed the students' trust. There was only one such person, the university's independent spirit, Kuno Aba. The young history instructor asked the students to abandon their mountain hide-away and come down. They were promised safe passage by the Soviet commandant. Now Aba was shouting into a megaphone: "Let's end the bloodletting. Life must begin anew, we have to recognize that we are outnumbered and act accordingly." The students yielded to the voice of sobriety and reason.

Dragomán, on the other hand, had urged them to flee; he suspected a trap, but his argument didn't carry much weight. He'd rather die here, he said, in this cave, which could still provide a good firing position. His left foot was injured but he wouldn't let them drag him away. He remained at his post. "Try to hold out for a few more hours, don't turn me in," he asked the other six, who were shocked by Dragomán's injury and awed by his courage.

From the hilltop he saw the boys come out into the open field in the Valley of Mercy and approach the young professor. One after another they threw down their guns and stood in a line, whereupon the militiamen, emerging from the woods, riddled them with bullets, all six of them. Dragomán had joined this band of college-age irregulars only the day before—they called themselves the *arrière-garde révolutionaire,* since most of them were studying Romance languages.

They didn't shoot, they were shot by others. Dragomán did kill someone, but all they could do was injure him. It was he who hit the commandant, and in retaliation his fellow students were executed.

Kuno Aba was frantic. This was not the way it was supposed to happen, he said, this was betrayal—they had been promised safe passage. He was struck in the face with a rifle butt. He stood over the six dead bodies, cursing, blood streaming from his nose and mouth. Then the men in quilted jackets threw the bodies on a truck, got into a car and rumbled off on the narrow mountain pass.

From his ledge Dragomán called out: "Kuno Aba, I saw you." Hurt badly, giddy with pain, using a stick for support, he groped his way down. "We both deserve to die," he said. "One of us should answer for those six boys' death, either you or I." He had two pistols on him and handed one to his friend. "One of us surely deserves a bullet," Dragomán repeated deliriously. A rock-strewn valley, approximate dueling positions: they both fired and wounded each other. Each limped away in a different direction without looking back.

Dragomán dragged himself to Jeremiah Tombor's house. The old man hid him, called a doctor, and nursed him back to health. The then seven-year-old Melinda drew pictures, told him stories, baked cookies for him. Kuno Aba also found his way home, to his sister's. He told her that he too, had been shot by the militiamen, and fell down, but after they left he crawled to safety. And the rest? he was asked. They are still there.

But they weren't there anymore, just bloodstained grass. "They must have come back and picked them up," Kuno Aba said.

Dragomán is in the garden listening to Kuno Aba's refashioned tale. Among the guests is Sandra, the deputy mayor–rector's wife, who drinks in every detail of the heroic story. Kuno Aba looks at Dragomán and waits for confirmation. Dragomán nods; nobody here knows that he was the seventh. But Kuno Aba relates further details of the story, each detail more flattering to himself. He is Kandor's great survivor, a martyr, the man who rose from a mass grave—an icon.

Dragomán puts down his glass then and says: "Kuno Aba, I saw you." The rector rises. "And just what do you mean by that?" Dragomán rises, too. "I saw you." Then Dragomán takes a coin from his pocket. "Heads or tails. One of us remembers it wrong. If you win, my memory's playing tricks on me.…Ah, you lose. You really believe what you said? And if you don't, why say it? The bones of the dead rise from the ground."

Because of the live show and the terrible mishap that is about to occur, that night in Tombor's garden will long be remembered by the assembled crowd. Everything is being done for the sake of the film. Tombor, like a hunting dog, is aquiver with excitement, waiting for things to happen, wanting his film to be action-packed. His henchmen are everywhere, his cameramen trying to capture every showdown and scandal. The deputy mayor is suspicious of his boss, convinced that all this is being staged for the film, for a mere show, for the TV screen, for the director himself, and not for the city.

The cameras keep trailing Kuno Aba. Clearly this old story

involving him and Dragomán is moving toward a climax. Mr. Barnag, the police commissioner and member of the old establishment, is also present this evening, sipping champagne. His job used to be to find out as much as possible about Tombor and his circle, but gradually he had absorbed the very poison he was sent to root out as a department chief in the old security apparatus. Certain expressions from banned and confiscated literature, with which he had to familiarize himself in his work, had seeped into his vocabulary, so in time he himself became an object of suspicion, and his career suffered. But with the transition, Mr. Barnag's career took off again; he jumped several steps in the official hierarchy, and he now openly presents himself as an admirer of Tombor and his friends—all of which has prompted Kuno Aba to raise his left eyebrow, making Mr. Barnag a little more circumspect.

Kuno Aba is sitting on a garden bench, cameras whir around him. Dragomán approaches, followed by more cameras. Both men are slightly drunk; behind the cameras stand the eyewitnesses, the chorus. Kuno Aba stands and edges closer to Dragomán. "The story is true as I recalled it, and that's the way it should be recorded in the history books. There were six of them, and I was the seventh."

"I was the seventh, Kuno Aba, and you know it. You persuaded the boys to come down. I begged them to stay, or run, but they believed you. And then the guns began to fire. You made a mistake; it was not what you wanted, and you have a cross to bear, I realize, but why the heroics? Atonement is not enough for you? You need a moment of catharsis, too, when you feel your pulse throb in your temples, and your heart skip a beat, and your knees begin to shake, when you finally understand that you're up against the wall, when you confront your executioners and say, let it come. *Or,* when you walk away from them with your hands in your pockets. When you get up in the morning and leave your sin behind, and retire at night with your sin still there next to you. There is a time to swell with conceit and a time to be humble. Tell me, Kuno, shouldn't I anoint you bishop of a fallible man's religion?"

"What I would like to know, Professor Dragomán, our esteemed *doctor honoris causa,* is what these riddles are supposed to mean. Do you wish to humiliate me with your insinuations in front of my fellow citizens, whose trust I deservedly enjoy? You left this place, *mon cher collègue,* while I remained locked as one with this city. You think you can cavalierly besmirch my good name. These are your methods, and those of your ilk. Stabbing someone in the back with a cynical comment. I am Dragomán, you say, international drugoman, I get stoned and say whatever I like, tomorrow I'll be somewhere else. Are you saying, Professor, that the rector of the university is lying?"

A man rushed up to Dragomán and grabbed his jacket sleeve. "Who do you think you are? Where do you get the nerve? Don't you know who you're talking to? We stick to him like glue, you won't get away with it." Kuno Aba's wife addressed the irate man: "Béla, don't." Then another man stepped up to him and pulled him away. "Ah let him go, can't you see on his face what sort he is?"

Dragomán drew himself up: "My answer to your question, my friend, is Yes, you are lying."

The rector slapped Dragomán in the face. Dragomán did not lift his hand. But when Kuno Aba moved to slap him again, he responded with a slight push. Kuno Aba fell backward and hit his head against the bench. For a moment he seemed to be trying to pull himself up, but then he fell flat on the ground.

Dragomán knelt next to him; the rector's upturned eyes were seeking him out. Then Dragomán said: "We should call the ambulance." He watched Sandra, the wife, as she stood looking at her husband. Everything should stay as it is, she finally said. Somebody wanted to pull her away, but she resisted. Dragomán leaned against a tree. Somebody said they should telephone the police.

Mr. Barnag stepped forward. "That won't be necessary. I witnessed everything. Please accept my heartfelt sympathy, Professor Dragomán. Your situation is quite clear. You were slapped in the face, whereas you only gave the rector a slight push. Though you did so in a judo-like move—you pulled, then you pushed. That's the way to do it: pull him up first, then send him flying. You didn't have to push hard, it was enough to point his skull toward the edge of the that oak bench, which, admittedly, requires muscle power and perfect aim. The ideological tension between you provided the necessary impetus. We are aware, moreover, of the hostility of outsiders—rootless elements, if you will—toward indisputable insiders. All in all, it is my impression as head of this brand-new investigation, that on a scale of one to ten, where one is manslaughter and ten is premeditated murder, we are still much closer to the former. Now whether or not the barely concealed drug addiction is to be considered an extenuating or an aggravating circumstance—we'll let the courts decide that."

Among those present several wondered if the story might not have political overtones. The widow knelt and held Kuno Aba's head in her two hands. "What happened? What did he do to you? Why did he take you away from me?" She looked up: "Tell me, what harm has he ever done to you? He paid generous tribute to you at the university, and this is how you repay him. He welcomed you, praised you, and you struck him down."

"If it's homicide, we're talking about ten years at least," someone said, and Mr. Barnag intervened: "Mr. Dragomán, by rights I should ask you to come with me; but if you give me your word that you will not leave town, and the mayor agrees to vouch for you, you'll be free to prepare your defense."

Dragomán turned to Tombor and said, "You set this up, too?"

He pushed the man and with that, killed him; everyone had seen it happen. Many of the guests had heard the exchange grow more emotional and personal, and turn from a high-minded philosophical debate into a fatal duel. The entire scene was on videotape, the pull and push could be seen as proof of malice aforethought or a defensive reflex. Some saw a possible aggravating circumstance in the fact that the "hyena" whom Dragomán kicked in the stomach had reported him to the police. To kick a man, just like that...brutal, no? Then too there was the mad young man with the erotics of fire. A series of ominous coincidences. They might just nail him for murder and put him away for a few years. Tombor would say that Plato was his friend, and so was Aristotle, but his greatest friend was truth.

"Out of sight, out of mind," said the scar-faced Svetozar, the man with the bird cage and the cat on a leash. He wasn't out of sight, though—if Dragomán should need him, he was ready to help. "Just say when, sir, and we'll take off. If you don't mind my saying so, you have a knack for causing all kinds of calamities and falling into meat-devouring plants."

A Suspect's Movements

Mr. Barnag, the police chief, offered to take Dragomán home, to any of his addresses, wherever he wished, though not beyond the country's borders, and not beyond a thirty-five-mile radius, whose nucleus would have to be the Professor's temporary domicile, Kandor's Crown Hotel. Actually, the circle of freedom encompassed a territory as large as a miniature country, with a number of villages, including Balatonújfalu and Old Hill—so even if Dragomán were condemned to spend the rest of his days within its confines, he could never explore it in its entirety. And were he to consider these allusions to imprisonment a tasteless joke—for there was every reason to believe that in the absence of a proven crime, all charges would be dropped—he might at least acknowledge that in thus limiting his freedom of movement, the authorities were being quite generous.

Mr. Barnag spoke without a pause. Keeping his hand lightly on Dragomán's elbow. When Dragomán asked why the police commissioner thought he could decide on his own where a foreign national could or could not go, Barnag raised his eyebrows.

"Bear in mind, sir, that I have the right to arrest you," he said. "The area of unrestricted movement I have designated for you is about fifteen thousand times larger than a prison cell. So your remark, made in jest, I presume, was uncalled for."

"The legality of your decision, Commissioner, leaves me breathless."

"What is your pleasure, then? The Mousetrap? The Crown? The Tango? It might be wiser if you came with me, for if I leave you here, you may be surrounded, even attacked. The rector, you see, was a beacon in our city."

After they passed through the garden, a broad-shouldered young man, who had been walking behind them, came up on Dragomán's right. Thus two men escorted him to the police chief's car. The young man sat in front at the wheel, Mr. Barnag in back, next to Dragomán. The excited guests had the impression that Dragomán was being taken into custody. "The perpetrator," somebody whispered.

"Drive me to Mr. Kobra's," Dragomán said. His request did not surprise Mr. Barnag. The police chief of Kandor, who before the 1989 political changes had been in the employ of the security police, kept under surveillance the very gentlemen in whose company he now openly and legally mingled. There was no lack of information in his files (though he didn't need to reach for them, he had only to close his eyes and jog his memory) about Mr. Kobra, or about János Dragomán, the academic sitting in the car next to him, or about a third friend, Antal Tombor, even though the latter now had easy access to the holders of the highest political offices—the same people, incidentally, who had once asked Barnag to keep an eye on Tombor, and to record his meetings with Kobra with the aid of tiny listening devices concealed in the ceilings of the two men's apartments. They had taken seriously Mr. Barnag's reports, which he illustrated by circling the names of prominent Kandoran intellectual groups and marking the links, the bridges, between the circles, referring to them, with an ironic nod to Solzhenitsyn, as "islands," in an archipelago of anti-government subculture, and highlighting in blue the names of persons who turned up at loyalist as well as dissident gatherings, those who were dangerous precisely because they were welcomed in both camps. It was conceivable therefore that Kobra was one of those persons—a moving target, a walking infection.

Mr. Barnag had been a history student and hoped to become an archivist; but after getting a classmate pregnant and marrying her with little prospect for an apartment or a job, Szilveszter Barnag said yes to a nice little man and his partner, a glummer, taller fellow, who offered him housing, and a good salary, plus benefits, in return for his pursuing his studies in the social sciences as an employee of the state security apparatus. He would not have to follow or interrogate anyone, or recruit agents, they had other personnel doing that, he would only have to analyze events and understand what went on behind the scenes—which were of our making, his employers added with a wry smile.

Before long, however, to test his loyalty, he was put in charge of covert operations. Until then Mr. Barnag had made sure his face was recognizable, if not memorable, to members of the Kandor archipelago, and he did this by appearing at every concert and first-night performance and art exhibit in the city, paying attention to the music, the play, the pictures, and never exchanging a word with anyone. He would stand by himself, peering at the program, sipping his drink: a man of medium height, in a well-tailored dark suit, his hair parted meticulously, his cheekbones slightly more prominent, his sideburns slightly longer, his gaze slightly more probing than that of the average spectator or theater-goer. Now it became more difficult for Mr. Barnag to remain the mysterious culture lover present night after night at cultural events, though never at private gatherings.

It's unusual to encounter a man on the balcony of our own apartment. We open the door, pass through the entrance hall and into our living room, and spot a man we automatically, almost unconsciously, associate with the city's cultural events sitting astride the balcony railing, trying to decide whether to jump, which would be his professional duty at the moment. It was a serious lapse in judgment to let himself be caught this way, the advance men were either blind or engaged in sabotage. He had only meant to look through some recent writings, and to remove, quite conspicuously, spare parts for the copying machine, thereby sending a message to the writer: he can write whatever he likes, we would not touch his manuscripts, but a private citizen is not permitted to own copying devices; it could compromise the security of the state. But the signal, meant to be subtle, turned comical when Kobra confronted Mr. Barnag on the railing of his balcony.

"Won't you come in? What brings you here? Practicing to be a stuntman? In case you haven't noticed, we're on the second floor."

"I am sorry, Mr. Kobra, that we must meet under such awkward circumstances. I am unable to give you an explanation for the all-too-obvious mystery of my presence. Please allow me to

233

leave through the front door, and do not ask any questions. Believe me, sir, the man standing before you greatly admires your writings. All your writings. I repeat, all. And that, coming from someone in my position, may seem like a surprising statement."

"What *is* your position?"

"Mr. Kobra, in your writings you often use the word 'acute.' Don't think I don't realize that you already know who I am."

"I have an idea what you are, but I still don't know who you are."

"My name, sir, is Szilveszter Barnag."

"Is that like a *nom de plume*?"

"That's what it says on my birth certificate. I suppose you will not want to shake hands with me, and naturally, you don't have to tell me your name. Don't hit me, please. I never go anywhere without my service revolver. Be well, Mr. Kobra."

THE LIGHT WAS still on in one of the front rooms in Kobra's house; a dark figure could be seen moving between two tables. Not wanting to wake up the family, Dragomán tapped lightly on a window. Kobra opened the window; he wasn't surprised to see Dragomán, but it seemed highly unlikely that the other two were dropping in for a friendly visit. Who was that brawny young man? Dragomán didn't look sick, though his usual roguish smile was slow in coming.

"We'll be on our way," Mr. Barnag said, and as he pulled his fancy trench coat closed, he bowed his head politely.

"The window doesn't tempt you?" Kobra inquired.

"I can now buy a collection of your most intimate thoughts at the corner bookshop. You've slipped out of the picture, Mr. Kobra, our binoculars are no longer focused on you. I owe Professor Dragomán thanks, however, for renewing our acquaintance."

Mr. Barnag waved good-bye from the back seat, as Dragomán made an indecent gesture at the departing car. Then he asked Kobra for a cup of coffee and told him what had happened.

"Maybe we should be with the body," Kobra said.

"You mean go back?"

"Anyone who might give us trouble will have left already."

Melinda told Dragomán over the phone that Kuno's body and the widow were still at the house. They would keep vigil awhile, the two of them, Kobra and Dragomán, should join them, the abbot was also there.

Kuno Aba's body was laid out on the long verandah table. His chin was propped up with a white handkerchief, his hair combed, his white shirt buttoned, but he was tieless. A policeman was posted in front of the house. A spokeswoman explained to the reporters and visitors arriving that for the next several hours family members and close friends wanted to remain in privacy with the deceased. Yes, Mr. Dragomán was inside. He had returned with Mr. Kobra for the vigil. No, there would be no autopsy. If they inquired at the mayor's office after twelve, the official on duty would give them the necessary information. The spokeswoman then asked everyone to leave.

Sandra sat on the deceased's left, Dragomán took one of the tall cane chairs on his right. Kuno Aba's lips had turned white, Dragomán's were white, too. The widow barely acknowledged his arrival; no one spoke. After a while Sandra looked at Dragomán: "Have you nothing to say?" she asked.

"He was my friend and rival, but never my enemy," Dragomán said. "Two dreamers cannot dream the same dream. Two actors cannot play the same role. He demanded that I bear witness to his words, confirm the veracity of his reminiscence. Why did he have to bring up that old story? He had everything; what else did he need? Why should a scholar want to be a hero? Why would a sinner want to be a saint? I just want to tell you, Kuno Aba, that we both have something to atone for. I've been wandering for a long time. I walk five or six hours a day—for my health, but also as penance. I will continue doing it until someone knocks me down, on purpose or by accident, just as I knocked you down. I'll be carrying you on my back from now on. You might say, I'd rather switch places with you. But that's impossible, so you'll stay on my back and keep choking me. I would like to ask for your forgiveness, if that were possible; I'd like to avert your revenge, I don't want to follow you, not yet. I would provide for your children if you had any; I would serve your widow, if that's what she wants; I would look after your papers, if I could hope for absolution."

"Be quiet," Sandra said, "and bring me a blanket for my back. I am cold." But Melinda was already bringing the blanket and wrapped it around Sandra.

Kuno Aba lay there as if he heard every word but had a toothache, hence the handkerchief under his chin. Now this man, will haunt them too; he'll hang around Melinda's living room, prowl the gravel garden path, or sit stiffly on the piano stool, and Melinda will hear such phrases as *grosso modo* or *per definitionem* at least a few times every evening, though once was too much. This group keeping vigil now had been Kuno's captive audience for his historical and political fantasies.

Fluvalism, he would say, and with his hand demonstrate the flow of a river. Streams come together, ideas fuse; dispersion and convergence is all. Neither continents nor oceans can teach us anything, only the great rivers do, these instructors in accumulation and confluence. This notion, for Kuno Aba, led to the conclusion that the images of the Leviathan or the Behemoth were passé—instead a multifaceted Central European monarchy must be restored, with Kandor as its center.

For Kuno, the rectorship, the academy, the deputy mayor's post, the chair in history, membership in institutes and learned societies, were interconnected and in many ways interchangeable roles. Kuno believed that excellence and status must, *grosso modo,* converge. His being rector was the major requirement. The rectorship for him was like a royal throne: it empowered him to make weighty pronouncements. He believed that the rector should regard himself as one of the anointed, the city's spiritual guide, who introduced, through indirection, mostly, the subjects for public discussion, or swept them into the basket of taboos. The actual words he would say in this office were a secondary, technical consideration.

Kuno Aba placed starched shirts, cryptic formulations, and parting sentences beginning with "Well then" between himself and his friends with such irrefutable self-assurance that they, in turn, put him on a lofty, though remote, perch of respectability. People were afraid of him, and didn't dare show him their blemished selves. They sensed what Kuno expected of them and devised an act that confirmed his view of the world.

I WOULD STAY in my chair if, in return, he could get up. But because he can't, I might as well rise. If they let me out the door, it means I am not under arrest. But I cannot leave Kandor until the investigation is over. I pushed a man who'd slapped me across the face. The way I see it, my friends, you want to ship me off to jail. It would not be proper, it wouldn't speak well of our friendship, if I gave you the slip right now. A gentleman accepts a challenge, he will not say that he need not bother with a fool, and leave it at that. "Madam," he said turning to Sandra, "what can I do for you?"

"Here is my car key; I feel ill, drive me home. Kuno will stay here with Melinda. When will they come for the body? Mr. Mayor, I'll be in the office Monday morning to make the funeral arrangements, I'm not up to it yet. I have to get used to speaking about my husband in the past tense. But you needn't worry; I will not kill myself. There is no reason at all why this man should be dead."

Like a stiff-backed footman, Dragomán opened the garden gate for Sandra and helped her into the car, then he got behind the wheel and began to drive assuredly, making all the right turns, knowing automatically which streets were one-way. Kobra, who could get lost in his own house, was full of admiration. When they stopped in front of his house, Sandra moved to the front seat, and Kobra stood on the sidewalk, watching the car recede. What were these two people going to do now, he wondered. Dragomán spoke up only once; Sandra was silent. When they arrived, Sandra got out and leaned against the gate post.

"Should I have stayed?" she said. "I was ashamed of my own curiosity: I would have liked to watch my husband turn into a corpse. Let the mayor do me the favor of taking care of the body. Between you and me, Professor, you killed my husband, that is a fact. You were the cause that led to the effect. Who knows what went through his mind? Maybe the gods were kind and let him have the privilege of falling in battle. In which case he died a hero. Will you come in? Or maybe you're afraid of a crazy widow?"

"I am afraid," Dragomán admitted. "I consider you a wild and unpredictable woman. I helped you get rid of your adoptive father turned husband. But the period of idol worship is over. You've already taken over the mayor's office and find it all rather tiresome. If you no longer feel like working, I will support you. I acquired a daughter and a grandson; if you like, I'll adopt you, too. I'll be your gardener, chauffeur, butler, if that's your wish.

Or I'll use my literary skills and turn Kuno Aba's life into a bestseller. But I can also make you a pot of tea."

"Let's be clear about one thing: I hate you. But I don't want to be alone now. There is no excuse for what you did. It's not you who's laid out on that table. You have no right to exist, you're a freak of nature. If you were in the electric chair, I'd give the nod. Coming in?"

"Is that an invitation?"

"Yes, it is. I am not used to being alone at night. Whenever Kuno traveled abroad, I went with him. I heard people call him a seer, a prophet, but nobody said he was crazy. Do you think he was crazy?"

"We're all crazy. And what do all these crazy people do? Crazy things. You know what today is? The day of calculated craziness."

They went into the living room: a large expanse of yellow parquet, a few tables and chairs on rollers, pale yellow walls. This vast emptiness led to another room, in which every nook and cranny was filled with art objects. If the first room left the entering guest unimpressed, this inner sanctum overwhelmed him.

"Will you sit in this chair? I dare you. And how about a pipe? Good, I am ready for you. I'll give you a wineglass to hold—I saw at Melinda's how it's done gracefully. You can even look out the window at a sliver of sky between the leaves. You must know that my testimony will carry a lot of weight; I will be asked if you were on friendly terms with my husband. It will be up to me to dispel any suspicion of premeditation. For a while you will be beholden to me, at my mercy. As was the rector; he was terribly afraid of my objectivity. I felt his tirades were redundant. But anyone who is given to verbal onslaughts must expect that. I admired the tension in him, the eagerness to bring the sacred into the world of politics. He wanted to turn political activity into a priestly duty.

"I did not wish to enter my husband's realm. In his spiritual world there are too many commands and tributes. Everyone knows his place but only because it is marked out for him. But don't suspect me of being a secret anarchist. You and I, sir, are not co-conspirators. You come and go as you please, while he lived for his city. He was serious and you are frivolous. A traveling man tends to exaggerate, but by the time people find out the truth, he is gone. On the way he kills someone, seduces his widow, then licking his chops, takes off again. I know that this is why you accepted my invitation, this is your plan. But I have plans of my own.

"Please lie down on the floor to demonstrate that you are really willing to make amends and be at my service. Yes, like that, now I shall walk around you, but you remain motionless, as if you were dead. Close your eyes and keep them closed. No noise you hear can be used as an excuse.

"If you open your eyes, I'll poke them out with this broomstick. Under no circumstances must you make the slightest move, even if I should dig you in the ribs like this; and if I should kick you with both feet, not sadistically, of course, you should take that too. Now I'll take off my shoes. Lie on your stomach and I will stomp all over you, except for your head; it will be more like a symbolic stomping. But I want it to hurt. And please don't hold back, feel free to moan and groan; I do want to cause you pain. There is nothing you need more now than a healthy dose of humiliation. Here I go, I'm stepping all over you.

"You took my husband from me, my advisor, my father. Your advice—what good is it now? Kuno must be made a saint, and you must help me make that happen. Your circle of friends could use their influence. His grave should become a shrine. You'll be the secretary of the Kuno Aba Society. You'll lead prayer sessions in memory of our founder. And I shall become the embodiment of his cherished ideals.

"We outgrow our idols, that goes without saying. To you I can admit that what I really am is a Sandrist. I always knew that I would begin a new life when his ended. My dearest darling, you died like a knight, in defending your honor. Yes, you were one of a kind and therefore irreplaceable. Now Mr. Dragomán, get up and make some tea."

There are many roads that lead from drinking tea to snuggling in bed. Dragomán did not choose any of them. He brought Sandra tea, bade her good night, and after kissing her hand and breathing a kiss on her lips, walked out the door. The professional eavesdroppers could see through their binoculars that the two figures moving about in the brightly lit living room had not disappeared in the inner recesses of the house. Then, as Dragomán left the terrace and walked down the gravel footpath toward the garden gate, the light in the living room went out, and the alarm system, which was occasionally tripped by the cat, turned on automatically.

THE WORLD SEEMED to be closing in on him. The day before yesterday, that crazy young man who jumped off the balcony; yesterday, Kuno Aba. Dragomán was at the point of agreeing with Barnag that it was generous of the local authorities to let him walk around freely. If he fled, most countries would ship him right back; he must let the investigation take its course. And if he got too close to the widow, the city would be rife with rumors that the two of them had conspired to do away with the rector.

He could take walks around the hotel, or shut himself in his room. He should notify the American consul, hire a lawyer, and seek out his friends' advice. Tombor, of course would say that both Dragomán and Kuno Aba were his friends, but his greatest friend was the truth. He'd clap, rub his hands and be off—the mayor must do his job. What he thought before going to sleep was his business. More often than not, he thought of nothing. He fell into bed like a log and slept till morning, when the urge to urinate woke him, and after that he stayed awake. A fine one he was, to invite Dragomán back to Kandor, crown him with laurels, then place him in the ring with Kuno, knowing that the two would clash. When they did, Tombor assumed an appropriately rueful expression and, privately, had a good laugh as he brought down the curtain. Next time he'll invite other players, and despite their misgivings, they will come, and put themselves in Tombor's hands. Or maybe next time Kobra will flash some bright new idea before Tombor's eyes, which Tombor will promptly adopt.

Kobra left Kuno Aba alone. On two occasions in the 1970s, Aba had made a point of ignoring Kobra, at a time when Kobra was under an official ban, and the target of a carefully orchestrated smear campaign. The image—an uneasy, stiff-necked figure walking past him—stayed with Kobra. Since then he had listened to Kuno Aba's ideas with singular indifference. The two of them could never be pitted against each other.

But why shouldn't Kuno Aba, Tombor's political rival, and

Dragomán, Tombor's rival in love, jump on each other? Dragomán was inclined to believe that Tombor had entrapped him. Who knew what connections the mayor might have with the highest authorities? Could Dragomán trust Melinda, the wife of the great manipulator? Could he trust the widow, who had said she hated him? "I am on more familiar terms with the spirit of this place than our illustrious guest," Kuno Aba had said. The spirit of the place ensnared Dragomán and preyed on him.

There was no one left now but his faithful escort, the Darnok agent, the scar-lipped, bird cage–carrying Svetozar. Dragomán had nothing against leaving Kandor incognito: in a cardinal's robe or in a sheik's headdress. A pilot's blue uniform would look good, too, or a Franciscan monk's habit; or he could disguise himself as a Hasidic Jew. Svetozar could get him a fake beard and fake sidelocks, as well as a Rolls-Royce, to make the caricature even more outrageous. Too bad Hungarians no longer wear a hussar's uniform. In your average post-modern city there are so many Scottish bagpipers and French lancers and hooded monks, people hardly notice them.

Or how about turning into a homeless person? That might be the best idea of all. All it would take would be a few days' worth of grime, a derelict look, an unshaven face ruddy from sleeping outdoors, a plastic bag full of odds and ends, and eyes would turn away. (They'd know they mustn't look because then he'd ask for money.)

He'd leave behind the international president, the man he was when he got here, he'd set him down in a chair and forget him. Dragomán would also love to shed his suspect self, slip out of it the way marrow slips out of a shankbone when you tip it, or a gob of yogurt from a plastic cup. He wanted to shake off the dubious individual who got mixed up in local squabbles in order to feel at home.

His sixth-floor suite, until yesterday so cozy, became strangely uninviting—a designated domicile, a place of confinement for the duration of the investigation. The desk clerk reports regularly to the police chief, who will drag out the investigation, if only because he loves spirited conversation. He'll do everything to make Dragomán's stay comfortable, but won't allow him to leave Kandor any time soon.

But why should we submit to claustrophobia? Dragomán muses. Why not enjoy the pleasures of a mole-like existence, the blessings of close quarters, tight spaces? Advice and precepts are aimed at the future. If he stays, lies down in his bed and turns to the wall, which will receive him with a certain gloating satisfaction, he may sink pleasantly into nothingness.

The past was that push, the slap Kuno had given him.

Dragomán can't help thinking that he should have left well enough alone, turned the other cheek. It was a sheer accident that Kuno Aba, after losing his balance (which, considering his trim condition, warranted further investigation), fell back against the bench, and hit his skull in a way that proved fatal. Could he have had a sudden heart attack? Even then Dragomán had no part in it.

Dragomán had sensed unusual excitement in Kuno that evening, perhaps because of the presence of cameras. How he came across to people seemed terribly important, but only because he was so eager to finish his life's work. Even when they were putting makeup on him in a TV studio, he felt he was serving his public. When Kuno Aba feasted on roast duck, he thought this would give him strength to realize his dream of restoring a Central European monarchy. Well, no more roast duck for the poor devil.

Go ahead, make light of it, but he did fall down, never to rise again. An eye for an eye? And you get up, just like that, and get yourself a drink? What excuse do you have? By rights you should be lying next to him. Even if it was an accident, it was your accident. Would it make Kuno feel better if somebody knocked *you* off your feet? Perhaps his wife, perhaps in their bedroom. He feels the stirring of disgraceful excitement in his groin, his arms feel the widow's firm back muscles, his fingers would love to take a walk on her belly. Burying his face in a pillow, an immature old man wonders if her undies are also black now. Is this nostril-flaring desire in him so repugnant—his thinking of thighs and tits and ass while he should be grief-stricken? You must punish yourself, don't leave it to Mr. Barnag; and don't ask your friends what to do. Be your own judge, pass your own sentence. Life or death? Pretend-life, or rebirth?

Escape in Slow Motion

What can you do with two such fatal occurrences behind you? You go out and walk in the square, stop at a friendly tavern, take a good look at things, for the last time perhaps, because the desk clerk has informed you that there is a message from Mr. Barnag, who has taken charge of unscrambling this mess and is personally conducting the investigation initiated against you—he requests, in a carefully worded, neatly typed fax that you see him in his office at three in the afternoon today, Saturday.

Just when you wanted to see your daughter, your grandson, and your friends at Old Hill—you had your heart set on it, there'll be a harvest festival in the Valley of Mercy, and up in the woods of Tobacco Hill, a Gypsy fair.

In the valley, in a natural amphitheater, a twenty-four-hour "preach-in" is getting under way, there'll be a procession of priests, each one will have an hour, and anyone getting tired of the nonstop sermon can nap in the stable.

This sounds more interesting than Mr. Barnag's invitation. You pushed a man who slapped you in the face. Anyone would have done the same under the circumstances. That he died as a result is his business. You didn't want to see him dead, you just wanted to have a chat.

True, you had watched him turn into a symbol. Kuno Aba had become more than a politician, he had become a seer with real power, one moment winking knowingly while mocking himself, the next moment the stern visionary again, issuing commands, making sure he's surrounded by fans, and that they included

243

young men with athletic bodies. "To the Empire!" they all cry and clink glasses. And thus shall the small become big.

But you yourself have pampered little ones in your time. Is it so bad to be small? Whoever is not feared is loved. If you want to know the meaning of sovereignty, take lessons from Habakuk. At least he's not small-minded, you yourself said of Kuno Aba. He may have been a prig but he was generous. Except about people who wore ankle socks and sandals, or couldn't sit or eat properly, or answer in a foreign language—they could not hope to be admitted to his school.

Kuno Aba liked the concept of an intellectual elite. One doesn't have to be born into a caste, but must know that we, originally small, represent something grand. We come from modest regions but represent an empire that existed for centuries, an extraordinary thing that at one time had been the normal framework of our existence. By declaring Kandor, the onetime coronation city, the temporary capital of this entity, Kuno Aba sought to restore around an empty throne first a virtual, then a real, monarchy, and also to raise funds for a few impressive gatherings.

Kuno Aba's visions of grandeur could have resulted in a few more spectacles. That scoundrel Tombor knew perfectly well why he needed Kuno Aba—he brought on board the well-connected old families, and attracted an assortment of intellectual snobs to the Kandor festivals. Tombor as well as the city needed all those who had a following.

Dragomán happened to like this presidential game of right and left, with Tombor poised in the middle. Kuno knew, of course, that the center had to expand in both directions, as long as it involved men of quality. And as for quality, it was enough if Kuno agreed with himself, and perhaps Sandra too, who after eleven o'clock in the evening made assenting noises ever more infrequently, while Kuno Aba paced and held forth, now and then even jumping on a chair, making sweeping hand gestures, and emitting terrible, absurd sounds when mentioning people he disliked.

You used to witness all this as you headed up the hill and passed their bedroom window. The loud ruminations could be heard outside and were so extravagant, filled with so many rhetorical flourishes, that a passerby might have thought a large audience had gathered to hear the rector. But the reality seemed more interesting to Dragomán, especially his realization that this fantastic performance was actually his way of courting Sandra, who worked hard all day in the mayor's office and was happy to be in bed, under the blanket, rubbing her feet, stretching her limbs, and curling up again.

NOW DRAGOMÁN COULD go to the tavern where he once saw a man go down on his knees, beat the floor with his fist, and shout: "I am guilty, I sinned." It happened long ago, the man had SS tattooed all over his body. "O God," he wailed, "if you sent somebody now to strike me down, I wouldn't make a move."

Dragomán passes the window of a chocolate shop and stops to look at the chocolate deer and chocolate hearts. Then he is riveted to a window filled with wine flasks and cheese, he pauses a moment, sits down on a playground bench and lights his pipe. This is where Habakuk likes to show how he can climb up one pole and slide down another, sit on the swing any which way, and do all manner of things that elicit a grandfather's boundless admiration.

From here they usually adjourn to a fur salon where Habakuk likes to stop and gawk. Mink, blue fox, Persian lamb, sheepskin, they have it all. No fake fur, though, every coat, even the catskin jacket, had been alive once, and will therefore outlast all others. Habakuk studies the women wrapped in furs, each wearing a different but proud smile, as if declining a compliment. Finally, he declares: "If you have the money, this is the one to get for Mommy," and he points to the most expensive coat.

Dragomán cannot pass the store that sells hunting gear without perusing the display case. But now it also occurs to him that it might be time to pay Mr. Barnag a visit, and have a long talk. He must clear his good name and get this whole nonsense over with. Yes, the only reasonable thing would be to go and tell him exactly what happened; his innocence is, after all, self-evident. In a civilized country such as this, he would expect nothing less than the dropping of all charges. Inside the store he examines a neat-looking canteen which has stirred his imagination for days. Filling that flask with some decent booze from the tavern would make sense.

What Dragomán might or might not confess to his Maker is of no concern to the authorities. The story fabricated so carefully by Kuno was fragile, it had broken into pieces on Dragomán, he shattered it, one might say. A well-dressed lady walking with her husband recognizes Dragomán and looks horrified. An older man in knickerbockers stops and says darkly: "Shame on you." Dragomán calmly moves out of his way and walks on.

He stops at the Tango bar, where Petra greets him with a little more reserve than usual. Deborah, too, blushes when she sees him. They bring him his coffee, cognac, and mineral water, then one of the girls switches on the TV and turns the set toward the customers. Besides Dragomán only a language teacher and his student are in the café, and a bald young man typing away on a laptop computer.

The TV screen shows close-ups of the rector's death. Thanks to the resourcefulness of a cameraman, the television station has obtained a videotape of the mayor's garden party and now replays from several different angles the altercation between János Dragomán and Rector Kuno Aba.

There's the slap, it's unmistakable: Dragomán's face hardens, he freezes. Kuno Aba may think it's not over yet, he is defending his honor, after all, perhaps he means to deliver another blow, but then, with the quickness of a practiced fighter, Dragomán grabs his wrist, steps back, pulling the wrist with him (maybe on purpose, or maybe he lost his balance), straightens the rector's arm and pushes him away with such force that Kuno falls back, hitting his skull on the edge of the bench.

The professor demonstrates his sense of theater, and his self-discipline, the voice-over intones solemnly, by being the first to kneel beside the corpse, that is—here the voice falters—beside the rector. He holds his face in his two hands, calls out his first name, takes his wrist, and puts his ear to his heart.

By then Sandra, too, is kneeling, you can make out Dragomán's words: "Close his eyelids." And so she does.

And that's how such things are done, the reporter says rather bitterly, then points out, in a more matter-of-fact voice, that the analysis of the video material, as well as of the various eyewitness accounts, is still under way.

"Oh, Professor, what did you get yourself into?" exclaims Petra. "You don't know who you're messing with. For the love of God, get away from here, the farther the better. I'll try to keep tabs on things and let you know when the mood changes. But right now these people are out to get you. Before, they idolized you, now they'll drag you through the mud. They gave, now they're taking away. They mean to put you in your place. Want me to talk to my brother-in-law? That scarface gorilla of yours, hasn't he found you yet? He sat here all morning, he must have been waiting for you. I'd show these people my backside, I'd moon them, so help me."

IT WAS AN accident that Dragomán had been invited to come to Kandor, an accident he had become a father and grandfather, an unfortunate accident a deranged young man had decided to jump off his balcony, and also an accident a quarrel between two friends had ended in death.

Since Dragomán has never given up his Hungarian citizenship, and since this is where the incident took place, his fate will be decided by a Hungarian court. He was released on bail, but remains under surveillance. Though Mr. Barnag was nice enough to include Balatonújfalu and Old Hill in the permitted area, the fair in the Valley of Mercy was out of bounds.

One of Mr. Barnag's men sits in the hotel corridor, keeps an eye on Dragomán, takes pictures of him, and reports to his boss on his cell phone. The prisoner feels protected here, though he can be visited and interrogated anytime. Svetozar, approaching him in the corridor, whispers as quietly as he can: "Maestro, let's hit the road."

But Dragomán wants to drink his cup to the lees. Now Mr. Barnag himself phones from the lobby: May he come up? Dragomán thinks for a moment. What could Mr. Barnag want with him now? He tries to dispel his suspicions, but then remembers that they may want to recruit him as an agent in return for protection from an assassin's bullet.

The longer Mr. Barnag thought about his man, the stronger the suspicions grew in his heart. Still, he was certain that as a friend of the mayor and holder of an honorary degree from the university, Dragomán would not sneak away like a common thief, he'd want to vindicate his name. The realization that Dragomán was a hostage to his own code of honor gave Mr. Barnag satisfaction.

But Dragomán didn't feel like seeing Mr. Barnag—he might just lock him up. He would rather slip into a monk's robe, or a pilot's uniform, take a taxi to the fairgrounds, melt into the crowd, and then sneak into Kobra's house, which was not far from the Valley of Mercy.

There'll be throngs, people from Budapest and even from abroad will arrive in droves, many expecting miracles from the sacred spring—waters of fertility are said to flow underneath the Stonedial. Couples will fan out into the forest, disappear into makeshift huts, looking for the hermit who will make barren women fruitful with the aid of the curative waters. Dragomán will wind up in a dark alley, surrounded by stray cats; beggars will descend on him, Gypsy children will tug at his jacket.

But skip the paranoia, please; let's analyze the situation with a cool head. To do that, however, we need to take a long walk. The Oriental man sits when he meditates, a European reflects while walking. As he wanders, he entertains ideas, images, responds to change by retaining in changing ways his essential self. A vehicle such as an automobile or a bicycle cannot take the place of his feet, and running is not the same as walking—while we are running, our body becomes the vehicle. It's the traveler who can let his mind wander most freely, for he is not bothered by the technicalities of getting there. Where else but on a train or an airplane can Dragomán daydream undisturbed?

It's all right if the representative of Darnok is on his tail, he doesn't mind the firm, though Svetozar should be notified somehow. He will not go to the hotel to leave Svetozar a message, his faithful tail may again look for him at the Tango, in which case Petra could tell him to see Mr. Kobra.

In situations like these it's best to remain cool, act as though it's business as usual. Circle Resurrection Square one more time, show one's face, and see what's going on. What might bear looking into is whether the mood in the square has changed from yesterday, when he was still greeted with smiles, and only a few angry glances. Dragomán is a great believer in an actively engaged observation of one's subject, all his writings start that way; without a provocative stance, the fine points never come to light. So he'll stroll in the square and through the neighboring sidestreets, walk along the lakeshore, wander through the marketplace, hit a few taverns, and after he's completed his rounds and given everyone the impression that this is quite normal for him, he makes such tours every day, he is the same man he was yesterday, after all, despite the weird stunts a few half-wits came up with—after doing and saying all that, he can get on the bus and go visit his friend Kobra, that oaf, that lug, that ox, because he wouldn't leave Kandor and adjacent parts without turning this evening into a farewell bash with family and friends.

But let's not fool ourselves: Dragomán also has quite different ideas, ones that reflect his stoic resolve just as strongly. Along the way he sees a costume rental place. Do they have a pilot's uniform? He'll rent it, leaving a nice deposit. In fact, he'll wear it and put his civilian clothes in the black leather case that's part of the costume. He does have a pilot's license, has flown a plane, while in the employ of certain shady African and Middle Eastern companies. Pilots are saluted, the hat and the pair of sunglasses work fairly well as a disguise. Dragomán's instincts tell him to get away from this place at all cost, even if an international warrant is issued for his arrest. He must extricate himself from the tangled affairs of this excitable town, he'd rest much easier if his case (if, indeed, there was one) were decided by some trans-Kandoran forum.

Tomorrow morning he'll cross the border in his pilot's uniform, in the company of Svetozar, and head toward Graz and Venice. There he'll board a ship for Cyprus, or he'll stay in Venice and gaze out a window overlooking the Grand Canal. He'll hear the seawater sloshing outside at floor level, and the huge wardrobe in his room will have a secret door leading to another room where a graceful desk will be at his disposal. He's already heard good things about the corner restaurant and café, so whatever the Crown has to offer, he'll find it there, too.

Aside from friendly chats with neighbors, he won't have to deal with anyone. He'll be an obvious stranger who doesn't have to suppress the local booster in him, the patriot who feels compelled to meddle in local affairs; he won't have to listen to outrageous lies with a self-indulgent smile that says: Oh but these outrageous lies have their place in the anthology of human folly. In Venice he'd be a traveler again. His incoming fees and outgoing manuscripts would cross borders electronically.

Whenever he wants to put down roots, Dragomán makes himself ill. That's the reason he became a pilot: it's so sweet and easy to glide across borders in a light, single-engine plane. Years ago, in 1967, near Trieste, he swam to safety from communism to capitalism. But he did not leave his own country in order to become an American, a Frenchman, a Swede, or an Israeli. Curiosity and loyalty are continually at swords' points in his soul. Who or what he really is is a dull, narcissistic question. Clearly, he is the sum of all the things he's picked up along the way. Dragomán is one with his memory freight, with the people he's known, and with those few sponge-holes where he's been twisting and squirming over the years.

A taxi pulls up, the driver leans out the window.

"Need a ride, sir?" Yes, that's exactly what Dragomán needs, all the more so as the driver is none other than Svetozar, who now sticks a magnetic FREE sign on the roof of the car and opens the back door. "The uniform is very becoming. I myself can offer you an assortment of priests' habits, a burnoose worthy of a sheik, along with the necessary makeup and facial hair. You could transform yourself in a roadside washroom, if you wanted. I do not doubt, sir, that you will match your behavior to your attire. In other regards, however—if I may be so bold as to give you advice—do not allow yourself to get carried away. A particularly dangerous figure: the strong-willed widow. So then, where do we go first?"

"To Mr. Kobra's house, if you don't mind. And I'd appreciate it if you could also pick up my daughter Olga, my grandson Habakuk, as well as Melinda and her husband, the mayor. I leave it to you to decide how to collect them. Habakuk sees you as a genie anyway; he's asked me if you can fly."

"Master Habakuk will fly with me yet...Nice little eatery over there," Svetozar said as they turned a corner. "The proprieter plays the bouzouki."

"Any news from home, Svetozar?"

"They're all crazy. They always say the same old thing, and play with their cigarette lighters."

"Ever had *cevapcici* in that nice little eatery?"

"No, only *razglednice*."

"I hope you drank red wine with it."

"I did, sir."

"And that was it?"

"Ah sir, you got me where I live. Somebody at the next table ordered grilled *süllő*, with its head and tail curling up, it looked so delectable, I ordered it myself—knowing full well that a fish course at that point would violate dining etiquette."

"Life is tough, Svetozar."

"So is fighting the battle of the bulge. Yet, our being is unbearably light, like that Slav brother, Milan whathisface, said."

It turned cool, the pounding of children's feet could be heard from the upstairs rooms, right over Kobra's head. Ready or not, here I go, one of them shouted, who in these parts is called the finder, not the seeker. After a few days in the country, little Döme had adopted the brash peasant-Gypsy accent of the local boys. Then there was a knock on the window, and János Dragomán appeared in his blue pilot's hat.

"What happened?" Kobra asked. "You a train conductor now?"

"Is this new? What is it?" Dragomán asked, pointing to a sheaf of papers next to Kobra's printer.

"Kid stuff."

"It's possible that what I've considered unusual in you, Kobra, is actually that at heart you're a hayseed. Your pulse, your speed, your frequencies are way too low. Next to me, a nervy and restless Kandoran, you are altogether too easygoing. One thing's for sure, if in kindergarten we had this test: who can walk around a chair the fastest with a bag of beans on his head, I would have beaten you hands down. But I am also pretty sure that the bean bag would never have fallen off your head. Making due allowances for gravitational pull, try to answer these two questions: First, am I guilty? And second, should I give them the slip? Let me remind you that to me a fugitive is a sympathetic character, even if his pursuers are well-meaning and earnest."

Svetozar motioned through the window that he was bringing more guests. He'd return for Dragomán at midnight. Kobra nodded. Svetozar disappeared.

"We'll see about that, in the meantime you'll have supper with us." In Kobra's study Dragomán chose the larger of two armchairs, which seemed more suited to his long legs. Now and then he turned to look at Maestro György Jovánovics's *frottage* on the wall: it was either a bird's-eye view of a city or the profile of a brooding man behind bars. He also tried to estimate the distance between where he was sitting and the farthest corner of the room: ten meters at least. Here Kobra could pace to his heart's content—at one time it had been a tavern, but now he was drinking a neighbor's home brew. A usurper of space, that's what Dragomán's friend was. And then there was the garden, where he could move about even more freely, far from watchful eyes, inside a tall fence, in undisturbed solitude. And beyond the garden, a hill and a meadow, a privileged space almost too good to be true. Enough, Dragomán thought, Kobra should let him have this house, he had enjoyed it far too long, it was his turn now. If this room were his, he, too, could come to rest and weave words as peacefully as a farmer's wife shelling peas. Would Kobra please leave this house, then, preferably by tomorrow morning, taking only a suitcase? In the name of divine justice, Dragomán would move in. Naturally, Kobra must leave behind his faithful wife, Regina, his two sons, Zsiga and Döme, as well as his grown children—Kobra must leave everyone and everything to him, the whole brood, including Kobra's elderly mother, and all his friends. Dragomán wants to sit at his desk, try his pens, scribble on his notepad, open his little boxes, touch the carved figurines, smoke his pipes, draw beautiful letters with his calligrapher's pen on fine Finnish stationery. He does have some nerve, wanting it all. Take Dragomán in, and he'll turn you out of your house. He liked Kobra's brandy, but his wines never impressed him, he always had something expertly nasty to say about them. But back to the question: was Dragomán guilty?

"You could have let him beat you up."

"Would you have let him?"

"No."

"But you still think I'm guilty."

"Yes."

"Because a crime just happens, like an accident?"

"Yes, mostly. It falls on you like a tree."

"But a whole forest?"

"Well, that is a problem...A warning, then: Everything will be yours tomorrow, if tonight you leave."

"Can I come back?"

"I wouldn't advise it. You and Kandor just don't get along. A therapist's positive outlook is no longer for you. I often wonder, incidentally, how your students in New York put up with you. I thought they felt pretty positive about themselves."

"I am more positive than any of them. The vagaries of fate, the blessings of stability—I praise the Lord for both. In America Laura and I had a log cabin, at the end of our property there was a stream, so when boring guests came, I rowed away. I watched birds with a telescope, owned a library of bird calls. All of that was destroyed by fire. An accident. My mother's and Laura's suicides were accidents, too. And now that I've found out I have a grandchild, I have to disappear."

KOBRA ROAMED THE world, too, but all his peregrinations taken together are nothing compared to Dragomán's travels in a single year. Kobra likes to sit in a hay cart or an airplane, but he remains in place, motionless in a moving vehicle—the world comes to him. Cars stop at his door, his wife picks him up, his friends lure him out of his den. He is a cave dweller who now and then finds himself pushed along moving walkways at airports. Most of the time he sticks to his cave and cherishes his inaccessibility, which, from the perspective of a morality that considers chatter the sole standard of proper human intercourse, is appalling selfishness. But Kobra believes idle talk to be the source of all ills. Most offenses, which then must be avenged with blood, stem from a swell of words. To lessen our woes it might be enough to keep our mouths shut, eschew bluster and facile wit, stop conquering with words. More time could then be spent on being idle, on backing down, on figuring out when words are really needed.

For Dragomán the world is full of beckoning mysteries, which either hit you in the face or caress you gently. He rides in a funhouse all day long; he hears words and tracks them down; he sees a face and follows it. He will travel to the ends of the earth for a lover, or an enemy, just to get even, to refute a theory, or to have a good laugh with a friend, as they did thirty, forty, fifty years ago. He visits old classmates and is pleased to note that B. is the same good-natured fool he always was, and that his third wife is as nice a woman as his second was.

He likes to read about a city, a canyon, an exhibit, a constellation, a skin color, a spice, a sexual custom, a social grace—for a long time Dragomán avidly pursued these things, so that the world, whose individual flavors he did not taste, should all be his. But Dragomán is not the proprietary type, he never wanted to invest in a house, a secure shelter, he was all for renting. When his house in America burned down, he didn't rebuild it but took cover in a rundown old house. He has slept in hundreds, maybe thousands of rooms, and when he checked out of them, he felt glad that they fell away from his body, because he'd learned where everything was in them, knew exactly which way to turn so as not to bump into a table on the way back from the bathroom in the dark, knew how to reach for a book or silence the radio, knew his place in bed, and that of his partner, his hand knew where the light switch was, and the doorknob, and he knew where to hit the floor when they were shooting outside, and how to reach the door in two leaps, and the elevator down the hall, when he had to clear out of the hotel because he was told they were coming to get him.

Usually Dragomán goes to places he knows he'll have to flee, and he is doubly glad and relieved to quit those rooms, as relieved as when slipping out of a vagina with a listless, wilting penis. Or when turning the light off in his faculty office and closing the door behind him. There are many border crossings in the world where the guards take their sweet time and fiddle about mysteriously. They note down and check off things, and ascertain that Dragomán's name appears on several of their lists, because once again his curiosity had got the better of him, he got mixed up in things, so now would he please step aside, his passport is still in their possession, and when his name flashes on a computer screen or shows up in a big black book, the guard's eyes light up too, his face tightens, he's on to something, a situation is at hand, the thing he's been waiting for with half-shut eyes; it's time to show his mettle: the swimmer is flagging, the prey is in sight—leaning against the handrail in his light overcoat and carrying two shoulder bags plus a huge, double-ribbed umbrella is the quarry, the man, Dragomán himself.

In airports where the toilets are filthy, the pipes rusty, the walls peeling, and the smell of unwashed feet and cheap cleansers mingle with the garlic breath of greasy, unkempt airport officials; where armed guards are very much in evidence; where nonchalance and punctiliousness go fearsomely hand in hand—at such airports Dragomán is usually told to step aside and wait while they go through his luggage and search under every shirt collar, although in the end the head of the security detail lets him board the plane, if only because it would not be a good idea to detain him, complications might ensue which are not worth the trouble.

Dragomán manages to whisk out everything that's important to him: his manuscripts in various stages of completion, perhaps a stash of pleasurable substances, for his private enjoyment. They swallow the bait, pass over the really dangerous stuff. They'd have to get up early in the morning to outsmart good old Dragomán.

He allows himself to detest certain people, and is able to despise, with youthful vehemence even at sixty, those he had already hated at the age of twenty or thirty—although with considerable forbearance he forbids himself to malign them. Every fact he sets down on paper is verifiably true, yet you will not find a word of slander in his writings. He never writes anything that proves to be libelous, his newspaper's legal department is never called in to smooth things over or correct his blunders. When he goes for the kill, it's always a clean cut, a well-aimed blow. Consequently he must sacrifice many an opportunity. He forgoes the cheap shots, bides his time, and then strikes. He is not vindictive, but he does strike.

"You, Kobra, want to avoid sinning at all cost. With you everybody gets resurrected, nobody receives a moral death sentence. There is an element of mawkishness in this forgiving kindness of yours; upon closer inspection, though, it smacks of cowardice. Let's let each other be, your conduct seems to be saying. With one quick smile you pay people off."

"But isn't that what you do yourself? You are forever saying good-bye, the moment you arrive you're on your way out; you announce in advance how long you can stay, you're busy, you must move on, catch a plane, meet people at your hotel, polish off a thousand-word piece, a three-thousand-word piece; and you also have to catch up on your sleep, that's a perennial problem, yet not a day goes by without your accepting invitations to parties that begin after midnight, though you know that at six a.m. you are wide awake, you're afraid of oversleeping, just as when you were a child, so you assure everyone that you won't keep them up late, if only because you'll probably miss the train you said you would be on, but then you arrive on a later one, and even then you are not reliable, because if I met only the later train, you'd be sure to catch the earlier one. You spend hardly any time with us, though enough to stir things up, there's always turmoil and turbulence around you, if you are on an airplane it's sure to be struck by lightning, wherever you stop over, age-old hatreds erupt, but even revolutions show perfect timing and break out only after you've already had a good night's sleep at the hotel, a decent breakfast, walked through the revolving door, enjoyed the morning sun, a leisurely stroll, and had a nice lunch down at the harbor, or in a well-lit modern restaurant, where good-looking boys and girls smile at you amiably, and where the maître d', the wine steward, and you enact a little drama that consists of a medley of "ahems" and "ahas," which are meant to reveal what kind of guest you are, whether you really know about wines, and can mutter expressively, meaningfully, and also quietly, otherwise it's vulgar…while all this is taking place, the revolution waits, though you've even had your demitasse, and are ready for a siesta. So while you doze with a newspaper on your chest, muffled noises are heard, faint at first, becoming more and more furious, until there is screaming under your window. It's a revolution, so you wash your face, at this moment raving desperadoes may be forcing their way up the marble staircase, tearing open all the doors. At such moments it's best to size up the situation, check out through the back door, and get lost in the crowd. Your best weapon is your feet. And your stupid mug, which brings a co-conspiratorial smile to the faces of thuggish rebels. This way, pal, they say, you can make it, climb in here and out over there, while I'm not looking. Sometimes things go wrong in these dazzling getaways, and you end up temporarily behind bars, under the protection of real scumbags...There is mayhem wherever you go. I am surprised, dear friend, that since you've been here there have been two only deaths—and you've been here for quite a while. Maybe you could even predict what kind of mishaps you'll bring down on us. Truth is, I wouldn't like a revolution now, or a conflagration, an earthquake, or even a family feud. You don't have to look for trouble; the usual ones suffice. Creeping dementia, my eighty-eight-year-old mother's broken hand, my little nephew run over by a car, the death of friends, the poverty of the poor, my ninety-three-year-old uncle's operation—all that is enough for one day."

"Your father was a merchant, mine sang and played the piano in a nightclub. He greeted each guest with a friendly glance and jokingly included them in his songs, eyes turned to him, he remained the center of attention. But the owner, the bartender, all the regulars were also centers of strength in that club, Father had to learn that he was one of many, his role was to offer wry, poignant commentaries on things that went on happening with or without him. He did not order the help about with a twitch of his eyebrow, or by whispering code words, as your father did in his store. I could mention more differences between them, but what they shared was their fatalism: they each stayed where they were, in the store, in the club, even though blustering madmen were on the rise. Each felt that these madmen's bark was worse than their bite, and that only the fuse burned, there was no dynamite at the other end. But what do you know: there was dynamite, and it blew up in their faces. And the bark in fact grew louder and louder, the madmen outdid themselves, because the monster that is in all of us cannot have its fill of evil. However many bodies are carved up, however busy the human butcher shop, the monster is not satisfied, the pleasure is slow to come. And then there is no turning back, he must have more and more of the same; no contrition, or confession, only new ways to kill even more people. Our optimistic fathers believed that evil would not come to pass. They believed this because they were good men, and a good man considers bad people childish and disregards them, which is a mistake. Maybe it's because they think that next to a good person a bad one turns gentle. But this happens only until the first transgression, until he discovers that he can slap a good man too, just for the hell of it. After that it no longer matters what kind of person he is beating to a pulp, it may be someone as innocent as a fish whose head is struck with a wooden hammer, its body cleaned and cut up and handed to the waiting customer. Once statements are made, texts formulated, declaring someone the enemy, it's of no importance what kind of person he is, his skull can be crushed with the heel of a boot just the same. Our fathers did not realize that the customer or the guest who always greeted them with a friendly smile, the neighbor who tipped his hat to them, was quite capable, in a fit of political fever, or tribal rage, of tearing his own brother to pieces; when the grinning barbarian in him slips out, he can hack his neighbor to pieces. Feed the monster the right words, and he'll break his chain and shriek with laughter. The family is proud of their son's heroic deeds, though by the time he returns home he is dripping with blood. Our fathers didn't understand that in this city, this region, volcanoes seethe under the surface; here the crust of civilization is thin, and therefore the landscape, and the human soul, more unpredictable than in older democracies. This is disquieting indeed, because you never know whom you can trust. If you have free choice, then for reasons of safety alone, you will choose boring decency and rationality, which will respond to challenge A invariably with solution B. That kind of certainty gives you courage, which will show in the way you carry yourself. When entering a room, your first thought will not be to see how you might slip out. Our fathers stayed, one in his shop, the other in the nightclub, though a piano player is more of a romantic dreamer than the owner of a hardware store. My father would often step outside the present moment and stare into the distance, at nothing in particular, or close his eyes, knowing that someone was looking at him—a guest's roving eyes had no interest in his partner and settled on the piano player. But then my father cast encouraging glances in every direction. Have a good time, he seemed to say to the guests, embrace your partner, it's all right, the night is different, daytime rules don't apply. Emptied of thought, he'd hum and sway. From his window at home, leaning on a thick pillow, he could watch for minutes on end a bouncing football or basketball, or kids on a slide coming down on their backs or their stomachs. From my window in New York I saw the same thing, so when all is said and done, I couldn't tell you anything deep about the differences between you and me. Except that you are home, safe and sound, while I am about to flee.

Endgame

Svetozar arrived with the guests he'd been asked to pick up, so Dragomán and Kobra's conversation had to be interrupted. They sat around the circular dining room table, Regina's two boys sitting on her left and right, then Habakuk and Olga, Kobra and Dragomán, Melinda and Tombor, nine people in all.

"This dinner is different from other dinners because it is a sad occasion, bidding farewell to János Dragomán. He is going abroad until the case is settled." As she made the announcement Regina raised her wineglass. "It would have been nice to see you around this table for much longer. Habakuk, Zsigmond, and Döme became good friends, and I have a feeling that you, too, liked it here. And then these tragedies. They didn't have to happen. We won't forget you. The place where you're sitting is yours always, wherever you may be."

The three boys crawled underneath the table covered with a white damask tablecloth, and reappeared in scary masks.

"A mature man doesn't skip town," Melinda remarked dryly. "You approve of this?" She looked at the two other men.

"It's damaging to me, but I approve," Tombor said. "Before they start harassing you, János, let them produce witnesses and more evidence. They aim at him but want to get me. Kuno will be made a saint, János is the devil, and I am his disciple. I can even tell you—for that's how such dramas turn out—who the next mayor will be, if they do get me. Want to know? The martyr's widow and spiritual heir. Ah, a miracle: there she is, the lady herself." Svetozar has delivered her too.

"Sandra, my young advisor, speechwriter, and right-hand girl, sit here on my right. You, too, should know that we are bidding farewell to Mr. Dragomán. Let's all drink to János's peaceful departure. And let's also drink to the memory of our friend Kuno Aba, and wish his stout soul eternal rest."

"You have a pleasant room," Melinda said, turning to Dragomán. "You have a bed and a table. The area of free movement allotted to you is sizable, if you walk it from morning to night for weeks you still couldn't traverse it. What is your problem?"

The bell rang. But apparently the garden gate had been left unlocked, because the visitor—Mr. Barnag—entered the house and walked through the kitchen into the dining room. For a moment the lights went out, a full moon peeked through the skylight. The three boys reappeared, this time with carved pumpkins pulled over their heads.

"If the mountain doesn't go to Mohammed..."

Mr. Barnag bowed politely toward Dragomán, but the host was annoyed. "Sir, this is a private party, to which you were not invited."

"Before you throw me out, I must caution you that I have a search warrant. A would-be fugitive from justice, Professor Dragomán, is on the premises."

Regina put another place setting on the table and casually asked Mr. Barnag if he'd just like soup, or a nice piece of flanken as well.

Tombor turned to Dragomán. "Did you throw that boy out?"

"I didn't touch him."

"Did you have a fight?"

"I said I'd make him some tea."

Tombor said, "We all saw the fight with Kuno, and the rector clearly hit Dragomán first; the unfortunate blow to the rector's skull should be considered a tragic accident resulting from a fall. Tell us, Mr. Barnag, do you have a valid reason for doubting the veracity of Mr. Dragomán's words?"

"The professor's refusal to come to the police or to make a statement made me wonder about the wisdom of releasing him," Barnag replied.

"I did not feel like coming to see you," Dragomán said.

Barnag went on. "What really interests me is your essay on the esthetics and erotics of fire."

"And what interests me is what you want from me."

"I simply want to enjoy your company. Give me a chance to do so, put me on the top of your list."

Melinda said, "See, János, we all want you to stay."

Kobra softened. "As long as you are here, sir, let's drink to Kuno Aba's memory. Incidentally, what is your opinion of our late rector?"

"I think he was an original, seminal thinker," Barnag replied. "He dared to assume responsibility. For you, for Kandor. He stood above petty destructiveness, he knew that the state is a sensitive organism that deserves tender care, like a tree."

Regina interrupted, "Care for some garlic sauce, Mr. Barnag? You know, Commissioner, an art historian once compared Mr. Dragomán's essays to garlic. It affects your blood pressure: reduces it if it's high, stimulates it if it's low, and relieves delusions caused by too much anxiety or excessive conceit. Take some horseradish as well."

Tombor spoke again. "I suggest that Sandra and Mr. Barnag withdraw to a corner for a private conference."

"With all due respect to Madame Sandra, regulations do not require that. In my profession nothing is more desirable than restraint, a sense of proportion. I don't want to disturb your dinner any further, the soup you let me enjoy should be immortalized by poets—it will remain a lasting culinary memory. And Professor Dragomán, would you be so kind as to stop by my office tomorrow morning at nine? In one of the pending cases I will question you as a witness, in the other as a suspect. It's nine p.m. now. You must be in your hotel room by midnight; my men will check on you. You must understand, sir, that after these two fatal accidents, you are no longer the person you were." Mr. Barnag bowed respectfully and took his leave.

Sandra broke the silence that hung in the air. "Kuno always said that this sinister character knows a lot about people and that he is a born collector: he files away little-known stories about everyone. What he said about how people respond to Kuno's ideas proved to be true."

"A versatile fellow," Kobra said, but didn't elaborate.

"Among other things, an acrobat," Dragomán added.

Kobra nodded. "A dependable character. He'd make a wonderful agent in the British Secret Service. His problem here is that the authority figures keep changing. Whom should he be serving right now? He did well to be loyal to Kuno, the city's longtime academic luminary. And Kuno was amused, I suppose, by the things he learned from this odd fellow. What's the name of the little bird that lives on the back of a crocodile?"

"Kuno a crocodile?" Sandra asked incredulously. "Where am I? Who are my friends?"

"We are your friends, Sandra," Kobra said, "even if we do make silly jokes, and don't take the word 'friendship' terribly seriously. Kuno believed that the art of politics is being able to tell your friends and enemies apart."

"Anyone who wants to accomplish something will have enemies," Sandra said. "Not just opponents, but enemies who turn bitter from a cutting insult. In the final analysis, what's important, Kuno said, is to know who is an idiot and who is not. One thing is certain: he wasn't an idiot. 'Serve and embrace' was one of his mottoes. He wanted his vision to permeate Kandor's institutions; he wanted to be Kandor's master thinker. He considered his rivals—Dragomán and Kobra—his enemies. Mr. Dragomán in his eyes was a frivolous seducer, and Mr. Kobra an intellectual lightweight. Kuno thought Antal Tombor was the right man for the job, as long as he accepted him as deputy-mayor and chief advisor. That's why he had me work in the mayor's office, instructing me to be loyal to them both, and letting me decide how that should be done. I *was* loyal to both. My husband thought it was generous of the mayor to make himself so vulnerable, so transparent. I think men play these games to turn others into loyal players, to win over hearts. The pursuit of fame is part of the game, it comes from the belief that adulation from others prolongs life. My husband is dead, so it makes little difference how many people admired him. In recent years Kuno became subservient to his own fame. He tried to be everywhere, which meant that he was present nowhere. He wanted me to learn this detachment from self, a life in the public arena required it, it is necessary psychic exercise to keep one's ego flexible. He demanded this flexibility of people—he felt one should be a first-rate bureaucrat during the day, and at night be able to play the cello with friends. For him, leaving a personal spiritual legacy was a top priority—he wanted his voice to remain in us even after he was gone. I was preparing to carry on the legacy, first as his adopted daughter, then as his wife, and trained myself to hear his voice when making a decision. If there is a man I know by heart, it is he. A disciple is the embodiment of the master. Instead of writing books, he devoted himself to his students. When I contradicted him, he rebuked me; but that was his job: to recruit a loyal following. A teacher is expected to impart coherent disciplines, not random ideas, though that aim can never be fully realized. Tell me, Mr. Dragomán, have you ever helped anyone die, actively, I mean?"

Dragomán answered, "I would hope only those who believe in an afterlife, and are therefore already there. For my part, I don't believe in existence after death, while Kuno believed there is another society on the other side, so in a sense we both got what we deserved. I saw him as someone for whom spiritual continuity in this world required continuous background lighting, that of the divine spirit; more precisely, the Christian version of that background lighting. He believed Christ's blood purges us of our sins. The crucified, himself a king, provides, through his church and through temporal rulers, moral justification and metaphysical luster to the complex structures of European hegemony. It's a great pity no contact had ever been established between Kuno and the pope. In this regard, too, I'm keenly aware, madam, of our loss. I could well imagine Kuno Aba as a high church dignitary. Yet, as I look at you now and listen to your words, I am not sorry that Kuno avoided the priesthood. You've noticed, I take it, that I prefer a secular republic in the belief that where theology intrudes upon politics, it's bound to produce a muddle. It's entirely possible, of course, that a muddle has practical value in our town, and it's therefore imperative that everyone pay daily homage, grandiloquently or grossly, to the god of muddle, for what is muddled is good. Or at least this is the impression I get when I read Kuno. Each place has its own brand of muddle, its own cultural hodgepodge, which may be interesting to the tourist or the anthropologist, but to the locals it doesn't mean all that much. Kuno's concoctions were too chauvinistic to be really palatable."

SANDRA CONTINUED. "Kuno said that if we don't have our own vision of ourselves, we'll follow the first comer. For us a monarchy is the legitimate form of government, our Hapsburg connection is almost five centuries old; only that monarchy can guarantee stability in a region as ethnically diverse as ours. The unity represented by the crown made a great deal of legal sense to Kuno. The restoration would have to be a Hungarian initiative, constituting an appropriate extension of our legitimate interests. Kuno gave the exercise of this extended sovereignty religious meaning: his Central European confederation would offer a political blueprint for Christian love and toleration. The reconstituted monarchy would need a queen through whom it could be reconciled with itself. This was my husband's wish, it's why he needed the city, the university, and all the rest—it's why he needed me. One can't live without ideals, people become savages or lifeless puppets without overarching ideals, Kuno said. And the latest is the wide wide world—right here. Kandor is the place; we can create an empire in miniature. Monarchy, this old-new formation, has sprouted in the garden of Central Europe; let's not pluck it out. Real conservatism needs democracy, Kuno said."

Dragomán said, "From now on you'll say, Kuno said this, Kuno said that?"

"If a student keeps quoting her master, then, in time, she is called master, too, and is quoted just as much. When listening to puffed-up pseudomasters—they may as well be called charlatans and cheats—you always sense that in their youth they were not humbled by tradition and continuity. After thirty you may discern a change in their attitude, but it isn't very significant. All this Kuno said. And you, sir, if I am not mistaken, never experienced that humility. An empty shell is what you are, yesterday's stand-up man, a balloon filled with vanity, a fistful of sand in a machine, wild hemp, which makes you cough and your eyes tear. Who invited you to come to Kandor? I did. Formally, the mayor did, but I planted the idea in his head, out of curiosity, and when he approved it, I wrote the letter and put it in front of him for his signature. I invited a murderer who didn't know he had it in him to be one; only that his reflexes were sharp and he could knock down any man who became too troublesome. My Kuno was an orator who tried to create balance and harmony among people, whereas you shot that Russian commandant as easily as if you were throwing a light switch. And that was why those boys had to die. You crippled Kuno with that shot—how could he have known that what he was attempting was impossible? For his good intentions, you humiliated him. But even that didn't satisfy you. You envied his stability, you couldn't stand that he was rooted here, and productive. With one kung fu move you pushed him out of your way. The guardian of Kandor's moral welfare is no more; in his stead we have Professor Dragomán, the dragon, who will corrupt our city."

"Don't forget the virgins and underage widows," Dragomán said. "Two vicious bites, one below, one above the waist, and it's done; their hands, head, and feet I don't even touch. I lure eager innocents into my cave and make seven-headed monsters out of them, and each of those seven heads then sounds off. Let the other students listen to their racket, since they are so intent on learning the truth, which in any case is like a many-faceted diamond that acquires its sparkle from the way the stone is cut. In provincial towns and universities scholarly lectures often turn into sardonic sermons. Small-town prophets believe they educate people if they pepper their explications with pipe dreams and nightmares."

"He's at it again, calling Kuno a provincial scholar, stripping away his dignity. In court I won't even say that you were friends. You conceal your envy with clever phrases, that's what I will say. You all heard what he said about provincial towns. Mr. Dragomán humiliated my husband, and then killed him; now it's my turn to humiliate him. Until now I didn't know what revenge felt like; now I know: it gives you wings." And Sandra at this point did fly out the door.

OLGA FUMED TO her father. "Did you have to get mixed up with that bitch? She ropes you in with her insinuations, and tightens the noose of your own guilt around your neck. You should have bashed her head in, too. If the rector was a protective umbrella, she is a viper. She's leading the mayor around by the nose, has made herself Melinda's sister and disciple, and dazzles Regina with her practical knowledge, her shopping secrets. And David Kobra could say to himself: 'What a body. Now if only she didn't talk so fast, if only she would stop showing off.' Important people are already sold on her; now she can start grabbing things for herself. She is a ball-buster, all right, her every word is a command. With those kewpie-doll eyes and military cheekbones she can't go wrong. What she needs is an impresario, Father, and if you don't watch out, it'll be you. She is what she was meant to be: an unstoppable avenger. She wins at every game, and her successes are a bitter remedy for obscure injuries. You mustn't see this woman again! Melinda, please stop him. Go away, Father, I beg you. I don't know what this bitch is up to, but she's up to no good, I feel it, it gave me the willies to stand next to her. I'll go home with the children now; you get in the car and leave the country tonight. And don't hook up with that shady Slav either, don't give in to your comfort, or to seductive strangers. Go alone and call me tomorrow from the other side. God be with you, my darling wanderer."

Dragomán replied, "One less woman to contend with, one less voice telling you to get moving, one more reason to fill our pipe and ask for another glass of this unpretentious Italian white.

"I assure you I'll consider my actions very carefully. I see no ethical problem here. I became involved in situations for which I cannot be held legally responsible. In a rash moment I pushed a man who slapped me in the face. I could have been more clever, I could have simply twisted his arm and held it, but such close physical contact with the rector I wanted to avoid.

"Drifting is not a problem for me. When, yielding to my nostalgic vanity, I came back, a voice warned me that there was a trap. No one set it for me, it was there all along. Is Mr. Barnag guided by the spirit of justice? God only knows what guides Mr. Barnag. Here everything is about something else. The rector is at the same time a priest. The honorary doctor is also a devotee of black magic, a sinister wizard. Gradually everyone inhabits his role, whether they like it or not. I should go on causing trouble until the good people of Kandor with the clearest of conscience stone me to death. The atmosphere of hostility makes court proceedings suspect; the establishment of facts is hindered by politics.

"But even if I am guiltless, am I not guilty? And aren't you expecting me to pay for my deed? And though authority is questionable, is there any other authority? A court competent to pass judgment and carry out the sentence? Other than my own mind, I don't know of one. I could lock myself up for a year or two; If I were found guilty of negligent manslaughter, that would probably be the length of my prison term. I could welcome the restriction of my movements, be happy that my designated domicile happens to be the hotel where I am staying. The lucky bastard has done it again, I can just hear it. And I could say—behind bars, under the watchful eyes of armed prison guards, in the library and the bowling alley of carefree convicts—there, Kuno, I've paid my debt, I've survived you, so farewell. I need you like a hole in the head.

"All of you are masters of self-imprisonment. There is no life outside Kandor, you all say, and if there is, it's nothing like this. It so happens you are right. But I can't stand being closed in. And I will not collaborate with my jailers, become the lover of my prison guard. What reason is there to put me in jail, and then, after a long detention, let me go?

"I have heard it said that as much as I would like to understand Kandor, I never will, because I have changed, paid too high a price for the privilege of seeing the world. A few right-thinking citizens will also say: He pushed to his death the very best among us, the best in us. He pushed *us* away.

"On the other hand, they asked me to be a target in their shooting gallery, so they could take aim, or at least point fingers at me, and exorcise that part of themselves that is most like me. Yes, I came willingly. We had our festive conventions. The metropolitan magic spread the siren song of their self-mockery. The presence of pacifist anarchists was in itself a provocation. In other words, I am no angel myself; but I won't try to prove my innocence to you, because in your eyes I am guilty, even if you do love me. This house is beginning to oppress me, I hear interesting noises outside, so let's join the fun. I hope we'll look out for each other, but if we drift apart in the crowd, God be with you. Thank you for all your kindness."

Drums roll, cymbals crash, a slender girl bows and scrapes, balancing on her shoulder like a wide collar a wooden contraption with a monster's head. An actor in tall boots claps his booted hands. Looking like a quadruped, or like two figures in a fight, he keeps shaking the skull and torso of his second self on his back; it is spattered with blood and flour and its eyes keep popping out.

The eyes of a giant wooden pig are lighted up, a screen in its mouth shows a pig slaughter in vivid detail, but in reverse order, from the sausage stage to the live animal. You can see blood being stirred in a pan, the eyes being cut open, the evisceration itself, in a close-up, and finally, you hear the squeals of the just-killed porker. It's like eating each other alive, like pouring our blood into a dish to make black pudding, frying it to a crisp in steaming onions.

"Here comes Strong John as marionette pummeling ghosts; first they get thrashed, then he does, sticks and saucepans are resorted to, but then the drizzle turns into heavy rain, and the show is cut short. There are spectacles everywhere, in churches, barns and taverns, tableaux vivants presented to the strains of a *cimbalom*. Clowns cavort on their wagons, grimacing and howling. Children run after their mothers, balls roll away, balloons escape, drivers are at their wits' end, beer, wine, and brandy are disappearing. A burly man stops cars and asks the drivers to taste his beer, which he has on tap in a fire truck.

A summertime Santa pulls his sled forlornly, his cotton mustache droops, as if melting. A creature of winter, he strayed into summer and feels out of place. Every now and then his red fur hat pops up in the bustle, he stops to talk, but after a few words walks on, discouraged. Yet he doesn't give up; he still hopes to find a better, colder world.

DRAGOMÁN GOES UP the mountain, treks through the forest, first oak than pine, there is the cave and there the cliff, his hiking boots have already touched the tail of a rainbow when he finally reaches the Stonedial, the rocky, ivy-covered plateau where twelve basalt slabs form a circle and where the rays of the sun are the hands of a clock. It seems that only here, from the perspective of stilled and imagined time, time petrified and turned to stone, can he truly see himself.

The horizon is crimson, wind blows from west to east, the lake's surface is pale, its shimmer is dying. If Dragomán were to take this steep trail, clinging to hillside shrubs, he could make his way down to the mouth of the cave where long ago he fired that fatal shot. Whether the right target is chosen or not, one shot follows another, a whole round. The trail down is steep, pebbles roll under his feet, some of the berries have turned red, others are black, the color now of the sky.

On the other side of the mountain torchlights cleave the night air, and in the great palm of the Valley of Mercy the faithful sit on benches listening to preachers who relieve each other every hour; the loudspeakers carry their exhortations closer: Submit to Him, He suffers for you. You through Him, He through you. A searchlight scans the cliff that serves as the backdrop of this drama. Dragomán sits on top of it, in the mossy cavity of a rock, the air is fragrant, the basalt exudes the warmth soaked up during the day. In a rock formation next to him a lizard rests for a moment. Stay, Dragomán feels like telling him. You don't mean that, the lizard might answer. Buses disgorge worshippers carrying church banners. Led by their priest, old women march toward that palm, the stone basin where they will remain all night. The priests will listen, too, and build on each other's thoughts. The faithful are intent: Yes, they will help, yes, they will take the first step and forgive; no, they will not do that, they will reject the sin of pride, they will not throw back their head in defiance, and will not flee the presence of the angel, should he appear and ask a question in the name of God.

IN THE TIME rendered motionless by the Stonedial, all exertions and contortions are reduced to a few tentative movements, and even those to a shadowy image, and that to a single dot which can only vanish. The elimination of all prospects is always imminent, but I can seldom exclude from my thoughts the notion of a future, of a time when I can still make things right, recover from my illnesses, make up for what I've missed. If there is no future and no redress; if everything remains as it was, if the future events do not modify those of the past, then each moment is complete in itself.

You are no better today than yesterday. As in a game of chess: where you put it is where it stays. If you lied, you lied; if you killed, you killed—no room for explanations. You didn't want to do it, you were drawn in. Few people choose sin, it comes to one's door, it pops in like a burglar, or lies dormant, under the doorstep, but always alive and fresh.

Of course, you were defending yourself, the situation demanded it, or a commander did, or the passion of the moment, a sudden surge of hate, not your true self but something peripheral; external, not your own consciousness but another's, his voice, yes, it was a voice that told you to do it.

I am the perfect fall guy: innocent cowards fault me for telling them to turn evil. But whom do I blame? Standing next to the basalt hands of the Stonedial and the steel column that marks the summit, I have nowhere to turn, I can only go round and round. A weak man who wants to cut and run, and leave behind, like a dog its turd, his unintended blunders and collusions. He twists and turns, but knows he can't slip away; what holds him here is the law, his conscience, his memories.

I could make my peace with the latter two, a voice whispers, a Mediterranean, Balkan voice—Svetozar's. Until things quiet down, he says, I should fly the coop, and submit to American-style justice, which is manifestly more reliable and impartial than anything meted out here. Unless we consider Mr. Barnag an atypical phenomenon. But it may not even be up to Mr. Barnag. If Kuno's friends are on top, I'll be found guilty; if it's Tombor's friend, I'll be off the hook.

But even my friends do not consider accidents to be really accidents; they don't believe there is such a thing; events taking place around me are inevitably my doing. And I believe the same about them: they, too, are accountable for what happens in their backyard. If they don't run away from it, they're clearly used to it, have learned to live with it. My friends soaked up all the Russian classics, and would probably find Raskolnikov's forced exile appealing, forgetting that Dostoevsky didn't choose to be imprisoned, he was hauled off in chains because he dared to discuss ideas in friendly company. He tried to make a distinction between truth and falsehood, as anyone would whose head is not filled with straw.

I can recall my past anywhere in the world. At Chicago's O'Hare, for instance, if I have a thirty-minute layover. Or I can bring up the wonderful subject of remorse in the bar of the Gramercy Park Hotel, where the pianist sometimes lets me take over for him. I provide background music that's smooth and dreamy or hot and swingy. Ladies sit next to me who have lines under their eyes and probably on their bellies as well; but then I am no youngster myself. Old girlfriends appear, new clients, editors, neighbors, actresses, drug dealers, and other people of dubious occupation. Hairdressers who claim to be dancers and who sometimes do dance, checkroom attendants who say they are magicians, and who do indeed make magic, forever stirring invisible pots. All I have to do is touch on my guilt, and they weave a nice little halo around my head, savoring my Kandoran misadventures.

But it's his grandson's request for a new installment in the saga that makes Dragomán appear at police headquarters at nine in the morning. He has to surrender his passport and is given a metal tag in return, the kind you get at the public swimming pool, after you've left your clothes in a cubbyhole. So long as his passport is in strange hands, Dragomán is, in an official sense, naked. But the young detective is unable to persuade him to give new answers to his latest questions. No, he did not know the gentleman. Yes, he did refer to an article of his, which has yet to appear in Hungarian. But the occurrence in question—a man leaping from the sixth-floor roof terrace into the blue-tiled swimming pool—has nothing to do with Dragomán's person or his work. There's no causal connection at all.

"Did the young man want something from you? Did he ask you for anything?"

"He offered to be my lover. I told him I wasn't interested."

"Obviously, you cannot be expected to avail yourself of such an offer, but a humiliating disappointment is sometimes enough to make one raise a hand against oneself."

"Suicide is a free gesture; by definition it can have no perpetrator other than the suicide himself, and it is therefore the stuff of literature, or an obituary, and not a matter for the police."

"You said 'free gesture,' a buzzword from your youth, when you were expected to be a leftist, and also to deviate from the official line in the direction of existentialism, isn't that right? At the moment this is indeed beside the point. Years ago you wrote an essay on the role of suicide in the drama of one's personal life. (I found it in a bibliography of your publications.) It's clear to me that in suicide the time and place are not without interest, they may be charged with symbolism. For if life is that which unfolds in time, it must cease at a given point—before a sharp decline, for example. Everyone has his version of the highest peak—in our region it's the top of Stonedial. One goes there to think something over, or to leap into the valley. That young man was preparing himself for a moment of truth. It had become an either/or matter for him. Whichever way it turned out, he had to draw the necessary conclusion. In the end he must salute like a soldier, press his cap to his side with one hand, grip his sword with the other, march out of the room, get on his horse, and ride away."

Dragomán looked at the flushed face of the young detective. Could this be the onset of an epileptic fit? Through a rear door Mr. Barnag entered, put his arm around the young detective and led him out.

Barnag sighed. "*Persona intacta,* even *pudica.* There are areas that are open to authors of detective stories but off limits to the police. Yet who doesn't know that inside every policeman is a would-be mystery writer? In the patrol car, on long trips, each weighs in with well-crafted stories. I regret, Professor, that my young colleague got carried away. He is what's known as a meteoropath, his mood shifts with the weather. The boy has a good head on his shoulders, though he lacks perseverance....But let's consider the case of the rebuffed admirer closed, and talk about our late rector. Tell me, sir, have you had training in any of the martial arts, karate, kung fu, and the like?"

"I trained for a year in California."

"You and Dr. Kuno Aba have known each other for a long time, were, in a sense, colleagues and friendly competitors. Was there, of late, tension between you two? Stemming from a revision of a certain historical event, perhaps? I would like you to know, sir, that you are not the only one with knowledge of what took place long ago in the Valley of Mercy. Some of the Russian comrades also knew about it. That colonel was somewhat careless. Lazar Moiseyevich was his name, I think. 'Let them kill each other,' a communications officer said, after learning of your family origins.

"That you were the one who shot him, we found out in the spring of '63. Fortunately for you, a little too late. Most of the imprisoned rebels had been released by then. You had spent time with us, a year and half, if I am not mistaken; it would not have been politically wise to put you away again. But you must have known that that we were watching you. Forgive me for saying so, but we were amused by the redundant summaries of your amorous adventures. Photographs taken on a number of occasions showed you in a compromising position, in one of the sentry boxes along the castle wall—always with someone different, but in exactly the same spot."

"And I have heard you called the Fouché of Kandor. You headed the department of dirty tricks. You offered Kuno your services as an honest-to-goodness conservative realist. He told me so himself. But if you were thinking of sinking your teeth into me now, be careful: they just might break. And now please return me my passport."

"I don't mean to offend you, Professor; however, my image of you is more subtle than yours is of me. But great minds allow themselves small acts of carelessness that mediocrities like myself can ill afford. I assure you that my confidential investigations never violated your personal rights.

"I know that your consul is quick to protest when we harass an American citizen. What we don't tell him is that we also found a packet of hashish on the unfortunate tourist, for the consul would take something like that much more seriously than we do. We tend to overlook it, knowing that where there is light, there's bound to be shadow as well.

"Our experts have examined the voluminous, indeed excessively rich photographic evidence of the tug-of-war between you and Kuno Aba, and have concluded that you bear no responsibility for what happened. Your behavior was evasive and defensive, rather than assertive and aggressive. It's obvious that the rector had more to drink than you did. And everyone was impressed that after the first slap you merely gave him a surprised look. You fended off a second blow by adroitly twisting his arm—an instinctive act of self-defense. It was his bad luck that his collision with the edge of the bench proved fatal, for his skull was struck in a most vulnerable spot. But if the rector had not drunk so much, he probably would not have staggered back as far. His being off balance, along with his aggressive demeanor, puts you in the clear.

"I mentioned before that I, too, could refute Kuno's revised version of the events in the Valley of Mercy, yet I would not have cried out: 'Kuno, I saw you.' For one thing, I did not see Kuno Aba, and for another, I would have let him say what he wanted; lying, in and of itself, is not a crime.

"You, Professor Dragomán, could not possibly imagine how much mendacity and falseness I come across among the Kandoran elite. And the lies are all different, it's like adding specimens to an insect collection. I smack my lips every time I stick a fat new one on a pin. They say writers peer into the dark recesses of life, that they are familiar with sin in all guises—well, if those gifted ladies and gentlemen could witness as much human ugliness as I do in my line of work, they would be shocked, and would perhaps be more appreciative of the dilemmas faced by crime fighters.

"When someone knows too much, he usually keeps quiet. When someone keeps contradicting people he doesn't know enough. As far as your case is concerned, incidentally, your chances are excellent. I haven't seen all the results of the official investigation, but I can tell you that statements made by several of our detectives are favorable to you. I must ask you, though, to continue to observe my instructions: Confine your movements to the prescribed radius, and remain in your designated residence. You have been released, but only conditionally. Still, within the liberal bounds, you are free to come and go and to do as you please. I invite you to discover the beauty as well as the seamier side of our city. Live your life, write your masterpieces, and enjoy your grandchild. Here, sir, is your passport. We'll see each

other at the rector's funeral. Our mayor will stand next to the
widow in the first row, right behind the casket, and you'll be on
Mrs. Tombor's left in the second row."

DRAGOMÁN HAD JUST made it back to the Crown and was
looking at his stubble in the elevator mirror. A few more days
like this, and it would be a relief to lie on a prison cot, his mind a
blank, his face blending in with the prison garb. Some people
never entertain the possibility that one day they will have to remove their own shirt and put on state issue, and get used to institutional rules, institutional food. Or if they itch for something
worse, they can get that, too, since the capacity to inflict pain is
always greater than the ability to endure it. But for the moment
let's forget about changes of shirts and stick to our shaving routine. Dragomán had just finished shaving and showering and was
getting into his clothes and pouring out coffee he'd ordered,
when the phone rang. A worried Colonel Barnag was at the other
end. Unfortunately, the situation was not as bright as they had
both hoped. He wouldn't say it had worsened dramatically, but it
did look less favorable. New circumstances had presented themselves, which called for a more thorough clarification and further
exploration on both their parts, and it was best to get that over
with as soon as possible. He must therefore ask Mr. Dragomán to
come and see him before noon. They could order in something
light, that way they won't even have to break for lunch. Mr. Barnag's voice turned bright and cheerful at the mention of a new
meeting.

DRAGOMÁN FILLED HIS shoulder bag with his essentials and
prepared to depart. He settled his account downstairs, paid for an
extra two weeks, and studied the train schedule. On his way out
he ran into Sandra just as she was entering through the revolving
door. She had come to hand-deliver a special invitation to the funeral; she was going to leave it with the desk clerk. The envelope
also contained an offprint of an article by Kuno with the following title: "Pariahs? Citizens of the World? A Strategic Proposal
for the Jews."
    Together they walked toward the square in the orange autumn
light. A street mime followed them, his left hand holding the in-

visible counterpart of Dragomán's bulky umbrella, and his right arm, doing what Dragomán's did not, encircling an imaginary lady whom he smothered with mock-impetuous kisses, and whose part he also played, first sweetly coy and then amorously biting back. Sandra and Dragomán turned around and tried to stifle their laughter.

At the taxi stand, an elderly couple and a young woman with a child were waiting ahead of them. Dragomán asked Sandra if she would drive him to the train station. Why not? She happened to be free. "Where are you going?" "Venice," he said. "Like this?" "Yes." "You have business there?" "I always have business," he said evasively.

"You came, you saw, you conquered, and now you leave? You made me a widow, and now you are abandoning me? You won't even come to the funeral? It might create an odd impression, you know; people may think you're nervous. But if you walked behind me, on Melinda's left, behind the coffin, and at the grave looked the mourners in the eye, you'd win them over, I am sure. Your otherwise debauched face would reflect the grief of the fellow sportsman, fellow sufferer, comrade in arms, and the case would be closed. Afterward, like a generous friend, you would do everything in your power to promote and popularize the legacy of my late husband. There would be a few TV interviews stressing the importance of building bridges between camps, and on Kuno Aba Day the memorial lecture at the Kandor Academy would be given by none other than Professor Dragomán, perhaps with the following title: 'Kuno Aba's Inquiries into the Dynamics of Multi-Dimensional Interdependence Among Regional Elites.' You and I could discuss the details later."

If he wished, Dragomán could take the next train. In any case, for the fugitive to hide out in the house of the aggrieved, the victim's widow, was the least likely possibility. Mr. Barnag would never think of that, and if he did, he would suppress the thought. At the same time, it would be entirely reasonable for the chief of police to exchange information with the rector's widow, provided the exchange was selective. The elderly couple have already left, a cab approaches, the young woman pulls her son along. Sandra tells Dragomán that her car is parked in a sidestreet. They might sit down somewhere first. Not a public place—Dragomán's face has become too familiar of late. And in her widow's weeds Sandra could be easily recognized. They might as well go up to Sandra's house, from her large terrace they could look down on the lake. Afterward, if he still wanted to leave, she would drive him to the station.

Dragomán got into Sandra's car and looked around, almost contentedly, contemplating the fork in the road. Here, around a one-story tavern laid out like a trapezoid, it divides into two winding cobblestone streets, which then begin their ascent up the hill. To the left is Kobra's house and Melinda's house, and to the right, Kuno Aba's. A sharp right. A woman is at the wheel, and if we are not mistaken her mouth crinkles into a smile. That he should divulge his secret and then have himself driven by her, of all people? Conspiring with the enemy can mean either betrayal or great success. At times like this, Dragomán with his long nose sniffs out the wind of fate, and like a dog picks up a scent.

The driver's perfume brings to mind the word "knowledge." These prominent cheekbones are stunning, elongating the eyes; the full, heart-shaped lips are another surprise, on them hovers a tiny smile, a mocking, suspicious smile, not an inviting one. Regardless of how this visit will end, the idea of revenge has been planted, and is sprouting quietly. But revenge can assume many shapes and guises. To best the one who's best—that's the real aim. In such an ambiguous situation the old Dragomán would have put his hand on the driver's leg, declaring his intentions, saying in effect: Count me in. But the driver's intention is to gently push that hand away. Dragomán senses that intention and the hand moves back of its own accord. Instead, he begins a meditation on local history.

At Florian Square he bursts out laughing; where the old Fisherman restaurant used to be, on the corner of Víg Street, there is a Chinese restaurant now. But the same aging beauties walk up and down, their lips heavily rouged, enticing. He used to love to listen to men swagger in the old Fisherman. They were glad to be away from their wives, and those who were here with permission acted even more cocky, telling everyone how they would shave off a little from their paycheck, and spend it here on fish soup, noodles and cheese, and a good bottle of Riesling, enough for all the regulars—though eventually they would get around to admitting that their wives made a far better fish soup (though this one is not half bad), to say nothing of their noodles and cheese. They made the pasta themselves, even if their hands hurt; none of that store-bought kind for them. All this had happened about thirty years ago, before Sandra was born.

"This is where I went to dance school," Dragomán says. "Me, too," Sandra replies. "Here was that espresso bar, the Narcissus," Dragomán says. "It's still here," Sandra answers. "That's where I said good-bye to Kobra, in that small square over there. There's the spot where the car picked me up. My neck hurt from craning it," Dragomán says. "I was here the other day, sitting on the porch of a retired army officer," Sandra offers. "He sells dry muscatel wine and aged sausage. His homegrown pears melt in your mouth. His wife has cancer and cannot stand up. She draws pictures in a thick sketchbook, until she is too tired to do anything."

The swallows have gone, and so have the storks, the afternoons are cool, it's time for woolen jackets again. Dragomán wouldn't mind sitting on that officer's porch with Sandra; from there they could watch herds of deer passing, and the clouds' shadows on the lake. Kuno Aba had thought very highly of the retired officer's apricot-and-plum brandy, a drop of it was enough to fire up your insides. The stone wall of Kuno's house loomed from afar, the metal garage door opened at the push of a button. Sandra was shivering, so they settled in one of the inner rooms and drank hot tea with rum. After a while Sandra stood and led Dragomán through the house, and then brought him to the guest room, which was so cramped their bodies had to draw closer. It all happened without words, with concurring movements, a quick shedding of clothes and turning of the key in the lock. Later, when Dragomán lay his head on the woman's left hip and observed the curve of her breast, her thigh, her belly, he couldn't resist saying to her: "You could be a trifle less perfect." But then it was Sandra's turn to take the lead. Dragomán, somewhat dazed, nodded in answer to Sandra's question: "Are you happy now?" But though his partner was even friskier than before, he fell asleep.

It was dark when he awoke. Sandra was next to him, leaning on her elbow. He would have to hurry to make the train. "If you want, I'll take you to the station," Sandra said helpfully, though her smile contained other meanings. Dragomán did what his hands wanted. He took her in his arms and caressed every part of her within reach.

Now Sandra is on the phone, the doorbell rings, they've come to take him away. He buries his head in her belly, moves up to her right earring, and holds her hand down as she's about to dial again. But no, she wasn't about to, she's just fine, everything is bright and cozy.

Kuno was overbearing—a father who lay in his adopted daughter's bed and bequeathed her his cherished ideas. Throw him into the well, push him off the edge of Stonedial, into the Valley of Mercy, a ninety-foot drop, get the master off her body, off the bookshelves and the floppy disks. And the others, too, get going, onto the diving board with you, old-timers, and from there a leap into the blessed void.

But first we must watch this woman take a shower, and dry and comb her hair, and argue with herself in front of the mirror. She must get over this, this had to happen, this act of sacrilege will bring her peace of mind. The second night justifies the first, the third vindicates the first two. But can she take more than three days of the impossible, the impermissible, the outrageous? She should be alone now, cut her hair short, brush it back, have a mass said for her dear departed, tend the flowers on his grave, publish his posthumous books—and not feel the stubble on the murderer's chin with the pad of her thumb. The guestroom bed is not wide, this was intimacy in close quarters; they've disarmed each other but also cunningly rearmed themselves.

From the time they threw off their clothes until they sat up once again properly attired in her overstuffed living room, filled with *objets d'art,* the lady of the house kept proposing to her guest that he remain. Nobody would suspect him of hiding out here, it would be the last place they would look, common sense and decency argue against it. What reason indeed would she have to hide him from the authorities?

According to a more conventional scenario, she ought to have stabbed him to death. Or worse. "Don't you think, János dear, that I ought to castrate you in your sleep with a good gelding knife?"

"You pose your question so enticingly, I am dying to stay. But let's just stay awake until we can see in each other's eyes what we might expect."

"I know I mustn't take the law into my own hands, but since you are an utter cynic, though not completely without morals, I can think of a solution whereby I will mete out your punishment. After all, I am the offended party. The man you took away from me was both my stepfather and my husband. His presence in my life may have been oppressive, but he was there for me, he built this house according to precise plans, he fortified it with heavy masonry, he built a prison around my mother, then around me, I nevertheless vanquished him and made him king of my castle.

"I have the strength to bend others to my will, and in a way that even makes them happy. I've embarked on a political career. For the time being I want to be chief administrator of the city. First, a job as a professional, then a political post—I must be able to switch from one to the other. At thirty-four I want to be mayor, and a forty, prime minister of this country. I will stay in office until I am forty-eight. Then I'll be elected president of the republic, which will be followed by high positions in the European Union or the United Nations.

"This place has given me the right to push forward my plans. When we cut things down to size, blow away the rhetorical foam, what's left is a down-to-earth realism that doesn't necessarily lack vision. What have you to do with all this, my dear Dragomán? If I so desire, the courts will convict you, but I can also persuade them, and the press, to find you guilty only of negligent homicide. In any case, public opinion would demand such a verdict.

"Taking my political ambitions into account, it would be riskier, yet more sensible, if I got you to become my slave. You're likely to receive a two-year prison sentence. Let me have those two years of your life. Give up your freedom voluntarily, and submit to my will on your own, out of common decency. Your meddlesomeness created a painful void in my life—try to fill it.

"For a month or two you'll hide out here, under my strict supervision. During that time we'll mail letters written in your hand from abroad, always with a different postmark. In the meantime I would testify that the two of you were old friends and that this contretemps did not suggest anything willful or premeditated—it was an accident, nothing more. You write a letter—I'll compose it, if you like—saying that you'd be more than happy to appear before the Kandor authorities in order to clarify certain details, something you have been willing to do all along, but this painful affair has so weakened your physical and mental state, you are in need of a few more weeks of recuperation abroad, after which you will report back. In the meantime you'll be a prisoner in my house. My own little house pet."

"Madam, I could not possibly help further your political ambitions; on the contrary, I would drag you back to inertia; we'd only get on each other's nerves. But while we were in bed, your majesty saw fit to start a tussle. Volcanic forces seethe within my lady. You would stamp your foot, strike your boot with your whip, and issue orders to shoot a hapless cur. Your cold fire and calculated excess make my heart sink."

"Don't go," implored Sandra. "I was talking nonsense. The truth is I am afraid to be alone. Do whatever you like, just don't go. Make the guestroom your own. There is a cabin in the backyard, use it as a hideout—be my little bird for a while. Warm me when I am cold, ask me if my head or my stomach hurts, bend over me when I cry in my sleep.

"Make coffee in the morning before I go off to work, tell me which perfume to wear, point out the most interesting article in the newspaper, pack my lunch, either a spicy salami sandwich or some smelly cheese—let them have a fit at the office. And when I leave, go back to bed, regain your strength, take a leisurely bath, walk in the garden, no one can see you from outside. Write your memoir in that cabin, a memoir whose main theme is that whatever may have happened, happened, it's over now, finished, done with."

"I am itching to know what my imprisonment would be like. Would we sleep in the same bed?" "If you behave yourself." "Would I be beaten?" "If you deserve it." "Could I hit you back?" "Not on your life." "Could I leave the garden?" "No way." "How about reading for pleasure?" "Only when I am not here.

"When I am around—except when I feel like reading—you must be ready to entertain me, service me, listen with undivided attention and approving, even rapt nods to my musings. And you must unstintingly rub my back, the soles of my feet, my earlobes, apply oil where needed, and trim my toenails. Furthermore, you must soothe my anxieties with tender sympathy, help me decide what dress to put on, not spoil my morning coffee by adding too much or too little milk, and know which jam tastes best with my toast—yes, you must decide even that, you have to know how much is too much. And make sure there's always herbal tea in the house, and know when to serve it with honey and when to make it plain.

"Without a word from me you must know, from the direction of the wind, the movement of clouds, that I am getting my period, which may make me irritable. In the evening, after I've got dressed, you will be enchanted by my looks, intoxicated by my perfume, you will give anything for another whiff behind my ear, and you'll wave after me as I drive off, a proper widow going to some respectable gathering, where someone will remark that black is very becoming to me. In short, what you need right now is to pay attention to someone else. And I also need someone to pay attention to me, I was a pupil long enough, the physical incarnation of a mind much loftier than mine.

"I need a slave, not a husband, for a husband wanders off, even if he stays at his desk; he feels he has a right to lock himself in his room. Let's be clear about this: you'll be my slave. If you should have some complaint, you can come to me for remedy. And if you start acting cold, I will turn mean and nasty and scream at you. And use filthy language. An ordinary male cannot take such treatment—before long you'll stop giving me the cold shoulder and caress me instead."

"I'm afraid you'd never judge my devotion to be completely satisfactory. Am I wrong?"

"You're right, I wouldn't. But you need not be perfect. Now and then I'd overlook your faults. In other words, what I promise you is paradise.

"People will think you are abroad, in hiding, underground; no one in his right mind will believe that you are here, with me, whom you have every reason to fear. And you really do, my poor friend, and always will, as long as you live. But what you'll be afraid of is not some bald, hulking bodyguard, who will go after you with a club and twist your arm and leg, just so I could hear

283

you whimper and be amused. No, what you're afraid of is that the expression on my face will remain stern even when you try your hardest to coax a smile out of me, or that in the morning, before getting into my car, I will say good-bye a little too inattentively, kiss the air, or merely pucker. There'll be progress, to be sure, and ever-more serious lovesickness—I will twist you around my finger as if you were a piece of string. Not enthusiastic enough, I will say about the thirteenth version of your study on Kuno, which you'll slide out under the door, because the door itself will be locked, and the only way it will be opened, in time for lunch, is if the slid-out manuscript serves our purposes and wins our approval. Get ready to remain my prisoner for as long as you live. It's nice to be a grandfather, but you could still be a father, too. You can do your own thing, but you must also take care of this house and keep alive the memory of our loved ones. Make sure you stay in shape, go on earning hard currency, take me to exotic lands, show me the wonders of the world, so I could pooh-pooh the wonders. Encourage and reassure me. Convince me that I am not the silliest person in the world, and even if I were, you'd love me just the same."

"I can just see myself in Kuno's slightly rearranged room, among his books and papers," Dragomán said. "I will run my hand over the fine wooden banister, which he touched so many times as he climbed the stairs to the bedroom. In his high-backed armchair I will rest my head in the same spot where he did when he wanted to rest his eyes, and then fell asleep. I would put my eyeglasses and my cup where he did. His suits would fit me fine, we're about the same size. And if—after a year of mourning—we step out in style and you call me Kuno by mistake, I wouldn't mind the slip. Kuno has skipped out of your life and departed for parts unknown. I will have taken his place, and at times will feel one with him. We'll live here as a threesome. For Kuno has been displaced only to the extent that he moved inside me. It's possible that to keep going as me is no longer feasible. To be there for your awakening, draw your bathwater, make your coffee, turn off the radio the minute you enter the kitchen, greet you in a properly cheerful mood, feed you and see you off as though you were going to school—all this is possible and desirable. You'll buy the food, I'll do the cooking, and won't set foot outside the house. I'll be an aging lapdog, a cozy blanket around your cold feet; I'll mutter words to relax you and growl a little to stimulate you. I'll lie through my teeth for you, and be your booster when you start bragging. I'll tend to the little injuries your stormy personality will be forced to suffer at the office. They are all idiots, I will say, don't pay attention to them. I'll be your professional trainer and masseur—I'll massage your fragile ego, so you'll feel good about yourself all day. And in the morning, when you get behind the wheel and wave to me, I'll look at you and wave back as I close the garden gate. Yes, we may indeed discuss marriage, but I'm afraid our contrary inclinations would not tolerate that holy estate. If I had a chance to make it out of here, I'd grab it. Go bark at the moon, my grandson, Habakuk, said to me the other day. Go on the lam, people kept urging after the war, and I've been heeding that advice ever since. My ancestors tried to go on the lam a couple of thousand years ago, when they felt the ground under their feet getting dangerously hot. Comfortable prisons are the worst."

"You will never leave this place. There is a pistol in Kuno's drawer—should I take it out, stick it in your back, walk you to your room and lock the door? Should I drive you to the station? Should I gag you and let things take their course?"

The phone rings, Sandra picks it up, listens, then hangs up.

It was a young man, calling her a Jew-loving bitch. He said she'd better not continue on her sinful path, because if she does, a whip will be used to decorate her back until she begs for mercy. His message to Dragomán: he's in for a freefall.

Another phone call. Svetozar would like to speak to the professor. He is sitting in the Stonedial restaurant, having ordered mushrooms cooked in garlic butter, smoked shrimp, and a bottle of Kandor rosé. As for the rest of the meal, he's undecided, but he is definitely of the opinion that with this light and noble rosé they might take their leave of Kandor. Coffee grounds and tarot cards point to the same solution: Away from here. Moments ago he saw shadows move and fall away from a tree trunk. He also saw two heads with the usual black stockings pulled over them, and club-wielding hands. They must be great admirers of the rector, those two; they kept whispering his name. The professor may have studied the art of kicking with champions, but let it be noted that that wasn't yesterday. "And I, Svetozar, would not rule out the possibility that there are people out there who may want to throw your body off the cliffs of Stonedial, onto the stage of that basalt amphitheater—only you would know why. With your feline nimblefootedness you may have a chance if not to break your fall with an expert kick, then at least to grab hold of a shrub growing between the rocks; after sliding a bit, you might grab another shrub, reducing the plunge by a third, and if you are able then to try out one of your daring jumps, you may, within a matter of minutes, walk nonchalantly onto the terrace of the Stonedial restaurant, whistling, your hands in your pockets, catching a popular tune played by the band. But because there is too much risk in this lively scenario, I think I'll finish what I ordered (leaving the rabbit stew for another time), and come get you. So, if possible, open the garden gate in exactly thirty minutes, I'll be there in my souped-up Jaguar. I have a gun license, so in case of attack I'll be at liberty to decide whether or not to use my magnum to defend myself. And if somebody around this telephone booth should overhear me, so be it. So, gentlemen there behind the tree trunks, let's not be foolish, let's not annoy each other, because I am likely to do something drastic. You'll be pleased to know, Professor Dragomán, that I've prepared a basket for the road, including a few bottles of beer. If you'll feel like it, you can even take a nap in the back seat. I am bringing a burnoose, a false beard, and a diplomatic passport issued by the United Arab Emirates. From the minute you open the gate, you speak only English and Arabic, and not a word of Hungarian. Behave with princely dignity and leave everything to your driver."

All Dragomán says in reply is that he's not leaving, he's staying here in the city. He'll return to the Crown to face the consequences. He will retain a lawyer, though, and contact the embassy of the United States, the country whose citizen he is, after all. He'll make sure not to travel beyond the territorial limit imposed on him. He has nothing further to report to Mr. Barnag. He is purposely saying all this on the telephone, so if somebody is listening in, they should forward the message to the appropriate authorities. The message is also for Sandra, and everyone else concerned. The next time he will speak it will be in a courtroom, *if* charges are brought, that is. And should the authorities detain him for not wishing to appear before Mr. Barnag, and indeed for not wishing, from this day on, to have anything to do with him, they should be aware that as long as he is deprived of his freedom, he will not utter another word. This statement will be conveyed through his lawyer to the authorities, and to the public at large. His daughter is soon to give birth, he'll have two grandchildren, he is staying close to them. "I'll be there in thirty minutes, make sure the gate is open," Svetozar says tersely.

DRAGOMÁN IS ROUSED from his catnap—Svetozar has jammed on the brakes. A car passed him and is now in front of him, moving at a snail's pace. But when Svetozar tries to pass this driver, he steps on the gas and is off like a shot. Svetozar has to stay in his lane because he sees a truck approaching on the other side. The car in front of him again slows to a crawl. Svetozar again tries to pass him and collides head-on with a truck that suddenly materializes from below an incline—he is killed instantly. Dragomán's face is bleeding, but he manages to climb out of the rear window. When he sees that Svetozar is dead, he runs off into the black night. Two men run after him, but in the dark they cannot find him.

He races across a field, then between two hillocks toward a forest where he suspects the border zone must be, or where he imagines it to be after noting the position of the stars. He comes to a thatched cottage, where he rests and lights a cigarette, but the flame of his lighter attracts two mounted soldiers who are faster than Dragomán is on foot, the pounding of hooves grows louder and louder, the soil is soft and wet, the horses seem hesitant as they stop in front of Dragomán. "You run fast for your age," the soldiers say and handcuff him.

Dazed from the shock and exhausted from running, Dragomán cannot answer the border guard's questions; he hears and comprehends them but no sound issues from his throat, his organs of speech have stopped functioning. But even if he could, he wouldn't give his name, or answer yes or no. Let them do with him what they want, he no longer exists; let them throw him in jail, he won't exist there either. Let this inquisitive, decent-looking stranger decide on a course of action, let him figure out who the silent trespasser may be.

IT FEELS GOOD to stretch out in a white hospital bed, in the midst of four sleeping males. He curls his toes, and hears voices out in the corridor lit by green bulbs. One of his neighbors moans in his sleep, the other is awake but buries his face in his pillow.

Dragomán feels as if he's slipped into a pool of water and is now swimming toward silent surrender. He's become a docile animal, sluggish as a guinea pig, and not much brighter. If it's put before him, he eats it. He stands all day long behind the French doors of this mansion's glass-enclosed lobby but doesn't say a word. Now and then he stands outside, in the driveway of the neoclassic castle, and observes the mountain that yields the best vintage in the country. Or he crouches down and looks up.

Friends appear and ask him if they've offended him. Why won't he talk to them? If he intends to punish himself, he should remember that he is punishing them, too. He shouldn't rush death, Kobra tells him. This is the year of his trials. If Dragomán were to say anything in reply, if he followed his friend down his labyrinth of words, then, as usual, Kobra would be right, and he'd have no reason to stand in a corner or behind the front door of this castle turned insane asylum.

Around him, patients and staff come and go, they've grown used to his not answering them. Tombor asks the doctor not to use electroshock, he'd be much happier if his friend were given some placebo tablets instead. Dragomán poses no danger to himself or to others. If he wants to just stand there, he should be allowed to do so. His friends will take care of the hospital expenses. When Dragomán receives a package, he doesn't touch it, or if he does, it's to place it on his neighbor's bed to indicate that it's for everybody. He eats only hospital food. He'll listen to anyone: one of the women doctors talks to him every night, and senses that Dragomán understands—he communicates approval. Everyone who passes him gets a momentary lift. Like an old gravestone with a strange inscription, he beckons you, but most people, sick or healthy, have other things to do, and after a while, leave him alone.

SOMETIME IN EARLY May, on one of their visits, Olga and Habakuk (Olga had regained her figure, the daughter she had given birth to was giggling already, especially if someone planted a wet kiss on her tummy) tried to make him snap out of his torpor. It's been half a year, enough of this silence, he should come home. Without waiting for an answer, they led him back to his room, put out his clothes, and told him to get dressed.

After ten minutes, Dragomán appeared in his checked jacket, white shirt, and tie, once again the respectable gentleman Olga had first laid eyes on. But in reality he was a puppet, docile, obedient, offering his hand to Habakuk, but stopping and staring into space if the child left him for a second.

Olga brought him home, and there he stayed. Occasionally Sandra took him off her hands, but she couldn't seem to get far with him and brought him back to Olga and his grandchildren, where he seemed content. During the day, under Bella's supervision, he hung around in the tavern. In the winter months he sat near the stove, in the summer he relaxed in the shade of a tree, on a garden bench, listening to the conversation, hanging his head and humming as though he understood everything, understood it only too well, he wished he didn't.

Olga regularly took him over to the Kobras', where he had his special place, which Regina declared his alone. He shook his head, feigned interest as he listened to Kobra's difficult-to-follow explanations, and nodded to signal that he should continue, or to indicate whether he wanted white or red wine.

As far as anyone could tell, he was fine. At dinner, though, he ate very little, felt cold, and his eyes grew so large you could get lost in them. His attention had highs and lows. He could watch Melinda knitting, watch the needles move, for hours on end, and he would even help set or clear the table. After a time these acts of silent assistance seemed unremarkable.

He liked to play ball with Habakuk, or a game of baci with people in the tavern; he enjoyed throwing copper darts at the corkboard, but hated the noisy pinball machines. Sometimes he would grope Bella or one of the female customers, and they'd wag their finger at him: No, no he mustn't; but they knew that the next time they walked by they would have another reason to admonish him. He chuckled at dirty jokes and because his hands trembled now, he'd keep pushing aside the cut-up pieces of buttered bread on his plate.

ONE AFTERNOON WHEN a storm was brewing and the sky rumbled majestically, Dragomán let go of his daughter's hand and sat down on the bench. "You don't want to come to the Kobras' with us?" Dragomán lowered his head and walked back to the beach. He loved to sit on a moss-grown rock, and didn't care if the crashing waves wet his trousers.

He disappeared, and for a long time after they had no news of him, until Kobra ran into him at the Frankfurt Airport. They stood on the moving walkway, going in opposite directions, and kept motioning and waving to each other, their ties slipping out of place.

"Off to St. Petersburg," Dragomán said, carrying twin shoulder bags with all his belongings, as well as a big umbrella, which he kept waving after his friend. "I'll call you," he cried. Perhaps he will. And one day he may turn up in his friend's garden, on the bench, and it will seem as though he had never left.